Wanderer

of

the

Wastes

KIT KARLSSON

First published in the United States of America October 2024 by Lake Country Press & Reviews.

Cataloging-in-Publication Data is on file with the Library of Congress.

ISBN: eBook: 979-8-9902729-7-2; Paperback: 979-8-9902729-8-9

Publisher website: https://www.lakecountrypress.com

Editor: Tara Sexton

Cover Artist: Fay Lane

Formatting: Dawn Lucous of Yours Truly Book Services

Lake Country Press & Reviews

Lake Country Press
Publishing & Reviews

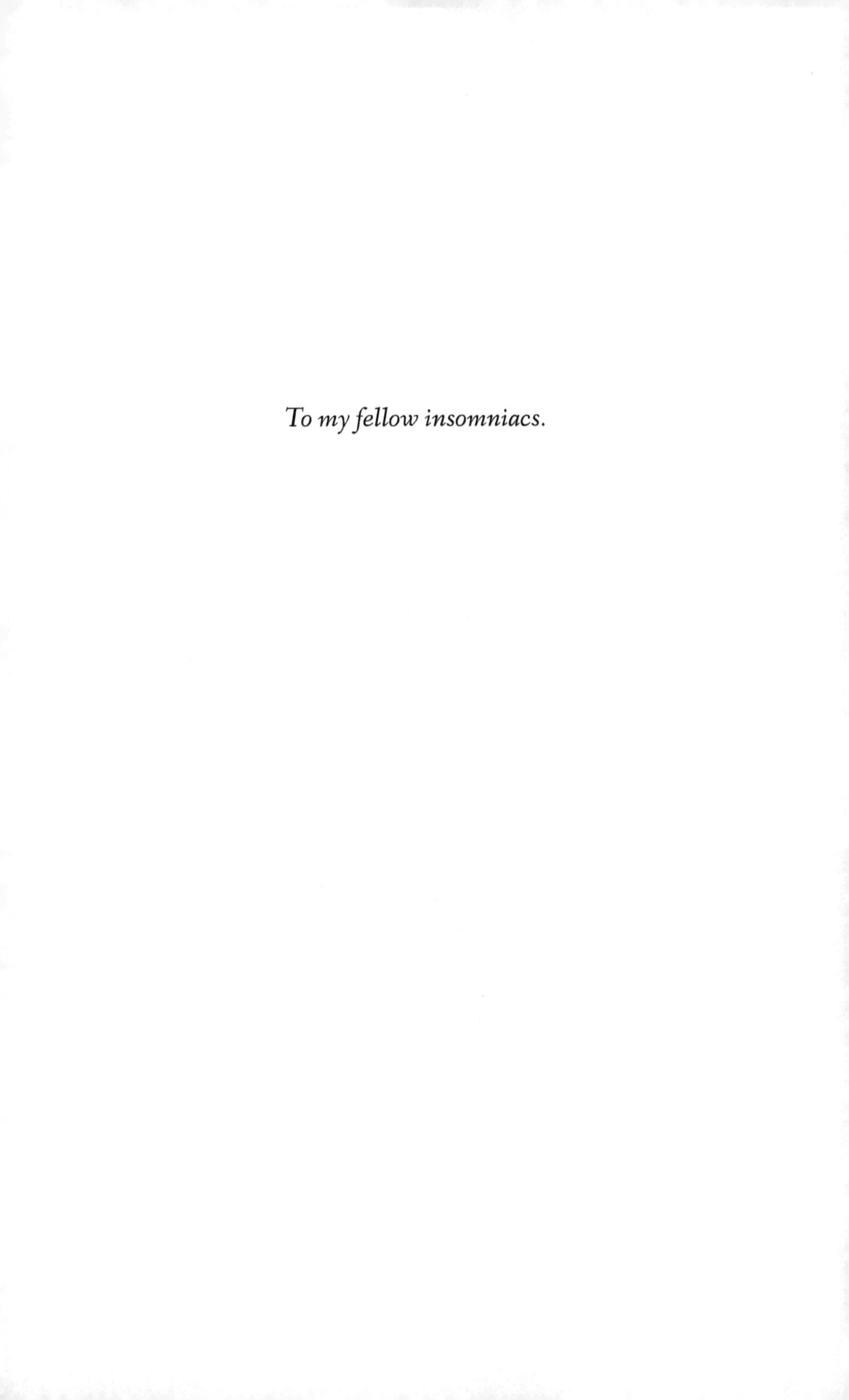

To my fellow insomniacs.

Author's Note

Hello Readers! I'm thrilled you've picked up Wanderer of the Wastes. Because I value your emotional wellbeing, I'd like to leave you with some warnings of what you will find inside besides snark, human-like dragons, and adventure.
Let's hope this is more of a "don't threaten me with a good time" type list, if not, perhaps this story may not quite be the right fit. If it's your fantasy jam, then carry on!
If you feel I have missed anything, please feel free to contact me.
Inside you'll run into:
Violence
Blood and gore depiction
Dead bodies and body parts
Torture
Physical injury/bodily harm
Scars
Physical illness
Sex
Cannibalism (listen, Alessi eats shifter flesh, which I feel kind of counts)

1

Kol shifted against the cold stone, pulling a book from his pocket and cracking it open on his lap. He ran a finger over its worn pages while the familiar ache in his back reminded him that this circular window frame was never meant to be a seat. But here, curled up beside the hallway's sand-obscured glass, was the closest he'd ever come to escaping.

"What are you doing?"

He straightened in his seat at his sister's voice and looked down. "You know." He looked at the book in his hand, *The Prince of Fire*. "Reading. Or, trying to."

"You're distracted," Mia said. Sometimes he hated that she knew him so well. "Nightmares again?"

"Yeah." They were always the same. He looked out at the wastes once more and the nightmare returned, half dream, half memory. One moment, the outline of his mother and brother stood dark against the crimson wastes, then they turned to face him. Where there should have been features, there were only shadows. The next moment, the vision vanished and there was only darkness and his mother's voice.

Find me.

Kol felt for the cool metal pendant around his neck.

"What were they about?" Mia asked.

He couldn't tell her. Their father wouldn't like it if Kol mentioned his mother again. Her name was a curse in this house.

"Nothing important." Kol smiled at his sister. "Just the dust bunnies under my bed. I swear, they're getting big enough to eat me." The twins, Alana and Nalan, passed him in the hall, casting Kol a disapproving look.

Mia stood on her toes. "Astor's coming. He wants you at the meeting."

"Hasn't he given up on me by now?" Kol asked. The hall was nearly silent, the rest of the family already at the emergency meeting his father called.

"Shhhh, there he is." Mia turned to her right, starting down the hall. "I'll see you there."

"I'd rather stick my dick in a meat grinder," Kol said once she was out of earshot. Moments later, heavy footsteps echoed through the space.

"Hey." Astor's voice echoed down the hall. As always, he was impossibly composed, with a tight-fitting white and tan jacket over a slim white shirt. Now that Kol was an adult, they were both muscular and tall, with strong frames, but otherwise they couldn't have looked more different for siblings—half-siblings, anyway—with Astor's golden hair and hazel eyes. Kol's hair was a straight black mess slicked against his tan skin, and his eyes were just as dark, like his mother's. Astor, on the other hand, was almost a mirror image of their father. His broad shoulders were tense, but that was to be expected. Usually, Kol would be happy to see Astor, but there was so much he wanted to tell him but couldn't, and that silence was a wall filling the space between them.

Kol met his brother's eyes for only a moment before turning back to the book. "Hey."

Astor tapped his foot as if searching for words. They had been so close once. Astor had raised him after his mother left, but now it was like they were a million miles apart, ever since—

"What do you think of the book?" Astor asked.

"Haven't read much." Kol flipped through the pages. He hadn't gotten far, which was a little embarrassing, but Mia was right. It was difficult to focus that day. "Only read maybe the first fifty pages before I stopped."

"Daydreaming again, huh?" Astor raised a concerned eyebrow and peered down at the book in Kol's lap. Despite being only seven years older than Kol, there were several shining gray hairs in the beard that graced his chiseled jaw. It suited him, giving him a wise look. "I'm surprised you can still climb up there."

"Desperation breeds ingenuity." Kol tapped his head. "Only good seat in the house."

"It's barely a seat. And it's odd you picked that book today, of all days. You know I'm going to ask where you found it," Astor said. There was a slight irritation in his voice.

Kol's face reddened. "I took it from your things. I figured you wouldn't notice."

"I did notice, and I'll need that back by tonight or we're in trouble." Astor ran a hand through his golden hair, cut short so it stuck out in a hundred different directions. "Besides, the book's incomplete. The last few pages are missing."

"You need it tonight?" Kol's heart raced. Tonight, their father would make the announcement he had dreaded all month.

"For the meeting," Astor explained.

"Why?" Kol asked. The reality he was trying to escape came creeping back in. It was a fate he hated, and yet he was helpless to fight against it. For himself, or for his brother.

"How about you show up for once and find out?" Astor asked.

A deep, uncomfortable silence hung in the air, lasting for several seconds before Kol sighed. He twisted his body to face his brother, whose eyes were still fixated on the leather-bound book. "Do the others know?"

"Not yet. A lot has changed. Now, will you come?" Astor's eyes were stern. "Something important is happening tonight, and you need to be there for it."

"I can't." Kol steeled himself for what would come next.

"You know you have to. It's part of living in the compound. Father will expect it."

"Father's a bastard and an idiot." Kol's eyes met Astor's, burning with intensity.

"Maybe he is," Astor said after a moment, "but it's not our place to question him. There is order here, and everything will fall apart if we lose that order."

Kol clenched his jaw. There was the biggest difference between him and his brother. Astor fit the system. He was the perfect son—caring, obedient, and faithful, even when their father was a belligerent oaf. Astor believed in the system, the order of the compound in which they survived. Kol, on the other hand, was a perpetual outsider despite being born in the cramped space. He never fit, no matter how hard he tried.

"Fuck father. I don't like what he does, and I'm not just going to sit there and condone it."

Astor took a breath, running his hand through his rough hair. "I have to leave, whether you're there tonight or not."

Anger rose in Kol's chest. "There's no reason for it. You know that."

"There is a reason," Astor said. "Naomi is due any day, and we're at capacity. Even just one more mouth to feed, and our agricultural efforts won't be able to sustain us longer than a few years. I'm a surplus male. It's an honor to make space for the next generation."

"Don't call yourself surplus." Kol sniffed, hoping his brother wouldn't see the tears working their way around the edges of his eyes. "And it's not honor, it's murder." Leaving meant death, and if Astor left, the wastes would have swallowed up everyone Kol ever cared about.

The vision plagued his mind again—his mother's figure outlined against the dunes as he watched years ago from a not-as-filthy window, palm pressed against it so hard it hurt, breath fogging up the glass. She should be dead, too, and yet he could still hear her.

Find me.

"You can't give up so easily. What if there's some way to survive out there?" Kol pressed his back against the metal again, his eyes turned toward the window. Faint light filtered through a layer of sand. "We could leave this place."

Astor scoffed. "Don't be ridiculous."

"People didn't always live like this. They could go anywhere they liked."

"And how would you know that?"

"Books. We could find a way if you could just stay a few more—"

"You'd need magic to live out there, and we don't have any." Astor crossed his arms and let out a heavy breath. "I taught you to read so you'd use your head, not lose your mind. Be careful, or you'll go mad just like..."

His mother.

He knew what Astor would say next, but it was a complicated thing, being compared to his mother. Some of his siblings whispered that he had already gone mad, but it didn't have the same sting now that he was a man—there was power in madness, and he had a feeling that someday it would put an end to his father's reign.

"I'd rather be mad than follow father's orders," Kol said. "At least my mother was sane enough to deny him."

"I shouldn't mention her," Astor said. "I'm sorry."

"It's alright." Kol glanced at the window again, his eyes tracing patterns in the silt. "You have a lot on your mind. So do I."

Astor took a breath, sorrow hidden beneath a forced smile. "I know how you feel about Father, but what if *I* want you there?"

It was difficult to deny Astor's pleading gaze. "Maybe."

"Please," Astor said in that way of his, the thin layer of obedient son peeling back for a second to show the man beneath. A scared man. A sad man. He was always the responsible one, the one their other siblings aspired to be, and now he would be rewarded with death. Kol's head throbbed. If he couldn't stop his brother from being sacrificed, he couldn't bring himself to sit there complacently, watching his father's smug face as he murdered another member of his family.

But if the brother who raised him didn't want to be alone that night, Kol would be there. Even if it broke him, and he knew it would. This was all their father's fault, overpopulating the compound and wasting resources. Kol took a sharp breath.

"I need a moment." Kol's fingers trembled against the book's warm cover. "But I'll go."

"Bring the book." Astor's footsteps echoed down the long hallway as he left.

Once Astor was out of sight, Kol sank down the wall and drew his knees to his chest, enjoying his last few minutes of solitude. With ten stepmothers and twenty-eight siblings, he was never alone. He was one of the only ones who didn't attend the meetings—even the younger siblings did—and the only member of the family who ever dared to question his father's rule. His mother had. That's why his father hated her. That's why she had to die.

Find me.

He cursed the fact he was too young to recall much of what happened. His eyes darted to a rare sliver in the window's filth, scraped clean by rain or debris, and looked to the twisting dunes beyond.

The wastes.

Many had left the compound, but none ever returned, victims of the poisoned air and acid rain.

Astor wouldn't come back, either. He would never see his brother again, just like he'd never see his mother.

A bitterness ached in the center of Kol's chest as he stared into the broken nothingness. He hated this dark place, this stone prison they were born in. He would do anything for Astor, if it meant his brother didn't have to leave—didn't have to die. Maybe he could find another way for him to live, but beyond the window's filthy layer was a world of burning air, of monsters and shifting sands. No human could survive out there.

A dark figure moved across his narrow field of view.

Kol's breath quickened, a wet film forming on the window where he pressed his cheek against the curved glass. The shape stumbled over the burned horizon, vermillion against the raging winds.

Sweat beaded on his brow. Nothing survived out there. Nothing lived, nothing died, except... he heard his mother's voice in his mind, faint words from a fading memory.

And from the Darkness came beasts with the faces of men. Monsters.

He could make out what appeared to be a creature on two legs, with tall ears and a wide tail. A pair of silver pinpricks glowed from the dark outline of its head. And it wasn't just coming towards him, it was running. At this rate, it would be at the compound in a matter of minutes.

He shoved the small book into his pocket before peeling himself away from the window. He leaped to the floor.

"Astor!" he called out in case his brother was still within earshot. There was no reply. As much as he hated the man, he had to tell his father.

Monsters with the faces of men. As he ran towards the meeting room, Kol passed dozens of the rounded windows, each filthier than the last. One of his father's oldest wives, Margaret, stood just ahead. She smiled at him, dimples marking her tan skin.

"Where are you rushing off to?" she called out as he brushed past her.

His chest heaved as he pushed his way down the hall. "There's something outside!"

"What do you—"

He missed the rest of her words as he threw open the meeting hall's thick double doors. His sisters' and stepmothers' voices echoed off the wide walls and tall ceiling, the chaos hitting Kol's ears the moment he was inside.

His family shot him disapproving glances as he swam through the crowd before stopping at his father's chair. The old man, with his gray beard cut harsh and angular around his jawline, exchanged hushed tones with Naomi, his youngest wife, her hand over her full and pregnant stomach. Astor sat on their father's other side.

Kol lowered his eyes, as was custom. "Lord Mendona." He tried to hide the fact he was panting, but the sweat on his brow likely gave him away.

His father looked away from Naomi, and his face twisted into a scowl. "*Kol.*"

There was no point in drawing things out. "I saw something outside," Kol said. His chattering sisters grew silent and their eyes burned into his back. "A monster. It'll be here any moment." He put his fist down on the table.

Lord Mendona laughed, leaving Kol dumbfounded.

"What?" Kol asked.

"It's not that kind of monster," his father said. Naomi's eyes widened, and she leaned away from her husband.

"It's a monster. What else matters?" Kol's voice was harsh.

"That," his father said, "is our honored guest."

At his words, the women in the chamber all started speaking at once, and Naomi leaned over to whisper something in her husband's ear. The man nodded.

Kol struggled to wrap his mind around what was happening. *Guest?* They didn't have guests—there were no guests to be had. There was nothing outside their compound, other than the two or three other surviving compounds whose communications had grown increasingly rare. Only Astor went outside occasionally for maintenance, and he'd confirmed this.

"Yes." Lord Mendona gave a smug side-smile. Kol hated that smile. It was the smile of a man with a plan, and Kol already knew that whatever this plan was, he wasn't going to like it.

"You've lost your mind," Kol said, his head spinning. "What are you thinking?"

"I'm thinking it's time you answered the door." Lord Mendona turned to Astor. "Take him with you and be sure he behaves himself."

Kol was beside himself. Astor nodded and grabbed his arm. Astor's firm hand turned Kol away from their father and led him out of the room. The door swung shut behind them. "I'm glad you came," Astor said. "Not what you expected, is it?"

"What's going on?" Kol's heart pounded in his ears. "And don't lie to me. Don't give me some story *he* cooked up."

"It's the truth, and I'd have told you earlier if father hadn't forbade speaking about anything I saw in the wastes. I was outside doing maintenance a few years ago when it wandered by," Astor said. "Our first contact with an outsider in over a century. I could barely hear its voice over the wind, but it handed me a bundle and asked me to hide it until it returned."

"What was in it?"

"Papers, books, clothing. Nothing very monstrous, I suppose."

"You didn't tell me." They told each other everything. The subtle knife of betrayal twisted in the center of Kol's chest. But then again, they didn't talk so much anymore like they used to.

"I couldn't." The two continued down the dark, curving hall, yellow lanterns casting strange shadows against the surrounding stone. "Three days ago, I received a letter. A bird delivered it to me while I was doing more repairs."

"A letter?" He had never seen a letter. Even if someone wrote a letter, there was no one to send it to, and no way to send it. Except, apparently, by bird.

"It smelled like vinegar. I almost gagged, but the most surprising part was that the bird read the letter out loud." Astor wrinkled his nose. "When Katerina found it, I had to tell father." Katerina was their nosiest stepmother, a trait for which she lost a hand. "I thought Father would be angry, but he wasn't scared."

Kol lifted a lip in disgust. "He doesn't have enough sense to know fear. Probably thinks he's a god."

"He's not as stupid as you think. He sees this outsider as an opportunity of some sort. A resource." Astor took a right down a long hallway, and Kol followed. The lights here were uneven, exaggerating Astor's shadow and the creases in his yellow coat.

"They usually don't come around here. You can only see shadows in the distance. Father said that they were just spirits or figments of my imagination and didn't want me causing an uproar."

"Are they people?" The idea of people living above ground excited Kol. There was nothing he wanted more than to escape this hole. If he could leave, that would solve all his problems, at least for now.

"This one's a little different... you'll see." They neared a double door, smooth and shiny with age. A faint memory crossed Kol's mind, a woman's hand holding it open, and he knew what this was: the forbidden door. Their gate to the rest of the world.

Kol's heart raced, and he wasn't sure it was from terror or excitement. Both, probably. This was the gate of banishment, but also the only way to escape.

Find me.

He could leave and run until the glow took him, until the poisoned air turned his lungs to liquid. The vision from his dream played over and over in his head, the wind rustling the silhouette of his mother's skirt. She turned to face him, but her face was only a shadow.

Find me.

Was it possible she was alive out there? The vision broke, and Kol was back in the dark hall beside Astor. He crossed his arms over his chest. Astor leaned into the double doors and whispered, *"The one who waits and the one who wakes will never find home in darkness."* The doors slid into the walls so fast Kol nearly jumped back. This was the only room in the compound whose locks he had never been able to get through on his own.

Inside was another room, lit only by one blue light. Yellow and black suits lined the walls like empty corpse-skins, all one piece. Kol ran his finger along one, feeling its soft, almost velvety texture. He pinched it. It was thick and spongy and smelled like soap.

Astor took one of the dusty suits off its rack and threw it to Kol. "Put it on," he said. "It should fit you." Astor grabbed another suit and sat on one of the six wooden benches in the center of the room to take off his boots. How was he so calm, so steady, always the older brother even here, at the threshold of another world?

"Thanks." Kol joined Astor on the bench. He took *The Prince of Fire* from his pocket and sat it beside him and started unbuttoning his shirt.

"Keep your clothes on," Astor said. "Just take off your shoes. They won't fit in the suit."

"This can't be safe," Kol said, slipping off his thin leather shoes. He had never been outside before.

"It's fairly safe." Concern twinkled in Astor's hazel eyes. "But you should know there are still risks involved with the old maintenance suits. Do you want to go forward with this?"

Find me.

"Yeah," Kol said, trying to contain the excitement that swirled alongside terror in the center of his chest. He had to see the outside, even if it meant confronting a monster. Astor had never let him join in outside duty, always said it was too dangerous. At eighteen, Kol was finally old enough. He was able to be with his brother for what might be the last time.

Astor's heavy hand patted Kol's shoulder. "I'm glad you're here for this."

Kol took a sharp breath. "Me too."

The room was hot, and the suit only made it worse. Without the flow of the compound's recycled air against his skin, there was nothing to stop his sweat from dripping and pooling in the suit's crevasses.

Astor stood, making his way over to the wall. His footsteps echoed, an empty sound. There was one large door on that wall, composed of six panels. He turned to Kol. "You'll feel some suction. Just stay still and stay close when the door opens. I wouldn't push these suits more than a few minutes." Astor pressed a button and the door clicked, then slid open.

A strong wind blew past Kol, as if all the stale air in the room was trying to escape. The stifling heat was replaced by a soft coolness, and a blinding, golden light. Kol covered his watering eyes, seeing nothing but streaks of gold and red.

"Walk forward," Astor said. "You've never seen direct light like this before, but your eyes will adjust." One after the other, they crossed over their home's tarnished threshold.

He could see just enough to walk until he stood beside his brother. Slowly, Kol lowered the hand that covered his eyes. Through the suit, he felt a soft, shifting surface beneath his feet. Once his sight adjusted, he saw sand, red-orange beneath him.

He looked up, eyes stinging as they focused on the shapes lining the horizon, shapes he'd never been able to see through the streaks in the filthy compound windows. They were like giants in the distance, looming and dark, their black, jagged teeth rising from the ground. They could only be mountains.

And between himself and the mountains was a sea of dunes. They seemed bigger now without the filthy window limiting his view. Red-orange gusts blew across the vastness in waves, gathering and spreading and swirling in little eddies with the wind. There was something strange in those sands, however.

A fine blue dust was mixed with them, moving with the wind but slower, heavier. It flowed like neither water nor air, but something in between. Astor either didn't notice it or ignored its strange beauty, but Kol knew what it was.

Glow.

The beautiful, poisonous reason humans couldn't live above ground. There wasn't a lot of it, but it was enough to keep him prisoner in his home. The glowing dust drifted through the air to dance between his feet, its faint blue light twinkling as if mocking him.

His eyes finally finished adjusting, and he looked up. Above, the sky was blue and infinite, beautiful and terrifying in its vastness. It could almost swallow him whole, as if he were nothing but one of the many grains of sand in this deadly, unfamiliar world. He felt his knees grow weak. Never before had his head been more than six feet from a ceiling.

Astor shot him a glance, sensing his tension.

"Don't worry, you're safe in the suit," he said, voice muffled. "As long as it holds."

It was like he always imagined. Better, actually. Terror gave way to excitement again, palms sweating, his heartbeat pounding in his ears. He had never felt so alive. Forcing his wobbly legs to obey, Kol spread his arms wide and laughed. "This is amazing!" He took a step forward but was stopped by Astor's iron grip on his wrist.

"Don't go any further," Astor said.

"Why?" Kol asked. He felt a pull in the center of his chest, as if the mountains to the east were calling to him, and he knew that in that moment, if Astor had not caught him, he wouldn't have stopped until he had been swallowed by the red-orange sand or drowned in that vast, blue sky. He could have fallen into that landscape.

Find me.

A gust of sandy wind blew over them like a wave, nearly knocking Kol over and obscuring the view with a red-orange haze. Glow blew in faint blue eddies on the ground, and the mountains vanished.

"You heard me. Stay near the gate in case your suit starts leaking," Astor said. "Besides, there are things you don't want to see. Nothing survives out here except—" He squeezed Kol's wrist as the shape grew closer, a dark silhouette emerging from the sandy cloud.

The monster.

In all the excitement, Kol had nearly forgotten about the dark, shambling shape cresting the dune that had previously concealed it. The sunset cast a long, black shadow to the monster's left, making it look impossibly tall. Kol squinted, the image blurred in the sand and wind. It swayed as it walked, like an animal. What kind of creature could survive out here?

Another strong breeze cleared the sand. What Kol had thought were wings and a tail of some great beast was in fact parts of a long, black cloak. It was soon right in front of them. It grunted and stopped walking.

"I received your letter," Astor said. The creature didn't answer, and Astor took a sharp breath. "That was your letter, yes? Are you Lord Mendona's guest?"

It spat into the sand from deep beneath its cloak, and for a moment Kol thought that was the only response they would get. Foreboding crept over him as the creature stood there in silence, ignoring Astor's question. Maybe it couldn't speak. Maybe it wasn't the same monster Astor had met three years ago. The creature let out a low growl, and Kol eyed the closed gate.

"Are you a guest of Lord Mendona?" Astor asked, louder.

The creature's head tilted to the side. "What do you think?" it asked in a biting tone. It had a woman's voice.

What was going on?

A hand emerged from its long, black sleeve—a human

hand, or at least some semblance of one—and threw back its hood to reveal not a beast but a woman with a long, straight nose and a mane of curling, silver hair. Kol held his breath. Two glowing, silver eyes stared at him with burning intensity, and above them a pair of black, curved horns grew out from between her steely locks. They weren't very long—perhaps the length of his hand—but that didn't make them any less shocking. He almost stumbled backwards.

She might have been beautiful by human standards—but he wasn't sure she was human. She brushed her silver hair behind her shoulders, a look of casual disdain crossing her face.

"You're... you're a woman," Kol said dumbly.

The woman rolled her eyes. "What gave it away?" she snapped, pushing past him to the gate. She had a sharp way of speaking, cutting every consonant as if with a knife. As she walked, he saw she wore little clothing beneath the cloak, leaving her bare skin exposed to the poisoned air and burning sands. She turned to Astor. "Do you have my things, little man?"

He nodded. "Of course. And my father prepared a dinner for you."

"Dinner?" She stopped, her eyes focusing on the distance as if deep in thought. He could almost see her salivate. "Things will get bad if I stay too long, but I never turn down free food."

Kol's mind ran a mile a minute. It was impossible, and yet here she was, living with no suit to protect her. Glow drifted around her feet and through her hair and didn't even burn her.

"How can you breathe?" he blurted out, his voice strange and muffled by the suit.

The woman pouted, a sarcastic glare in her eyes. "How can you breathe?" She mocked his voice, pressing her finger over the clear plastic shield in front of his lips. "Shut up."

Kol nearly went cross-eyed watching her claw-like nail

leave a dent in the material. He imagined it rupturing, the air poisoning him as he melted in the suit which would become his coffin. It didn't make any sense how she could look so much like him but be unaffected by the glow's poison. "But how—"

She withdrew her finger. "Food now, questions later. I haven't eaten in a week." She backed up, and then to Kol's disgust, picked her nose without breaking eye contact.

"And... you *are* the princess of witches, yes?" Astor tried to hide his doubt. "The one I met three years ago?"

In a single bound, the woman was inches from Astor's face. She was taller than him, just barely, but that with the horns and her overall demeanor made her feel larger and more imposing than the distant mountains. Kol sensed his brother's discomfort.

"Why, do you doubt me?" she asked, smiling. Her canines were long and fang-like, and they showed when she spoke. "Do you think I'm an *imposter?*"

Astor cleared his throat. "Of course not, you're just..." his voice trailed off.

"Not what you expected?" the woman asked. "Nothing up here is what you'd expect, hole-boy."

There was panic in Astor's eyes. "Yes, Princess. Sorry, Princess. Right this way." Hesitating, Astor turned to the door and pressed a series of buttons in the wall—a curved bow, a crescent moon, a triangle and one that looked like a mouth with two fangs — and then twisted the metal handle. It blew open as if sucked in by a giant breath.

They stepped inside. As the door shut behind them, the woman set her eyes on *The Prince of Fire*, still on the bench where Kol left it. She bumped into him as she strode past, picking it up.

She flipped through the pages, sniffed it, then looked at Kol with curious eyes. "Where'd you get this?"

"I hid it like you asked, but my brother Kol here found it." Astor said. "I'm sorry if that's not—"

"I didn't think anyone would read it." She sniffed the book, then met Kol's eyes. "Did you like it?"

"Uh." He swallowed. Would she be upset he hadn't read the whole book? "So far."

She held the book open in front of him and pointed to a faded inscription with her claw-like nail. "A.H.," she said. "That's me." She winked. "You're not bad looking for a book-worm. I can only hope your taste in women is as refined as your taste in books."

"Huh." Blood rushed to Kol's face.

"She's just messing with you," Astor said. "Don't pay attention."

"Dark gods only know what might have happened if *he* had gotten ahold of my stuff. Thanks for hiding it, humans." She shoved the book into her pocket and sniffed the air. "What is this place?"

"The gate. Beyond it is the seventh settlement. It's a human compound." Astor reached for a lever on the wall beside him. Glowing, blue dust gathered around Kol's shoulders. "Hold still, we need to get the glow off before heading inside."

The woman stretched, cracking her knuckles. "You can't keep the glow out forever, you know, but I'll take a free bath." As she stretched, the black glove she wore on her left hand flexed, reflecting a thousand strange, dark colors in the light. It reminded Kol of an iridescent serpent struggling to break free. The brothers took the suits off, hanging them back up on the racks.

"Hold still." Astor pulled the lever, and the room began to rumble. "This might hurt."

"Ah," the woman said, recognition sparking in her eyes. "This place was built with the old magic. You know—"

She didn't get to finish her sentence. Air came from all angles and whipped around them, burning Kol's eyes and skin. He was simultaneously freezing and hot, his skin both contracting into goose pimples and sweating. Across from him, the woman shut her eyes and faced the ceiling, the air blowing her long hair around her like a silver storm. She smiled—at home in the chaos. When it was over, she shook her entire body like a dog, then made her way over to the door connecting the airlock to the rest of the compound.

"Let's get this over with," she said.

Kol rubbed his raw, aching skin. The hair on his arms was gone. Reaching up with a panic, he was relieved to find that the hair on his head had not met the same fate. Astor's face was red —the cleaning winds had hurt him, too, even if he didn't otherwise show it. He eyed the woman, who had the same pallid disposition as earlier, her face a pale, bloodless gray. Unharmed. Inhuman. She wasn't human. She couldn't be. Not with those horns, and not if she survived out in the wastes.

Astor shut the door behind them, and the strange trio continued into the compound. Little light shined through the filthy windows. The sun was setting, but the lanterns on the walls had not yet been lit. Shadows fell across the woman's face, her eyes glowing dimly within them. As they made their way toward the meeting room, Kol's eyes followed those filthy windows, his gaze jumping from one thick, domed glass surface to the next.

She pointed at them. "This is all you see?" The evening sun's golden light barely filtered through their sandy films.

"Usually," Kol said.

The witch made a face. "They're windows. What's the point of having windows if you can't see through them?"

"You can see a little. I saw you," Kol said. "Though I thought you were a—"

Astor cleared his throat, signaling Kol to stop. "Hasn't always been this way. We clean them, but the sands are shifting in our direction. We'll be buried completely in a few years if we don't do something." They were near the window where Kol read earlier that evening. "Everyone's waiting for you in the great hall, Miss... may I ask your proper name? You signed your letter only as 'Princess of Witches'."

"Alessandra. Alessi is fine," she said.

"Right, Alessi—" Astor began.

She cut him off. "*Princess* Alessi, to you." She brought a claw to Astor's chin, laughing when he stiffened in response. The look in her eyes was clear—she could kill him if she wanted to. And in his eyes was that flicker of fear he held all day, that wave of dread about to drown him. She was strong enough to survive the wastes. Astor never would be.

She lowered her hand and Astor staggered back beside Kol, rubbing his chin. Frozen, both brothers watched Alessi take long strides toward the room where everyone waited. Her long black cloak, cleaned by the gate's winds, trailed behind her. When she reached the door, she stopped, waiting expectantly.

Gathering himself, Astor hurried towards her. "This way, *Princess* Alessandra." He opened the door to the great hall, and they walked inside.

The witch smirked as the room fell silent.

2

Kol leaned forward in his chair, watching the witch spit chicken bones onto her plate. She picked one up and scratched between her toes, which were conveniently resting on his father's white tablecloth. Her fangs left gnaw marks on the bones before she threw them to the floor. He didn't know what to make of her. She looked human—mostly—but she *felt* more animal than human, like some untamed force of nature forced into a cloak and shoes.

To Kol's right, Lord Mendona, like the rest of the clan, looked on with an expression of disbelief. Naomi sat beside him stroking her heavily pregnant belly, which her green dress barely concealed. Locks of auburn hair flowed over her full breasts. Sometimes, Kol forgot that she was only six months younger than him. She had arrived via tunnel from another compound to the south, expecting a grand life, and now looked on with disappointment as Lord Mendona failed in his third attempt to start a conversation with the witch.

"I hear on the surface, there's a weather mage known as a Rainsinger who controls the weather, winds, and seasons,"

Lord Mendona said, attempting small talk. "Is it possible there's a new Rainsinger? The winds have been burying us, which was never a problem before."

Alessi removed another bone from her mouth and waved it, tendons still hanging. Kol winced as bits of meat and saliva fell to the stark-white tablecloth. "I'm eating," she said with her mouth full. "Why does everyone want to talk while they eat? You can only do one at a time."

Lord Mendona's eyebrows knitted together, and a smile crept across Kol's face. Finally, his father had met his equal in persistence.

"So, the weather—" Lord Mendona began.

Alessi rolled her eyes, swallowing. "Are we really going to do this?" she asked, her voice lilting with dismay. "Let me eat in peace. It was a long journey."

A vein throbbed in Lord Mendona's forehead. "It's my food, Princess. I'm allowing you to eat." He smiled, exposing his black teeth. "If this doesn't satisfy you, I may know something else that can."

Something snapped in Kol. "Don't talk to her that way."

He slammed his knife down on the table, the hollow sound reverberating through the space, causing his mothers and sisters to freeze. The disrespect. His father used to speak to Kol's mother that way, taking her wrist in his hands, his nails leaving jagged marks on her skin. Old memories washed over him, as fresh and vibrant as the blood dripping from his mother's fingers all those years ago.

"Control yourself, *boy*," his father said through gritted teeth.

The woman winked at Kol, causing his face to redden before she stood and faced his father. She gave an exaggerated bow, hand outstretched.

"Oh, gracious sir, let me thank thee for this meal," Alessi

mocked, waving the chicken bone like a conductor's wand. Her face grew serious, and she stood to her full height, towering over the aged man. She poked the center of his chest with the chicken bone, and he stiffened in his seat, leaning back as if trying to escape. "You don't own me, you don't tell me what to do, you don't tell me when to *eat*, even if it's your food. If you piss me off, I'll eat *you* instead." She winked at Kol before sitting again and sliding another chicken thigh into her mouth like nothing happened.

Through the crowd, Mia's wide eyes met Kol's. She was scared, but also excited. Even Naomi eyed them with curiosity. Neither he nor his mother nor anyone else had ever spoken to his father like Alessi just had, and Lord Mendona's initial curiosity turned to a rage burning in his eyes like embers. Kol knew that rage. His father couldn't punish the woman, but he *could* punish Kol for speaking up. He would feel this later, likely with the business end of a whip.

Still, it was worth it.

Lord Mendona forced a smile, quelling his rage, and motioned for the other women to continue their meals. They did, but in silence, eyes turned towards Alessi. She did what had long been on all their minds. Kol forced himself to take a sip of his gruel. Besides *Princess* Alessi and his father, the rest of the family ate porridge, not meat, due to the difficulty of raising animals underground. They watched on in silence as the witch cleaned an entire chicken's corpse. No one had ever made his father so uncomfortable, and nothing had ever made Kol so happy.

Gathering himself, Lord Mendona tried to start the conversation again, his voice an artificially even tone. "Now tell me, what's the outside like these days? Has the glow let up?"

"Fine. I'll play." Her plate was empty, except for a few

bones. "Glow's receding, but no one cares about that. What you have to watch out for is the dragons."

"Dragons?" Lord Mendona asked.

"You know, dragons. They'll swallow you whole, crunch your bones." She crushed a chicken bone in her fist, letting it fall to the floor in pieces. "Barely escaped three of them getting here."

"And you traveled by yourself, Princess?" Lord Mendona asked. Alessi nodded nonchalantly, turning over her gloved hand.

Dragons. Most records of them had been erased centuries ago, their pages torn from books and records. All Kol knew of them was from rumors and stories. He scooted his chair forward and rested his chin on his hand. "You seem like you can handle some overgrown lizards."

He held in a groan as Astor's heel slammed down on his toes below the table before leaning close to him. "Do you want to get yourself killed?" Astor asked under his breath. "Stop speaking out of turn!"

The witch smiled, amused. "Overgrown lizards?" She pushed against the table with her feet, rocking her chair back on two legs. "Of course, you've never seen a dragon, living in this *hole*—"

"What are they like?" Kol pressed. Astor's foot stomped down on him again, but Kol didn't mind. There was more out in this world, and he had to hear about it. He thought of earlier, that sky that could swallow him whole, the mountains at what seemed like the edge of the earth. He longed for another taste.

"Dragons, hmm." The witch hummed, and after a moment said, "They're like people."

"People?" Kol asked. "I thought dragons were monsters."

"Yeah." The witch raised an eyebrow. "So are people. Who doesn't know what dragons are?"

Lord Mendona interrupted. "We haven't heard much of the outside world — nothing about dragons, and only rumors of monsters." He hesitated, then said, "Humans, living on the surface in any form... I'd have thought it impossible."

"Only because you don't understand it." She grabbed another thigh from the middle of the table and chewed at its end, working a long canine into the marrow. This was her third chicken, an excess by any standard. "Now, will you tell me what's going on? I appreciate the welcome party—and the food, most of all—but this is a lot of humans in one space."

"I was hoping you'd give us a little demonstration." Rotten teeth were on full display in Lord Mendona's smile. "Since my son was kind enough to keep your books safe from the... what were you running from?"

"Dragons, remember?" Alessi raised an eyebrow. "And you'd like a *what*?"

"Right. And I want a demonstration as proof that humans on the surface have become monsters, capable of magic. And that we're safest down here."

Of course, that was his father's reason—a desire to scare the rest of the family into submission. However, Kol was more hung up on another word.

Human.

Humans lived on the surface.

Alessi gave a long whistle, raising both hands. "That's a lot to unpack, mister. Is this why you invited me to dinner? To be rude and then demand I give you some excuse to stay here in your hole?"

"Those horns. They're proof—" Lord Mendona began.

"These horns were a gift—they give witches the ability to steal magic. I am not a monster." She stroked one horn. "But the magic I use is taken from monsters—or Belgarri, which we call the intelligent non-human creatures living on the surface.

Witches have no magic of their own, and this is what makes us human." She pressed her thumb to the tip of one horn, and dark red blood trickled down the side of her hand. She licked it. "Just like you."

"You don't look like us," one of Kol's stepmothers said.

"Your hair!" exclaimed another.

"Like I said, the horns were a gift." Alessi took a lock of hair between her fingers. The silver glowed, like threads spun from moonlight. "Humans were never supposed to have magic. It leaves a mark on you, first leaching the color from your body, then changing you in other ways. But in exchange, you receive great power."

"Show us!" Mia said. "We wanna see!"

Alessi clenched her jaw. "Magic can't be used willy-nilly for old men and petty reasons, but I'll tell you what you want to hear. With this gift, silver ones like me can survive in the wastes, off the magic of strange monsters. But if humans like you come into contact with the glow, your eyeballs will roll into the back of your throat for you to choke on as the skin crawls off your body and your intestines are ejected through your mouth. Instant death. It's a sight to behold, cruel and unmistakable."

Lord Mendona smiled. "Thank you, Princess."

"Always happy to provide for power plays," Alessi said mockingly. She sighed. "I expect my belongings after this meal so I can get out of this cultish hellhole."

Kol's mothers and sisters chatted quietly, brows creased, eyes wide. Fear was written across their faces. Kol clenched his jaw, forcing more porridge down his throat. This is what his father wanted—fear of the outside. Fear led to control which led to power, and Kol was sick of it.

Alessi was right, this place was a hellhole. And he could never leave, lest the glow claim him. But Alessi had survived. There was a way, and with this knowledge, something stirred deep within him: a realization coupled with determination. He had to get out, and she could show him how.

"You can't leave yet," Lord Mendona said.

"Excuse me?" Alessi's voice raised in pitch.

What did he think he was doing? Did he seriously think he could keep her here as a prisoner, or make her one of his wives?

"You can leave at dawn. It's too dangerous to open the gate at night," Lord Mendona said, a sly smile on his face.

"You don't understand." Alessi stood. "You'll all be in danger if I—"

"No need to worry, you are safe here. Nothing gets in these walls." Lord Mendona turned to his gossiping wives. "Now, onto our other business of the night."

Alessi sat, anger written across her face.

Kol's heart sank into his stomach. In all the chaos, he almost forgot about his brother's impending banishment. But if Kol were to find some way to leave instead, there would be enough space for Astor to live a little longer, at least until he could figure something out.

"I have one last announcement," Lord Mendona said. "When the Princess leaves, my son will leave with her." He patted Astor on the back, a pained expression spreading across the man's face. Kol's heart dropped.

"I don't remember agreeing to this." There was irritation in Alessi's voice. Kol would have been irritated in her position, too. "Fine. Which one?" she asked, apparently oblivious to all indications that he intended her to take Astor.

"Astor," Lord Mendona said. "Make him a witch."

Alessi picked her teeth. "It doesn't work on men."

"Excuse me?" Lord Mendona said.

"Witch magic turns most men into mindless monsters. I've only ever met one man who didn't transform into a Sorgin when given witch blood. The magic is more stable in women.

But the other boy..." She looked at Kol, sniffing the air. "He has a strange smell about him. He's different. He might make it."

"You don't want him." Lord Mendona scowled. "He's untrustworthy, like his mother."

The witch snorted. "What did *she* do to earn that crown?"

"Tried to kill me."

Kol flinched. "You lying bastard!" He dropped his fork on his plate with a *clank*, and the room grew silent. She hadn't tried to kill his father, no matter how much she'd hated him. She'd never.

Alessi sniffed the air, eyes glued to Kol. "And where is she now?"

Lord Mendona cleared his throat. "Gone."

"Dead?" the witch asked. "Or out for a stroll? Be specific."

His father opened his mouth to speak, but Kol cut him off. He couldn't bear his father's version of the story.

"My father accused her of treason, so she left for the wastes before he could banish her. She took my brother Caliban with her," Kol said. "They're dead."

"Are you sure?" Alessi leaned toward him, a glimmer in her eye.

Kol leaned forward. "Of course. No one survives out there." Except her. That twinkle of hope returned. Maybe his mother had lived. If magic was real, and humans like Alessi could use it, maybe it really *was* her voice he heard.

Alessi sighed. "Taking your son—this is the only way you'll let me out?"

Lord Mendona nodded.

"Fine. I'll take the older one, Ass-whatever, with me in the morning. But I don't think you'll like what happens." Alessi combed her claw-like fingers through her hair. "And even if he survives drinking my blood, even if he can breathe the air, he knows nothing of the outside. He won't last long."

"He can use a sword," Lord Mendona said.

"What for? A dragon would use his flimsy human sword like a toothpick." Alessi laughed.

"I can learn if it's my only chance of survival," Astor said. "I'm not useless."

"You're right. To the dragons, you're useful as a tasty snack," Alessi said.

Astor turned back to his porridge, which Kol now realized was untouched. He had never seen such an expression on his brother's face. Worry. Fear. Uncertainty. All masked with a thin veil of bravery. On the other side of him, the witch drummed the table with her fingers, sending several dishes vibrating to the floor. Glass shattered under Kol's feet. Alessi's eyes met Kol's—hers glowing a faint silver, like a light at the end of a tunnel. Like the brightest, most focused fires he'd ever seen. For a moment, he thought he might burn alive under her gaze.

She broke away, and Kol felt himself breathe for the first time in what felt like minutes.

"Since you're keeping me here until dawn, I imagine you have some lodgings for me?" she asked.

Lord Mendona tugged at his collar. "Of course, Princess. Only the finest. And you could stay longer, if you'd like." He looked calm, but Kol heard his foot anxiously tapping beneath the table. *Tap tap tap.*

"Absolutely not." She felt at her pocket, where the rectangular outline of Kol's book—her book, if she were to be believed—jutted out. She stood abruptly, sending her chair clattering behind her. "Take me to my rooms. I'll deal with you in the morning."

The mothers stopped their whispers, and all eyes turned again to the witch.

"Astor will show you," his father said.

The witch shook her head, then pointed to Kol. "That one.

I want him to show me." And with those words, her eyes caught his again, trapping him like a snake beneath her bare foot.

Kol felt himself go almost as pale as the witch. At this point, she must have just been messing with his father. She smiled at him, a mischievous, sideways smile. This woman was as beautiful as she was deadly, able to escape dragons and traverse the wastes. He couldn't look away.

Lord Mendona rolled his eyes. "As you please."

"Which room?" Kol asked. The compound was large and sprawling but taking into account the levels reserved for farming with the aid of ancient, magic lights, there were no spare rooms. Even Kol shared a room with Astor.

Lord Mendona took Kol by the wrist, drawing him close. Kol felt his father's breath against his ear. "The old wing," his father whispered. "Room five thirteen."

"Hurry up," Alessi said. There was a glint in her eye he didn't like.

"This way." His voice wavered. Would she see it as a weakness? What could she do to him? Crush his bones like a dragon? As Kol led her out of the meeting room, she went out of her way to crush a chicken bone beneath her black boot. It felt like a threat. Silence suffocated him as they walked down the long, steel hall that led to the old wing.

Alessi broke the silence. "Your dad's a dick."

At least he wasn't the only one who thought so. "Yeah."

"I can smell dried blood on your back," she said. "From the last time you went against him, I assume?"

"Yes." They still ached beneath his skin.

"I understand dickish parents better than most. A little tip," she said. "Don't stick your neck out for a stranger. You'll get your head cut off." She made a slashing motion with her gloved hand.

Kol raised an eyebrow. She was almost... friendly. Scary, but friendly. "Thanks."

They were nearing the old wing, lit only by flickering lights. "Is this it?" Alessi ran her finger along the wall, smiling, showing off her fangs.

Monstrous. And yet, human.

Kol swallowed as the door yawned ahead of them. Memories stirred. He'd gone through that door once before, with his brother. Caliban, his full brother. His dead brother. Sweat beaded on Kol's forehead, and his hands shook.

"What are you doing?" Alessi asked.

"Thinking that I've been here before." There was an edge to Kol's voice.

She smiled, fangs gracing her lower lip. "Do you know what they say about people who think?" She jumped into his path and looked at him, her eyes inviting him to play some game he didn't know the rules to. To catch the punch line of a joke he didn't understand.

"I don't know," Kol said after a moment.

"That they're thinkers. It's not hard." Alessi felt at her pocket. "Do you know what they say about people who read?"

Kol decided it was a good idea to play along. "That they're readers?" he guessed.

She shook her head. "That they're so lost in other worlds, they forget to explore their own. Then they fade and wither like burning pages, like ash, until there's nothing left. Not blood, not words, not ink." She looked at him expectantly. When he remained silent, frozen, her face fell. "It's a quote. I thought you read the book."

"Not, ah, entirely," Kol said, his face reddening. She laughed again. "I want to ask you something."

"What?"

They stopped at the door, its carved archway bearing the

number 5 1 3 and the mark for *east*, two straight slashes against a crescent moon. He pressed his hand against it, watching it glow. Was he really doing this? Maybe he was mad. "Take me with you tomorrow, instead of Astor."

She crossed her arms. "No."

"Why?"

"Do I scare you?" Her voice was softer now, without its edge.

"No." Kol gritted his teeth, eyes fixed on her horns. How easily one of them could pierce his throat, or his heart.

She brought her face close to his, and he stiffened. Her breath had a metallic, sweet smell to it. "Do not lie to me. I smell your fear." She was close enough to rip his throat out with those fangs, to slit his veins with those claws and let him bleed red onto the ancient floor. "I ask you again: *do I scare you?*" Her voice had lowered to a growl, vibrating through his chest. Her colorless gaze was petrifying. Sweat dripped down his temple in the stale air.

"A little bit." His voice cracked.

She backed away, a too-pleased smile on her face. "That's better."

"Are you... toying with me?" Kol asked.

"A little bit," she said, mocking his voice. "You're weak. Even weaker than your brother. If even I scare you, you wouldn't last a day up there."

"You looked at me earlier," Kol said, "like you saw something. I thought—"

"Everyone knows magic has a color, but did you know it also has a smell?" she asked. Kol remembered Astor's story about the vinegar smell. "For a second, I thought *you* had a smell, too. But it turns out you just smell like regular ass."

"I don't smell like ass," Kol muttered. He sniffed his armpit, detecting an unpleasant musk. The door opened and Alessi continued ahead into the unlit hall behind door 5 1 3. But he wasn't about to give up. "I'm less likely to turn into a Sorgin, you said so yourself. So, take me instead."

"Even if you didn't turn, you'd be dead weight until you're tragically picked off by any number of creatures. I'm not taking you, interesting and desperate as you may be."

She thought he was interesting, at least, but it was no use. He was trapped here. His heart sank. They stopped at a door, and he stood in the threshold searching for words, light from behind casting his shadow into the dark space. It ended at the faint light of another room that waited on the right, door wide open. He could see a made bed and a single lightbulb that glowed from within, casting it in warm, flickering light. There was nothing more he could say. He had no bargaining power, no skills to offer. He was worthless.

The witch hummed to herself, running her hand along the book in her pocket. He had taken the book from his brother's things because he had already run out of books to read in the library, run out of worlds to escape to. So not only would she not take him with, but she was taking his last escape, leaving him to stare into dirty windows and hope for streaks of light.

"I should probably thank your brother." She turned around, saw his dismay, and smiled. "If he hadn't hidden my things for me, the red king would have got them for sure. Asshole dragon's been hunting me for years."

"What does he have against you?" Kol asked, seeing a possible in.

She placed her gloved hand on the back of her neck. "It's a long story and none of your business." He could tell by her tone not to push any further.

A breeze from the compound's vents pushed the door shut behind him. Alessi's silver eyes glowed in the dim light, and an awareness sank into his heart. This woman traveled across the wastes, alone. This princess, this strange princess, could defeat dragons. She did whatever she wanted, like freedom herself. She terrified him, but as his eyes adjusted, he couldn't look away from those twisting horns that towered above, that crooked smile, that dark cloak.

She was a burning pyre, and he, a moth.

"If you take me with you, I'll do anything," he said. To buy Astor some time. To get out of there.

She opened the door and pushed him out, preparing to close it again, but he put his foot in it.

"Anything?" she asked.

"Anything."

"That's a dangerous word when there are fates worse than death." She tilted her head again to the side, an amused look on her face. "You're a strange man, Kol." She slammed the door, and he was alone in the darkness.

3

The vision returned that night.

He saw the outline of his mother's form against the wastes, holding his brother Caliban by the hand. Caliban was so small then, though he was older than Kol by two years. Their mother turned to face him, shadows consuming her features.

But this time there was something different. He was falling into a deep chasm.

Find me.

"Where?" Kol cried out in the void. He could barely hear himself. The hot wind nearly drowned out his voice, whipping his hair behind him.

Find me in the Valley of Dragons.

"How do I get out of here?" he called out to her.

You already know.

He was back in the hallway with Astor outside the gate. Astor leaned in, and whispered, *"The one who waits and the one who wakes will never find home in darkness."*

The memory of earlier that night replayed. He and Astor

moved like blurs, the next several minutes passing in seconds. They talked about the suits, Astor told him to take his shoes off, then Kol stood beside Astor again as he pressed the code for the second door: a curved bow, a crescent moon, a triangle and one that looked like a mouth with two fangs.

He sat up in bed, clutching damp sheets in his fists. Of course. She wanted to leave, and he knew the way out. *That* was his bargaining power.

But it was dangerous, that terrifying vastness of the sky, the uncertainty of venturing out with a practical stranger, whatever monsters lurked the wastes above. And Astor wouldn't like him leaving. Should he tell Astor? No—best to talk to the witch first. He rolled over, dangling his feet off the edge of the bed. It was hot in the room they shared, but it always was, the air growing a little staler each day. He cradled his head in his hands.

I'm waiting for you.

His temples throbbed, and he felt at her pendant around his neck. It was cool and smooth until the metal dragon's carved teeth cut into his finger. Why now, of all times, could he hear his mother? Why was it that now, if she was actually alive, she wanted him to join her? She should have taken him the day she left for the wastes. At least then — he stopped himself.

She couldn't be alive.

It was impossible. His mother spared him by taking Caliban instead that day, and yet, he resented her for it. Like he wasn't even good enough to die at her side.

Was he finally going mad, hearing her voice? There was something, some possibility he wasn't. Alessi said glow caused a near instant death, but in that memory, his mother and Caliban were... alive. Breathing. Walking. He had written the memory off as a product of his childish imagination, but after seeing Alessi, he knew it was possible. Unlikely, but possible that they were still alive. And if he left the compound, that would make room for Astor to live a little longer, at least until the next baby was born.

His temples throbbed. He couldn't believe what he was about to do.

Kol stood, hitting his head on Astor's leg, which dangled off the bunk above him before walking out the bedroom door and down the hallway. He thought about saying something to his brother, then changed his mind. Astor would only try to stop him. He took a breath of the stale air, then rubbed his eyes before walking out of the small room, entering the compound's main hallway, and taking a right.

He would go to the witch and convince her to leave this place together. He was her ticket out, and she was his.

The hallway formed a circle around the compound's entirety, curving gently to his left. Soft, blue moonlight filtered in through the thin layer of sand on the windows, casting ghostly circles against the opposing wall. He stretched as he walked. The library was ahead on the left, a metal door set in a curved archway.

Something moved behind him.

He startled, then calmed himself. It was probably just Katerina snooping around again. He hated when she did that. "Katerina!" he shouted. He heard shuffling and continued toward the sound. "I thought you were in—"

There was blood on the floor, a long smear of it stretching from the center of the room to one wall. Feathers were strewn about the body of a headless, brown-speckled chicken. It was one of his father's most prized possessions—the chicken that would be slaughtered to celebrate the birth of Naomi's child.

Whatever tore off its head had also ripped flesh from the hen's breast, leaving fang-marks. To the left of the carnage was a set of bare, bloody footprints, leading into the shadows.

"Who's there?" Kol called out. "Show yourself."

There was no answer.

"This is one hell of a prank," he said, thinking of Mia. She enjoyed her pranks, and so did many of his siblings, but none would risk their father's wrath to pull off something like this. "Come out!"

His words echoed through the space. Whatever had done this was long gone, and every hair on his neck stood on end. He picked up the chicken, smearing blood across his palms. It must have gotten out of its pen and come upstairs looking for food, only to meet its untimely demise. He covered his mouth with his bloody hands, feeling the sticky liquid against his face.

He remembered the witch. She could have done this, but his father slaughtered three chickens for her—there was no way she was still hungry. *Something* was with him in this darkness. And it wasn't good. A heavy air settled over the place, distilling a singular truth in his mind: he needed a weapon, and fast.

But what? A sword hung on the wall, but it would be an unwieldy mess in his hands. He never learned the art of sword fighting like Astor. He couldn't be trusted after his mother left —as fruit of a poisonous tree, he was lucky his father even fed him.

A shuffling noise echoed through the hall. Kol held his breath.

Kol bent down, reaching for the twisted metal bar his sisters used to reach high books. It was bent in the middle, and with enough force, probably sharp enough to split a skull—crude enough for him to use. The sound grew quieter, and he made his way out the door and into the hall, careful not to make a sound. It was between him and his quarters, so there was no turning back. He rushed down the curving metal hallway, cold bar clutched tightly in his hand, cutting into the creases of his palm.

The noise came from behind. It was a shuffling, wet sound.

Something, or someone, followed him. It could be the witch. He looked at the makeshift weapon in his hand and imagined smashing it through the stranger's skull. Could he do it? Would it hold up against her horns? What unimaginable terrors could she release on him? She was called a witch for a reason.

The shuffling sound grew louder, and he started running, his mind racing almost as fast as his legs. His chest heaved and he fought for air.

Ahead, the door to the old wing glowed a faint blue, and he pushed it open. He pressed his back against it as the shuffling turned into dragging, and he felt the door thrum against his skull. He could call out for help, but no one would hear him—he was far away from the sleeping quarters, where everyone was. He was alone, with this... thing. Whatever it was.

He sniffed the air, which smelled of smoke and was accompanied by an oppressive darkness more felt than seen. Some instinct, some latent knowledge, told him it wasn't of human origin, and it wasn't the witch. Her presence was different, more intense. This was like a shadow. His chest heaved against the door. The hall in front of him was empty. No more shuffling came from the other side, no more motion. Another feeling came over him, a supernatural coldness that reached under his skin and into his mind.

Open it.

He opened the door to reveal the hallway. It seemed to grow longer and longer as he waited, frozen, to be certain the noise was gone—that this thing, this intruder, was gone. If he were to head back the way he came, whatever it was would be on the other side of the compound by now.

A hand pressed against his mouth and throat. He let out a sound, but it was muffled.

Whoever it was dragged him backward, into the darkened hallway he just emerged from. He clumsily aimed for his attacker with the makeshift weapon, but his sweaty fingers slipped, and it clattered to the floor. Some part of him said that this was it. This was where he would die. He tried to cry out, but only flesh-muffled sounds left his mouth.

"Hey!" a woman hissed. It was the witch. "Calm the hell down, will ya?"

She removed her hand from his mouth.

"What are you doing?" Kol demanded. Her claws cut into his cheek as he scrambled away from her, eying his metal bar which slid to the opposing wall. Blood dripped down onto his chin. He could still reach it if he was fast.

"Calm down. I'm not going to hurt you." She pulled a stone out of her pocket, shook it, and watched it glow. It wasn't blue like the poisonous glow outside, but a gentle yellow light. "I told your idiot father it would be bad if I stayed too long. Something followed me here."

"What's going on?" Kol raised his voice again. "We—"

"Shh! They'll hear you."

Kol swallowed hard. "What will?" he whispered. Something moved in the darkness to his right, and he heard metal on metal.

The witch's fingers teased at the rim of the black leather glove that stretched all the way to her elbow, then peeled it off. Blue-green scales covered her skin and black claws tipped her long fingers. It wasn't a human hand, but that of a monster.

"The hell happened to you?" Kol asked.

"Long story, no time."

Kol eyed the metal piece again, and crept closer to it. "What"—he lowered his voice to a whisper—"What followed you here? How did it get in?"

"There are three dragons following me, blue, gold, and red. I have no idea how they got in," she said. "The blue dragon is a lyramancer, and that makes him dangerous. Lyramancers have a way with sound, so don't listen to anything he says. Damn dragons..."

Kol cleared his throat. He found the witch—or the witch found him—and now was his only chance to convince her. "I want you to take me with you."

"Right now, really?" she whispered, tension in her voice. "Did you not just hear what I said? It's dangerous up there."

"I know."

"Why should I take you with me?" Her tone was quiet and harsh.

"You need two codes to get out. I know both."

"And why do you want to leave your safe little hole, hole-boy?" Her sideways smile returned, tempered by the severity of her eyes.

What could he tell her but the truth? He had nothing else to offer.

"My mother," he said. "I had a dream where she spoke to me, told me to find her."

"Everyone dreams. Your mother's dead," Alessi said.

His heart sank. "Maybe." He shook his head. "But what if she was a witch?"

"If she really was your mother, that's unlikely at best," Alessi said.

"Then, I need to leave to make space for my brother. If I leave, he doesn't have to."

"Foolish." Alessi took a sharp breath.

"Look," Kol whispered. "I don't have anything to offer you but a way out. I'll admit that, but there's nothing for me here. My days are numbered, eventually I'll be sent into the wastes just like Astor. And if you don't take me with you, I'll burn out my own lungs to deny my father the satisfaction."

She stood, making her way out of the dark space. "There may be nothing for you here, but there's nothing for you out there, either." She looked both ways before walking into the hall to the right. "But that's your problem. Let's get out of this hellhole."

"Let's see Astor, get your things—"

"Got 'em." She gestured to a crude pack swung over one shoulder. "And there's no time. Those dragons will be on us in moments."

Dragons. In the same compound that was safe for so many years, where he, Mia and Astor called home.

"What about my family?" Kol asked. "Will they be safe?"

"If we're fast, the dragons should follow me out without destroying much. But I have to leave, and I have to do it *now*." She picked up the pace, and so did he.

They reached the gate's interior door. Alessi pounded on it for a moment, then whipped around to face him. "Alright, mister useful. Open the damned thing."

Kol repeated the words he heard Astor say earlier. "*The one who waits and the one who wakes will never find home in darkness.*" The double doors swung open. Kol stepped through the door, but apparently not fast enough. Alessi dragged him into the suit room by the back of his shirt then latched the door behind them.

"They're close. Hurry." She pointed to the exterior door. "Open it."

"I'll die without a suit." Kol looked from her to the door, then back to her.

Something flashed in her eyes. "There's no time. I'll give you my blood once we're out and this door is shut behind us. You'll have a few seconds."

The symbols on the wall glowed a faint blue. He punched in the sequence he remembered Astor using earlier.

Nothing happened. His heartbeat pounded in his ears.

"Open the door," Alessi said, baring her fangs.

"I can't." Did he do it wrong? Did he remember the code incorrectly? Sweat plastered his hair to his head. "It's not opening."

"Then I'll break it down." Alessi rammed her shoulder into it, and the door bulged at its hinges.

"Stop!" Kol yelled. "You'll kill everyone if you do that."

"I don't care." Her hand met his mouth again, pressing his lips tight against his teeth. Blood dripped where the claw-like nails on her other hand tore into his shoulder. "Why are you so loud? Open the damned door!"

"Give me your blood," Kol said. "Take me with you, that was the deal."

"Once we're out." She tossed him aside as if he weighed nothing, but he pushed himself to his feet. Without her blood, which she said was a human's only chance of surviving on the surface, he would never make it before she opened the door to the outside and killed him. He knew what glow did to people. He remembered Mia's mother's body after she was banished. He saw it through the window for nearly a year. The melting flesh, the sores...

One didn't survive out there without magic.

The witch rammed her shoulder into the door again. It creaked. She braced herself against it, pushing the screaming metal.

"Stop, this wasn't the deal!" He pushed against her with all his lean weight, but she didn't budge.

"Get out of my way!" She swatted at him with her vicious claws, then threw him to the side again with what looked to be only a simple motion. He landed with a thud on the floor, hitting his head.

The world spun around him. "Let me put in the code again, maybe it'll work.'

"It better work," Alessi said.

Dizzy, he rose to his feet and stumbled over to the wall. He paused, fingers hovering an inch above the buttons. "Give me your blood first, so I know you're not planning to kill me."

Something glimmered in her eye again. A spark of truth. If that door had opened the first time, she'd have left him for dead.

A shuffling sound came from the hall, and Kol got an idea. It was cruder than he imagined, but it would work. Still on the ground, he gathered himself until he could take a deep breath, then yelled, "She's in here, assholes!"

"What the fuck's wrong with you?" Her hands met his mouth again, pressing his lips tight against his teeth. She straddled him, pinning his legs with hers and both arms with her free hand. "Look, I was never going to take your brother. It's none of my business if your asshole of a father wants to murder the guy. It's not *my* problem, hole-boy! I'm doing you a favor. You don't know how bad it is up there!"

She pressed harder, and with a lurching motion, Kol twisted his head and loosened her grip against his mouth. If she wouldn't give him her blood, he'd steal it. He bit down, but she didn't bleed. That was supposed to work—this was his last plan to take her blood. To survive in the wastes.

"Nice try," she said, shaking her hand, "but it'll take a lot more than that to make me bleed. Give me the damn code." Something banged against the interior door.

"No." Her hair fell into his face as he stopped struggling. "Your blood or we both die here." Her eyes glowed, and in them he found both his life and his death. She was a predator. A creature that killed, that ate, that murdered. His only bargaining chip, the one he now bet his life on, was that he wouldn't put the code in without first receiving her blood.

Whatever was banging against the door was louder now. Its pace increased, the sound bleeding into his heartbeat. The floor was cool against his back.

"Fine. It seems we've reached a stalemate." She raised a hand as if to strike. "This will probably hurt."

Kol shut his eyes to prepare for the blow. When it didn't come, he looked up at the witch, silver hair falling around her shoulders as she brought a claw to her wrist. She tore into her flesh, sending a cascade of warm blood spattering across his face, his shirt, and the ground around them, then forced her wrist to his mouth.

"Drink, you stubborn shithead," she ordered.

Her blood seared his tongue as if he were drinking a metallic, boiling tea, and the stench of vinegar and smoke was overwhelming. He gagged, struggling not to pull away, and she placed a clawed hand on the back of his head.

"You got yourself into this," she said. "Don't blame me if you turn into something you don't like."

The pounding on the door continued, accompanied by a dull roar. It reverberated through the floor and straight into his skull.

The pain subsided, and he shut his eyes. He was alone with the overwhelming cascade of scarlet. Her dark red blood had a strange texture, thicker than his own, which he remembered from when he bit his tongue or licked a paper cut. Hers was like mud, and as its fouler tastes faded, he tasted only a strange, chemical sweetness. The same chemical sweetness as her breath across his face. And he wanted more of it.

She removed her wrist, and he pushed himself to his feet, head burning. Silver light sparkled in her hair like particles of dust. It covered him, too. His eyes adjusted to a dark world of vibrant colors.

Alessi inspected him. "Good. Now we leave before this gets ugly. Open the damn door."

He shook his head and gathered his senses before punching in the code again, and the door started to open. He looked back.

Kol hated to leave Astor in that place with such unknown dangers. Maybe they could go back for him. Maybe they could—

Just as Kol opened his mouth to say something, the pounding stopped. He and Alessi listened in the silence.

"Kol? Is that you?" Astor's voice came from behind the door, but before Kol could answer, the witch dragged him outside into the silvery moonlight.

The witch pushed against his back and sent him stumbling forward into the wastes. He coughed. Sand was everywhere— in his mouth, in his eyes, between his fingers, sticking to the sweat on his chest. But if he was alive, maybe so were his mother and Caliban.

Maybe he wasn't mad after all.

4

Alessi watched the man collapse outside the gate, squirming on the ground as if a thousand eels pulsed beneath his skin. Some part of her always enjoyed the suffering of men, though another part felt pity.

"Weakling." She lifted her lip in disgust. Had she really just given this human a literal taste of her magic? He twitched then grew still, dark eyes wide and reflecting the silver stars above.

"Fuck. Guess I killed him," she said to herself. She poked him with her boot, but he gasped, wide-eyed, clutching at his bloodied chest. She jumped back, hand gripping the cloak-concealed dagger at her waist. He wasn't the monster known as a Sorgin yet, but there was still time for the change. The man's chest heaved, and a minute passed. There was no sign of distortion. No color leeching from his body, no glowing eyes, no claws... just an idiot groveling in the filth. What was he thinking, forcing her hand like this?

She turned around, cloak sweeping the sand around her feet. "Get up."

"Fuck, do you have cyanide running through your veins?"

"C'mon. What you're feeling is no worse than a hangover," Alessi said in a gruff voice. "Welcome to the Western Wastes. You're lucky, you know." This guy had no idea what he had just gotten himself into. But, then again, neither did she.

"I don't know how much you drink," he said, rubbing sand from his eyes, "but I've never heard of a hangover that bad."

Her hood hung partly over her face, shielding her from the sandblasting winds. Glow danced around her feet as a blue dust, pooling in low areas, heavier than the air or the sand particles she inhaled. It was faint—they said glow was the essence of magic, and witches couldn't see it as well as Belgarri. When she looked back at Kol, light blue glow had gathered in his hair, which was ruffled by the breeze. She sniffed. There it was again: that odd, oily smell. The same scent on him as the night before.

She stopped, then turned and walked until she stood directly in front of the boy. Placing her hands on his cheeks, she stared into his eyes. "You have any magic, human?" Humans weren't supposed to have any.

His dark eyes glimmered, illuminated by the glow gathering in his hair. "No." There was something odd about him. Enough to strike her curiosity, but there were plenty of curiosities out in the wastes.

"Then did your mother have any magic?" she asked, pressing her hands harder against his face. "You thought she was a witch."

"No." He shook his head. "No magic."

"Are you sure?"

"Yes." He tried to look away, but she held him tighter, peering deeper into his eyes.

His father was definitely human, and his mother couldn't have been a witch. It was rare for witches to have natural children, and as far as she knew, her mother was the only one ever to have one. If his mother had magic, she would have to have been one of the Belgarri —and you could always tell species by the color of their eyes, same as the color of their magic.

But Kol's eyes, though a dark, chocolate brown, were the brown of a magicless human. They didn't glow in the low light. She let him go. He was delusional if he thought his mother was alive— his human mother was dead, her bones likely carried away by the rat-like Arratoi that were so plentiful in this region. There was something odd about him, though she didn't know what.

"You're weird." She pushed him away.

He massaged his cheeks. "I have to go back, tell Astor what happened. Just for a second."

Alessi raised an eyebrow. "It almost got us. If you head back now, it'll kill you for sure."

"I heard his voice." Kol wiped sand from his eyes. He coughed, covering his mouth, and a thin trickle of blood ran down his arm. His insides would probably bleed for weeks after drinking her blood. He did it to himself, though.

"That wasn't Astor."

"But he—"

"It's a lyramancer, remember? Some people call them mimics. On the other side of that door was a monster and nothing more." A gust of wind hit them from the east, blowing her black cloak back and revealing her thinly wrapped torso underneath. "Let's hurry before they catch up again."

The wind whipped at them, and the boy covered his eyes with one hand. The underside of his arm was already red and raw from the wind and grit. "People are rarely hunted without reason. Care to share?"

She narrowed her eyes, then took a breath. He'd probably die soon, anyway, so who could he tell? "I pissed off the wrong dragon," she said. "The red king, Bakar. A real nasty bastard, even eats his own sons."

Kol's eyes widened. "Nasty bastard sounds right."

"A prophecy said his son would kill him, so he's eaten every one he's had. And that's not even the worst of it." She bit back more words. She didn't want to get too personal with the human.

Luckily, Kol didn't press any further. Alessi pulled her cloak back over her as they made their way south. Ahead was a vast, sandy nothingness, gigantic red-orange dunes stretching as far as they could see. The same color as Bakar's eyes that night he... *Bastard.* There was nothing she hated more than him except perhaps her mother.

She trudged forward, and the human followed her. His presence felt like something between that of a curious pet and a leech. She only knew their direction by the setting moon, swallowed by the dunes, and the constellation the Hunter of Seven Stars stretching high above. It would be a long night, but there was a village in this direction. She was tired, and by morning she would need to rest.

Then she could figure out what to do with the troublesome human.

What that meant, she wasn't quite sure. She could kill him —she probably should, actually—and yet something prevented her from doing so. The other witches said that blood was powerful magic that bound fates—bound witches to their sisters, to the witches they turned, and to the Sorgins they created.

She wasn't so sentimental.

And she had other concerns. Money was tight, and business was slow. A thought crossed her mind, sending a smile creeping across her face. He could be the solution to her problem. Humans like him were rare on the surface, a delicacy from an older time. He'd sell for what, ten thousand? And all she had to do was keep him alive until they hit the next major city.

She grinned, feeling her fangs press against her lips. What an idiot. She almost felt bad for him, but money was money. "You shouldn't have asked to come with me," she said. "You'll miss your hole."

"Maybe Astor, but not that hole." He followed her, the first hint of twilight showing in the sky. "I wish I got to say goodbye."

It was too late now. Alessi looked at him out the corner of her eye. That look on his face—a pure sadness—wasn't a common one. Those on the surface were too broken to feel such emotion. "You can spend your whole life looking for closure. You'll never find it. So, find your peace now."

"And what if I did turn back?" he asked.

"You drank my blood." Alessi smiled. "Congratulations, now my scent is on you. They're after you, too."

"Then, some day," Kol said, "I'll find a way to save Astor and the others, and then I'll come back."

Alessi shook her head. Naïve human. He spat a mouthful of sand, then wiped his mouth with his arm, leaving a trail of sand-filled saliva. Some spit blew back in the wind, landing on her face.

She wiped it with one hand. "You're gross."

"You're one to talk," Kol muttered.

She shot him a sideways smile, then rolled her eyes. "This will be *fun*."

He froze again, then keeled forward. She caught him with her right hand, claws cutting thin lines in his delicate human flesh.

"Don't tell me I'm turning into one of those things," Kol said.

"Fuck if I know. Probably." She stayed there as he retched

into the sand. When he was done, he stood, wiping vomit from his mouth with a filthy sleeve.

He wasn't a Sorgin; he was just sick. Her acidic blood was eating his insides again. Hopefully *that* wouldn't kill him, fragile thing he was.

"You really are—" she began.

"Gross, yeah, you said it already."

That wasn't what she was going to say this time, but she let him think so. *You really are human,* she was going to say. The taste of magic she gave him would keep him alive for a little while, but no longer.

He retched into the sand a second time.

"Sharing blood is primitive magic. You'll need rest while you recover. And..." What else could she tell him? That she would sell him off in the next major city between the western wastes and the dragon lands in the east? That she was on her way to murder what was possibly the most powerful creature to have ever lived?

"What?" Kol asked.

"Nothing. You'll feel better later." She pulled herself from her thoughts and smiled. Human meat untainted by magic was a delicacy in many villages, and largely the reason humans had nearly gone extinct. He was an opportunity—a gift from the gods. She bounded a few steps ahead and walked backward, her hands outstretched, face turned upward to the moon.

Another gust of sandy wind came from the west, blasting his face. "Ouch." He covered his eyes with one hand.

In his current state, he would probably wind up on some fat Belgarri's plate. "You'll be fine," she said. "But you need new clothes. You share my immunity to glow, but no one's immune to the sand and wind."

"No shit," Kol muttered, looking away.

A faint yellow light glowed ahead on the horizon. She gathered her cloak around her shoulders, letting it shield her from the next gust of grating wind. There was no break from it. The boy had no such protection, and without it, one couldn't survive in the wastes. She had to keep him safe. For now.

"We'll stop at Vico," she said. "It's a small village but should have what we need."

"A village with... people? Dragons?"

"No dragons in these parts. As for people, I wouldn't exactly call them that." Alessi pointed to the growing light on the horizon, the telltale sign of civilization. "We'll be there by dawn. Then you can get some rest."

It was like leading a lamb to the slaughter.

5

The light grew on the horizon until they arrived at
Vico, a village of brown and white buildings sitting at
the bottom of a basin. Some roofs were thatched with
dry, broad leaves, and others were lined in stone panels. All
buildings showed signs of wear and bore a layer of sand. Glow
landed on the rooftops then flowed off them like water, pooling
on the sides of the streets, the fiery brightness of the rising sun
slowly overshadowing its brilliance.

Kol paused at the top of a dune, his heels sinking into it. He
took a moment to shake some of the sand out of his boots, which
he quickly realized was a pointless exercise, then threw a
glance in the direction from which they had come.

"You good?" Alessi asked.

"Yeah." He wasn't. Nausea came and went, and he was
spattered with blood. Dirty, sandy scabs covered gashes on his
cheeks and shoulders. His raw skin burned, and memories of
that night flickered before his eyes like a dream he couldn't
wake from. Everything hurt, and yet he knew he was where he
had to be. He still felt that pull towards the wastes, away from

his home—he would go back some day, but for now, he had another goal.

Find me.

He had to learn the truth about what happened all those years ago. If humans on the surface were as rare as Alessi said, someone would have noticed something if his mother passed through here. This was his chance to get information. To find his mother, if she truly was still alive.

The hairs on the back of his neck stood on end as they trudged through the empty twilight streets of Vico. The cobblestones beneath his feet were rough and broken, but he was grateful the basin the village was situated in gave him a break from the wind. He followed Alessi to a building marked with a wooden sign shaped like a crescent moon. Alessi brought her gloved hand up and knocked on the door.

A panel slid open, just wide enough for Kol to see a pair of glowing eyes. They weren't like Alessi's, however—they were a vibrant purple, their violet light illuminating the door's black paint. Other than that, what little he could see of the person's face appeared human.

Beasts with the faces of men. He recalled his mother's words. *Monsters.*

"Hi Rosaria," Alessi said.

The violet-eyed woman spoke. "Who's—oh. You again." She sounded less than pleased, then looked at Kol. She gave a displeased snort, and Kol looked down at himself, clothes filthy with sand and torn by Alessi's claws. "What is that?" Rosaria's eyes locked hungrily with Kol's.

"Dinner," Alessi said.

Kol's heart raced, fear and surprise mixing together. "What?"

Alessi laughed. She elbowed him in his sore ribs, and he shuffled away from her, but she drew him close again. Sweat beaded on his brow. "I'm kidding, I'm kidding," she whispered to him. She looked back to the innkeeper with a grave face, and said, "I'm not."

"Very funny," Rosaria said. "But the last man you took upstairs nearly burned the place down."

"First, I didn't take him with me. That was an asshole bounty hunter who followed me from Carpacia. Second, he's gone now," Alessi said. "This is someone else."

"You and your, um, *snack* will have to find another place to stay," Rosaria said. "Though he does look delicious." Kol could *hear* her lick her lips.

"It was one time. It won't happen again, I promise," Alessi begged. "I can't sleep out in the dunes. The vultures start pecking at me like I'm a corpse."

"You're thin enough to be one," Rosaria said. Alessi shook her shaggy mane in protest. "But I don't need a promise, I need collateral."

"Just four hours." Alessi reached her hand into her pocket, drawing out two silver coins.

"No." Rosaria shook her head. "You're a liability." The panel slid shut.

"I can be collateral," Kol said. He had surprised himself a hundred times in the past twelve hours, but he couldn't stand to stay out in the dunes any longer.

The panel slid open again, and the violet-eyed woman raised an eyebrow. "I'm listening."

"If you let us stay here, and something goes wrong, you can eat me. I'm weak, you'd be able to catch me."

"He's very weak," Alessi added, nodding. This made Kol feel worse, but he didn't show it.

The woman's eyes inspected him, but the blood and vomit on his face and shirt were enough to prove the point. She turned to Alessi. "Fine. But it'll be three copper for you and your... snack."

Alessi nodded. Chains jangled on the other side of the door, which swung open to reveal a stone room cast in an array of colorful lights. "Witches," he heard the innkeeper mutter under her breath. He eyed the woman—this strange, man-eating woman—but aside from her eyes she seemed as human as him.

"What's it been, six months? You look like hot shit," the woman said, "and not the good kind. And did your friend here drink some dragon piss or something? I know corpses that smell better than him."

Alessi smiled. "Something like that. And you still find him appetizing?"

"The worse they smell, the better they taste." The woman smiled, flashing too-sharp teeth. "Some men are only worth their meat. Enough years in this business, and you learn to lower your standards."

Kol caught a whiff of himself as they stepped over the threshold, sand chafing his legs. He smelled like noxious fumes, like chemicals and poison. "I think I need a bath."

"That'll cost extra." The woman handed Alessi a key.

Faint music played, accompanied by soft female moaning. Kol's face reddened further. Colorfully burning fires cast a dancing rainbow against the wall behind him, the flames' motion and heavy incense in the air nearly causing him to lose his balance.

"What is this place?" Kol asked Alessi in a quiet voice. He eyed the yellow stains on the violet-eyed woman's white shirt, giving her a wide girth as they passed.

"Technically, it's a brothel." Alessi took a key from the disgruntled woman. "But I like it because they rent rooms *cheap* in hopes you use their services." She shot him a sideways glance. "I don't have spare coin, so don't get any *ideas*."

"Aren't princesses supposed to have money?" Kol grumbled.

Alessi led him up narrow, twisting stairs. "Maybe," she said with a bitterness in her voice. "But this one doesn't." She traced a claw-like nail along the cold stone walls, lifting it so as not to disturb faded paintings that hung along the way. "Thanks back there. I'll try to keep her from eating you, but no guarantees. It's nice to get out of the sand for a bit."

"Thanks," Kol said. With him as collateral, however, he hesitated to think what would happen if the mimic from earlier caused any damage. "What if that mimic dragon catches up to us?"

"They shouldn't if we don't stay too long," Alessi said. "The blue dragon will have exhausted his magic after last night, and red dragons are notoriously bad at tracking. I'd say we're at least a day ahead of them."

They approached a thick, wooden door. Alessi inserted the key with a clicking sound, and it swung open to reveal a small room. Another faded painting of a man, woman, and what appeared to be a child with its face scratched out, hung opposite a bed too wide for one person, but too narrow for two. Kol looked closer at the child. Someone sketched over it with the head of a horse, its eyes two crimson splotches.

He shivered, a cold breeze making its way through the open window, moonlight scattered across the wooden floor. "That woman," he asked, "wasn't human, right?"

"Right," Alessi said.

"A monster?"

"To be specific, she's a kind of Belgarri known as an Otsen. They're wolf-people. They'll eat anything, though you really tested that limit." Alessi scrunched her nose. "Luckily for us, they despise dragons, so there aren't a ton of those around here."

Kol looked out the room's dingy window, carved out of the wall at an angle. In the distance, the pinkening dunes reflected the dawn's brilliant rays.

"Get some rest. We'll leave in a few hours, before *they* get here." Alessi plopped onto the bed, facing away from him. Her long, silver hair draped over her like a blanket. She sprawled out on the bed in such a way as to preclude any possibility of sharing it.

Kol sighed, eyes turned to the floor. Of course, she wouldn't share with him, she barely knew him. He barely knew her. What would happen when he woke? Would she push him out the door and say *good luck*? Leave him to die on his own?

After a moment's hesitation, he laid on the floor. He had to sleep. His bones ached, and his raw skin stung. He rolled onto his back, and for a moment, he imagined Alessi's irregular breathing was Astor's. He thought of home, the hole in the ground he cursed for so many years, and when he shut his eyes, the vision returned. The silhouette, his mother's shadow of a face.

Find me.

Then the sensation of falling jerked his body awake. Sweat trickled down his brow, and he buried his head in his hands. He felt dizzy again, as he did in the desert. He sat up, looking at Alessi's still form. She rolled over, facing him.

He couldn't sleep, but he couldn't survive the crushing silence. Her crushing gaze. He had to say something.

"What's going to happen to me?" he asked.

"Death, and maybe taxes." Her voice had a sarcastic edge to it.

"That's not what I mean. When we leave here." Kol took a

breath. "I want to stay with you. I need information on my mother."

"You're crazy. She's dead."

"She isn't. I don't know how to explain it... I just *know*," Kol said. "Then when I find out how she's survived up here, I want to go back and free the others."

"Those are some lofty goals." Alessi rolled onto her stomach. Her voice was muffled by her flat pillow, and she didn't turn to look at him. "I can't fault you for them, but I have bigger concerns than aiding your delusions."

"My mother had money," Kol said. "She was from a wealthy family in Tortaka. If we find her, she would reward you."

"*If* we find her, sure." Alessi groaned. "But dead women rarely pay."

"Then, I can help you. Like I did tonight. Are you banned from other inns?"

"Every inn from here to the eastern islands."

"I'll talk to people for you. I'm good at that, always solved arguments between my sisters. You won't even notice me."

"I have a feeling I will. Look, here's the deal—when we leave, we'll head towards the nameless city to the north. But you're doing *everything* I tell you," Alessi said.

Kol's heartbeat quickened. She was taking him with her— she was really taking him with her. "And what will you tell me to do?"

"Carry my stuff because my back hurts like crazy, pickpocket for me, talk to people for me..." she continued with a list of menial tasks for him. It seemed that everything she disliked doing, she would have him do instead.

Kol kept his voice steady, masking his excitement. It didn't matter what he had to do; this was working. "Alright."

"The nameless city isn't a major city but should be large

enough for our purposes. If we're lucky, we should be able to lose those dragons in the crowd." Alessi rolled over. "Hopefully, that's the end of it, but that bastard king's put a bounty on my head."

Dawn was a red-gold liquid pouring over the clouds and drowning the stars. "Why does that king hate you so much?" Kol asked.

"Lots of people hate me. Go to sleep."

"Out! Out with ya!" The gruff woman's voice jerked Kol awake. He hit his head on the bed frame. "You only paid for four hours!"

It took him a moment to remember he wasn't in his bunk, sleeping beneath a snoring Astor. The previous night's events flashed before his eyes: the headless chicken, blue glow gathering around his hair, dunes as far as he could see. His lower back cracked as he pushed himself to a standing position.

On the bed, Alessi was sound asleep, drool trailing out of the edge of her mouth.

The woman banged on the door again. "Out! Out! I don't care what you're doing, just finish and get out of here!"

Kol placed a hand on Alessi's shoulder, shaking her.

"Hey!" he shouted. She stirred but didn't wake. "*Hey!*" he shouted even louder. He kicked the bed, pushing it back a few inches.

Alessi whipped around to face him, drool smeared across the side of her face and sleep in her eyes. "What?" she snapped, fangs bared as if to bite him.

He drew back his hand. "It's that woman—"

"Out with ya!" the woman's voice came again from the other side of the door.

Alessi jumped out of bed, bumping into Kol, and nearly sending him tumbling into the stone wall behind him.

"Oh shit, what time is it?" She squinted at the sunlight pouring in through the slanted window. "Why didn't you wake me up?"

"I just did."

"Damnit, should've called a crow..." Alessi licked her filthy hand, slicking back her hair.

"Out! Out!" the woman shouted again. "Or I'll eat the man as your late fee!" The door made an empty sound as it rattled against the frame.

Alessi threw open the door with such force that the irritable innkeeper pressed herself against the opposing wall. "Yeah, yeah, we heard you," she growled.

The woman's eyes followed Alessi, then Kol, down the twisting steps with what he could only describe as a mixture of hunger and suspicion.

Alessi grunted as they walked into the blinding sunlight, shielding her face with her hand. "Thanks, Rosaria."

"Whatever." Rosaria slammed the door behind them.

Someone bumped into Kol's side as they entered the street, sending him staggering back a step. Not only were there people, but there were *lots* of people, or Belgarri, or whatever they were. He turned in a full circle, nearly tripping on his tattered pant leg as he took in the new sight. The people, less than amused, shot him hard stares as the crowd parted around them. Their eyes glowed like the innkeeper's and Alessi's, but all different colors, mostly shades of reds and purples.

"Here." Alessi handed him a coin. She placed one hand on his shoulder, and with the other, she pointed to a building ahead. "Time for some new clothes. You stand out far too much."

"Thanks," Kol said, overwhelmed by the vibrant reds,

blues, and greens around him, eyes all burning with the intensity of miniature suns.

"Don't thank me, it's for my own good. Anyone here could be my enemy, so we don't need to go attracting attention," Alessi said, whipping her silver hair behind her shoulder with one hand. "This is your first test. I want you to pickpocket that guy over there." She pointed.

The guy, as she said, was a man at least seven feet tall wearing furs and studded leather boots. Kol's eyes widened. "Him?"

"Him." She held out her hand and made a grasping gesture.

"I'm pretty sure that'll attract attention," Kol said, unconvinced by her plan.

"Just come up behind him, slip a hand in his pocket, and take a few coins. Easy, yeah?"

He eyed the man again. He was bigger than Kol. Bigger than Astor, too, and pure muscle. His entire body was clothed in furs. "No, not easy."

"Look, I don't have enough coin for both of us. Make yourself useful or I'll have to ditch you here." Alessi crossed her arms.

She would take some getting used to. But for now, he needed her.

Kol swallowed. "Fine." He wove through the overwhelming crowd. "Sorry," he said, reminding himself to breathe. "'Scuse me." Glowing eyes turned toward him with hints of curiosity and irritation.

His target leaned against a stone wall talking to a shorter man. The shorter man's eyes glowed a faint red, and his prominent front teeth were razor sharp in his mouth as he spoke. Tiptoeing in his now-ruined shoes, Kol snuck up behind the target and slid a hand into his warm pocket. At the bottom of the pocket were coins of varying size—too many to count—and he curled his fingers around a few. He gritted his teeth, then carefully withdrew his hand. The man didn't seem to notice and continued conversing with his equally oblivious friend.

Kol looked at the coins for a second before stuffing them into his pocket. He did it. He made his way back across the street to where a smug Alessi waited on the other side.

She took a fist and ground it into his head. It hurt, though it seemed to be an affectionate gesture. "I knew you could do it," she said. "Let me see what you got."

"Hey!" The violet-eyed man, who Kol now recognized as an Otsen wolf man, had noticed them. His friend pointed at Kol.

Shit.

Alessi lifted one arm, and her cloak followed it like a wing. She tucked it over Kol. "Run!" she said, and the pair took a right down a dusty alleyway between two buildings. Glow lined the alley's center and lowest point.

Kol's heart beat in his throat as they ran. The walls were so uneven he had to duck at points, and at others he had to follow immediately behind Alessi, but after jumping over a few piles of refuse they emerged between two buildings unscathed. Sweat plastered Kol's hair to his face, and his chest heaved like it never had before. There was not as much space to run in the compound.

Alessi laughed.

"What's so funny?" he asked, an edge to his voice.

"You." She took her cloak off him. "I haven't had that much fun in ages. Let's do it again."

"Let's *never* do that again." He coughed, clearing his lungs of dusty phlegm. "I don't think I'm cut out to be a thief."

"Maybe not," Alessi said, holding his stolen coins in her gloved hand. "But this is enough for some food and new clothes so you can blend in." She put a hand on his shoulder and peered into his eyes.

Kol struggled against her, but claws dug into his flesh. "You're doing that thing again."

"Your eyes will be a problem," she said. "They mark you as human. And there are a billion Belgarri up here that would literally kill to eat a human. You guys were a delicacy up until you nearly disappeared, you know."

"I didn't know that, actually. But if my eyes are a problem, I'll hide them." Kol looked around. At least some of the Belgarri already recognized him, or so it seemed, with their piercing stares. Several had the same violet eyes as the innkeeper. "So, what are these monsters?"

"Belgarri. Look at their eyes. Wolf-people, rat-people--"

"But they look like *people* people."

"For now. They're shapeshifters, and if you're lucky, you'll never see their native forms."

Shapeshifters. *Monsters with the faces of men.* It made sense, and yet, it was hard to believe.

Alessi walked into the street, and he followed. He turned in a circle, taking in the stone and wood architecture around and above him. A cold breeze met his face, but this time he wasn't chilled. They approached a building, a shop with words Kol couldn't understand written across the side in scrawling font. Or at least, he thought they were words, but the letters looked more like chicken scratches. They went inside, where a shop-keeper sorted piles of cloth.

"Reynor," Alessi said.

"The wife said you had an interesting *snack* last night, witch," said the violet-eyed shopkeeper. He looked Kol up and down as if inspecting a slab of meat.

Alessi traced her clawed fingers over black iridescent robes for sale. "Gossiping already, hey?" She waved a hand dismissively.

"I'd like to know what *he's* doing here," the man said in a low voice, "since he's a—"

"Customer?" Alessi finished his sentence. "And eating your customers is bad for business."

The man huffed. He stood at least a head taller than Astor, his shoulders unnaturally broad. He had the musculature of a warrior, and the scars to prove it. "Fine. But you know I still don't sell to you, after what happened last time."

"You say that, but you know you're not too good for my money. You're no better than your whore of a wife." Alessi picked up the garment, holding out another coin.

The man smirked at her. "Don't speak that way about my wife," he said, taking the coin. He looked at Kol, hunger in his eyes. "But that collateral..."

"You can't eat him," Alessi said. "Kol, ignore him. He likes to tease, but he's all bark and no bite. He's nothing more than Rosaria's own personal *bitch*." That last word flew off Alessi's tongue like venom. "Pick something out."

Kol nodded and turned away. When Alessi wondered to the other end of the store, Kol busied himself looking at clothes until he froze, feeling the man's breath on his neck before he took a long, deep... sniff?

"Can I help you?" Kol asked.

"You have a smell about you," he said. "How was a human like you touched by magic?" The shopkeeper took another step forward, hungry eyes glowing.

"I drank her blood," Kol said after a moment.

"No, this is something different. Old magic. I've smelled it before." He sniffed again. "On a woman who passed through here maybe fifteen years ago, had dark eyes like yours."

"Really?" Kol asked. This could be useful.

"Yeah. You don't forget a sorceress like that." The man took another step towards him.

"Where was she going?"

The man scratched his head. "It's hard to remember."

This could be his only lead. "Tell me what you know. I'll pay you."

"East," he said. "Something about the Valley of Dragons, but that's in the red king's territory."

Find me in the Valley of Dragons. So, it was true.

"You're not planning to go, are you? They call it the Valley of Dragons for a reason. It's dangerous there." The man took another step toward him, practically salivating.

"It's dangerous here, too." Kol stepped away, but the table's edge met his lower back.

The man sniffed the air. "You both smell so unusual. And I *do* like them rare." He licked his lips and took another step closer. He was right in front of Kol now—if he were to reach out with those arms, Kol doubted he could escape.

A small book hit the man on the side of the head with enough force to nearly knock him over. On the other side of the store, Alessi stood defiantly. "What part of 'you can't eat him' do you not understand?"

As Alessi berated the shopkeeper, Kol turned his attention back to the reason they were there. Various items of clothing were folded on tables in the open space, while others hung from the ceiling. It was chaos but organized roughly by color. Reds here, blacks here, blues here, yellows by the door. He dug through a pile of stiff shirts and rough materials before seeing a cloak made of the same strange material as Alessi's.

It shined an iridescent blue in the light, and as he slipped it on, his fingers found a hood like Alessi's to protect his face from the sand. It was cut differently, though—closer to the body than Alessi's, resembling a long jacket. The material was thin and gossamer in a way that suggested it may be waterproof without adding bulk.

"Perfect," Alessi said, appearing at his side and rubbing the material between her thumb and index finger. "Let's get going."

Kol looked down at his ruined pajamas. "I need pants. And probably a new shirt, and maybe some—"

"Ugh. Fine. Get what you need." Alessi thumbed through another pile of dark clothing, and it shined in strange hues of purple and blue in the sunlight. "What about these?" She tossed him a pair of burgundy pants. They looked worn around the edges and had a foul smell to them.

"Uh..." Kol said.

"What? Something wrong with them?"

He sniffed them again, confirming they were foul. He searched for words that would not offend her selection. "These aren't the same as the jacket," he said, clutching it to his chest.

"What, you care about matching now?" Alessi asked. "You're covered in vomit, not exactly a fashion icon." She pointed at the jacket. "Only outer clothes are made of Onari skin because it tends to chafe, and there's a lot of sand in this region. You get the picture."

"Alright," he said. He would have to ask her later what an Onari was.

She tossed him a new pair of dark leather boots, then a black shirt and black pants. "Those boots are good. Hartzen leather, should last you a while. And the shirt will match your pants since you care so much." She muttered something under her breath he couldn't understand, though the shopkeeper chuckled.

Kol slipped the boots on. "Thanks." They not only fit but seemed to shrink to the size of his feet. He nearly fell backwards in surprise. There was so much about this world he didn't know—Onari, Hartzen, dragons...

She jingled the coins in her pocket and picked up a long, red shirt. "Something for me, now."

She held it against herself, looking at her reflection in a cracked mirror before peeling off her own tattered shirt. Kol's face grew hot, but he couldn't force himself to look away from the tattered bindings covering her chest. She slipped the new shirt over her head. It snagged on her horn, and as she struggled the shopkeeper laughed.

"Witches," the shopkeeper scoffed. "No modesty."

"Is that what you tell your wife as she's shagging other men?" Once the shirt was on, Alessi grabbed an assortment of other supplies and a small pack before putting coins in the shopkeeper's open palm. "Always a pleasure doing business with you."

"Wish I could say the same." The man walked behind a desk, where he stored the coins in a leather pouch. "And don't bring stolen coin next time."

"We'll see about that," Alessi said as they left. They rounded the corner, avoiding a group of elderly, red-eyed women. Their gossiping chatter cluttered the air. Alessi turned to Kol. "Alright, go change."

He felt at a tattered sleeve and looked around. The streets were not packed, but there were people—*Belgarri*—about. "Where?"

She pointed to the alleyway to her right. It was empty, though littered with refuse, and Kol walked into its shadows. His feet disturbed the glow that pooled in the gutters. It seemed dirtier now, during the day, its light dampened by that of the sun. Carefully, he peeled off his torn pants, stained with blood and vomit and covered in sand. He held them between his thumb and index finger. They were in worse shape than he imagined. He slipped on the new ones, leaving his old pants in the dirt before taking off his tattered shirt.

Something moved in the alley ahead, then a rat skittered by his foot. He thought of the man he robbed from, and looked back, checking that Alessi was still there.

"What if he comes after us?" Kol shouted.

"Who?" Alessi leaned against a wall outside the alley, facing away from him and inspecting her claw-like nails. The wind rustled her silver hair, sending sparks of glow tumbling to the ground.

"That man from earlier," Kol said. "You know, the one I"—he lowered his voice—"stole from."

Alessi grinned, tilting her head back to look at him. His face reddened, and he slipped the new shirt over his head. "No way," she said. "He's not going to follow us for that kind of chump change."

He remembered the man's towering figure, his muscled physique. He looked strong, but there was more to the surface than met the eye. "Alright."

"You're taking forever. You done putting your makeup on?" Alessi asked.

Kol zipped up his new pants. They were too large around the thighs but fit fairly well for the most part. He brushed his hair with one hand, surprised by the iridescent blue dust that fell from it. "There's glow in my hair."

"Yeah. It might be the only thing up here that likes you."

Kol rejoined Alessi in the street. He eyed her as they walked, side-by-side, toward a gate on a hill ahead. By the shape of the city, and the decreasing concentration of buildings, he could tell they neared its outermost border. That archway, though only a marker, was the gateway to a new life. "So, you are taking me north, like you promised." Part of him expected her to abandon him by this point.

Alessi nodded. "Yeah. Unless you'd rather I leave you here to fend for yourself." For a moment, there was a change in her expression, however slight. Worry crossed her face, and that sideways smile faded.

Find me.

A crowd approached, and they wove their way through the mass of bodies and multi-colored eyes.

"You can leave if you want," Alessi said. Her eyes were downcast. "If you don't like where I'm going." They stopped at an intricately decorated metal archway at the entrance of the city. Scratch-like letters glowed above it, a faint blue not unlike the doors back at the compound. The same color as the glow, likely more brilliant in the night than in the overwhelming sun.

"And where is that?" Where was her final destination, and would it align with his own goals?

"If I tell you now, it could ruin everything. But this path I've chosen is a deadly one." Alessi took a breath, still avoiding his eyes. "This is my last journey to the eastern kingdom."

Eastern kingdom. Where the red king was.

Find me in the Valley of Dragons.

Alessi's smile was gone, and her slumped shoulders told him she did not want more questions. Besides, the only other questions he had he wasn't sure he wanted answers to. He flexed his toes, feeling sand between them. Same socks, new shoes. His socks were Astor's, borrowed that night without permission and now he may never be able to give them back. It was such a silly thing to be bothered by.

They crested a dune, at the top of which was a partially buried gate.

"Wait," Kol said, stopping. He pulled up his new hood to shield his eyes from the sand and the blinding sun and looked north. At this height, far away, he could barely see the compound's dome on the horizon. Or at least he thought he could.

The reality of the situation took the breath from Kol's

lungs, and he paused. Was Astor looking for him? Would Astor be there when he got back? There was a good chance he'd never see his brother again. Silently, he faced the hill and they continued north. He threw one last look over his shoulder to the crowd of glowing-eyed people gathered at the bottom of the basin.

"Homesick?" Alessi asked, studying the expression on his face.

He wiped his eyes. "A little. But I had to leave. I know I did."

Find me.

"It'll hurt less with time," Alessi said.

"I don't see how."

"You'll miss them for a few days, maybe a few months, or a few years. Then you'll start to forget, and you'll realize you're better off on your own." Alessi looked back at him and smiled, but not with her eyes. "And you'll feel better."

6

He'd dreamed of home the night before, between pecks from opportunistic vultures and nibbles of crawling wasteland parasites. He dreamed of running from a shapeless darkness down black hallways and through glowing doors. Then, when he stepped over the final threshold and turned around, Astor stood there.

"Astor!" he'd cried out before his brother's form was overtaken by nothingness, and Kol fell into a world of shadows.

Find me in the Valley of Dragons.

That woman the shopkeeper saw was his mother; he was certain of it. And if what the man said was correct, she was alive—or at least she was alive fifteen years ago. He knew the glow didn't kill her, but now something else bothered him.

The man called her a sorceress. Was she like Alessi? Or was she something else entirely?

The moon was high overhead as they walked through the western wastes in the direction of the nameless city. A cold wind bit Kol's ankles as he eyed Alessi, seemingly unbothered by the chilly weather.

"What's the difference between a witch and a sorceress?" Kol asked.

"Why would I know?" Alessi asked in a gruff voice.

"Because..." Because she was a witch. Should he press more? Maybe he was in over his head. And yet, this witch was helping him, but not without a cost—his back ached where her heavy pack dug into his shoulders. Their equipment had increased, too, with two sleeping bags and two canteens now.

Kol shook the glow from his hair as they crested another dune. He would ask a different question.

"What is glow, then?" he asked. "Why is it everywhere, and why doesn't it hurt witches, Belgarri, and sorcerers?"

"Gods, you're hung up on sorcerers tonight. No one really knows," Alessi said after a moment. "Some say glow is the blood of a god, other say it's the remnant of a living weapon designed to kill all humans during the Darkness. All I know for sure is that it's attracted to magic and kills those without it."

Crests wove like snakes through the sand, as if the western wastes were a million writhing serpents governed by the wind. Rivers of glowing blue made their way through the lowest point, and Kol could almost imagine the glow was water. He was finally free, like the people before the Darkness, like the people in books.

Something howled and yipped in the distance.

"Koyotles," Alessi said. "Not quite Otsens, not quite coyotes, but mongrel beings left to wander the wastes. They're small and harmless as long as they're not too hungry."

She cupped her hands around her mouth and tilted her head to the moon and howled. The Koyotles went silent for a moment before howling back.

Kol did the same, letting out a long howl in the direction of the moon.

But what howled back next—whatever it was—was not a

Koyotle. Instead, it was low and coming from the opposite direction. It echoed through the vastness of the sands, over glow stirring around the desert surface like waves.

Alessi looked over her shoulder before quickening her pace, prompting Kol to follow. "Come on, let's hurry. We're almost there."

"What was that?" Kol asked.

"I don't know. But it howled even worse than you."

A breeze rustled his hair. Clouds hovered in the distance, blocking out the stars, and the sand gave way to a strange substance gathering on the dunes, purple-white in the moonlight. This wasn't glow. Kol paused, leaned down, and took some of it in his hand. Sand was beneath it, sticking to it. His fingers burned from the cold, but he didn't let go.

Alessi rolled her eyes. "What in the hells are you doing?"

Kol looked down at his hand, only disappointed to see that the strange substance disappeared. "There's something wrong with this sand."

"It's not sand, it's snow. Really dirty snow. Put that down." She swatted the remaining snow from his hand.

Something small, white, and cold landed on his finger before disappearing. This had to be the snow she mentioned. He'd read about it, but it was so different from how he had imagined. He looked up. More snow fell from the sky, onto his eyelashes and melting into the leather of his cloak.

It mixed with the glow, creating a blue-white radiance spreading across the landscape. It was strange to him that, just a few days prior, glow was so deadly, when now it was just a part of life. Part of the landscape. Another feeling crept over him, a slight numbness of his extremities, with the occasional stinging pain.

Alessi held out one hand, letting the white flakes land on her skin before disappearing. The snow filled the sky above them, casting it in that same alien radiance. Her silver hair reflected the luminescence around, and she spun, throwing snowflakes off her body. It was impossible not to watch her.

Alessi stopped, shivering. She hugged her arms to herself. "So cold."

The snow came down in waves now. Kol tried to keep his voice steady, to hide his awe as the world around him turned gray, blue, and white. "It's beautiful."

"It's deadly. The citadel's just north of here, we need to hurry up and get there before the storm gets much worse," Alessi said. "We'll freeze to death if we stay still, so let's get moving."

"It doesn't seem so bad to me," Kol said. "I kind of like it."

Alessi rolled her eyes. "It's the middle of summer."

"It's summer?"

"Yes, dumbass. That's why I didn't bring a coat. Hurry up." She pushed him, sending him tumbling forward. It might have hurt if there weren't a pile of snow and sand to catch him.

Kol's palms stung as he pushed himself back up. "So what? It's snowing in summer."

"It's not supposed to, hole-boy." Alessi faced the clouds, which were now closing in. "Your father was right. There's a new Rainsinger."

"Rainsinger?"

"Storm mage. He's young and moody, and he's terrible at cards."

Kol lifted more of the sandy snow into his hand, watching it fall between his fingers.

"I told you to put that disgusting stuff down. Look, we're almost there." Alessi pointed to the horizon. Through the falling, luminescent snow, he could barely make out a gray mound. "Put your hood up and pray nothing smells you."

They continued in silence, Kol's hood bouncing as he

walked, snow building around them. Soon, they reached the city gates, carved and glowing not unlike the gate in Vico. This gray stone gate, however, was much larger, stretching into the blue-white sky above. Above it was the place for a name, but there were no letters he could recognize.

"We call this place *Zeniko Hirata*," Alessi said.

Kol raised an eyebrow. He knew a few old human languages from the compound's library—or at least could recognize them, but these words were completely alien to him.

"It means '*nameless city.*'"

"Okay, but why doesn't it have a name?"

"It will. Belgarri have old customs, they're waiting for a namesake to come along. It may not happen in your lifetime, or mine, but that's a problem for them."

Ahead, the city streets wove between gray and white buildings like a labyrinth. When the snowflakes stopped, Kol could see a tall, stone wall stretch to either side for as far as he could see, like great arms wrapping around the city.

"I see why you picked this place," Kol said. They walked underneath the gate, and more people became apparent. However, while the eyes in Vico were reds and purples, these were every shade of green, blue, gold, and yellow.

The colors changed, bodies moved, but one man stood still amidst the torrent. His eyes were a fiery red-orange, and his hair the same color, and he was muscular in a lanky way only exceptionally tall men could be.

Alessi pulled Kol behind a snowdrift, then peeled off her glove. Blue scales reflected the yellow light around them. A crowd of people pushed by and strange yellow lights reached from poles along the street.

"Who's that guy?" Kol asked. As he spoke, the man turned around and headed in the direction they came from. His presence was different from the other Belgarri, familiar and deadly.

Kol couldn't stop looking at him. His eyes burned like embers, glowing in the night.

Alessi turned, grabbing Kol's hood between two fingers. Then, she yanked it down over his face with such force he nearly landed in the gathering snow.

"What was that for?" he complained, massaging at his sore scalp. Her grip relieved him of a few strands of hair.

"Shhhhh," she hissed. "Keep your eyes covered."

"Who was that?" Kol asked after what felt like hours.

"Red dragon," Alessi whispered. She raised an eyebrow, inspecting the man. "Sent by the red king."

Kol's heartbeat quickened. "One of the dragons from the compound?"

Alessi studied him. "It's likely, there aren't a lot of other dragons out here, but he's leaving the city. Probably going to regroup with the others."

Kol's eyes were glued to the man as he disappeared into the crowd once more. He felt it again—that pull he felt that first time he saw the wastes. Something compelled him to talk to the red dragon, and it took everything in his sense and willpower to keep from chasing after him.

The vision flashed before his eyes again.

Find me.

Kol shook his head, grounding himself. There was another familiar face weaving its way through the crowd, attached to a scarred and muscled torso. "Now it's that guy from Vico." His heartbeat pounded in his ears. "Should we even be here?"

"He's not here for us. It's not uncommon for Otsens to travel between the western cities for work," Alessi explained. "Of all the Belgarri, they may be the most dangerous, but also the most money motivated. You find them working as mercenaries." Seeing the concerned expression on Kol's face, she added, "Don't look so down in the dumps. You're safe as long as you're with me."

"Sure."

She gestured to the passing crowd, their strange and colorful eyes glowing in the dim light. "But there is something you should know. We have enemies among the Belgarri here. Some want to see me suffer for my mother's sins. Some haven't tasted human flesh for far too long. Some, I may have... a history with. Others will kill us both for the hell of it. Do you understand?"

Kol nodded. He looked to the street again, but both men were gone. He felt exposed and claustrophobic as they walked on, surrounded by strange and colorful people and sights but unable to see their full view. He turned his eyes to the ground and checked his hood, which greatly diminished his field of view. All he could see were feet. Large feet, small feet, feet not unlike those of his mothers and siblings, except that snow lined the street and all these feet were bare. He shivered.

Alessi stuck a hand in her pocket, jingling change. A few hungry eyes turned her way.

"Where are we going?" Kol asked.

"I know a place."

Kol remembered the woman from the inn the night before, her shirt stained with something neither beer nor saliva.

"Not another one," he said, exasperated.

"A brothel?" Alessi asked. "No, this one's just a regular inn. No one goes for the beds, only for the beer."

"Hmm."

"Yeah. You drink?"

"Not yet." There was limited alcohol underground, and his father drank what little they had or made. "But I could go for a taste."

"You haven't had a drink? How old are you, thirty?"

"Uh." Kol remembered the small party Astor put together for him with cake from the kitchen and a new book, which he finished in less than a day. That was only three weeks ago, but now it felt like another lifetime. "Twenty."

"Twenty and you've never had a beer?" Alessi gave him a look he didn't entirely like.

"It's not exactly easy to come by where I'm from," he explained.

Alessi laughed again, putting a hand on his shoulder. He winced at the pressure. "We'll have fun tonight," Alessi said, "just don't trust the locals." Together, they burst through a pair of heavy doors and into a room full of strange men.

"As long as fun doesn't end with one of us dead," Kol said, his voice drowned out by the sounds of the tavern. Scarred men with glowing yellow and emerald eyes wearing fur and feathers filled the wood-lined space. Flaming torches cast their shifting shadows on the high walls.

Alessi punched him on the shoulder, sending stinging pains throughout his body. "Eh, we're fine. I'll kick those dragons' asses when the time comes." She pushed her way between two leather-bound warriors, one with an ax on his belt and the other with a sword. "Coming through!"

Kol squeezed after her, following closely as she swam through the crowd. There were posters up on one wall with men and women colorfully drawn on them. At the top was a red-haired man marked:

Prince of the Eastern kingdom as he would appear today, courtesy of King Bakar of the Eastern Kingdom. Forty thousand gold.

The man's face was like a memory of a dream, familiar yet strange. Beside it were two posters of the same silver-haired woman, one marked:

Princess Alessandra of the Badlands, courtesy of Witch Queen Miren. Thirty thousand gold. Wanted dead or alive.

And the second marked:

Princess Alessandra of the Badlands, courtesy of King Bakar of the Eastern Kingdom. Thirty thousand gold. Wanted alive.

He looked closer at the witch, her sideways smile, those curving horns. It was a terrible drawing, but its expression was unmistakable: that was Alessi. Even her own mother wanted her dead.

When they reached a wooden bar, she looked back at him, hood covering her horns. It wasn't much of a disguise, but hiding her distinctive horns did help.

"You passed the first test, making it through the crowd." She gestured for him to sit on a simple stool beside her, and they both put their elbows on the bar. Alessi held out a silver coin, a broad smile spreading across her face.

"Oh. *You.*" An irritated Bartender set down a glass he was polishing with a white-and-blue rag. "I thought I told you not to come back."

"I'm hurt." Alessi faked a pout. "Give me two of your finest. Take the damn coin, silver should cover us for the night."

"Not with the way you drink," the bartender muttered under his breath. The man wore a chain around his neck, and at its end was a curved glass. It was a common magnifying glass, not unlike the ones his father stocked in their library. Maybe Kol could gain his favor.

Kol checked his hood, then pointed to the glass. "Nice gear."

"Thanks." The bartender smiled for a moment, his yellow eyes flashing. He leaned in. "It's a family heirloom; we've collected human relics for generations. It was a weapon before the Darkness."

Not exactly. "Do you know how to use it?"

"No." The man shook his head. "It can't amplify magic, so I think it's broken."

"It was more of a tool than a weapon," Kol said. "It magnifies things visually. You can read with it if you want. But—most people don't know this—if you hold it at the right angle in the sunlight, it can start a fire."

"Ah, a fire-weapon!" The bartender smiled and nodded. The look of joy faded from his face when he turned to Alessi again. "And you're with *her*?"

"Yeah," Kol said. "We're traveling. On... business." He hoped the man wouldn't see through his lie.

The bartender looked from Kol, to Alessi, then back to Kol. "Lots of that sort of business out here," he said before returning with two glasses full of amber liquid.

Kol eyed it suspiciously.

Alessi held it to her lips, and within moments it was empty. "Drink. It's beer. Still can't believe you've never had one. I've been drinking since I was a child."

"Which would be what, five years ago?" Kol asked, but Alessi smacked the back of his head. His eyes watered. "How old can you be?"

"Never ask a lady her age," she said, downing yet another glass. She burped.

"Lady. Right." Kol sniffed the foul liquid and took a sip. It was terrible.

Alessi laughed at his scrunched face. "Try it again when you're a man."

"I am a man." He took another sip, then another, and found it slightly less terrible, though he found its metallic edge to be off-putting. The glass wasn't even half empty when his vision began to blur.

Through Kol's blurred vision, he saw a large man with a mane of black hair walk up behind Alessi. She spun around to face him, flexing her clawed hand. Kol thought she might attack him for a moment, but she gave a false smile.

"Ah. Kyan," she said with her eyes narrowed.

"I see you have a new pet. What happened to the last one, the pretty-boy with feathers?" Kyan asked. " Did he stop letting you peg him?"

Alessi's face reddened. "It wasn't like that."

"Here on business, right?" Kyan asked in a biting tone. He looked to Kol. "Hey, how much is she charging these days?"

Kol shot him an irritated glance.

The room filled with laughter. Alessi gave a wry smile. One of the man's companions tugged at Kol's hood, pulling him from his chair. The room spun around him.

"Fuck you," Kol said. The lackey kicked him in the shin, and Kol landed a sloppy punch in his solar plexus. The man stepped back.

"What the hell are you?" Kyan sniffed the air. His breath smelled of blood and rotting meat.

"Leave him out of this," Alessi said.

"Why should I?" Kyan lowered his head, looking directly into Alessi's eyes. "I want everyone in here to see what trash you are. He almost smells like a dragon."

"Not funny, Kyan," Alessi said.

Kyan lifted the corner of his lip. "Well, he's nothing I've smelled before. Have you really stooped so low as to sell yourself to beasts?"

Kol checked his hood.

"He's a basilisk," she said. "If you look him in the eye, he'll turn you to stone."

She was clever, he had to give her that much, but Kol knew when it was time to leave. He started getting up, but another man pushed him, and he fell to the ground with a curse, head spinning.

"Sure doesn't hold his alcohol like a basilisk," Kyan said.

"He's weak, doesn't even have magic." Alessi rolled her eyes. "It's just like you to pick on someone like that. Leave him alone."

"A broken one, eh?" Kyan laughed again. "Even a dragon would have been better. Why don't I have a go at him, he'd better be good in—"

"Whatever. He's nothing to me."

"If he's nothing to you, how about we eat him? Men with no magic are useless, after all."

Alessi was silent, glaring at Kyan.

Kol stumbled to his feet, steadying himself against the bar. The room spun around him, and a warmth spread through his veins. He cursed himself for drinking so much so quickly.

"You can eat him," Alessi said. A murmuring crowd gathered, pouring in through the doorway. "But only if you can beat me."

Kol didn't like those odds. Any chance of getting eaten was worse than none.

"This can only be settled with a *hartu*, dragon shagger." A wicked smile spread across Kyan's face. His teeth were a little too sharp, as were those of the onlookers.

Kol, on the other hand, scrambled back into his creaking chair. His shin hurt, and his eyelids drooped. His glass, nearly empty, sat in front of him.

He's nothing to me.

Somehow, those words hurt worse than the kick to the shin, and they haunted him as he continued to drink. The tavern was lively around him, indifferent to his misery.

"You alright there, sonny?" a man's voice came from beside him.

Kol's hood bunched on the top of his head as he groggily looked up to see a man with a pinched face and protruding front teeth that reminded Kol of a mouse, wearing a long, red robe. The man stepped back in alarm.

"I'm fine," Kol muttered. "Go away." He waved a hand dismissively.

"I haven't seen one of you in forever." The man took the seat next to him, and a bare, fur-framed torso appeared beside the mouse-man. Kol looked up and recognized the purple-eyed Otsen from earlier.

This caught Kol off guard. "Who do you think you're—"

"I heard you're traveling with the Wanderer." The mouse-man leaned closer to him and Kol leaned away.

"The what?" Kol asked groggily.

"You know. *Her.*" The mouse-man said. "Trouble."

"Alessi?" Kol looked at Alessi over the man's shoulder to see her down yet another glass of amber liquid.

"Now tell me, what does... *Alessi* want with you?" The shorter man looked around the room as if to check he was being followed. "Considering she just bet your life on a *hartu*. A game. No one beats Kyan, not even her."

Kol thought for a moment. He remembered her arrival at the compound, the dinner party, his father's words. His face flushed. "I don't know. I thought she was going to help me."

The mouse-man covered his mouth and laughed. He tapped his foot against the warm wooden floor. His Otsen wolf-man companion stepped closer, and Kol took the last sip from his glass. He didn't seem to recognize Kol, or at least if he did, he didn't show it.

"I'd rather accept help from the Beast of Alon himself," the mouse-man joked, looking to his companion. The violet-eyed man grunted in response. "She never does anything for free."

The bartender brought Kol another drink, and he swirled it in the glass. He wasn't afraid—he was too drunk to be afraid.

He took a sip, holding the liquid in his mouth for a moment, noting the metallic taste.

Blood, he realized. That was the strange flavor layered on top of the alcohol.

Beyond them, in the center of the room, Alessi leaped at her rival, grabbing his beard in her clawed hand. The way she whipped him to and fro seemed unnatural for a woman, but then Kol reminded himself of her magic. Two other men tried to separate them. Alessi bit one then pushed him backwards with blood spurting from his arm as she dove again at her rival.

"Why are you traveling with that monster?" the mouse-man asked.

"I have to," Kol said. "We're being followed."

"Witch magic. Trickery. Illusionists, the lot of 'em, I'd know. They like to lure men away from their homes and drain them of all that they are—" The mouse-man winced as Alessi slammed her rival down on a table, shattering it to pieces. He raised his voice over the noise and continued. "We could get you out of here before she loses the bet."

Kol looked to the violet-eyed man, who stood with his arms crossed. "I can't. She said—"

"That he's dangerous? Otsens do get a bad rap, but Bartu here is as friendly as they get." The scarred, violet-eyed man forced a smile, which looked rather unnatural on his grizzled face. "She only told you that to scare you out of coming with us. She's an old... acquaintance of ours."

"I'm not sure I believe you."

The mouse-man sniffed the air. "You have an odd smell to you, a mix of things. You drank her blood, yes?"

Kol's heart nearly skipped a beat. "Maybe."

"There are other things you can do to keep the glow at bay. Witch's blood is bad stuff. Poison. It'll rot you from the inside out until there's nothing left, until you're just a shell of yourself. I've seen it happen."

Kol scoffed. "I think you're lying." His eyes unfocused, reducing the mouse-man to a blur.

"She'll kill you. They eat people, you know, witches. That's how they get their power." The short man stood, and so did Kol. He swayed, steadying himself against the bar as the brawl continued beyond.

"And why should I believe you?" Kol asked, slurred words like mud in his mouth.

The mouse-man eyed his companion, who nodded. "There are... *other* humans here, on the surface. We work for them, smuggling humans to the highlands." He reached out a pointed finger, tracing a tall shape. "There are pillars there, reaching high into the sky. Remnants of what once was, coated in earth and ash. But at the top, the air is clean, and there are humans. I can take you to them."

Kol shook his head. "I don't want to go there."

"Then where do you want to go?" the mouse-man asked.

"I have to find someone," Kol managed.

The two men looked at each other and smiled, only to duck when a piece of wood came flying their way. It narrowly missed Kol, smashing to pieces on the wall beyond him. The Otsen made a series of hand signals, and the mouse-man nodded. The brawl drew to a stop behind them, and Alessi downed yet another glass of blood-beer. Now, she appeared to be playing a game of dice with her rival.

The mouse-man leaned in. "We need to leave before she realizes we're here."

Kol froze. "I don't know..." his voice trailed off, and he saw double. Alessi had just called him useless, then bet his life on a drinking game. And yet, he couldn't leave her. Not until he knew more about this strange world. "I can't. I have to stay... with Alessi." He forced the words from his drunken mouth.

"I tried to do this the easy way," the mouse-man said. Kol felt a pressure against his ribs and looked down to see a knife. His heartbeat pounded in his ears, and suddenly he felt even more sober than he did when he walked into the place. The mouse-man continued, "But you're coming with us."

Kol followed the two men through a pair of beaded curtains and out a narrow door. He took a breath of fresh, cold air, and swayed, dizzy from the blood-beer. Yellow glowing stones on poles cast diffused light onto the snow around him.

"Hold him still," the mouse-man said.

"Right." A woman's voice came from behind Kol. He struggled against her arms, but they held like ropes, muscled and sinewy. She had to be at least as strong as Alessi. The smell of vinegar filled the air.

He looked back at the mouse-man to find gray fur erupting from the man's face and neck, and claws piercing through his fingertips. Beside the mouse-man, the violet-eyed man's furs and leather cloak twisted and bent as he grew into a shaggy, monstrous wolf. The furs, which he still wore, graced his neck like a collar, making him look even larger than he was. The creature opened its vicious mouth, saliva hanging like strings.

"Thank you, human," the wolf said. "I thought I'd lost her scent until I smelled her on you in Vico."

"What do you want?" Kol gritted his teeth.

"We want you to scream, bait," the mouse-man said.

Kol fought, but the woman's arms were iron, her carved muscles cutting into him when he moved. Memories flashed before his eyes, of being together with his mother and Caliban, then of days spent alone in the library. He must have read something useful. He thought harder, his chest heaving, then remembered something he read about escaping assassins. Or maybe it was bears. Either way, confusing them could be his only chance.

"I taste like socks!" Kol blurted, unsure of what else to say. And he was still wearing Astor's socks, known among his siblings for their pungent odor.

The wolf shut its mouth and tilted its head. "You *what?*" the wolf asked, spit flying in Kol's face.

"I taste like socks." Kol lifted one foot. "I smell like them, too." He hiccuped again.

"Enough of this nonsense," the mouse-man said. "You're drunk, boy."

The woman sniffed behind him. "He does smell pretty bad."

"See?" Kol said. Then, due to the stress or perhaps that strange blood-beer he drank, he hiccuped once more, then vomited. The wolf jumped backwards, narrowly missing it. Vomit landed on the snow and dotted Kol's face, and he couldn't bring a hand to wipe it.

"So, I know why you smell like vomit, but why would you taste like socks?" The wolf lowered its head to the ground, sniffing the air.

"Because of my socks, of course." Kol kicked off one boot, then extended one filthy, socked foot. "They're... they're my brother's."

The wolf lifted its lip in disgust.

Kol had never been so grateful for Astor's stinky feet, though the thought of his brother still stung him. It was working.

"Hurry up," the mouse-man said, pacing. "Draw Alessandra out."

The wolf, Bartu, drew closer, giant violet eyes meeting Kol's. His claws cut into the wet ground, leaving muddy streaks behind them. The air was cold and heavy around them, and

Kol could see his breath. He spat at the wolf, and the woman holding him shifted, making a sound in disgust.

Bartu made a face and sniffed the air before looking to the mouse-man. "I don't know, boss. There's something weird about this one."

"He smells like the witch's blood. Ignore it!" the mouse-man said, hands thrashing wildly in the air.

"No, there's something else." The wolf sniffed again. "It's clearer, now."

Kol wrenched free from the woman's arm, swinging a punch at the mouse-man. The mouse-man gave Kol a swift kick to the ribcage, knocking all the air from his lungs. His eyes watered.

"What do you mean? Are you going to turn down a perfectly good meal because it smells bad?" The mouse-man brought a clawed hand across the wolf's face. "You're an idiot."

"Look at him," the wolf said. The mouse-man grew closer, and Kol could smell his rancid breath.

The mouse-man walked towards Kol. He had an impossible radiance about him, almost an aura, which was enhanced by the glow clinging to his hair and tunic. He brought a hand to Kol's chin, razor-sharp nails cutting lightly into the soft flesh of Kol's throat as he tilted his head up. Kol steeled himself as the mouse-man peered into his eyes like Alessi had the night they met..

"Oh... *that* could be a problem—" the mouse-man was cut off, ripped from Kol's view almost too fast to see. The woman holding Kol shrieked and released him, letting him tumble to the snowy ground.

"Kol, you IDIOT!" Alessi's voice rang out.

Relief washed over Kol, who turned to see her slam the mouse-man against the tavern's wall by his hairless tail. Blood splattered across her face, but he could tell by the black color it wasn't hers.

"Bartu! Heytor!" the mouse-man yelled to his companions.

The other woman who had been holding Kol traced a shape in the air, its light hovering for a moment before Alessi tackled her to the ground. She had horns. It was another witch, but this witch was different from Alessi. Her hair was the same silver, but she had skin like a night sky freckled with silver stars. The wolf neared Alessi, the smaller mouse-man gripping its long ears in one hand like reins. He held a black, twisted blade in the other.

"Watch out!" Kol yelled. He scuttled backward as the women brawled.

The short, muscular attacker cut into Alessi's shoulder with a claw-shaped blade, but she rolled just in time to avoid a bite from the wolf's vicious mouth. She staggered to her feet just as the mouse-man took the end of her silver hair in his talons. She yelped as he lifted her up, her feet dangling over the ground.

"Let's see how you like it!" The mouse-man flung Alessi against the stone, but not before she made one last swipe at him. She fell with a sickening crunch.

"You think you're so much stronger than us, with your stolen power. I know you cut that arm off dragon woman!" The mouse-man held up a chunk of torn hair, letting it fall to the ground like a thousand silver threads. "No witch is ever going to—" The mouse-man wheezed and doubled over.

Alessi smirked, though it was more of a grimace, as she pushed herself to her feet. Her clawed hand was covered in black blood. "You let your guard down."

The mouse-man's eyes widened, blood dripping from his mouth. He fell backwards, catching himself and grasping at his throat. It was sliced deep along the side, black blood pouring out of it.

Alessi slashed again, and the mouse-man keeled over.

Bartu's eyes widened. "What did you do?"

"It's only fair," Alessi said, "since you were going to eat my friend, here." She grinned, blood dripping across her face and over her eyes as she took a breath. Bartu snarled, but it was already too late for him. Almost too fast for Kol to see, she slashed Bartu's throat, which bled black into the snow.

"They would have done the same to me." Alessi stood, limping over to the other silver-haired woman who lay motionless. A wild snarl contorted her face. Alessi rolled the witch over, then pinned her to the ground with a boot to the chest. Alessi lowered a clawed hand to her throat, and the witch's eyes widened.

"Please," she whimpered.

"Don't kill her," Kol said.

"Why?" Alessi looked back at him, her eyes narrowed. With one arm, the woman tried to drag herself away, but Alessi's boot held firm. Frayed hair caught the light around Alessi's like an asymmetrical halo. The other witch screamed.

"She's the same as you, isn't she?" Kol asked. "So why kill her?" This was worse than sending someone to the wastes to die. What cruelty would he need to dole out to survive? Someday, would slaughter be like nothing to him?

"She would have killed you," Alessi said, "then me."

"But she didn't. All she did was restrain me." Kol looked to the carnage around them. The dead wolf's tongue lolled out of its open mouth. Dark blood painted the stone wall. The power required to do something like that... and she was outnumbered, too. No ordinary human could do something so simultaneously powerful, horrifying, and impressive.

This was what Alessi was capable of. She was a monster.

But she saved him.

The other witch let out another whine, crawling further away. Alessi tilted her head to the side, studying her.

"You attacked me," Alessi said to the witch. "Why?"

The witch didn't answer.

"Who are you? Do I know you?" Alessi asked.

The woman coughed, droplets of blood landing on her lip. "N-no," she rasped.

Alessi nodded, seemingly satisfied. "Then why are you here?" she demanded.

"There's a bounty on your head."

"Whose bounty?" Alessi demanded, shaking the woman. She didn't answer. "Fine. I know who it was, that fucking *bitch*," Alessi roared at the witch. "You leave us here. If you follow us, I really will kill you. Understand?"

The witch smirked, then spat blood and saliva across Alessi's face. "Bitch!" the woman hissed.

Alessi made a fist and for a moment, Kol thought she'd kill her after all.

Instead, Alessi removed her boot from the woman's chest, and her eyes met Kol's. "Come on, let's get out of here before anyone else shows up to the party."

"You saved me again," Kol said. "I was worried you wouldn't come."

"I'm sorry." At first, Kol thought she was mocking him but the edge to her voice was gone. She was sincere, for what may have been the first time since they met. "Let's get out of this place." Though limping herself, she dragged one of his arms over her shoulders and pulled him forward.

As they rounded the corner, Kol looked back one last time to see the other witch crawl to what remained of her friends.

7

As Alessi stepped, she could feel heat radiating from her shoulder across her chest, confirming what she feared most: the Arratoi's claw-knife had dragon venom in it. It was stupid of her to take a dragon blade for that human. She gritted her teeth. This hole-boy was too much trouble. He was completely unprepared for this world, but business was business, and ten thousand gold was damn good business.

"Thanks," Kol said.

"For what?" Alessi muttered. She envied him—his wounds had already closed, but hers had yet to heal. Witches were particularly vulnerable to dragon venom.

"For saving my life," Kol said. "Again."

Alessi grumbled. Guy didn't know how much trouble he was. "Did those hunters mention anything to you?" Her eyes e turned downward and there was a hint of indignation in her voice. She tucked her frayed hair into her hood.

Kol spat yet another mouthful of sand, squashing it into the ground with his shoe. "Nothing really."

Alessi's eyes pierced through him. "Nothing?"

"I shouldn't have listened."

"What did they tell you?"

"That they knew you."

She narrowed her eyes. "They didn't. What else?"

"That witch blood is poison."

"A lie. Did they say anything else?"

"That you were going to kill me." As Kol said those words, Alessi furrowed her brow. "Do you intend to kill me?"

Not exactly. "Don't be ridiculous. What else did they say?"

Kol gritted his teeth. "That's it." His eyes were clear, determined. He was telling the truth. "Were those guys with the dragons who followed you to my compound?"

"No." Alessi said. "They were only after my bounty." A feeling overwhelmed her, the nagging sensation that she was being watched. She whipped around. "Who's there?" she yelled into the dunes.

Only a slight echo responded from the sea of red and orange, winds silently whipping the sand into ridges. Maybe it was just nerves. Those dragons had been on her tail for almost six months, ever since leaving Carpacia. And what a mess she left there... she had to do something about those dragons.

Alessi shook her head. "I have a plan, and you're coming with me." Ahead, the telltale pink lights of a village faded into the night sky. "Those dragon bounty hunters are cowards, so they're waiting for a moment of weakness to ambush me." She winced again. She wasn't sure she could beat them in her state. "We have to set a trap for them."

"Do we have a choice?"

Alessi shrugged. "Not if we want to live." A gust of sandy wind blew from her left, nearly sending Kol toppling over. "That *asshole* king should come after me himself. I'd show him."

Kol shot her a disbelieving look. "He sounds pretty strong. I'm sure you could fight him, but would you really want to?"

"Yeah. There are only two guys I wouldn't fight, and they're both actually women. One's the Queen. The other is a Zaharran, and I'd take a million red kings over that bitch."

Kol furrowed his brow. "Zaharran?"

This know-nothing hole-boy. She looked forward to getting rid of him and his stupid questions. She grunted. "They're older than the Belgarri—some call them gods—but I know they're just monsters like the rest of 'em. There's only two here; one's an immortal on an ego trip and her brother is a librarian with a terrible sense of humor."

Kol paused for a moment. "Odd to call them gods, then."

"People look to false gods when the real ones fail them. And sometimes it's the false gods who help you."

The village yawned ahead of them, built between two boulders. The buildings were common stick and brick constructions, and candles shined from their windows. Human shapes darted about, eyes glowing as they grew closer to the village's glowing blue archway.

"This is Brusa. We'll stop here, rest up," Alessi said.

Kol hoisted the backpack higher on his shoulders. "Alright." If there were more questions brimming behind those curious dark-brown eyes, he didn't ask.

They walked beneath the village's glowing archway and onto a busy street. Alessi looked around them. Over the past several days, they had climbed steadily upward. The air was thinner here, and she felt herself taking deeper breaths than usual. Distant mountains marked the horizon, smoke rising from the volcano Kur at their center. Eyes watched them pass, but Brusa was a terraced farming village, not a popular destination for bounty hunters. Still, because of its location, the two would probably stand out like a sore thumb.

Alessi stepped in front of Kol, prompting him to dig his heels into the cobblestone road, but he still couldn't stop in time. He bumped into her back, and she looked at him over her shoulder.

"What?" he asked, a perplexed look on his face. Part of her felt bad about using him this way, then selling him off to the highest bidder. She had invested in him, after all—but maybe it wasn't the best move to take a dragon blade to the shoulder for him. She couldn't do something like that again.

"Here. Protect yourself next time." Alessi reached into her belt, unsnapping a small dagger she kept. It was of sentimental value to her, one of the items she left with Astor that day in the wastes when she ran from Bakar. A gift, more useful in reality to Kol than it was to her with her claws. She handed it to him.

He took it hesitantly, as if not quite sure to make of the gift. "Thanks," he said, meeting her eyes. He inspected it with some amount of suspicion before sliding it into his pocket.

She turned away from him, heading toward the town. "Come on," she said. "I know a place."

"Another brothel?"

"Another brothel."

8

Something twisted in Kol's chest. She was one strange princess, far too willing to stay at a house of ill repute to save some coin.

They neared the brothel. A drunk staggered outside the stone building, collapsing on the ground before them, babbling incomprehensible syllables. Alessi crouched next to the man, her claws outstretched. The drunk's eyes widened as she stuck a hand in his pocket, rummaging around, before he vomited onto himself and the stone pavers beneath.

"Oh ugh... don't..." Kol tried to hide his disgust as Alessi reached into the man's dirtied pockets and pulled out handfuls of copper, silver, and lint—but mostly lint. She licked her lips, stuffing the coins in her own pocket.

Kol stepped back, eying the babbling, frothing drunk. "Gross."

"Come on, you've pickpocketed for me," she said. "You know where my money comes from." They headed toward the brothel, marked with an illegible, haphazard sign hanging above the door.

"So, do you work?" Kol wiped his nose, feeling sand grate against his skin. "Do princesses... need to work?"

"Usually, but now I'm a freelancer." Alessi felt at her hair, tragic and frayed.

"You're unemployed, you mean?" Kol asked.

"If you must know, I am 'available for hire'." She threw her head back. "But money's money, and business is business." She had a severe look on her face. "That's how things are in the witch kingdom."

The inside of the inn wasn't unlike the others they stayed at. Given the nature of the places, and Alessi's familiarity, Kol tried not to let his imagination wander. Why would it even bother him if she was *more* than a thief? If she sometimes resorted to more... physical measures? They were practically strangers.

The wallboards creaked as wind whistled in, cooling the room. He faced the wall as Alessi stripped, watching her shadow undress. This was a woman without modesty, and yet he faced the wall.

"If you're going to make us share a room, can I at least take a peek?" Kol asked, half-joking. Her hand came crashing down on his shoulder. He deserved that.

"I'd get two if I could afford it," she said. "But like I said earlier, it seems you're stuck with me."

"Did you ever steal from your mother?" Kol asked.

"No point. Think for a moment. Where would that money come from?" Alessi asked.

Kol thought for a moment, his mind racing to old books. "From the citizens. Taxes."

"Right. Witches don't pay taxes or hoard treasures," Alessi explained. "The witch kingdom doesn't work like that. We're a nomadic kingdom."

"I haven't heard of that before." Kol was taken aback. In every book he read, a kingdom was defined by its lands.

"A kingdom of people, with no land," she explained. "No taxes. My mother rules out of respect, not force. I'm a princess in name only. The strongest witch always rules."

"And your mother is the strongest witch," Kol said.

Alessi paused. "She was."

"Was?"

Alessi took a breath. "A long time ago, she challenged me to a duel."

Kol thought for a moment. "I see now. She was worried you were stronger."

Alessi shook her head. "Others were. She wanted to prove them wrong, but... stealing magic takes a toll on someone. She's taken so much dragon magic that she's unrecognizable in form and spirit. She wasn't the same as she once was."

"So, you ran away?" Kol asked. "Because you didn't want to fight your mother?"

"There's more to that whole mess, but only one witch walks out of a witch's duel. Even after all she'd imprisoned me, I still didn't want to kill her. That was three hundred and fifty years ago."

There wasn't a wrinkle on her face. "You don't look a day over eighteen," Kol said.

Alessi must have sensed his incredulity. "Magic slows the aging process, so don't look at me like I'm some kind of geriatric. She was going to force me to fight. I forfeited the fight because I didn't want to *kill* my mother, and I left before she had me executed for the act."

"Nice lady," Kol said with an edge to his voice. "Killing her own children. Sounds familiar." The queen would probably get along with his father.

"It should. You're not the only one with something to run

from," Alessi said. "The moment I became a threat, I wasn't her daughter anymore."

This new world outside his compound never ceased to surprise him. And this was not the kind of princess he imagined —this was a princess who had to work for everything she had. She paused, and then he watched her shadow tend to its wounds. They were deep; Kol saw them the night before. He remembered her bloodstained fingers, the peeling mars in her flesh. He was there when she stole the bandage cloth from a stranger's clothesline earlier, and he'd watched all day as she hid her pain.

Kol turned so he could see her out the corner of his eye. She struggled to wrap a bandage with one hand, her fingers slipping. As embarrassed as he was for her, it was hard not to watch. He was bewitched by that nude form, that naked shadow of hers on the wall.

"Do you want help?" Kol offered hesitantly.

Alessi chuckled. "Do you want to help, or are you just peeping?"

Kol's face reddened. "I want to help. I owe you."

"Fine."

He turned around. Her simple tunic and pants were removed, and she was clothed only with bandages, many stretching the length of her body. They formed a bloody, yellowed second skin. She handed him a strip of cloth.

His hands shook. "Where does it go?" he asked.

"Where do you think? My upper arm." She held out said arm, where dark red blood oozed out from a gash beside her shoulder alongside black pus. "It's a bitch to reach." He knew what to do. He was often in charge of tending to the wounds of Mia and his other younger siblings, but mostly Mia. She always had a knack for getting into trouble.

The wound was deep in her muscle, oozing red-black pus.

"That dagger did a number on you," he said. After a moment, he took her arm in his hands. The pus crusted around its edges.

"The Arratoi had a dragon claw blade. Dragon claws have poison in them," Alessi explained. "Prevents witches from healing."

Kol wrapped the bandage around her arm, and his eyes rested on *The Prince of Fire,* which she had laid on the bed. "You went through all the trouble of hiding that book," he said. "Why?"

"Full of questions tonight, huh?" Alessi scoffed. A mischievous smile reached across her face, and she lowered her voice before adding, "A friend gave it to me a long time ago." She reached up, wrapping her arms around his chest. Her hot breath tickled the hairs on his neck. "A *special* friend." *Special* rolled off her tongue with both familiarity and an edge, like intoxicating venom dripping from a serpent's mouth.

Kol's breath grew shallow, and he felt blood rush to his face. "Careful, or I'll think you're hitting on me." He forced his voice to remain steady, and turned away again so he could only see her shadow.

She let go and laughed. Her shadow pointed at him. "You're hilarious, hole-boy." She was having too much fun with him.

"Just what kind of friend gave you that book?" Kol asked.

"You know. The kind of friend you—" Her demeanor changed, and he could feel the electricity in the air. "The kind of friend who gives you books and expects them back."

"Hmm." He was peeking again, out the corner of his eye. She had a muscular torso and full breasts, which were pushed up and supported by her bandages. It didn't surprise Kol she had other men in her life.

"I kept it so that bastard would follow me, but he never did." There was not a hint of laughter in her voice now. She stood. "Turn around." Her breasts were covered in the once-white linen bandages, now stained pink and brown. She winced.

Kol swallowed, then faced the wall again, her naked shadow slipping a shirt back on. It was hard not to look at her body, her injury. That had to hurt. She reminded him of Astor in a way, always putting forward a strong facade. "Maybe we should stay here for a bit so you can recover," he suggested carefully.

"Don't worry about *me*," Alessi said. Kol watched her shadow peel the bandages from her breasts, then re-wrap them. "I'll be back to normal in a few days. I'm done, turn around for good this time." He did. She wore a straight face and ran her fingers through her ruined hair. "What I'm really worried about is my hair."

"Oh." Kol's eyes darted to her arm and shoulder. The bandage he had just replaced was already black and crimson.

"I need you to cut it." Alessi held out a dagger—his dagger—and he took it with a shaking hand. He felt his pocket, and confirming it was the same one she gave him earlier. She must have taken it when he wasn't looking—he would have to put it in his shoe next time so it would be secure.

"I don't think you want me to," Kol said, looking from the dagger to her and then back to the dagger. He cut Mia's hair once, and she cried for nearly a week because of the asymmetric bob he gave her.

"I do, or I wouldn't have asked. Just cut it all to the same length. That blade should be sharp enough."

"Cut it with a... with a dagger? Don't you have a pair of scissors or a—"

"Shut up and do it. All to the same length."

"Fine." Kol's eyes darted to a large mirror on the other side of the room. She wouldn't be happy if he messed this up.

Drawing a breath, he took a handful of her hair into his left hand before raising the dagger with his right. Her hair was softer than he expected, reminding him of down though he had expected a texture like reeds or coarse linen. With a slight sawing motion, the clump of hair fell to the ground.

She reached up and inspected his handiwork. "More even, use a single motion." She demonstrated with another handful of hair on the other side, and it was at that moment Kol began to realize how much hair she really had. It was thicker than his or any of his siblings' hair, and its color and texture was curly and simultaneously finer than the finest silk in his father's closet. Questions bubbled forward.

"Your hair," he said. "Why is it gray, and not white, if it's lost its color?" Their eyes met in the mirror.

"Gray? You call this gray?" She raised one eyebrow, running her fingers through what remained of her hair's long segment.

"If it's not gray, then what is it?" Kol asked.

"Silver. Like a spider's web."

He read in a book somewhere that spider silk was not, in fact, silver, but he was not about to say that to the foul-tempered witch. "Silver, then." It was shinier than the gray of his older stepmothers, he supposed. Another clump fell and clung to her shoulder, its bandage already soaked in blood and pus.

"You don't look so good."

"I know." Her voice was tense—she wanted him to drop the subject. Her fingers curled into claws.

Kol cleared his throat. "I've been thinking. If you're being followed, why stay at places like this? Lower-profile places might be better."

Alessi sighed, her face distraught. "This is a brothel—it's anything but high profile."

"But they found us. The Otsen, and the mouse-man—"

"Arratoi."

"Right. The Arratoi. Maybe we should stay out of the cities after this. Others might know you're injured," Kol said.

"There's a certain protection to being around other Belgarri, but"—Alessi twisted on the bed so she faced him, a glimmer in her eye—"you may be smarter than you look."

Kol laughed. "What's that supposed to mean?"

"It's true I didn't want the Arratoi to find me, but..."

"But...?"

"I'm looking for someone. I thought, maybe, I'd run into him in a place like *this*." She gestured to the dingy room around them.

"And who's that?" Kol asked. Who was it she would make herself vulnerable to see again?

Alessi picked up the book and shook it.

"Oh. Him." Kol's heart twisted in his chest, but he tried not to show it.

"We could use his help." Alessi narrowed her eyes and gave him a look that drained all the warmth from his body. He knew better than to ask any more questions and focused on cutting her hair. More silver locks fell to the ground around her.

"He tends to hang out at these kinds of places. A place like this is where we met, actually." Alessi clutched the book to her chest. "He said he'd find me. When he didn't, I went looking for him." She shook her head, and Kol withdrew the blade for a moment to avoid cutting her. "I shouldn't have tried. It was never going to work."

"You don't know that," Kol said, letting one last lock fall through his fingers. Her mane of hair was more voluminous, freed of its own weight now that it barely reached her shoulders. She looked rougher with short hair, but it fit her.

"I'll wait for him to find me, and if he doesn't, then I'll *make* him come to me," Alessi said. "But you're right about one thing. We'll stay in the forest at night until we reach the red king's country." Her fingers brushed over her hair's newly severed ends, narrowly missing his hand.

"I didn't know—" Kol began.

"You almost died yesterday," Alessi said. She crossed a hand over her bandaged chest. "I didn't mean to put you in danger. I was careless, and you're so... fragile."

"I'm not that fragile, and what happened back there wasn't the kind of mistake I plan on making twice." Kol stroked the scrape on his arm. His chin was scabbed over, and several of his ribs were sore—likely fractured. "And now I have your dagger." He tucked the blade back in his boot, but his mind lingered on one word. *Fragile.*

"It's still true," Alessi said, apparently unaware of the ill effect her words had on him. "You're—"

"Gross. Yeah."

"No." She shook her head. "You're only human."

He searched for something to fill the silence that followed. "And what if your *special* friend can't find you in the woods?" Kol asked.

"There's no place he can't find me if he really wants to." She tapped the book. "But I have a feeling he's close."

9

The next night, they slept beneath the stars. They were strange stars, unlike any Kol remembered from his father's books, or even his own musings, but stars that glimmered and shifted in the dusty air. They swam through the sky until one landed on him.

They weren't stars—they were some kind of bugs with vibrant yellow glowing bodies. He shook it off. Sweat dripped down his brow, moistening his tunic and cloak, but it was still a welcome break from the stuffy rooms they shared.

They were out of the wastes and in the western woods now. Kol had never seen a forest before, but he recognized the gnarled bark and reaching limbs from stories he read in the library. The heights dizzied him, but at least he didn't have to sleep on the floor—and it was safer, or so he hoped, as long as he didn't fall and break his neck. Alessi even stole him his own hammock, which reminded Kol of a sail with each end tied to a tree branch above. And he felt like a sail, too, the way the wind whipped him back and forth.

A strong gust hit him from the side, and he thought he

might fall. He sat up, hugging the gnarled tree branch above him, and knocking a plume of electric blue glow around him.

"Stop swinging around, you'll break your neck." Alessi looked down from where she sat on a branch above, cross-legged, eating some sort of purple fruit from her lap. Kol had never seen one of those before. He raised an eyebrow. "Don't look at me like that," Alessi said. "We're not in an inn. Isn't this what you wanted?"

Bark fell from the branch and onto Kol's face. He shut his right eye. "I guess. But I thought we'd be a little closer to the ground."

"It's safer up here. You should thank me." She smiled, fangs showing like a beast's.

"I'm not so sure about that." Kol's black hair blew across his face, obscuring his view of the silver-haired witch.

Alessi laughed, more of a cackle than a laugh. And yet, the sound made something stir within him. It was nice to see her happy, even if just for a moment. What was this feeling? He smiled. She threw one of the purple fruits at him, leaving him to fish it out from wherever it rolled within his hammock.

She laid back against the broad branch of the ancient, twisting oak. "You'd be nothing but a snack for an Otsen or a Nara on the ground."

Oh, she loved to tease him. But he was getting used to it. "Not with you around." He threw the purple fruit back to her.

She missed, bringing a hand to a shoulder. "Ouch."

Kol winced sympathetically. "I guess an apple a day will keep the dragons away? Or are you still able to handle dragons yourself?" He looked down, feeling himself grow dizzy.

"Not while I'm sleeping. I'm a very heavy sleeper, you know." There was more to those words. She was a heavy sleeper, true, but his suspicion was correct. She couldn't do much with that wound on her shoulder. It still hadn't closed.

She stood on the broad branch, and Kol felt dizzy thinking about how long it took them to climb to that point and how far down the mossy earth waited below them. Alessi jumped from branch to branch, climbing the tree, each time sending a fresh drop of sweat down Kol's brow. She stopped when she reached the highest branch, and Kol craned his neck to look at her standing against a gradient of pink and navy, the speckled sky stretching where the sunset's last remaining colors receded. Her hair, which he'd cut neatly below her jawline, rustled in the wind. She threw back her head, turning to the stars.

"What are you doing?" Kol leaned forward, nervously steadying himself as the hammock rocked. Far above them, a star left a silver streak against the darkness before breaking apart, cascading in fiery showers across the sky.

She looked back at him over her shoulder, wearing that sideways smile he hated so much. "I'm trying something." She brought a hand to her shoulder and sniffed the air. "He's near, but he won't show himself. Sly bastard."

"You'll fall."

She shot him a look, and he knew what she was going to do before she did it. She crossed her arms over her chest and fell backward, shoulders first, toward the ground below.

Panic rose in his chest as she fell, his hammock twisting as he watched while time slowed down. A fall from this height would certainly kill him, and though she was tough, she did not seem to be immortal. He scrambled out of his hammock, but no matter how fast he climbed down the tree, he wasn't fast enough. Moments later, when he expected to hear a sickening crunch, he heard nothing. He looked down below to see Alessi cradled in the wings of a feathered stranger. He stood like an owl with a craning neck, masculine yet graceful.

"Holy shit," Kol muttered under his breath. He almost expected an attack, but the stranger only studied him. Kol scrambled to the tree branch below him, then the one below that. He wasn't fast like her. He couldn't dig his claws into the tree and run straight up or straight down, his magicless self left to fumble and fall and get splinters in his palms.

"Who's this?" the creature asked. It was a deep voice, and though its language was human, its tone was not, as if a thousand voices of varying colors and shapes were braided into every word. Now that Kol was closer, he realized that this was not a monster like the others he had met, but an owl-like being with wide, silver eyes set in a bird-like face. He held Alessi in his wings, long enough to stretch far behind him.

The owl—or whatever it was—let Alessi down, and she bounced to her feet just as Kol's own toes met the leaf-covered earth. Kol reached for his dagger only to then curse himself for leaving it in his hammock. The creature had a vaguely male physique and smelled of ash and decaying leaves. Glow landed in his feathers like a crown, casting his face in an eerie blue. Kol watched him with caution, neither man moving. The stranger's presence was different from Alessi's, and different from the Otsens and Arratoi he had met. It was an older presence, heavier somehow, pressing down on him and demanding his full attention.

He remembered his conversation with Alessi, and it made sense. A false god. A Zaharran. "You're her book friend," Kol said. "What's your name?" Though Alessi was not treating him as an enemy, Kol eyed him with suspicion.

"He's—" Alessi began, raising a finger.

"Him first," Kol and the creature said in unison.

Kol looked from Alessi, to the beaked stranger, then back to Alessi again. After a moment of silence, Kol went first. "I'm Kol Mendona. My father is Lord Mendona of the seventh settlement. Who are you?"

"Who," the owl-man hooted before chuckling at his own

joke, "is correct. My friends call me Az, but you can call me Azazel."

"Azazel..." Kol's voice trailed off. But there was more to this stranger. A familiarity, a memory—he had read about Azazel in several ancient religious texts. "You're the owl god?"

"Hmm. Been a while since I heard that name," the owl-man said. "Are you one of those polygamist compound humans?" The owl man drew closer, inspecting him. "How are the breeding programs working? It's a shame your kind was so... *delicious*." He licked his lips.

Alessi rolled her eyes. "Yes, Kol, this is one of the Zaharrans I mentioned. A real asshole. Come on now, enough games, Az."

Trust him, he will help you.

The words startled Kol. It had been days since he heard his mother's voice. The man's silver eyes blinked before his shape shredded and turned to twisting shadows. He then reformed as a man, with the same starry-black cloak covering him. Kol nearly fell backward into the moss, cooled by the night air.

Azazel tilted his head, now that of a man with a tawny-brown beard. He was tall but not broad-shouldered in that form, and glasses sitting on his hooked nose magnified his eyes, a similar color but duller than Alessi's. The stars in his cloak seemed to stay stationary, as if the item were merely a window into the skies.

"Never seen someone shift before?" Azazel asked.

Kol remembered the Otsen's shifting form, mouth open wide, spit hanging like strings. It sent a shiver through his body. "Only once."

"Once! Have you been living under a rock, boy?"

"Quite literally. Compound, remember?" Alessi elbowed Azazel, who flinched, massaging his arm.

"You've been watching me." Alessi's face was serious. "Why didn't you show yourself?"

"Of course I've been watching you, my *acolyte*," Azazel said, his words like a bite.

"Of course you've been watching, you pervert." Alessi crossed her arms.

"Now, that's not exactly fair," Azazel said.

Kol stepped between Azazel and Alessi. Something was going on here, and he didn't fully understand. Azazel didn't seem like another bounty hunter, but he also didn't seem like a friend if he never came back for Alessi. "How did you find her? Did someone send you after her?"

Azazel shook his head. "I sent myself, thank you very much."

"Then why are you stalking her?"

Azazel rubbed the back of his head. "Competing interests, you could say?" He shrugged. "My sister and I disagree on many things, and Alessi is one of them. I've taken her under my wing, so to speak."

"She knows you're not a real god," Kol said.

"So? I kept her from breaking her neck. Could your *real* gods do that?" Azazel looked to Alessi. "Why do they keep calling us gods, anyway? I get that we're formless, immortal, and seemingly all-powerful, but 'god' seems excessive."

"Your sister insists," Alessi answered.

Azazel sighed. "Of course, Lilith would do this." He sounded exhausted.

"Where did you come from?" Kol asked. "I couldn't even get to the base of the tree before you showed up out of nowhere." During their trek in the woods, he hadn't so much as heard a twig break behind them. It was a silent journey. Too silent.

"Anywhere, everywhere. That's what's so special about me." Azazel winked at Kol, then turned to Alessi. "I'm flattered you have such belief in my abilities, but believe it or not, I can't watch you all the time."

"So you just *happened* to be watching me when I fell right now? And when—" Alessi began.

Azazel cut her off. "No need to bring that up. You're lucky I caught you before you really broke your neck." Azazel scratched his head. "I know you like attention, but there are better ways to get mine."

Alessi smiled. "You know you love it."

"I don't. Also, you owe me a book."

"Should have come for it earlier." She brought the book from her pocket again, but when Azazel reached for it, she pulled it away.

"Keeping my books again, I see." Azazel sighed. "How long have you had that one? A week?"

"Three years." Alessi's voice was flat, and her eyes narrowed.

"Oh. Has it been that long?" With a flick of Azazel's wrist, a glowing, teal circle traced through the air before him. He reached in, grasping at something, and Kol did not see the hand emerge from the other side.

"Yes, you big oaf." Alessi asked.

"Time doesn't pass for me like it does for you. Three years is a breath in the eternal library. No sun, no moon, only stars and books... you can get lost in time there. Or lose yourself between worlds."

"I'm a fugitive. I could have used your help months ago," Alessi said. "Look, I need you to meet me in the Eastern kingdom. I'll let you know the exact timing later."

Kol looked from her to Azazel. She still held her left arm like it hurt—the wound was there, and it wasn't getting any better. Maybe Azazel, the eternal librarian, knew the cure.

"Got yourself in trouble again?" Azazel asked. "I'm worried about you."

"You sound like my father," Alessi said, "if I had one."

"I can't be your father, but I can be your *daddy*." Azazel laughed.

"That was one time." Alessi brought a hand to her forehead, exasperated.

Kol's face reddened. He'd hoped it wasn't true, but it seemed Azazel was *that* kind of a special friend. Azazel put a hand on Alessi's shoulder, and an unpleasant feeling grew like a fire within Kol. This man was a trespasser, an interloper in what he had with Alessi, but at the same time Kol didn't know if he wanted Azazel gone or if he wanted to *be* Azazel.

"So, why do you need portaled?" Azazel asked. "I'm not your free ride everywhere, you know. This is an art." He traced a shape with his hand, and it hovered in the air the same vibrant blue as the glow that freckled his feathers. Behind it were rows and rows of bookshelves with small, owl-like creatures flitting about with books in their beaks. One shelved a book, then took another in its mouth and flew away. It was like looking into another world.

"I need portaled," Alessi said, "because I'm going to kill someone."

"Who?" Azazel hooted.

"The red king." Alessi clutched at her wound, her stance weakening.

"You know I don't want to help with that. Anyway, you shouldn't think about that right now, you don't look so good." Azazel reached forward, putting his hand on her good arm.

"Shut up," Alessi said, shaking her head. "I oughta—"

"Hey hey hey, calm down. Now's not the time for theatrics." Azazel looked concerned, and the fact that he probably was legitimately worried about Alessi grew Kol's jealousy to a roaring flame. "There's a druid temple around here; I've got an old friend there. I want them to take a look at you."

"You don't get to tell me to calm down." Alessi coughed and clutched at her wound. "And a druid is more likely to purge me from this Earth than help a witch." She wrenched her arm away from Azazel and took a step back. Her discomfort was clear at the mention of the druids.

"As much as I hate to admit it, he might be right. You can't keep going like this." Kol walked closer to her, positioning himself between her and Azazel and placing a hand on her good shoulder. Disappointment spread across Azazel's face, so strong as to even overshadow the man's worry, legitimate as it may have been.

"You're a couple of babies." Alessi rolled her eyes. "It'll take a lot more than this to kill me." And with those words, she collapsed.

10

Kol caught her this time, and Azazel shot him a possessive glance. "Alessi? Can you hear me?"

He guided her to the ground so she could rest on the cool earth. Her skin was almost hot enough to burn him, a gentle steam rising from it, and the bandage on her shoulder was completely soaked through, leaving black pus on his forearm. A putrid smell like rotting meat emanated from it. She seemed so small in this state, almost like a different person—and it was all his fault. If he had been strong enough to defend himself, she wouldn't have gotten hurt.

"She's even worse than I thought," Azazel said.

Alessi groaned, clutching at her shoulder.

Azazel tilted his head, looking at her unconscious form from the side. "That's it. We're taking her to the druids."

Alessi's eyes fluttered open. She hissed, pushing Kol away. He reached after her, but she batted his hand away.

"No." She struggled to her feet, leaning over and bracing her arms against her legs.

"They can help you." Azazel reached out, but she swatted at him with her vicious claws.

"I'm fine," she said.

"Your flesh is liquifying," Azazel said. "Once the venom spreads to your brain, there's not much anyone can do. You have to act now."

"Nonsense, this isn't the first time I've been infected with dragon venom. Those old druid bitties won't be able to do anything," Alessi walked far ahead of him. "Useless bunch of con artists."

"It's worth a try," Azazel said. "They're my friends—"

"They were your brother's friends, not yours. Besides, why would they help a witch?" Alessi drew her lips into a grimace. "We've been killing them for centuries."

"Witches have been killing everyone for centuries." Azazel sighed, bringing a hand to the back of his neck.

"That's not the point," Alessi said. "They've always hated us. People never really change."

"I've lived long enough to know that's usually not the case. Will you take a chance, for me?" Azazel's eyes darted to her wound. "You have nothing to lose and no better options."

Alessi's eyes locked with Azazel's, blocking Kol out of the intensity passing between them. It was like he was in a glass bubble between two raging storms, two forces of nature, so close and yet so apart from them he couldn't feel the wind on his skin. What did Alessi see in Azazel? Power, probably. He could never be like Azazel, he could never have that—he was, and would always be, only human. This thought sank in his stomach like a rock.

"Fine," Alessi said. "But I'll be pissed if they burn me at the stake." Azazel smiled, then Alessi gave a weak laugh.

"I can't deny it's nice to see you again," Alessi said. "I thought you were gone for good." Alessi put a hand on his shoulder, and Kol remembered her soft touch the night he cut her hair. His face reddened.

"You know I can't leave you alone for too long," Azazel said. "I live to meddle in your life."

Alessi winced, grasping again at her shoulder. She pulled away from Azazel. "Then can you make yourself useful and portal to the druids?"

"I can't just portal willy-nilly. I've only got about two good full-sized portals in me per Alon day," Azazel explained. "I spent my second on your little stunt back there."

"What about the first?" Kol asked.

Azazel winked at Kol. "Take a guess."

Alessi elbowed Azazel. "Fine. I guess you're sleeping alone tonight."

Azazel pouted. "Seriously though, let's get that shoulder fixed before you get anywhere near the red king. You know what happened last time, with Bakar of the eastern lands."

"One doesn't so easily forget a dragon like the red king. I have everything but a way into the castle," Alessi said. "And a way out." She looked better, though Kol could tell she was faking it. Any second, she could keel over again.

"I won't get you in, but I can get you out," Azazel said. "I still hope you change your mind about going in."

"I won't, and I don't need your help getting there. I'll find some way in, just get me out when I call your name." She brushed aside a branch with her hand, then let it snap back into Kol's face.

"Hey!" he said. "I'm still here!"

Alessi shot him a sideways glance, pausing for a moment to let him catch up. "Right, forgot about you."

Azazel looked at Kol as if he had completely ruined their moment, and maybe he had.

"Why are you going to kill the red king?" Kol asked.

Alessi clenched her gloved fist. "It's a long story."

"Sounds like a suicide mission," Kol said.

"It is," Alessi said with a flat voice. "No return journey for this one."

His heart dropped. So, she was serious about it. He didn't like this plan. "I hope whatever he did is worth your life."

"I made a mistake a few years ago and paid for it dearly. That's all you need to know, *hole-boy*."

Kol clenched his jaw. The venom in those words was like a slap to the face. *That's all you need to know*—as if he wasn't capable of understanding. As if he was nothing but a commodity only for carrying her pack. Useless. Weak. Human. Azazel wouldn't have let her get hurt like that. Azazel would have been able to help her. But he couldn't be Azazel, and he couldn't be what Azazel was to Alessi. His attention turned back toward the conversation.

"My tail feathers are fine as they are, so don't go threatening them," Azazel said.

The bitter feeling only grew within Kol. He knew what it was now—jealousy, even if he denied it. He strained his ears as she grumbled again.

Azazel pointed his finger to the broken woods, where burned trees stood, their ancient trunks snapped like twigs. He took his owl form again. "Not much further." His voice was almost human, but on some syllables his many voices broke through as if held back by a thin veil.

A fog rolled ahead of them, and Kol focused his eyes on the dark outline of caves behind it, black shadows in openings of white stone. A chilly breeze came from their direction, rustling his hair and carrying with it the scent of earth and rain. Somehow, he couldn't shake the feeling this place was familiar. It was like he had been there before in a dream, or a book. Dry grass crunched under his feet as he took a step in the caves' direction.

Alessi leaped onto a tree branch hanging above him, then laid down. "Stop." She pressed a finger to his forehead. Her injured arm hung loosely at her side.

"What?" Kol asked. The caves looked dark and safe, as far as he could tell.

"Don't go near there," Alessi said. If even Alessi didn't want to go near, something was wrong.

"They're just caves."

Alessi pointed at the caves' many mouths. Fog flowed out of them like breath. "They're natural portals, used as a prison over the years. You could fall between worlds and never get out. I've heard even the Beast of Alon is imprisoned there," Alessi said.

"And even he can't get out?" Kol asked.

"The druids keep him sleeping, but one day he'll wake up and finish what he started." Azazel's face was grave. "This prison is only for the worst Belgarri. The ones truly deserving of the word 'monster.'"

Alessi leaped from the tree, flinching as she caught herself with her injured left arm. Her bandages ripped loose and hung black at her side, covered in pus and her too-thick blood. Kol could almost still taste it, metallic and sweet.

"The druids will take care of you, I know it," Azazel said.

The bushes rustled, and Kol braced for an attack as a silver-haired child tumbled out, landing flat on her stomach. The three watched in shared confusion as she pushed herself to a seated position, drew her knees to her chest, and started crying. Snot and tears streamed down her face.

Alessi lifted her good hand as if to block the child from view. "Ugh, what is that?"

Azazel inspected the girl. "A druidling, by the looks of it." He took a step forward, and Kol imagined the owl's talons wrapping around the child's throat. The girl's cries intensified, as did Alessi's visible discomfort.

Kol stepped between them. "I'll help." The girl wasn't much younger than Mia. He offered a hand to the crying child, and the girl looked at him with eyes as silver as Alessi's. "You alright?"

Alessi rolled her eyes.

"I hurt my knee," the girl said. She had an unusual accent, lingering on the vowels and cutting the consonants short, and it was so strange and heavy Kol barely understood her. She wiped her nose, then took Kol's hand. Her fingers were gooey.

"Don't *touch* it!" Alessi hissed. "Gross!" She brought a hand over her mouth.

The girl pushed her silver hair behind her ears. Her coloring was like Alessi's, and her presence felt similar, if lighter. What was different, however, was that this girl had no black, curving horns on top of her head.

"You're with her?" The child's eyes rested on Kol, then darted curiously to Alessi before lifting her boogery chin. "The elders say witches are dangerous."

"They are," Alessi muttered, gaze fixed on the trail of boogers running from the girl's nose.

Despite these words, the girl reached for Alessi with a fearlessness only small children had.

Seeing Alessi tense, Kol caught the child by her hood, freezing her in place. She pouted, and Kol kneeled before her. "Where's your mom?" he asked.

"Elder Enira says she's"—the girl wound up her face and took a sharp breath—"sleeping."

Kol lost whatever progress he made with the child as she broke into tears again. Fuck. He looked around, unsure of what to do. He was hesitant to say much more about the child's dead mother.

"Quick. We should eat it," Alessi hissed. The girl cried louder.

"Now's not the time for your jokes." Azazel shot her a stern look. "If her elders hear this, they'll think we're hurting her. And I don't want to deal with angry druids."

"Kol, do something!" Alessi's voice broke, and she paced hysterically.

Alessi needed him. He felt a little better—he could handle children. She was at that tender age when comfort and emotion overpowered logic. "It's ok, it's ok," Kol said to the child. "When I was your age, I thought my mom was sleeping, too."

The tears lessened. "With my mom?"

Kol nodded. "Right."

"They're sleeping together?"

Alessi rolled her eyes, and Azazel brought a hand over his mouth to stifle a chuckle.

Realizing where they sensed humor, Kol paused. His face reddened. "... sure. I know it's hard right now, but you'll be ok." Kol patted the girl on the head.

"Ok." The child wiped her nose again. She seemed to have lost interest in Alessi and fixed her eyes on Azazel. "You're a god. Are you the wolf god, mister?"

"I'm an owl, druidling, though this form can change." Azazel ruffled the child's hair. "But I knew the wolf god."

"You were friends?"

"Brothers." The girl's eyes lit up, and he continued. "I'll tell you more if you take my friend here to a healer."

The child took Kol's fingers in her hand and led them further into the forest. Alessi walked beside them, though at a distance.

"Oh, don't keep touching it," Alessi said.

Azazel smirked. "Oh, you just don't like them because—"

Alessi gritted her teeth. "*Don't.*"

They broke through the trees and entered a clearing full of silver-haired women rushing about with baskets in their arms or children on their backs.

"Elder Enira!" the child called out, running to one of the older women. She looked at them, her creased eyes stern. She put both hands on the child's shoulders.

"Isolt! I told you not to talk to strangers." Her voice reminded Kol of his grandmother's, during the brief time he knew her. There was little use for the elderly underground.

The child pointed to Azazel. "He says he knew the wolf god."

The old woman's eyes widened as they met Azazel's. "Is that you, Azazel?"

Azazel smiled. "It is."

The woman took a breath, then paused. "I never thought I'd see you again."

Azazel walked up to her, then took her hand and kissed it. "Likewise. You're as lovely as you ever were."

"That was a thousand years ago." The elderly woman looked away from him, her cheeks blushing.

"You..." Alessi's jaw dropped. Kol tried not to laugh at the dumbfounded expression on her face. Apparently, she was nothing special to Azazel.

"Better late than never." Azazel winked, then his face grew serious. "My friend needs your help."

Elder Enira narrowed her eyes at Alessi. "You've brought a witch into our woods."

Alessi hissed at the woman. "What about it?"

"We don't help witches," Enira said.

"She's not like the others. The queen sent men after her. One cut her with a dragon blade," Azazel said, gesturing to Alessi's arm. "No one hates the queen more than she does."

"Is this true?" Enira asked.

Alessi nodded.

"I'm sorry," Enira said, "but there's—"

"I didn't come back here for polite greetings," Azazel said, his voice severe. "You owe me a favor." He walked closer to Enira, dry grass crunching under his feet, and placed a hand on her shoulder. "Remember?" Understanding passed between them like electricity.

Enira straightened her old, bent spine. "So be it." She wrinkled her brow, seeming to mull it over. "If it's for you, I can make an exception to the rules. But only once."

"Thank you," Azazel said in his many voices. "Let's take care of this before it gets any worse." Kol followed Azazel's eyes to the forest, a white fog creeping around its edges.

Enira turned to Alessi. "How far have you walked with the wound?"

"Far," Alessi answered. "It's been three days and at least fifty miles."

"The venom's already in your blood, girl." Enira reached out to touch Alessi's arm, fevered and red, but the witch shied away. She reached forward with speed Kol wouldn't expect from an old woman, placing a firm grip on Alessi's wrist. "You have to do everything I say, but even then, it may already be too late."

<h1 align="center">11</h1>

The evening sun burned on the horizon, filtering through the trees and leaving long shadows like fingers across the grass. It was hot, though not as hot as the wastes, and a southern breeze caressed Kol's skin.

"Come," Enira said. "We don't have all night."

Alessi walked into the clearing where Kol sat with an irritated look on her face, wearing the long robes she had begrudgingly shed her sand cloak for. They draped over her in green and gold, contrasting against her gray-pale skin and making her look more sickly than she was.

"This won't take all night, will it?" Alessi reached for her shoulder.

"Tssk! No scratching," Enira scolded.

Alessi grumbled in response. No, it wasn't just the robes making her look sicklier—she *was* sicker. The corners of her eyes and mouth were creased with pain, and her jaw was tensed from clenching.

"You're lucky you've lasted this long," Enira said, wringing her hands. She led them between two rows of gray stone buildings. "Most don't last more than a day after being infected with dragon venom. You're strong, but you've got some powerful enemies."

"Tell me about it. How long will this take?" Alessi asked.

"An hour. Maybe two. It really depends how... *progressed* your condition is." Enira turned to look at them, raising one eyebrow. "In a hurry?"

"Yes. Powerful enemies and all that," Alessi said.

"You're safe here," Enira said. "If you leave before you heal, you'll die in your current condition."

Kol tugged at his sand cloak. Enira had cleaned it for him that afternoon, an unexpected gesture. He thought back to earlier that evening when, shortly after receiving his clean clothes, he heard her screams from across the temple as the druids bathed her, and she'd spat curses he had never heard before.

Enira's silver brow creased, and the woman seemed lost in thought.

"You will be able to heal her, right?" Kol asked as they walked beneath an ivy-colored archway, cast golden in the evening light. Ahead, an altar lay in the shadow of a stone pit, lit only by candlelight. It would be night soon, and the shadows cast by the thick, green trees around them grew longer by the second. A cool breeze rustled Kol's jet-black hair.

"I said I would try," Enira said. "We'll know by morning if this works."

"And if it doesn't?" Alessi asked.

"Let's just say this purification ritual is not without risk."

Alessi looked down, balling her hands into fists. "If you druids were the healers they say—"

"Healers, yes. Miracle workers, no." Enira's voice was flat. "You're lucky you're not dead already."

Dead. That word rang in Kol's head. Alessi couldn't die.

She was so alive just a few days ago—alive enough to spite his father, alive enough to save him from the mouse-man and the Otsen. She was so pale now—and it was all his fault. His heart sank to a pit in his chest. Maybe she'd be better off with just Azazel. But if Azazel cared about Alessi so much, then why wasn't he there? Maybe she had noticed, too—a disappointed look crossed her face.

Enira walked to the altar, standing in front of it with the dignity and poise of a statue. She held an open hand out to the altar, gesturing for Alessi to lay on it. "You shouldn't have walked so far with the venom."

"How the hell else was I supposed to get anywhere?" Alessi spat.

"You could have had your boyfriend carry you." Enira sighed, and Kol blushed. He probably could carry her, not that Alessi would have let him, but did Enira mean him, or Azazel? "You know the risks. I need you to say that you want to go through with this."

Alessi sat on the altar's edge. "You already—"

Enira cut her off. "I need you to *say* it."

Alessi grunted, turning her gloved hand over as if inspecting it. For a moment, it was almost as if he could see through the glove, to the scaled hand of a beast—of a dragon—concealed.

"I want to go through with this. If I die, I deserved it." She crossed her gloved arm over her waist. "Hate to go out this way, though."

"I fucked up." Kol clenched his jaw. "You saved me. You don't deserve to die, so don't say that you do."

"You have no idea what you're talking about." Alessi clutched her gloved hand tightly in her other. "Besides, you may be an idiot, but I'm the reason you were a drunk idiot. Let's get this over with."

Enira's treatment *had* to work. The elder turned to a shelf filled with glass bottles of powders and pickled monstrosities.

"It'll be ok." Alessi reached out, placing her fevered hand gently on Kol's arm. Her hard exterior cracked, and she forced a smile. This was the most authentic expression he had ever seen on her—pain, hope, anger. And she was attempting to comfort *him*, even though she was the one suffering.

A commotion erupted outside. Outside the window beside Alessi, a procession of silver-haired women followed Azazel. Compared to their straight, well-kept hair, Alessi's was a bird's nest.

Alessi gave them a dirty look. "If they knew what a selfish prick he is, they wouldn't be all over him like that."

"I'd imagine you're familiar with being all over him," Enira quipped.

"You're one to talk," Alessi said. Disappointment spread over her face like a shadow. One woman fed Azazel a peeled grape, and he smiled in lustful satisfaction. Kol sat beside Alessi, and both watched in disdain.

"How could he party like that when Alessi's about to... when Alessi might die?" Kol narrowed his eyes. "What kind of man is he, anyway?"

"Don't judge him so harshly. He hasn't been the same since we lost Fenvir." Enira trailed off.

"Lost him? He's dead!" Alessi said.

"Worse. He fell between worlds," Enira said. "He's trapped in eternal, unending suffering." The candles flickered one by one, and the candle at the end of the row went out. "Are you ready?"

Alessi nodded. Enira rolled up Alessi's sleeve, rubbing a metallic blue powder into her wound. Alessi's flesh sizzled, but Kol winced more than she did.

"Actually, there's something you should know," Enira said.

"I don't care—" Alessi began.

Enira cut her off. "Did you ever hear what really happened to Fenvir? How he fell?"

Alessi paused. "I heard one of your kind killed him," Alessi said. "Then you drove Azazel crazy and now you're about to kill me, too."

Enira chuckled, working the blood-pus-paste further into the wound. "You're the princess, yes? I've heard about you."

"So what?" Alessi asked.

"It was actually your mother who betrayed Fenvir, around the time she left the druid order," Enira said. "I knew her, then. She seduced him and ate his heart."

Alessi massaged her gloved hand. "I didn't know she used to be a druid."

"Most consider her a traitor and a cannibal, so I'm not surprised she never mentioned it," Enira continued, massaging the paste.

"Why would she seduce a Zaharran?" Alessi asked. "That goes against her stupid witch code."

"That was before the codes," Enira said. A cool breeze sent the candles flickering. "I'm surprised she never told you about your—"

Alessi hissed. "That's enough of your nonsense."

"Later, then." Enira pulled out a yellow vial, pouring a substance with the texture of syrup over Alessi's wound. Alessi made a face as it filled the gaps in her flesh. It hardened like amber. Enira lifted a candle to it, orange tongues licking Alessi's wound, and the blood-amber began melting.

"Gah!" Alessi said. From where he sat beside her, Kol saw her jaw clench. He yelped as she placed her left hand on his knee, her claws digging into his maroon pant leg. When the melting amber liquid pooled on the floor, a black substance swirled within it.

"That's some of it," Enira said, "but not all. We'll try again tomorrow." She walked across the room with a slight limp, then ground something with a mortar and pestle, orange in the candlelight.

"I haven't seen this magic before. This isn't the same as witch magic," Kol said. The smell of moss and moist earth filled the air. Somehow, this magic felt different, more organized.

"Do I seem like a killer to you? Do you see bodies littered around the room?" Enira asked in a sarcastic tone. "Of course it's not witchcraft." Alessi stuck out her tongue as the Druid packed a black, powdered substance into the wound, then wrapped it with a clean bandage. "I hoped I could do more, but this is the most I can do for you."

Alessi grumbled, massaging her wounded shoulder. "At least you didn't manage to kill me."

Enira shot her a stern look.

"Thanks," Kol said, eyes turned to the ground in a combination of shame and relief. Now, she just might not die because of him.

"Don't thank me yet," Enira said.

Something clattered high above him in the small room he shared with Alessi, and Kol stirred. Cool air pooled around where he slept on a cot in one of the druids' many sprawling stone buildings. It poured in from the open window, and the dust made him cough. It was supposed to be a storage room, but several young druids begrudgingly moved their sacks of flour to make room for them both.

He heard the sound again, the empty sound of stone on stone, and he sat up, pushing himself to his feet. He rubbed his eyes and stretched, his back and ribs aching. He had insisted on staying with her in case something happened overnight. It was a kind gesture she probably couldn't understand, and she was miles away from letting him sleep in a real bed, because that would mean sharing. She wanted him close, but never too close.

She'd share with that stupid owl. Kol didn't like what he felt, especially after what had just happened, and yet her words rang through his mind. *Special friend.* Alessi's bed was empty, and Kol could only imagine where she was. But *he* was there for her when she was at her worst, when she was about to die, not Azazel—and yet, the way she looked at Azazel... He feared his jealousy was about to swallow him whole. He leaned out the open window, feeling the cool night air against his flushed face, and took a deep breath.

"Couldn't sleep?" Alessi's voice came from where she sat on the edge of the peaked roof above him.

Kol startled. "Oh, you're up there." Relief washed over him as he craned his neck up to look at her. The moonlight cast her in a blue-white hue.

"Yeah, where else would I be?"

"Well, you weren't in your bed." Kol's voice was flat, and an unpleasant feeling clutched at his heart. "I thought you'd be with *Azazel.*" The name rolled off his tongue like a curse.

"That stupid owl?" Alessi blew air out through her nose. "It's not like that."

A momentary relief flooded Kol before her wounded shoulder dripped black ooze onto the roof beneath her. "Shit."

She glanced at the wound in disdain. "The ritual was a bunch of chanting and snake oil." She shrugged. "The wound still won't close." She brought a hand to her chin, and the bags under her eyes less were pronounced than before.

"You look better, though. And you're not dead."

"Yet."

Kol wasn't sure how to follow that up. Pebbles fell to the

ground beneath him as Kol pushed himself off the sill, grabbing at the stone wall's uneven edges and climbing onto the slate roof above. "What are you doing all the way up here, anyway?" He sat beside her, feet dangling over the roof's edge.

"Sitting," Alessi said without turning to face him. A breeze blew past her, carrying a new scent to him. The air had a peculiar tang to it, somewhere between blood and fruit and rotting flesh.

Kol looked around at the sprawling temple complex, two large buildings flanked by dozens smaller, like the one they were on. "That was you on the roof, then. You woke me up."

Alessi scoffed. "It's not my fault you sleep like a princess."

"And princesses need sleep." As Kol spoke, a thick glob of half-dried blood trailed down Alessi's arm.

"You're—" he began.

"Gross. I know." She gave a weak smile, completing the joke. She wiped the half-dried blood with her good hand, then flicked it onto the ground below. "All the spells and powders in the world couldn't fix me."

"Why?"

Alessi kicked at the air. "Maybe it's fate, but I meant what I said earlier. Some people deserve to die." She massaged her gloved hand. "And I'm one of them."

"You don't deserve to die," Kol said.

"You don't know me."

He edged closer to her. "But I do. You saved me."

Alessi laughed. "You're too trusting." She shook her head. "Do you ever wonder why I rely on brute strength instead of using magic, even when I'm a witch?"

Kol hadn't thought of it much before.

She raised her hand. "I've deserved to die ever since I stole this magic. I fucked up, Kol. I did a terrible thing and everyone

I loved died for it." Alessi shook her head. "I'm a traitor and a monster."

"I don't know what happened to you," Kol said, "but people change. Maybe you're not the same person who did those things. Maybe *this* Alessi doesn't deserve to die."

"Don't be ridiculous." Alessi gritted her teeth. "It's about time I pay what's due. Fate is catching up with me."

"But your wound is better," Kol said with a forced smile. "Enira helped, even if only a little bit."

"Never trust a Druid. They're born with their magic, so you never know why they do the things they do. We steal ours fair and square."

"That doesn't sound fair to me," Kol said. She sat close enough for him to feel the heat radiating off her body, and off her wound in the fresh night air. Her hair rustled in the breeze, and he wanted to touch it, remembering the night he cut it with his dagger.

"And their religion is ridiculous. Worshipping Zaharrans... this is Lilith's doing." Alessi pushed herself to her feet.

He looked up at her. "If Zaharrans aren't gods, then what are they?"

Alessi stretched her arms high over her head and yawned. "If the world is a dream, they're the dreamers." As she stood against the night sky's navy, with the stars and moon the same silver-white as her wind-tousled hair, he realized she was beautiful in a haphazard, terrifying, bone-chewing kind of way. And he kind of liked that.

Go with her.

"What are you going to do after this?" he asked. "After you recover and escape from those bounty hunters?"

"If I recover," Alessi said, "I was planning to head east to the Valley of Dragons." She narrowed her eyes. "And from there, the red king's castle."

Kol's heart fluttered.

Find me in the Valley of Dragons.

This worked perfectly. Maybe it was fate that that they met. Or maybe it was magic that drew them together.

"I'm going with you," he said.

Alessi raised an eyebrow. "We'll probably die."

"I have to go to the Valley of Dragons." Kol turned his body to face hers.

"Fine. But we can't do anything until my wound heals. And until we lay a trap for those assholes."

Kol drew his knees to his chest, old worries creeping back in. This world was full of enemies. "And how do we lay the trap?"

"We'll bait them, then send them where the wolf god sleeps." She settled back on to the roof beside him, leaning back and crossing her legs. "With some luck, those assholes will fall between worlds and we can wash our hands of them."

The wolf god. Fenvir. He'd heard stories. Kol thought to what Enira said earlier, about Miren's betrayal. To eat the heart of the one you love—to devour their very essence—was something he had difficulty imagining. But maybe that was what witches do.

"Fenvir was a Zaharran like Azazel, right? He must have been stronger than your mother at the time," Kol said. "So, why couldn't he stop her?"

She then looked him in the eye, her face sullen. "I guess he trusted her. Love is a destructive thing, Kol. Don't forget that." She leaned against him.

Kol tried to steady his breathing. Her blood soaked through his cloak, but he didn't care. He gazed out on the sprawling buildings before them. They were a pallet of gray between the white light of the moon and the blue glow gathered along the forest floor. A gentle golden luminescence shined from every street corner.

Then, the stars above faded and the world around him disappeared, and he was in darkness. He grasped at the emptiness beside him—Alessi was gone. He recognized this void of a landscape as one in his visions. It had been so long since he last had it that it sucked the air out of his lungs. He saw the outline of his mother and brother in the wastes, the shadow of her face, then fell through an endless space, wind whipping his hair back.

"I'm going to find you!" Kol yelled into the void, the wind nearly drowning out his voice. "We're going to the Valley of Dragons!"

He's coming.

12

K ol found himself back on the roof, his chest heaving.

"Are you alright?" Alessi asked. She had one hand on each of his shoulders, shaking him.

"*He's coming*," Kol said breathlessly.

"Who?"

Something moved in the forest beyond, and Alessi stiffened. Fog spilled from between the trees and Kol almost thought he saw the outline of a deer, then a badger.

"Fuck. They found us," she whispered.

The trees swayed and shifted. A familiar vibration emanated from the forest.

"It's those assholes," Alessi said. "Two are illusionists, but the red dragon has control over fire. Watch for him to strike."

"Shit." A red dragon. Like the red king.

"Come on, you need to get out of here." She stepped forward defensively.

Kol brought a hand to his forehead.

He's coming.

The voice rang through his mind until it was all he could

hear, like an overwhelming echo. He couldn't stand. He couldn't move.

Alessi held him by the shoulders, again shaking him to his senses. "Now's not the time to loiter around. I can't face them like this, we've got to get Azazel!" Alessi leaped to the ground, landing in a crouching position. They were near the druid temple. She hissed, grasping at her oozing left shoulder. "Azazel! Fuck, I oughta cut off this cursed arm."

There was no response.

"Stupid womanizing owl," she muttered as Kol clambered to the ground beside her between two stone buildings. A few silver-haired women peered into the street, whispering.

Face him.

"We can't run this time," Kol said. "We have to face them."

"What did I just say? I can't," Alessi said, clenching her jaw. The motion in the trees grew closer, as if some giant *something* was making its way towards them.

She can't keep running.

Kol leaped to the ground, then turned to face her. "You're the most powerful witch in Alon. We can face them. Together."

"We?" Alessi snorted. She stopped walking, and Kol bumped into her, more blood smearing across his cloak.

"I'm here for you." He put both hands on her shoulders, her wound smearing warm blood across his palm. When he looked into her silver eyes, he saw fear. Hesitation. "You can do it, Alessi," Kol said. "I don't know what you've done, but whatever it was, stop punishing yourself for it. Become what you're supposed to be." When he removed his hands, they were covered in an iridescent silver dust.

"I can't," Alessi said.

"Alessandra?" A man's smooth voice came from the woods. "I've *finally* found you."

Alessi inhaled sharply through her teeth, and she massaged

her gloved hand. Kol could tell by her reaction this must have been someone she knew.

"Kol?" Astor's voice now came from the woods. "Let's go home." The voice was so real it made Kol's heart ache. Memories flashed before his eyes—Astor on his birthday. Astor teaching him to read. He and Astor stepping out of their home and into the burning wastes together. But this wasn't Astor.

"Damned blue dragon. Come on," Alessi said. "If we can make it to the caves, we might have an advantage." She crouched beside the building, gesturing for Kol to follow, before they both ran away from the temple and into the brush.

Fog pooled around Kol's feet as they approached, the smell of earth and rain permeating the air. They crouched low in the bushes, pine needles crushing beneath his hands. Something stirred in the distance, and a long, shadowy neck reached high above the trees, glowing eyes searching out the darkness.

"It's an illusion," Alessi said, "but that doesn't mean it's not dangerous. Blue dragons mimic sounds, but golden dragons create shapes. They can hurt you, so be careful."

"And red dragons?" Kol asked.

"Fire. But not regular fire—they give life to it, give it a purpose. Some can create a fire that will hunt you for the rest of your life until either you or it is extinguished. Wait here."

Alessi started as if to run out into the clearing before them, then froze. A clawed hand reached from the shadows behind her, grabbing what was left of her silver hair. She let out a shriek of protest.

"Not so strong now, are you?" A man stepped into the clearing, silver moonlight illuminating his golden hair. The shadowy monster in the distance drew closer, flattening trees. "Seems my little pet managed to find you."

"Do you know what else is little?" Alessi spat on the dragon's face. He wiped it with one hand, balled that hand into a fist, then punched her in the face. She fell onto the ground.

"This isn't the Alessandra I remember. You're *pathetic*," he said.

"Fuck you, and it's Alessi now." Alessi lunged at his legs, only to take a sharp kick to the ribs.

Kol inhaled sharply, feeling her pain before shrinking into the shadows. The man kicked her, and each time glimmering golden light fell from his body like dust, coating Alessi's similar silver glimmer until hers was almost too faint to see.

Kol had to help her.

The man kicked Alessi as she struggled to her feet. "The bounty's nice, but I'd kill you for free after everything you've done."

"That's a lot, coming from you. The red king was our enemy, and now you suck his dick." Alessi spat blood again. "Don't underestimate me."

Something wrapped around Kol's ankle. It pulled him backwards, sending his chin into the stone before pulling him across moist leaves and flinging him into the clearing. He rolled to a stop, ribs screaming, and turned to face the misshapen thing. The dark shape from earlier—the illusion, the shapeless monster—had found him.

"Hang on," Alessi said. To his surprise, Alessi leaped over it and landed beside him. She crouched over him, snarling, claws borne. She swayed.

Her body is weak. If she does not use her magic, you will both die.

"You have to use your magic!" Kol cried out. His arms bled where he rolled against rocks and brambles, and when he wiped the dirt from his brow, his hand was covered in crimson.

"I can't," Alessi panted. "It'll kill me in this state. We have to run."

The shapeless, faceless thing was all around them again. It reached for Alessi, and in an instant, Kol pulled his dagger from his boot and slashed at the creature. Kol plunged his dagger into it to no avail. He couldn't grab, hit, or touch the thing, which appeared to be solid only when it wanted to be.

"That's not going to work," Alessi said. "It can touch us but we can't touch it. I need to—"

Her eyes shut, and she collapsed to the ground, the wound on her shoulder reopened and oozed a black goo. Just like earlier in the forest with Azazel, only this time, she didn't get up.

"Shit shit shit!" Kol shook her. The dark shape grew closer, wrapping a shadowy limb around Alessi's waist. A mouth full of teeth formed in the shadows behind her.

"I'm fine," Alessi grumbled, half-awake.

"No, you're not." Kol put his hands on her shoulders, smearing his palms with pus and blood. He held her to his chest, rocking back and forth. The monster neared, and the dragons drew closer like cats playing with their prey before delivering the final blow. There was nothing he could do. Without Alessi's magic, this could be the end.

He heard his mother's voice, more urgent this time. *Save her so she can save you.*

He would try, but Alessi wasn't making it easy. "You can do it," he said. "Come on!"

The light in her eyes had faded to a grayish color. She was getting weaker.

As the monster dragged her toward its open maw, Kol pulled her body over his, clutching her tightly to his chest and digging his feet into the ground. Her arm bandages fell into a bloodied pile to reveal pus-filled flesh and a gaping, swollen gash.

Her hair was in his face, silver dust dancing across his

vision. There was something else, too—a stream of black dust falling from her shoulder. For a moment, it looked like her wound was getting worse, but then he looked closer. No, it wasn't getting worse—it was closing.

"It's healing," Kol said.

Alessi stirred. "Don't be ridiculous!" She hissed, slashing at the monster's tendril. The branch broke off in Kol's hand, sending them tumbling closer to the beast.

"Your wound is closing. I don't know how, but it is!" Kol shouted at her. The creature was directly in front of them now, snarling fangs dripping with shadowy saliva. Its shape was amorphous, something between a serpent and an octopus. He kicked at the creature with one leg only to be met with icy teeth. He threw Alessi to the side. His legs burned for only a moment before they went numb. He looked down but saw only darkness.

They had come so far. From the compound, through the wastes. And now, he was being eaten.

Only moments before, they were on the roof, and she leaned against him. Now, she writhed on the ground.

He felt something, then. Now, he would never understand it.

He would never find his mother.

He would never find out what happened to Caliban.

She could have saved you. He heard his mother's voice.

What could he have done differently? To make Alessi accept her full power, this duty, this part of herself? He felt his consciousness start to fade as if he was dissolving into the nothingness, becoming one with the shadowy illusion. Where was she now? Would they find each other in the shadowy nothingness?

"Fuck OFF!" Alessi's voice came from above, and Kol fell out of the creature's grasp, landing with a thud on the soft earth below. "You want me, right? Then come for me. Leave him out of this."

As she stood, more black dust fell from her shoulder. Where the gaping, pus-filled wound was only moments before, there was now not even a mark. It was impossible.

This is only the beginning.

Alessi pulled Kol to his feet, supporting him on her shoulder as they ran back toward the caves. He looked again at her wound, just to confirm. It was gone. How was it possible? Moments ago, he was about to be eaten, and she was about to die, but now there wasn't even a sign of black, venom-encrusted pus where the wound had been. Her left arm, blue and scaly, was no longer covered by her glove.

"You saved us," Kol said.

"Maybe I should have put more faith in those druids," Alessi said between heaving breaths. A fire started in the brush, illuminating her silver hair in orange light and sending dancing shadows across her face.

This is only the beginning.

He knew it wasn't the druids who did this but didn't know what else to tell her.

He's coming.

"Will you use all your your magic now?" Kol asked.

Alessi smiled. "I don't let second chances go to waste."

He's here.

The fire spread in lines on either side of them, trapping them against the caves. The golden-haired man walked out of the smoke and stood before them. He was tall, with broad shoulders. His eyes, which were the same gold as his hair, were youthful other than the lines creasing around them.

"Where are you morons?" the golden-haired man growled. The other two dragons emerged on either side of him. The red-haired man appeared muscular and young, standing with slouching shoulders. His hair and eyes were every shade of red and orange, as if he was made of living fire. A small, weasel-like creature sat on his shoulder.

"The new guy got lost," the blue-haired man said.

The golden-haired man gnashed his teeth. "Again?"

"I wasn't lost, Viktor," the red-haired man said. "My tracker—"

"Shut up, Red," the golden-haired man—Viktor—said before turning his attention back to Alessi. "I could have sworn you were on death's door."

"Rumor travels fast, doesn't it?" Alessi asked.

"Not as fast as your scent." Viktor sniffed the air. "Like rotting flesh and body odor."

"I'll rip out your throat for that," Alessi said.

"Throat? I thought you could do better than that." Viktor winked. "Long time no see, Alessandra. Wish we were meeting under better circumstances, but alas, you're a traitor and a bitch."

"Alessi," she corrected him.

"You know him?" Kol asked her.

"Biblically, much to my very drunk disappointment."

Red looked to his golden-haired companion. "You and a witch?" Red let out a long whistle. "You never fail to surprise me, and always in the worst ways possible."

"They used to work together," the blue-haired man added.

Alessi snorted. "You could call it that."

The golden-haired man lifted his lip in disgust. "We were on a team together before the war. Or to be specific, before Alessandra started the war."

Kol's heart dropped.

"I was set up!" Alessi said.

Viktor snarled. "Thousands died because of you." He shut his eyes and flared his nostrils, gathering himself. When he opened his eyes again, they glowed like miniature suns. "But let's not get into this now. It's time to pay. The red king wants you alive to stand trial, and we're here to bring you to him."

Alessi straightened up. "I'll go with you if you can beat me."

"What?" Viktor raised his eyebrows.

"Yeah," Alessi said. "If you can defeat me in battle, I'll go with you willingly."

"You're lying," Viktor said.

"I'll take a blood oath. Remember that?" Alessi twisted her pinky in the air. "We've done this before."

Viktor's face reddened. "That was a long time ago."

"But you'll do it," Alessi said. "This time."

Viktor paused, then nodded.

"If you win, I go with you," Alessi said. "But if I win, you three go back to the western wastes and try again. And if you break the oath—"

"He dies," the blue-haired man finished.

Viktor smiled, sending a shiver down Kol's back. "Don't do this," Kol said. "There has to be another way."

"This is the only way," Alessi said. "I have a plan."

Viktor and Alessi each brought a claw to their palms, then, with a fluid motion and so in-sync that they could have each been a reflection of the other, they brought the claw across their flesh. Blood dripped into the dirt below—Alessi's a dark red, and Viktor's black—and the two approached, then shook hands.

Viktor nodded to the blue-haired man. "Lysander, come on."

"That's two on one." Kol balled his hands into fists.

Viktor laughed. "She should have specified, but she didn't think this through, as usual."

"I'll be fine," Alessi said. "Stay alive. I'll be back."

Alessi, along with Viktor and Lysander the blue dragon,

stepped through the smoke. Her silver hair was the last thing Kol saw before she disappeared entirely from view. For a moment, there was only the crackling of wood, the smoldering of embers. Thick smoke filled his lungs, and he coughed.

Viktor's voice came through the smoke. "Oh, and Red? Kill the weird human."

Kol turned to face Red. The man stood at least a head taller than him, taller than Astor and maybe even Alessi. One arm hung at his side, and the other scratched the back of his head. He didn't look like he was going to attack—but then again, what did Kol know about Dragons? If they were as cruel as Alessi said, maybe he would strike at any moment.

"Viktor's an asshole," Red said after a moment. "And that witch is going to kick his ass. I'm just here for the job."

Kol paused as he reached for the dagger in his boot. "You think so?"

Red nodded. "She's done it before. Guy's brain is eighty percent ego, or he wouldn't have agreed to fight her." He yawned, sending the weasel on his shoulder skittering to the ground, where he transformed into a young, goateed man.

"This is Parker, and I'm Red," the dragon said. "And we're both famously unmotivated."

Kol wrapped his fingers around the knife's hilt, then stood with it at his side. A feeling washed over him—a feeling of help-lessness. The only thing keeping him alive was their laziness and curiosity. He looked at the small dagger. It could do nothing against the wrath of a dragon. He might as well be standing there naked.

"We're not going to kill you," Parker said. "Humans are endangered."

Trust him.

"They're not endangered. Not technically. And I wasn't going to kill him," Red said. He yawned, fingers tracing his chiseled jaw, and Kol felt himself relax. There was an aura about this man—a bewitching aura, not unlike the one he felt around Alessi—and it was impossible not to fall under his spell. His body was marked by a supernatural perfection, and his muscles rippled with the very embodiment of power. This was an apex predator in his own domain, beautiful and horrifying if not a little tired. It was difficult to look away from him.

He's here.

"Who are you?" Kol asked.

"Red."

"That's not a name."

"Why would you care?"

Because he was looking for someone. "It's not like I'm complaining, but why aren't you trying to kill me, unmotivated or not? Isn't this your... job, or something?" It was like they had met before, but he couldn't place where. If the man wasn't a dragon, he might have even thought him to be Caliban.

Your fates are tied together.

Tell me how, he asked.

All in due time.

"This is a temp job until the king finds somewhere permanent for me. I'm after your friend, that's the only reason I'm working with those assholes." When he turned his head again, Kol realized where he had seen the man before. He was the poster beside Alessi's in the tavern where he met the mouse-man. He was the missing prince.

"You're the—"

"The prince?" It was like Red could read Kol's mind. "Probably not. I get that a lot, though." The man sat on a log, and the fires died down to a thin flame around them. Now, the flame was a welcomed warmth in the cold night air. "I'm just a bastard from the wastes, and I don't get paid enough to deal with this shit." He leaned back and scratched the back of his head. "You look like hell. When Viktor and Lysander get back, run into the caves."

The caves. Where you could fall between worlds. Kol sat across from him, still too cautious to get close. The man was too symmetrical, too finely formed, and yet there was a touch of feminine grace about him. He was inhuman. Perfect. Another memory surfaced from the mouse-man's village. A red-haired man clad in furs, standing in the snow.

"You've known where we were for a while," Kol said. "I've seen you before, you were watching me."

The man smiled and nodded.

"Red can't track worth shit, but I had your scent the whole time," Parker said.

"You didn't tell the others?" Kol asked.

Red shrugged, then his burning eyes met Kol's. "It's your lucky week. Something's telling me not to."

Kol's heart raced. This man had to be a clue, some hint as to what happened to his mother.

"You ever get a little voice in your head?" Red asked, laying back on his log. "They say it's glow madness, but I'm not sure."

"What's that?" Kol asked.

"Yeah. If you breathe too much glow—I imagine it would affect you more, since you're..." the man sniffed the air. Then he sat up, leaning forward with his elbows on his thighs and a quizzical look on his face. "Human?"

Parker chuckled.

"What?" Kol asked.

"You don't know?" Parker asked. "Might be for the better."

This is just the beginning.

"Know what?" Kol stood.

"You smell like magic. Could be a curse, but—" Parker began.

Alessi dove through the smoke, landing beside Kol and

looking at him with both eyebrows raised. "Good, you're still alive."

"You look surprised," Kol said.

Alessi shrugged.

"What happened?" Kol asked. Red stood, and Parker assumed his weasel form before hopping back on Red's shoulder.

"Time to go, I guess." Red sighed.

"I won," Alessi said. "These idiots have to go back to the wastes, and soon, preferably."

"I can help with that." Another head popped through the smoke beside her before stepping through. Azazel, looking far too pleased with himself. Red waved his hands, sending the fire dying down and revealing a displeased Viktor and Lysander. Viktor had a bleeding gash over one eye, which was puffy and swollen.

"Where were you?" Kol asked.

"Busy." Azazel winked. Blue flame came from the tip of Azazel's finger as he traced the outline of a new portal. The familiar red-orange dunes of the western wastes waited on the other side. "Out you go," Azazel said, ushering the dragons through. With only a menacing look, Lysander stepped through the portal, his blue hair the last thing Kol saw of him. Viktor reached the threshold, then paused, with Red behind him.

"We'll catch up to you again," Viktor said. He stepped through.

"And I'll kick your ass again," Alessi said.

"I know you're heading east. It'll be different next time because you'll be on *our* turf." Viktor sneered. "And we won't be alone." He stepped through the portal.

"Nice meeting you, I guess," Red said, bringing two fingers up to his forehead. His eyes burned like embers, and Kol almost felt himself falling into them.

"You don't have to go with them," Kol said.

"I do, until I find a permanent job," Red said. "Until then, I've got a feeling we'll meet again." He stepped through the portal, which snapped shut behind him.

Azazel stretched his arms into the air and yawned. Alessi placed a hand on his shoulder and pushed him back, fangs borne, fire in her eyes. "I called for you!"

"I was a little preoccupied," he said, massaging the sore spot where she pushed him. "Besides, I knew you had things under control."

"You didn't know anything, you womanizing owl," Alessi said. She pushed him again.

Kol couldn't help but smile but couldn't fully explain why. It was like her affection for Azazel was a wall between her and himself. Like he was a remnant of a past Kol never had the chance to be a part of. And it was lifting.

"Owww!" Azazel protested. He looked back at Alessi with wide eyes and added, "Your arm..."

"It's good enough to punch you with, and maybe I oughta." Alessi spat into the dirt. She grabbed Kol's hand with hers, pulling him back in the direction of the temple. "Come on Kol, I need a fucking nap."

As they walked away, Kol looked over his shoulder at Azazel, who watched them with a knowing expression.

<h1 style="text-align:center">13</h1>

Alessi rolled over in bed, her three hours of sleep weighing on her eyelids like a bag of rocks. Azazel's voice drifted in from outside. She groaned, rolling onto her back, and pressing the pillow against her ears. He was the last thing she wanted to hear.

She should have been in so much pain, but she wasn't. Viktor had nearly snapped her neck the night before, the bastard, but now it wasn't even sore. It was a surreal feeling, accompanied by a discomfort that ate at the edge of her mind like a lightbeetle chewing on dew leaves. With the sound of female laughter, she sat up and maneuvered herself to the edge of the bed. She stood, nearly stepping on Kol's still form. She fought the temptation to run her finger along his sharp jaw, through his dark hair, however foolish that might be. He still slept soundly in his blanket on the floor, though how he did so, she wasn't sure. Must be exhausted. Amazingly, he was unscathed—he must have talked his way out of a confrontation with the apathetic red dragon.

Maybe he was smarter than he looked.

150

Birds sang as she walked outside, sweltering air making the space between her shoulders sweat. She walked right past Azazel and his gaggle of fangirls.

"Hey, Alessi." Azazel reached out a hand.

She rolled her eyes and blew past him. "I didn't ask for a wakeup call." There was something else on her mind. Clear of the gaggle of druids, the old song came to her mind, and she hummed it quietly to herself.

"There once was a woman named Oasis
For where she walked
The desert bloomed"

High Queen Oasis was the only person Alessi's mother feared, other than perhaps Alessi herself. There were only maybe three mages in the world capable of healing a wound such as hers. And at least one—Oasis—was dead. Enira could be another, but she wasn't so sure. She massaged her healed shoulder as she walked between the stone buildings. The elders lived in the largest building at the top of a hill. Behind it, a smaller building was connected by a vine-covered porch.

It almost seemed to grow larger as she neared it, until she stood at its carved, wooden door. It was warm to the touch as she knocked on it, making an empty sound. The raspy voices of old women came from within.

Enira answered the door. "Oh, it's you." She began to shut the door, but Alessi wedged her foot in the doorframe. "What do you need?" She inspected Alessi's arm. "You're healed, there's nothing more I can do for you."

"I have a question for you," Alessi said.

Enira studied her for a moment, her eyes resting on Alessi's healed shoulder. She hadn't tried to hide her healed wound, the space where it had been exposed by the hole in her shirt. "You have more than one question, don't you?"

Alessi gritted her teeth. Azazel had terrible taste in women. "Maybe."

Enira stepped outside, gently closing the door behind her. They walked together through the empty morning streets, side-by-side. "Your shoulder is healed. That's good."

"Did you do it?" Alessi asked.

"Well... it's hard to say."

"I need to know." Alessi stopped, looking into Enira's eyes until the old woman sighed and looked away.

"No," she said. "But I would appreciate if you kept that from my acolytes. I'm getting on in years, and they don't need reason to doubt me."

"Then whose work is this?" Alessi demanded.

"Who do *you* think did it?" Enira sighed. "I have a feeling you already know."

Oasis. "It's impossible," Alessi said.

"They say she lives on as a ghost, manipulating lives from the other side," Enira said. "Even we have felt her spirit, or heard her voice, in the caves where the boundary between worlds is thin."

"There's no such thing as ghosts," Alessi said.

"And how would you know?" Enira asked. "Is it so bad to believe in something greater? The everlasting?"

"There are no ghosts because... because..." Because her team would have come back to haunt her. To curse her.

"These things aren't for us to understand," Enira said. "There are some things in life best left mysteries."

"Enough of this nonsense," Alessi said. She gritted her teeth. "Where was Oasis last seen?"

"You can't be serious." Enira scoffed. "She's dead, a ghost!"

"Where?" Alessi asked through gritted teeth.

Enira eyed her carefully. "North of Vico, heading into the western wastes."

"I heard she went south to Carpacia," Alessi said.

"Lies spread by the red king. When he sent his men after her, he told them the truth—she was seen north of Vico, heading into the western wastes."

That's where Kol was from.

"You've grown fond of your companion." Enira smiled. "I hear you used to travel alone."

Alessi was getting tired of Enira's nosiness. "He's cargo. Human meat is a delicacy—I'm selling him off in the nearest citadel."

"You don't have to go to a citadel to sell something like that," Enira said. "I can tell by your face you've had many opportunities, and yet you didn't take them." She raised an eyebrow. "Maybe you're not as heartless as I thought."

"Watch me," Alessi said. "If you think I'm going soft, you're wrong."

"Whatever you tell yourself."

"Don't tease me," Alessi hissed. They had walked in a circle and were now at the large building again.

Enira laughed. "You remind me so much of *her*, in her better days." She reached for the door, and as her fingers grasped the handle, she stopped. "You should be careful. History has a tendency to repeat itself."

"Always am."

When the door shut behind Enira, Alessi made her way back to the small building she shared with Kol. Things were changing, and somehow Kol was in the middle of it. Alessi wasn't sure she liked that. If he was connected to the mad queen Oasis, and if the rumors of Oasis' last days were true, this could get complicated.

But on the other hand, this could make him even more useful. He could be the missing prince. The posters just showed a younger version of the red king. No one really knew what he'd look like, anyway, since Oasis was pregnant when she disappeared. She shook her head. Impossible—the missing prince would be a Red Dragon, and Kol was only a human. But if he was somehow the missing prince, that left her with two options: kill him herself, or hand him over to the red king to be eaten or used however he had intended to use Oasis.

"Dragons really are like people." Kol's voice sent her jumping backwards.

"You scared the shit out of me," Alessi said, straightening. "Of course they're like people. I told you."

"I didn't think you meant literally," Kol said. "Like the other Belgarri. I'd imagined monsters, but they were just... people."

Azazel approached the two, arms crossed. Kol shot him a dirty look. "Where'd you go at such an odd hour?" Azazel asked. "Always a busy body."

"None of your business," Alessi said. "I could ask you the same thing about yesterday, when I almost got my ass handed to me." Alessi made her way back to the small room she slept in. Time to pack her things, then get going.

"I was busy," Azazel said. "Like I said."

"With whom?" Alessi stopped, hands on her hips.

"Lenina, Ataria, and—what does it matter? You live long enough, and all the faces start to look the same." Azazel sighed. "We were having such a great time until you showed up."

"Sorry our almost dying interrupted your orgy," Alessi said. "Don't forget that you owe me."

"Right, right. But what am I to do if you take your new *friend* on adventures instead of me? What of the good times we had? I'm always willing to share, but—"

Alessi cut him off. "Enough. Kol, stay here. Mommy and daddy have to talk about this *outside*."

She didn't as much as look back as she herded Azazel

outdoors. "What the fuck is wrong with you?" she asked through gritted teeth. "Are you losing your mind? We're so close, and you're wasting your time with druids?"

In contrast to her fury, Azazel looked relieved. "I was just trying to get you alone, Alessi! It's all in good fun."

"Now's not the time, you pervy owl."

"Out in the open like this? No, no, I'm not a barbarian." His face grew grave. "There are dangers out here. I wanted to tell you to be safe on the road."

"I will be," Alessi said.

"Those dragons will catch up to you in a matter of days. Don't forget they can fly."

"I'll head to Oniby for a while. It's off all the major paths, and it's got some killer brew. We'll be fine. And you'll be where we agreed when the time is right? In the dungeons?"

"Of course." Azazel's eyes traveled to her shoulder.

"You know something, don't you?" Alessi asked.

"It's that boy..."

"What about him?"

"I have a bad feeling about what you're going to do. If you go forward with this, I can't watch."

"Then don't." Her voice was low, like a growl.

"He's innocent, Alessi. If you do this, you're as bad as—"

Alessi opened the door, startling Kol and sending him tumbling into a pile of dusty books, which landed on the floor in a heap. His head bled where his forehead hit the stone floor, and he held it with a crimson hand. Of course, he was listening. Her heart was like a stone in her chest, but when she looked to Azazel for reassurance, she found only an empty space where he once stood.

Lousy owl.

<h1 style="text-align:center">14</h1>

They left the druid temple that morning and found themselves back in the wastes by noon. Kol pondered the conversation he overheard. What could Azazel have meant by that? What, exactly, was Alessi planning to do? A gust of sandy wind came his way, and Kol used his cloak to shield himself from it. There was a hot western wind that day, and the sun's heat combined with the merciless sands set his skin on fire.

If he couldn't trust Alessi, who could he trust?

He brought a hand to his head, finding it covered with crimson only moments later. The thin cloth Enira had wrapped around it did little good to contain the blood, and there was also no time to slow down. Alessi pulled him by the wrist, and he followed, lightheaded. The sun glinted off her blue, scaled arm —the arm of a stranger, the arm of a dead woman he never met. Would he wind up like her, too?

His wound stung with fierce intensity. "Did you really... did you really kill a dragon and steal her arm? Do you kill people?" Would she kill him, too?

Alessi huffed. "What of it?"

"I guess I want to know why." Kol stumbled over the words like there was cotton in his mouth.

"The arm is stolen, and so is my magic. That's how witches get magic."

"But it changes you." Kol was dizzy. "Do you ever worry you won't be yourself anymore?"

Alessi whirled around. "I'm a witch. This is what I am made to do." Alessi bore her fangs. "What do you think these are for? Smiling?" She bit into her arm, sending lines of her too-thick blood falling to the sand below. "My body changes, but that's the price of stolen magic. Nothing comes easy, and nothing comes free."

"It must hurt," Kol said.

"Not as much as it used to."

Lights danced around the edge of his vision. Kol coughed, the pressure sending another cascade of blood onto his hand from where he'd injured his head. It flowed from his palm and dotted the sand, his crimson beading into little domes on top of Alessi's darker, rosewood blood. Kol fell to the ground beside it, cheek pressed into the sand, mixing their blood together with a finger and watching it swirl. It was beautiful. It was hypnotizing. He could almost fall asleep.

"Hey, stop being a freak." Alessi slapped his cheek. It stung.

"I'm not." Kol nearly slipped out of consciousness.

"Don't go dying on me. You're not even bleeding that much."

Kol looked at the blood and his ruined shirt. "Is this what you call not much?" He brought up his hand from the puddle, spreading his fingers for her to see. Sticky liquid dried on them.

Alessi crouched in front of him, touching her own fingers to the wound. She brought her clawed hand up, pressing it against his skin, and he felt a stinging sensation. "Whatever. We'll take a break."

She ripped Kol's pack off his back, rummaging through it. She pulled out her own ruined bandages, which he saved from before. "Wrap these around your head."

Kol fumbled with the bandages for a moment, but his fingers were weak, uncoordinated. Alessi rolled her eyes then took the bandages into her own clawed fingers, reaching to the bottom of his shirt with her free hand.

Kol resisted as she peeled off his jacket, then his tattered tunic. "The hell are you doing?" Were these the same claws she planned to kill him with? Rip out his throat, or tear him limb from limb?

"I thought you said you were dying. Don't you need some help?" she asked.

"No..." But he did.

Kol looked away from her as she wrapped the stained but clean linens around the wound, binding it tightly tying it on the side. "Why bother?" Kol asked. "You're just going to kill me, anyway."

Alessi shot him an irritated glance. "I'm not going to kill you."

"But you said—"

"I changed my mind. Drink this." Alessi held out her dragon hand, pointing her fingers at the ground. Streams of water snaked their way out of the sand. She maneuvered the water to Kol's mouth, and he drank.

"Thanks," Kol said.

"I'm using my full magic again because of you." Alessi shrugged. "You helped me back there."

The water helped, and Kol started to feel better. But there was something on his mind. "You were, or are, going to kill me. I can't tell if you're a princess or a murderer."

"Why can't I be both? Or I could murder you now and settle this for sure." Alessi's voice was low and stern. "Look, I was going to feed you to some freaks, but I changed my mind. Ok?" He could hear the sincerity in her words.

Kol managed a slight smile. "I told you you're not a bad person."

Alessi's nostrils flared. "Ridiculous." Eyes narrowed, she turned her head to face the setting sun, the breeze blowing her hair behind her like dusty tendrils. "It's getting late so might as well take a break before you bleed to death. I hope we're rested in the morning because we've gotta make it to the wall."

Kol wanted to ask about this wall, but he was too tired. Too much had happened, and he'd lost too much blood. She said she changed her mind, but could he really trust her? Would she change her mind again? Maybe he shouldn't trust anyone who —at any point—had planned to feed him to 'some freaks.' He had put all his faith and hope in a stranger without even thinking what motives she might have.

He was a different person when they met. So much had changed in just a few weeks.

He laid down in the sand, curling up from the heat and pain. His lips were chapped, and he felt his every heartbeat pulse through his forehead. Who was she, really? This thought worked its way through the fog of pain many times that day. Whatever the truth may be, it didn't matter. Friend or foe, he was stuck with her, lest he be left to die out in the wastes.

***

The sun rose in a dusty haze as they set off, Kol following behind the faster Alessi. The wound in his forehead didn't throb quite so hard now, and he had energy to ask the questions that had crossed his mind the previous day.

"So, the wall..." Kol began. There was more he wanted to ask, but he stopped himself. What would happen when they got there? And what would she do to him there?

"They call it the wall, but it's not really a wall," Alessi explained. "It's a mountain range. You can see it, there." She pointed, but Kol could see no mountains, only heat rising from the sand in waves.

He squinted, studying the horizon harder. "I don't see it." But, as those words left his lips, it was as if brown specks stretched from beyond the curve of the world, coming towards him. He blinked, and they were gone.

"Human eyes are weak," Alessi said. "The wall is the divide between territories. To the west is witch land, to the east is the realm of dragons. Witches are usually forbidden there."

"Then why are you going?" He was almost caught up to her now, his chest heaving. He lost a lot of blood the day before—he was lucky his wound nearly closed during the night.

Alessi huffed. They both knew the answer, Kol just didn't like it.

He pressed. "How far is it?"

"Far," she said without looking back. "Now stop with all the questions. I'm tired."

"No," Kol said. "You talked about killing me. You owe me some answers."

She gnashed her teeth. She may never tell him the truth—he was no longer foolish to believe otherwise—but he had to at least try. Had she really changed? Was there anything meaningful between them? She paused, biting her lip. Maybe she would humor him.

Or maybe she would kill him, after all.

But all she said was, "Why?"

"I have to know more about you," Kol said. "About this journey."

"Fine." Alessi sighed. "Go on, ask away."

He eyed her clawed arm, peeking out from beneath her sand cloak. "When you took her— the dragon's—arm, did you cut yours off?"

Alessi rubbed her arm. "No. Hers... replaced mine, you could say."

"How?"

"These aren't for decoration. Our original gift allows for magical replacement." She tapped her horns. "Witches steal magic by devouring it, and the magic replaces our original bodies." She pricked her thumb on a fang just to make a point. "Flesh, blood, bone... these things are all sources of power for a witch."

Kol tried to imagine her in the act. Blood dripping down her face, the screams of her victim. It was hard to picture her like that—even when he knew what she was capable of—but that was a part of her as real as any other. "You really killed a woman and ate her arm."

"A dragon," Alessi corrected.

"What's the difference?" Kol asked. "They walk like us, they talk like us. You're a cannibal."

"Not technically."

"But you are, at least in spirit."

Alessi paused. "It depends on your definition."

"Viktor and the others have something serious against you," Kol said. "I think it's about time you tell me what happened between you and the red king." Alessi pushed forward without looking back at him. He couldn't see her face, but he could feel the guilt and shame overshadowing her from the darkest corners of her demeanor.

"I will tell you," she said. "But not here." She stopped,

throwing back her shoulders, and turned to him. She smiled, but not with her eyes. "You're going to get sandblasted." She gestured to his bare arms, which burned like they were on fire. "I thought you put your cloak on ages ago."

"I'm fine." He couldn't push any more. A breeze blew even more gritty sand against arms, leaving them red and raw.

She drew water up from the ground and threw it against his skin. It was almost an affectionate gesture. When done, she looked ahead, standing on her toes. "We're almost there."

"To the wall?"

"To the skyship we'll take to the wall. There's one abandoned in this airlift."

Kol fished his bloodied iridescent cloak out of his pack. It was shredded up the back, likely where it caught on a branch or gnarl, but he liked the way its two new tails blew in the breeze. Alessi stopped walking, and when Kol caught up with her, he saw why. The wind blew something free from the sands. He took a breath, taking in its incredible form. It was a curved shape, peaked in the middle and rounded at the bottom. Its top was flat, and what remained of three dusty pillars stretched high above it. Though it resembled the tall ships from his father's library, it also had wings.

"This is *your* skyship?" Kol asked. It was incredible, but it was a wreck. There was no way that thing was going anywhere, but what intrigued Kol the most about it, however, was what was beneath it.

Shade.

He started across the sands and towards the strange shape, but Alessi caught him with one hand.

He shot her an irritated glance. "What?"

"That's not it." She didn't look at him, her eyes fixed on the ship. Her face was blank, and Kol looked from her to the shape and then back to her. The ancient wood creaked in the relentless wind. "Don't go near it, only dangerous things hang out around downed ships. Come on, we're almost to the lift."

Kol jogged to catch up with her, his feet leaving wakes in the sand. He wondered if he should be worried about whatever was waiting in the lift.

She continued. "The ground's too dangerous between here and the flats. We can't take the main path, or those assholes will find us. We could take the skyship straight to the Valley of Dragons, then continue across the flats."

A high-pitched sound interrupted them. It was loud and grating but had a fluid quality to it, and he looked ahead to see a waterfall of sands cascading into what appeared to be a massive hole. With another sound almost like a breath, a column of air blew the sand from the hole and into the sky above, where it rained down on them. Alessi shook herself off like a dog. Kol coughed, spitting sand. It was everywhere. He took off one boot and shook it—not like it did any good.

"No time for that." Alessi made her way to the edge, too close, and Kol resisted the urge to call her back. She lowered herself to the ground and worked her way to the dusty cascade.

"We should wait," Kol said, but the ground released another breath, showering them with more sand. The ground rumbled, and the waterfall of sand flowing over the edge grew in intensity. It was like the whole world was being sucked into the dark pit before them. He stepped back. "I don't like the looks of this."

"Neither do I, but there's a ship down there," Alessi said.

Kol could see over the edge now. If there was ever a ship down there, it must be completely buried in sand. "This is a bad idea. I don't think there's a ship down there."

"There is. I know because I put it there," Alessi said. "It belonged to a target from my bounty hunting days, so no one knows about this but me and a few friends." Alessi gestured for him to draw closer. "Hurry up or you'll miss it."

Kol lowered himself beside Alessi along the hole's edge, feeling the coarse sand grate against his hands as he made his way to the edge. If she was planning to kill him, this was her chance—one flick and he'd tumble into the abyss, never to be seen again.

"Look." Alessi pointed. Along the edge of the cliff were tendrils as if the roots of some plant desperate for water, perhaps miles away, snaked their way through rock and sand to find the desolate hole.

Kol squinted. "I don't see anything."

"Look closer."

He scooted a little closer to the edge and followed Alessi's fingers again. There was something now, further than he could see before. It was like the broken boat in the dunes, but with four green, translucent wings emerging from its hull. Alessi eased one leg over the ledge, and Kol realized in an instant what she would do.

"Don't do this." He wheezed, throat dry and full of sand.

She furrowed her brow and swung her other leg over the ledge. "Wait here." She climbed down, her hands gripping thin cracks likely formed by the roots Kol saw earlier.

He watched for a moment before crawling backward, keeping his eyes glued on Alessi. "There could still be someone down there," he shouted. He wasn't sure he wanted to meet anyone who had business in this part of Alon.

"Then I'll kill them. I'll untie it and ride the lift up and get you."

There was no bottom in sight, and his legs tingled from the dizzying heights. This may as well be a portal straight to the world of the dead. Kol stiffened as the ground rumbled beneath him, sending cascades of sand and stone tumbling over the ledge.

"Ah!" Alessi cried out, hanging by one hand over the yawning abyss. It was as if something stirred far below, and Kol stilled his imagination as what might live in a hole this deep, or what might have dug it in the first place.

"Hang on!" Kol pushed himself to his feet, eyeing the ancient roots hanging over the precipice. More rocks tumbled into the hole.

"Don't get too close!" Alessi yelled. She grabbed at a crevasse, but as the ground shook again the rocks pinched together, and Kol watched as she struggled to maintain her grip. A wet sound came from somewhere far below, like a mouth opening and closing. Beneath it, however, was the sound of water sloshing against stone. Looking at the roots reaching from its walls, he supposed that once, this hole may have been filled with water.

He felt around the lip of the opening, pulling at one of the ancient roots. It broke in his hand, bits of wood falling into the opening. He felt at another, this one newer, younger, more supple—but it didn't budge. He drew the dagger from his pocket and hacked at the root's base until it came free, sending him over the edge. Alessi dangled by one hand, her wide eyes turned toward the darkness below. She clawed at the stone with her other hand. The ground shook.

Let her die. She's served her purpose.

What do you mean? Kol asked. This was the first time his mother's voice told him to do something against his conscience, and it felt... wrong.

"What's taking so long?" Alessi yelled.

Leave her there. She wouldn't save you.

"She already has," Kol said out loud.

"Are you seriously talking to yourself at a time like this?" Alessi screamed.

You heard her back there, if you save her life, it will be the end of you.

You're wrong. She's changed, he replied.

Kol lowered the root, and it hit Alessi in the face.

Alessi shot him an irritated look. "You trying to kill me down here?"

Don't say I didn't warn you.

"Come on, take it!" Kol shook the root in her face, and she did. "It's only fair." She was heavier than he expected. As he pulled her, and his boots slid across the gritty sand and toward the cascade of crimson pouring over the edge. He hadn't considered what may happen if he wasn't strong enough to pull her up. A wet, squelching rumble came from somewhere below.

"Hurry up, beefcake! Use those muscles," Alessi yelled. "Before it gets us both!"

Every muscle in his body strained as he pulled her from the blood-red pit. Kol heard wood snapping—the ship, he imagined —just as Alessi rolled back onto solid ground. A gust of foul-smelling wind met Kol's face.

Something big was coming out of that hole, and it was coming for them.

"Change of plans," Alessi said, taking to her feet and running back in the direction they came.

Sharp pain ran up Kol's chest and shoulders as he dropped the root and followed her. She kicked sand up behind her. She was so much faster than him, especially with his injury, and no matter how he tried she only got further and further ahead. He pressed a hand to the wound on his head and resisted the urge to look at the monster that flapped behind him.

Curiosity got the better of him. He twisted his body to the

side, throwing a glance behind him. He tripped, landing in hot sand, but he couldn't take his eyes off the beast, its brilliant green reptilian eyes focused on him. It didn't just look at him, it looked through him. Tip to tail, it was at least the length of the gargantuan hole's diameter, which was at least ten times his height. This dragon smelled of moisture and sand and had a roughness about it that the other dragons they met lacked.

Kol scrambled to his feet. "The hell is that?"

"It's a feral blue dragon," Alessi yelled from up ahead. "They're like regular ones, but dumber and a lot more dangerous."

The creature flew from the hole and landed, lowering itself to the sand on four short, squat legs. It reminded Kol more of a winged salamander than a dragon. It was faster than Kol expected. It threw itself into the air, slit pupils resting on Alessi. Without thinking, Kol stepped between them. He held his dagger out in front of him, gripping its small hilt in his firm hands. Hot air blew in his face like breath.

He was about to die, he was sure of it—armed with only a tiny blade against the great beast. Was it worth it, dying like this to save Alessi? Was he a hero, or an idiot? The dragon was upon him now. He shut his eyes and braced himself for the inevitable.

One, two, three heartbeats. No impact, no claws tearing into his flesh, no teeth around his neck. Nothing.

Hesitantly, he opened his eyes. The dragon was gone, and his blade had no blood on it. He looked around, nearly tripping over himself as he spun. Relief flooded him as he saw an unharmed Alessi.

"The hells just happened?" he asked. "Where's the dragon?"

His eyes rested on Alessi, who pointed to a bleeding black mass in the sands beside them. It was the same dragon, but the lights in its eyes were extinguished. The smell of its magic was gone, replaced only by the fleshy smell of rot and death. It let out a wet breath before it went still.

This is only the beginning of what you can do.

His heart sank. What was going on? What knowledge really awaited him in the Valley of Dragons?

Alessi stood beside him. "Lucky strike." There was hesitation in her voice, as if she didn't fully believe her words. She probably didn't, but Kol couldn't allow himself to think too hard about the startling reality this could mean. Her hands bled from cuts obtained in her near-fatal fall into the lift. Black and purple bruises formed around her fingers and wrists.

"You alright?" Kol asked.

"Never better." She slapped him on the chest, leaving a bloody handprint on his cloak. She then walked up to the creature, toed its face with her boot and looked at him with a sideways smile. The dragon's tongue lolled out of its mouth. "Congrats. I don't know how you did it, but you're a dragon slayer now. Don't tell anyone about this, or you'd have a bounty on your head in less than an hour."

Dragon slayer. The idea made him sick to the stomach. His mind raced. Was this dragon a person, like the one Alessi killed? Did it have a family? Friends? Was he a murderer?

Alessi must have sensed his tension. "Relax. Ferals are pests, spending their days eating livestock and villagers. They stayed in one form for too long and killed their human minds and bodies."

"That's... sadder than I expected," Kol said.

"It's an intentional act, stemming from the desire to kill a part of yourself. When a Belgarri goes feral, what's left is an animal. No more thought, no more suffering, only instinct." Alessi shrugged, poking the corpse with one finger. "You can't tell me you've never wanted to escape somewhere."

The desire to escape. He knew that feeling well, though in a different context. "We should bury it. Or at least try to." He looked into the dead dragon's eyes. The life he ended, however miserable it may have been, was still a life. How did Alessi live with herself, after so much death?

Alessi opened her mouth as if to say something, then wrinkled her brow, thinking. After a few moments, she said, "No. Traditionally, you'd carve out its heart and eat it." She must have seen the look of disgust on Kol's face because she then added.

"I'll pass," Kol said.

The creature twitched, and Alessi let out a disgruntled sound. "Maybe it's not as dead as I thought. Better make sure, or it'll wake up with a grudge." She reached down with her scaled hand, letting her claws break the skin between two armored plates.

"Please don't do this," Kol cut in. The creature twitched again.

"Don't what?" She kicked it, and Kol struggled to hide his disgust. "It's just a dragon."

He tasted bile. "Leave it alone. It's dead."

"You're not going to do it, and there's no way I'm letting this amount of magic go to waste. I could use a recharge." Alessi sliced the creature's chest open with her claws and began feeling around inside.

Kol heard wet noises. He turned away so as not to see the horror and crossed his arms. "You wouldn't like someone doing that to your corpse."

"It was never like us. It was a dragon," Alessi said. "Their human bodies are nothing more than a costume. They were animals first, and that's all they'll ever be."

"Please stop," Kol said. The wet noises ceased. He tried not to look.

"You wanted to learn more about me. This is what witches do. If you don't like it, you should have picked a better travel companion." Her words were forced. She emerged beside him, gore smeared up to her elbow, a dark shape in her hand. "It easily could have killed you, anyway. You're lucky the damned thing flew right into your blade, cut its carotid." She took a bite and looked at him, chewing, black blood dripping down her chin.

He hadn't cut its carotid. He looked at the creature. It was bloodied past the point of being able to discern any specific wounds. Kol looked away, tasting vomit in his mouth. He could see why dragons didn't like her. There was too much to process. He knew what Alessi was, he had an idea of what she had to do for her magic, but it was like the majority of him could deny it, having never seen it in action. This was not a part of her that he liked. He clenched his jaw.

"What now?" Kol asked, looking away from the bloodied witch. The setting sun's orange fingers stretched across the sky, the first hints of stars visible on the eastern horizon.

"We're both a little worse for wear, so stopping for a few hours won't hurt. Your head, though—that must hurt," Alessi said, studying his face. She laughed, mouth full of blood, and a chill went down his spine. "You're full of surprises, aren't you? I'd better not let you out of my sight."

After retracing their footsteps for what felt like hours, the orange dunes were cast a silver-blue as day turned into night. Kol's head no longer throbbed, and ahead loomed the broken ship from earlier, half buried in sand, wind whipping around it. The other ship likely looked much like this one now, crushed by the dragon. He shook his head at the thought of running into another feral dragon, or worse.

Alessi sniffed the air. "It's empty. We'll rest in there for the night."

"So much for it being dangerous"

"I didn't think we'd be out here after dark. I guarantee you some monster has made it their den, or some bounty hunter has stayed there within the past fortnight, but whatever's in there won't be half as bad as what's out here once the sun sets." Alessi gestured to the twilight wastes, the white-speckled sky high above them. Dark shapes blinked in and out of existence on the horizon. "We'll just have to keep our guard up."

The ship creaked in the wind, and with one leap, Alessi stood in its door. Due to the angle of the ship, the door was higher than Kol's head, and he was neither as nimble nor as graceful as Alessi. He clambered over the side, heavy pack weighing him down. He fought through the pain that spread from his chest.

She offered a hand. Kol took it, and she hoisted him onto the tilting ship. Moonlight shone through its empty windows, casting blue-white light across its dry floor. A hammock hung between two pillars, and judging by its condition, Kol guessed it was used recently. Alessi crawled into it without hesitation.

"Sleep." She pointed at the bare floor.

"Someone's been here," Kol said. He laid out his blanket and crawled beneath it, shutting his eyes. It was difficult to relax, and the events of the day replayed in his head.

"Yeah, but the sleeping bag hasn't been touched in at least three days, whoever owned it probably left it behind or got eaten by that dragon," Alessi said. Then, quieter, she added, "How's your head?"

"As mad as ever." Kol brought a hand to his forehead. There was no longer any mark where the wound had been. "Wait," he said. "It's totally healed."

"Impossible," Alessi said under her breath.

She was right. It shouldn't. No matter how much he tried to make sense out of what was happening, Alessi's wound, his head, the dragon, it didn't make sense. He replayed the events in his mind, searching for a clue, a detail, anything that might lead him to the truth—but there was nothing, and each time he tried, he felt a little worse. Discomfort grew in the center of his chest.

He thought of his mother's words.

What are you not telling me? he asked. When his mother's voice did not reply, he rolled onto his back, sight resting on Alessi's glowing, silver eyes.

"Why aren't you trying to sleep?" he asked.

"I don't know. You?" She traced a shape in the sand on the floor.

"Something's bothering me," Kol said. "Something's bothering you, too."

Alessi took a sharp breath. "Maybe."

"You first."

"I've been thinking a lot lately, and... how well do we really know ourselves?" Alessi asked.

"Like our identities?"

"More than that. Who we are, what we want... If we change our minds, does that mean we're different people?"

Kol stared at the ceiling above them, moonlight leaking through it. "Like I said, people change."

"But how much can they *really* change?" Alessi asked.

"Is this... is this about the..." The whole murdering him thing? Kol couldn't bring himself to finish the sentence.

"I've done terrible things, hurt innocent people. Friends." Alessi took a breath. "I'll do it again, even if I don't like it, because that's who I am."

"You don't have to be that way," Kol said. "You could change. It's within your power."

"That takes us back to the beginning. *Can* I change, or am I stuck playing the hand I was dealt?"

"If you play by the rules, that's your choice," Kol said. "But you could always put the cards down and walk away."

"Maybe," Alessi said.

There was almost too much on his mind to form into words —how could he express his concern? His fear? Part of him wanted to keep it to himself, but another part still wanted to trust Alessi despite everything. Even if she told herself she was a bad person, her actions had suggested otherwise.

"I think there's something wrong with me," Kol said. In the distance, more dark shapes blinked in and out of existence, leaving trails of colored dust behind. When he rested his eyes on Alessi again, her hair and skin sparkled silver. He reached out a hand to her, then stopped. That color was her magic. It was alive. Every ounce of his body wanted to feel it, to breathe it in, to cover himself in it. "I've been hearing things."

"Your mother. You mentioned it."

"Right, but now it's like... I'm seeing things, too. Not always, but it's happening more often."

"What do you see?"

"Colors," Kol said. "When we first met, you said magic has a color. Can humans see it?"

Alessi scrunched her brow. "I've never heard of it happening."

"And then there's what happened with the dragon," Kol said. "I didn't—"

Alessi sighed. "Who knows? But if you keep searching, you might not like the answers you find. Travel has a way of bringing out the truth about oneself. Or, you could go back home, crawl back in your hole, and wait to be sacrificed by your cultish system. Not a life for me, but hey, who am I to judge..."

"I can't go back," Kol said.

"Doesn't it scare you? Seeing magic, killing dragons?"

"Yes, but..." He remembered his mother's voice. *Find me in the Valley of Dragons.* "I have to get to the Valley of Dragons. I have to find my mother."

"Because the voice in your head told you to? Then it doesn't matter what's going on, because you've already made up your mind." Alessi rolled over. "Look, I've seen some real weirdos up here, but you by far are one of the weirdest."

"... thanks?" Uneasy, Kol rolled to face away from Alessi. "About earlier... people are always changing. A bad person would have let me die today or pushed me into the lift. You didn't."

Alessi was silent for a moment, then said, "You are definitely one of the weirdest people I've met, but that's why I like you."

A warmth like fire spread from Kol's heart, through his chest, and to his limbs. Alessi was a complicated woman, but that was what made her human. As for him... his eyes followed the dark shapes on the horizon, colorful dust rising behind them. He squinted. He could see more of them now. They were Belgarri, and they were hunting.

What was happening to him?

He shut his eyes. Sleep didn't come easily, but when it did, the vision did not return to him.

15

A day passed, and the pair made their way out of the wastes again and into another forest not unlike the one where the druid temple was located. He hadn't seen magic that day and also hadn't heard his mother's voice since defying her at the lift. Alessi was in a better mood. As Kol walked, she ran or climbed trees or danced over roots, humming to herself. Her silver hair rustled in the slight breeze. He jogged to catch up with her. The trees around them were crooked and strange, their wood shades of red and purple and blue.

He nearly ran into her when she stopped, her hair slapping him across the face when she whipped around. She smelled of lilacs and smoke. And sweat.

Well, mostly sweat, but he didn't mind.

"Stop staring," she said. "I can feel you staring."

His face reddened, but before he could say anything, Alessi put a hand over his mouth. She craned her neck upwards, sniffing the air, then her eyes darted to the space behind him.

She dug her claws into a nearby pine, its bark shredding

under her touch. "Azazel?" she asked, but only the wind answered.

"Pretend everything's normal." Alessi turned her eyes forward, placing one hand on Kol's back, guiding him along the path.

"What is it?" Kol said.

"Something's following us."

"Something's always following us."

"This is different." There was an edge to Alessi's voice. "I hear something, but I don't sense any life."

Kol's eyes widened. "Shit."

"Monsters stay in the woods. Let's get to the nearest village, try to blend in. Should be safe enough, but..."

"But what?"

"In these parts, the villagers might be worse than the monsters."

The walk through the forest was tense, and Kol wasn't entirely sure what to say, so he kept his mouth shut. He sensed Alessi's apprehension in the sweat on her brow, the weight she carried in her shoulders, and the caution with which she placed her every step.

After some time, the cold wind disappeared.

"I know what it was now," Alessi said. "I don't think it was a monster. It's a spirit." Alessi reached into a tree, grabbed a handful of red berries, and popped them into her mouth. The juices dripped down her chin, red like blood. "Probably from the dragon graveyard we just passed through."

An unintelligible babbling floated to them. They rounded the gnarled trunk of an ancient tree, and a young boy stood in a clearing. He was a mud-streaked child of four or five years old, wearing what appeared to be a tattered burlap sack. A line of blood ran across his neck.

Alessi turned around, hand over her eyes. "Another one? Why is it always me?"

Kol thought back to the druid forest. Unlike the druidling, the boy didn't react to them. He faced away; blood dripped from his neck and down his side. He was around Mia's age, and severely injured by the looks of it. The boy continued mumbling to himself. He kneeled next to the child.

"Where's your mom?" Kol asked.

Alessi paced nervously. "Don't talk to it!"

The child pointed back to where they just came from. The dragon graveyard. A chill went down Kol's spine. As he looked at the child again, noticing that not only was there a line of blood across the child's neck, but blue and purple bruises mottled his upper arms. His pupils were dilated, and on his forehead was a dent larger than Kol's fist.

"What happened to you?" Kol asked, digging some clean bandages from his pack.

The boy only pointed again to the graveyard.

"Hold still." Kol dabbed the cloth on the boy's bleeding forehead. The boy continued mumbling.

"Leave it alone," Alessi said. "It might be dangerous."

"He's just a kid. He's harmless," Kol protested. The boy looked at him, red eyes glowing like embers.

"That kid's a dragon." Alessi kept her distance from the child. "He's no more harmless than a cobra."

The boy mumbled again, and this time Kol could almost make out the words.

"Daddy ate me and mommy's underground. Daddy ate me and mommy's underground." The boy twitched, his head jerking to one side. He met Kol's eyes. "Beware."

Kol stepped away from the child.

"Some batshit kid isn't our problem," Alessi said, pulling her hood over her eyes and buttoning her cloak. Only her mouth was visible. "But if you insist, tell the village elder and they'll send someone for him. We'll have to stay at an inn here because I'd rather not be out after dark."

Alessi narrowed her eyes at the woods, where a dark shape shifted. Green eyes glowed from the shadows, and the boy took off running towards it.

"Hey!" Kol called out. "Come back!" He started to run after the child, but when the child's foot hit shadow, it was like the boy dissolved—there was a breeze, the dust of red magic, and nothing else. Kol stopped, a perplexed expression on his face.

Alessi seemed unperturbed. "So,, it was the boy's spirit who followed us. How irritating. Let's go." She set one foot on the wooden bridge that stretched before them, over a small brook. Reeds grew along it, and Kol reached out. It was soft against his fingers, like a feather.

Alessi knocked it from his hand. "What is it with you and touching everything?"

"They're just reeds. They were also in the druid forest."

"Those aren't *your* reeds. They're dragon reeds, brought over from Belgar. If you'd touched that much longer, your fingers would have turned to stone."

"Shit." Kol looked down at his hands.

"We're not in the wastes anymore. This is the red king's territory, and shit gets weird around these parts." Alessi brought one hand to her temple and placed another on Kol's shoulder. "Just... don't touch anything without asking me first, yeah? So many of these things are cursed, or poisonous, or *alive*." Something that appeared to be a rock scurried across the bottom of the river, and Kol jumped back from the water's edge.

"Alright." He readjusted his pack, and the pair made their way over the cobblestone path into the village. As they left the forest, Kol looked back one more time, and he could have sworn the shadows shifted. When he looked to the town, villagers eyed them with suspicion.

"Newcomers," someone whispered.

"They don't look like us," added someone else. Three more people walked up.

"Stupid nosy dragons," Alessi mumbled, claws squeezing Kol's wrist.

Kol stepped close to Alessi as they pushed forward. He tried to look away from the people gathering at the road's edge. Ahead was a familiar sign: a crescent moon.

An inn.

Alessi pushed the door open. It wasn't like the doors in the human villages, but lighter and round in shape. Inside, a middle-aged man greeted them with a smile that quickly faded.

"Travelers!" The man tried to sound eager, but there was a nervous edge to his voice. "What brings you to these parts?"

"Business," Alessi said. "We'd like one room, please." Her grip on Kol's wrist was iron, and the man seemed to notice.

The innkeeper looked from Alessi, to Kol, then back to Alessi. "Ah, I can't do that. I don't allow that sort of business in my fine establishment."

Kol's face flushed, but Alessi only looked frustrated.

"Not that kind of business," she hissed through gritted teeth. "I sell... services."

"Services? You're not helping your case."

"... Surfaces. I sell tables," Alessi said.

The man crossed his arms. "Then where's your stock?"

"It's with my coworker back in the Queen's Country. Mind your own business." Alessi shook her growing mane of hair, which was already longer than it maybe should have been. It rippled down to her shoulders.

"I am minding my business." The innkeeper gestured

around them. "This is my business. I can do two rooms if you like."

Alessi brandished her claws, looking like she was going to fight the man.

Kol rolled his eyes. "Just pay him."

Alessi mumbled something about a scam before fishing two copper coins out of her pouch. The innkeeper smiled, throwing the coins into the air before catching them, and handed them each a key. The staircase they took to the upper level was broad and decorative, stretching up from the first room and into a hallway above. The floors were graced with wood that was the deepest red Kol had ever seen, and the doors were all rounded like the entrance to the building.

"Indoor forms only! I don't want claw marks on the carpet!" the man yelled from the lower level.

Their rooms were next to each other's, and when Kol lifted the key to the door, the end of the key moved almost as if it were full of angular worms, twisting and squirming. He almost dropped it.

Alessi rolled her eyes. "Just hold it up to the lock."

He did so after a moment of struggle, and when he held it close to the keyhole, the door opened as if pushed by an invisible hand. The sun had already set, and the forest-filtered moonlight cast the room in blue and green. Tall, tube-like plants shot up near his window, but Kol remembered Alessi's words. He knew better than to touch them, no matter how smooth they looked or how curious he was.

A smaller round door led to a balcony decorated in dark metal twisted into intricate patterns, much like the decoration on the doors. He leaned against the railing, watching the wind whip through the distant treetops, and he wondered what happened to the boy in the forest. He was likely a spirit and one of many mysteries he would encounter in his travels.

This was a beautiful place. Strange, but beautiful. So much of this upper world was.

"Don't fall for it," Alessi said. He turned his head to see her on a separate balcony, beside him. She leaned over it, her hair rustling in the wind. "All of this is fake. They use their enchantments to conjure up images of beauty, impressions of serenity, but it's just an illusion."

"There must be a lot of dragons here," Kol said. Looking down, there were several people gathered. A few eyes glinted gold in the dimming light, and a fog began to roll out of the forest beyond.

"Yeah. Golden dragons. Do you know why they call them that?" Alessi turned so that now she faced her room but still leaned over the balcony's edge.

"Their eyes?"

"Yes and no. Gold was always hard to come by, but there was a time after the Darkness when it was nearly nonexistent on the surface. Yet, kings and those who fancied themselves kings wanted to look stately, so they'd bring in dragons who could create the illusion of gold. Golden Dragons."

"So?"

"So, they can't be trusted. As often as the dragons helped the kings, they'd eat them, or sell them out."

"Shit."

"Shit's right. Just be careful. I wouldn't have come this way unless I had to. Everything comes with a price, and some things shouldn't be seen," Alessi said. "After all, we're in the Valley of Dragons."

16

Kol didn't sleep easy that night. He tossed and turned, the too-soft mattress somehow digging into his side and his shoulders. After he'd finally gotten to sleep, something that felt like a wet finger traced across his face. Horrified, he sat up straight in bed, pushing himself away from a shadowy thing that reached out from the dark space between the mattress and the ornamental wooden frame beneath it. With any luck, it was just a bug. Kol bit his lip, working up the courage to approach it. He realized whatever touched him wasn't a finger but a leg with at least three jointed sections curling upward. He grabbed a nearby travel brochure— *Welcome to Wellston!*—and swatted at the thing.

The shriek that came from it was far louder than what he imagined a tiny creature could create, skittering out from its dark space and across the floor. It moved like both spider and shadow, and though it didn't have a face, Kol imagined it to be very upset by the indignant way it carried itself.

"I didn't mean to disturb you," the thing said. It had a high-pitched whisper. "Enjoy your stay."

"I'm sorry!" Kol whispered, not knowing what else to do as the creature slipped into an almost invisible crack in the wall. Kol sat back onto the bed, burying his face in his hands, his eyes still heavy with sleep.

"Hey!" Another voice startled him. It was a woman's voice. Figuring it must be Alessi, Kol rubbed the sleep out of his eyes and made his way to the balcony. "You won't believe what woke me up. There was a weird little spider thing, are those common—" he began, only to look over to Alessi's balcony and see that it was empty. He then turned to the ground below him, where a woman stood with her hands on her hips and hair the color of golden morning sunlight. She had an amused expression on her face.

"Spider thing? Have you never seen a sprite before?" she asked, and blood rushed to Kol's face.

The wind blew, pressing Kol's thin night clothes against his body. "I thought you were someone else, sorry. You weren't talking to me, right?"

The woman laughed again. "I am now."

Kol pinched himself. She was beautiful—he couldn't deny that, but why would a beautiful woman be talking to *him* from his window? "Okay. Well." Kol fidgeted with the hem of his shirt. "I'll... I'll go back in now. Goodnight."

"You've got a funny smell, has anyone ever told you that?" the woman said just as Kol turned around.

"I don't know why they would've." He looked back at her, too embarrassed to admit Alessi had told him so on several occasions. "I don't think it's true."

"You do, but people can't smell themselves, you know."

A smaller but similar-looking woman and a blue-haired man joined her. The man was close to the first woman's age, perhaps a year older than Kol, but the new woman carried herself in a youthful way, with more spring in her step. She may have been even more beautiful than the older one, with a wry smile on her face to match. They had to be sisters. Kol leaned against the railing as they talked, taking in the sweet, moist smell of the breeze.

The man turned to him. "You're new around here."

"Just passing through," Kol said.

"That's what everyone says."

Kol raised an eyebrow.

The younger woman spoke up. "Don't mind him. We're going into the forest; do you want to come?"

Kol brought a hand to the back of his neck. A cold breeze blew by, and he thought of the boy from earlier, and of Alessi's anger if she found out he ventured out with a stranger again. "I don't know, aren't there *things* out there? You know, dangerous things?"

"Like witches? Not this far east of the border," the younger girl said, crossing her arms. She looked to her two companions. "It's safe, we go all the time."

"What's out there, then?" Kol asked.

"Ghosts, sometimes," the older woman said. "Loved ones. The boundary between worlds is thin here."

The boundary between worlds. Ghosts. He found himself again at the filthy window, watching his mother and Caliban disappear into the red-barren wastes. He never understood why his mother took Caliban and not him, but what if he could ask? She wouldn't answer when he asked her in his mind, and he was beginning to suspect something was wrong. No, something was definitely wrong, and he needed real answers—including if his mother was truly alive, or if he was going mad.

"Can you talk to them?" Kol asked.

"Only if they want to talk to you."

Find me in the Valley of Dragons.

I'm in the Valley of Dragons, Kol said in his head. *Where can I find you?*

Go with them.

Are you alive? he asked, but there was no reply.

He glanced nervously to Alessi's balcony door, still shut. She wouldn't like this, but he needed answers. "Fine. Give me a minute."

And so he slipped on his cloak and shoes, making his way down the elegant steps and onto the moonlit cobblestone. The women met him with smiles, but the man stood with his eyes down, hands in his pockets.

"Where are you from?" The younger girl jogged next to him. She had a pleasant face with piercing yellow eyes, glowing ever so slightly.

He wasn't sure how to respond. He was from a hole in the middle of the western wastes. "Nowhere, really."

"Nowhere?" the man scoffed.

"He doesn't have to tell us where he's from," the older woman said. "But he must not be from around here if he's never seen a sprite before."

"Right. What are those?" Kol asked.

"They were here before we were, they're like part of the land," the younger woman explained.

"They like cozy places, like under mattresses and in coat pockets," the older woman added, "but they're harmless and will leave you coins if you're nice to them."

Kol felt the inside of his pockets and was relieved to find they were empty. He likely wouldn't be getting any coins after his encounter earlier that night.

The man, walking some distance from him, grumbled words Kol couldn't understand.

A glowing shape appeared, floating with a long, blue tail following it. The older woman pointed at it. "He's back!"

The creature turned its deer-like head toward them and drew closer. It floated, legs moving as if walking on air as it approached. It lowered its head as if to bow, its two sets of antlers bobbing up and down. The older woman walked up to the creature, leaning her head against it. It whinnied.

"What is that?" he asked. The creature came close to him, but he shied away.

"Yuhin, I missed you," the woman said, running her fingers through the creature's fur. The younger girl did the same. The creature nuzzled Kol. Despite its appearance, it was cool to the touch, and had the sort of wet feeling to it only cold things do. Kol pulled his hand away.

"Yuhin's just an Orien. He was our pet growing up," the tall woman said.

"Is he... you know..." Kol began.

The man spoke up for the first time since they left the dragon village. "Dead? Yeah. But so is everything else in this forest."

With a nod, the creature climbed into the sky, its blue tail trailing between the trees high above.

"He's so beautiful here," the older woman said. "So free."

"What else is here?" Kol asked.

"All kinds of things," the woman said, holding a glowing blue orb on the tip of her finger. "Spirits, monsters, old deities. There's even a creature called a hegia that will answer any question you ask."

"Really?"

"Yeah, but they're hard to catch," the younger woman chimed in.

"Do you come out here every night, then?" Kol asked.

The older woman shook her head, golden hair bouncing on her shoulders. "Not every night." She pointed up, where the full moon shone between the pines. "They're always here, but you can only see the dead during the full moon. It's part of the wolf god's curse."

The hair stood up on the back of Kol's neck.

The younger woman must have seen his disturbed expression, because she laughed, and added, "That's just the word for this kind of magic. Not all curses are bad." She hiked up her pants, sticking a foot in the water. "A curse is magic attached to a place, a thing, a person— anything, really. The caster can go a thousand miles away, or die, but the magic lives on."

Ahead, blue light pooled in a crevasse in the ground. The water was so still, he almost mistook it for a sheet of glass. As Kol grew closer, he realized that the rock beneath the water had been cut into steps, and the woman waded until she was knee-deep in it.

The younger woman looked up at Kol, a quizzical expression on her face. "I'm surprised you didn't know that."

"Why?"

"I thought all dragons could sense curses."

Dragons. He panicked for a moment before remembering she couldn't see his eyes. He was careful to keep his hood drawn, though he supposed it was dark enough now he might be safe.

"You should take that off," the younger woman said. She must have seen him fidgeting with his hood. "How else will you swim with us?"

"Swim?"

The women giggled, hands over their mouths.

"Fine," Kol said. He might have been about to make a terrible decision. "I'll swim, but I'm keeping this on. Don't want it getting stolen or something."

The younger woman's eyes rested on his pendant. He always wore it, to the point he barely thought about it. "That's a rare pendant. Where did you find it?"

"My mother gave it to me," he said.

The younger woman looked like she was about to say something else before her sister interrupted her.

"Oh! The water sprites are out!" The older woman pointed to blue lights dancing in the trees.

The perfectly still water before him reflected the full moon's light. He didn't belong in such a pristine place, with Yuhin's glowing blue tail dancing through the trees, or the other sprites floating on the breeze. Several landed on the pond, illuminating its crystal-clear waters. They were the same brilliant color as the glow, which cast blue-white light around the edges of the leaves concealing it. The man and the older woman climbed onto a boulder high above the pool, where they sat together, speaking softly and looking into the forest. The young woman gestured to the water.

"Get in," she said. "There was a time when people travelled from all over the world to come here. Broken bones, broken hearts; they say these waters can cure anything."

Despite the beauty of the water, Kol hesitated. Though it was shallow at the end by the woman, he couldn't see the bottom of the pool where the spirit lights floated.

He also wasn't entirely sure he could swim.

"Okay." He took off his shoes one by one and rolled up the bottoms of his pants. "But just to where you are." He hoped it was too dark for them to see his eyes. Their color, not the vibrant gold of his dragon companions, could betray him.

Go in.

"Of course," the younger woman said.

After a moment's hesitation, he peeled off his sweat-stained shirt, leaving in the grass as he walked to the edge. When he stuck a foot in the moonlit pool, he realized while it looked like water, it didn't feel like water. It felt like nothing at all—like air though perhaps a little thicker, and it rippled strangely as he moved through it.

"What is this?" He sat beside the woman and took a handful of the liquid in his palm, letting it run between his fingers.

"Starshatter. This pool's only here once a month, during the full moon, so we always come out. They say the red king used to bathe here, and that starshatter is the key to his eternal youth. And do you know the craziest part about starshatter?" She stood, waves crashing over Kol as she dove into the deepest part of the pool. She popped her head up, and to his surprise, her hair was completely dry. "You can breathe in it!"

Kol eyed her with suspicion. "Are you trying to drown me?" he asked, half-joking.

She shook her head, kicking away from him. "I'll show you, put your head under."

Kol sank below the surface, watching nervously as the woman sank to the bottom of the pool, sitting cross-legged. Then, she took a breath. Her yellow eyes glowed brilliantly, and her hair flowed like golden fleece. She kicked her way to the surface.

Her eyes met his with a burning intensity. "Your turn," she said.

Kol, now with his head above water, laughed despite the tension. "If I die, Alessi's going to kill me."

He swam to the other side of the pool and dove. After a moment of hesitation, he lowered his body until he sat on the terraced bottom, legs crossed, facing the woman from across the pool.

He looked into her eyes, glowing like suns framed within her bronze face. He didn't want to drown, but he couldn't look away. The dragon needed no magic to bewitch him as she had.

He fought against every instinct, every fiber of his body to force his lungs to empty of air.

He opened his mouth, letting the thick fluid fill his lungs.

For a moment, he felt as if he were drowning. Then the pain and shock subsided, and he breathed. The liquid felt thicker than air, pouring down his throat and into his lungs like water, but he felt more alive than ever. He pushed himself forward, off the terraced steps, to where the woman waited for him, and—

17

Kol lurched forward in his bed, cool white sheets folding around him. Sweat pooled around him, and he slicked back a few moist hairs that fell into his face. Memories of the night before flooded his mind. He might have thought it was a dream if he wasn't soaking wet. He pushed himself out of bed, making his way to the balcony, where he looked for sign of the three strangers. There wasn't a soul in sight. Returning to his room, he threw open the decorative door and made his way to Alessi's. He knocked three times.

There was a low grumbling inside, then some mumbled swears, but no other movement. It was definitely her. He knocked again, six times now, and louder than before. He heard shuffling, and more grumbling. The door opened to reveal Alessi with her messy mane of hair poking out in all directions. That night, she hadn't slept in her cloak but instead a short-cut gown hiked halfway up her hip. The first rays of sunlight filtered in through the balcony behind her.

"What?" she growled.

Kol took a step back. "The craziest thing just happened.

There were dragons in the forest, and some sort of ghost deer with all these lights, they took me to a pool made of starlight and it was like I could breathe underwater—"

Alessi rolled her eyes. "You had a dream."

"Three dragons called to me from the balcony."

Alessi crossed her arms. "Did they?"

Kol swallowed. "Did anything strange happen to you last night?"

"Yes. An idiot woke me up at an ungodly hour to tell me a story about ghost deer and breathing underwater." She slammed the door. "Go back to sleep!"

Kol returned to his room, but no dreams came now. He sat on the edge of his bed, facing the balcony east, and watched the sun rise through the rounded archways.

———

Later that day, Kol followed Alessi through the crowded city square, barely keeping up with her coattails. He wondered if what he felt last night could have been a dream. His clothes were dry, after all, but he was wet. He told himself it was sweat, but he felt different after that experience. He felt lighter, freer. As the pair continued into the town, his eyes combed the crowd in search of the three strangers, but he was only disappointed. Alessi stopped, letting him catch up.

She gave him a sideways smile. "Still thinking about that sex dream, ey?"

Kol's face flushed, which she must have thought amusing because she snickered.

"It wasn't a," he started loudly, then lowered his voice, "*sex dream*."

"But you keep muttering about a woman."

"There were two, actually."

Alessi raised one eyebrow. "Two? Adventurous, are we?"

"No!" Kol dodged an elderly dragon making his way past with a basket full of leeks. "There was also a man."

Alessi raised both eyebrows and looked at him with a mocking expression.

Kol sighed, exasperated. "*Not* like that. They took me into the forest. The sprites were out."

Alessi's expression changed to a serious one. "Sprites?"

Kol nodded. "Yeah. The deer, and all these glowing orbs. The woman—the younger one— she said they could only be seen during the full moon."

"Who's filling your head with garbage?" Alessi gently tapped the side of his head.

"The dragons, two with golden eyes, one with blue eyes like Lysander."

"What were their names?" Alessi asked after a moment.

Kol thought for a moment. He meant to ask, but realized he never got the opportunity to. "I don't know."

Alessi huffed, blowing air through her nose. "Just a dream."

"But—"

"We're leaving this evening to be in Dunvara in two days' time. The flats can only be crossed at night because of the dragon day guard."

"Let's hope there's not a night guard."

"There is. But we can hide from them. The day guard consists of yellow dragons. They have unique eyesight." Alessi made circles with her thumbs and index fingers, raising them to her eyes. "They see the color of one's soul. You can't hide from them."

Kol swallowed.

"I'd rather stay here another day." Kol looked around at a shop selling clothes with the same angular ornamentation as at the inn. He picked up a broken piece of glass off the ground, and it sliced a line in the soft flesh of his palm.

"Don't you remember what I told you?" Alessi gestured at the bustling street. Hanging signs were decorated in golden, angular filigrees. "None of this is real."

Kol looked at his bleeding palm. "This is real." He held up the glass.

"Belief is what gives an illusion its power. That glass may very well be real, but this environment, the scent of honey in the air"—Alessi took a deep breath— "isn't real. This is a place of darkness and death, a trap for those who stay too long." Alessi stepped around a group of children who ran by laughing.

Kol shrugged. It didn't matter to him whether or not the place was real, in the way Alessi wanted it to be, but he also wasn't convinced it was an illusion. Two armed, red-haired men walked down the other side of the street.

"He'll be here tonight," one of the men said. His armor was redder than his companion's, which was a copper color. "'Bout time the son of a bitch king came to this territory."

"Word has it he's here for a woman," the other said. "Though, I'm not sure if it's to kill or to fuck her."

The first laughed. "Both, probably."

Alessi stopped, jaw clenched. Kol nearly ran into her.

"Fine." She spun around to meet his eyes. "We'll stay one more night. You get your wish. Looks like that bastard red king landed in our laps."

One more night. But meeting the red king so soon? Kol's heartbeat quickened. In her own words, confronting the red king was her last mission. This could be the end of everything. And though they had reached the Valley of Dragons and he felt his own mission was nearly complete, his heart was like a stone.

He had to be careful with what he was about to say. "What happens if you… don't go after him?"

Alessi froze. "What did you just say?"

"What if you don't confront him?" Kol cleared his throat, tension filling the air like poison. This was dangerous. "I don't know what happened to you but killing him won't undo it."

"It's not about what happened to *me*." Her voice was a growl, and her eyes glowed beneath her hood. Those were the cold eyes of a predator, not a friend. At that moment, she was not the same woman who leaned against him at the druid temple, who led him through the wastes. She stepped towards him, and with her every step forward he stepped backwards until his spine met the cold stone side of a store. There was nowhere to run.

"What are you doing?" His heart pounded in his chest. Her arm pressed against his neck. Pressure built in his throat, and he coughed. Curious onlookers gathered to watch what they probably thought would become a bloodbath.

"What if you don't confront him?" She mocked his voice. "Don't speak of what you know nothing about." Alessi's spit flew in his face. There was so much anger behind those cruel eyes, but behind the anger was sorrow. She wanted to say more, he could sense it, but she held these emotions back like a tidal wave, its waters leaking around the edge of her hard exterior.

"You shouldn't—" Kol began, but she shoved off of him with enough force to leave him dizzy.

"Fuck off. You don't understand anything." And with that, she left him, pushing her way up the street.

"Wait!" He took after her, feeling like an idiot. She was right. he didn't understand, but how could he? He could see her, but no matter how fast he ran after her, she was always at least ten paces ahead. It wasn't long before she disappeared. He failed. He leaned over, hands on his knees, catching his breath. If he had learned anything from books, it was that vengeance was a double-edged sword.

He wandered through the streets for what felt like hours. Gray clouds rolled through the sky above, and the air held the heavy, sweet scent of a coming storm. Just when he was about to give up, he saw Alessi standing in front of a wooden board in the center of town. It stood on two stout, wooden poles covered in nails from years of use and had posters tacked across it.

Kol walked up to her but keeping a safe distance. "I was worried I'd lost you."

She ripped her claws through one of the posters, leaving three long tears. When the torn paper curled up in the cool wind, Kol saw why—it had her face on it, like the poster he saw earlier. This was the bounty the king put on her. She shredded the remaining remnants of the paper and threw them to the wind. She then turned to the poster beside it, shredding it in a like manner, but she stomped this one into the ground.

These were her two wanted posters—one bounty offered by the red king, and the other by her mother. And only the king wanted her alive. A few raindrops spattered Kol's cloak, but he didn't look away. Alessi stood as if frozen, the torn paper dancing in the wind around her feet. Thunder shook the ground beneath them. The streets cleared, leaving only the pair.

Kol stepped closer. "Are you alright?"

She bore her fangs, and sorrow and fury burned in her eyes. "Do I look alright to you?" She turned away so that her hood covered her face. "Dumbass."

"I'm sorry," Kol said. "I want to understand, but—"

"That bastard has to pay for what he did." Alessi wouldn't meet his eyes. "It's the only reason I'm still alive. This is my chance. He doesn't travel with his entire guard, so maybe I won't die for nothing."

Kol didn't know what to say. He watched her as rain began

to fall, water soaking into his cloak and plastering his black, windswept hair to his face.

"Don't look at me like that." Her eyes met his again, water dripping down her face like tears.

Kol paused, searching for words. There was no easy way to say this. "I'm worried you're just looking for a way to kill yourself." It didn't feel right, everything ending like this. "If you fight, you should fight to win."

"Even if I won, I don't know what I'd do after. Sometimes I feel like this quest for vengeance is my only reason for living." She punched the wooden board, splitting it in half before slumping against one of its squat support poles. She let herself slide to the ground. Hesitatingly, Kol joined her.

They sat inches apart as the dirt turned to mud. There was a person beneath those horns—a scared, sad person. It was easy to forget sometimes that at her core, Alessi was no different from himself, or Mia. He reached out a hand, half expecting her to bite it, and placed it on her shoulder.

"I want to understand," he said.

Her shoulders shook, and she leaned into him, burying her face in the crook of his arm. He stiffened, unsure of what to do. It was as if a beautiful, volatile beast laid in his lap, and moving could mean the death of him.

"You're crying," Kol said.

"Crying is not weakness," Alessi said. "Weakness is the fear of expressing yourself."

"What happened all those years ago?" Kol gently stroked her hair.

She didn't answer at first, but then slowly said, "It's a long story."

"You don't have to let me in," he said, "but if you want to, I'm here to listen."

Alessi took a breath, steadying herself. People cleared as the rain continued to fall. Puddles formed around them, and the air grew cold, but her body's warmth radiated through to him. And she began.

"I was alone before I met you, but it hadn't always been that way. Before dragons and witches were enemies, I was trained to be part of an elite team that would apprehend criminals from the different kingdoms. We were chosen when we were children and trained together for decades, witches and dragons and other Belgarri. Viktor, I, and the six others were like family. We lived together, worked together, trained together. We were everything to each other.

I was still young when the queen gave us our first task, a target on what was called the death list. This was important because I was the only witch on the team that still had no magic. Witches were only allowed to take magic from those on the death list, but our information was incomplete. We were given an address and a time and were told the target would be the only one there. With some prying, I was able to learn the target was a blue dragon, but nothing more."

"I told the queen that our information was incomplete, and she said to go through with it. So, we arrived at the address, did what we thought was our duty, and..." Alessi trailed off. Her blue clawed fingers flexed, tapping her knee.

"It was the wrong person," Kol said. Things were starting to make sense.

She took a sharp breath. "Yeah. We found out when the real target got home, a general in the red king's army. We had just killed his wife, and I was caught red-handed, literally, in the act of stealing her magic. And you can imagine how that looked."

Kol remembered how she ate the dragon's heart back in the wastes. What a sight to come home to. His stomach churned.

"Given who I was, the king took this as an act of war. He demanded I be turned over to him for punishment, but my mother imprisoned me instead. And when he couldn't get ahold of me, he boiled my teammates alive, skinned them, and served them to guests. He said it was justice." Her claws, which had been tapping on her leg, sliced through her pants and into her flesh. Dark blood dripped around the shredded fabric.

She continued. "Only Viktor was spared because he was a dragon, but no part of him I recognize survived the red king's prison camps. He's like a different person now. Broken, cruel."

"I'm sorry," Kol said, but his mind raced. The queen gave them the job. The queen gave them imperfect information. The queen knew that Alessi would take the target's magic because she did not yet have her own.

Alessi drew her legs closer to her chest. "Before you say anything, I know my mother set me up."

"You shouldn't blame yourself," Kol said.

"I let myself be fooled. That's on me. After my mother challenged me—a prisoner—to that duel, I escaped and swore vengeance on the red king for killing my friends. Everyone I love is dead, and I have no other reason to live once this job is complete."

"That's not true," Kol said. "You can find new meaning."

"Some people deserve to die," Alessi said. "I'm one of those people." She pulled her bloodied claws away from her leg, and Kol placed his hand on hers. She had finally let him in, after all this time. Though she had plenty of opportunities to betray him, she hadn't. She had saved his life more times than he could count, and no matter how many times she insisted she was a bad person, he knew it wasn't true.

"If you saw yourself the way I did, you wouldn't say that," Kol said. "And you wouldn't throw your life away for vengeance." However, he knew her well enough to know she would not see herself that way. And that if she had already made her mind up about something, there was nothing he could do to stop her.

18

There was a pit in Kol's stomach the rest of that rainy day, as if at any moment the world as he knew it might end. Evening rolled around, the sun's honey rays filtering through the lifting storm clouds and onto the buildings and streets. Kol watched in silence as Alessi downed shot after shot in the inn's parlor, growing more agitated by the moment. Her foot tapped anxiously.

They sat with a bar stool between them. It was strange to feel so close to someone, and yet so far away—so aware of a situation, but so powerless to stop it. She didn't want to do this. He could tell that much. But she felt she had to, for her honor or for her twisted sense of justice. It was not justice when the king killed her friends, but it was also not justice for Alessi's life to end like this. The time grew near—soon it would be dark, and she would leave. This could be the last time he ever saw her.

She must have caught him staring at her.

"Hmm?" She downed another shot, following it with a sharp breath. Orange light danced in her hair, and he thought of the day they met, and the day she stood against the star-speckled sky. His face reddened.

"Uh." There was something he wanted to say to her, but he held the bittersweet words between his teeth, unable to spit them out. He was glad he met her. He was sorry he couldn't change her mind. He felt there was something between them and regretted he would never know what could have been. "I'd be lost without you."

"Literally," Alessi gave him a forced half-smile. "You couldn't find your ass with two hands and a map." The bartender brought Alessi another drink, and she stirred it absent-mindedly with one claw. "I thought about what you said." Then, in a whisper, she added, "I'll win, and be back in the morning." She eyed the door, the sun's last golden rays cast across the room. "That's my cue."

She said she was coming back. He smiled. Their eyes met for the first time in a while, and she made her way over to him.

She leaned in, pausing with her lips inches from Kol's. "Thanks. I've decided to live, for now." His heart raced, and he thought for a moment she might kiss him before she whispered, "Don't go outside tonight. Don't talk to anyone until I'm back and lock yourself in your room." Their lips were so close, he had half a mind to kiss her himself.

"Alessi, I—" Kol stopped himself. Now was not the time.

"What?" Alessi asked.

"I'd better see you in the morning," he said. "We'll celebrate."

Alessi nodded. He watched her disappear out the inn's rounded door, its gold filigree vibrating as it slammed shut behind her. Kol sighed, and the innkeeper shot him an expectant look.

"You didn't tell her," the innkeeper said.

Kol looked at the innkeeper out the corner of his eye. "Tell her what?"

The innkeeper smirked. "I know a man in love when I see one."

"It's not like that." Kol shook his head, turning away from the innkeeper, before walking up the grand staircase.

His legs felt like they were made of lead, and a numbness crept through his mind and body. Once he reached his room, he waved his strange key to open the door before returning it to his neck, where it hung on a string. He plopped onto the bed, feeling the cool sheets against his skin, and turned to face the window. Blue-white light filtered in. Alessi was out there, somewhere, risking her life. He wanted to be anywhere but that room. He wanted to be with her. He shut his eyes, his emotions a jumbled mess inside his mind, and thought of golden-haired women and pools of starshatter.

"Hey!" a familiar voice called out. He sat up in bed to see the room cast in moonlight, cursing himself for having fallen asleep. Now there would be no way to know if he was dreaming. After walking over the smooth wood floor to the balcony, he saw the golden-haired sisters waiting for him below, and waved to them.

The older one gestured for him to come down. "Are you coming tonight? It's the last night of the full moon."

He remembered Alessi's words. *Lock yourself in your room.* She'd kill him if she—he stopped himself, and realization sank in once again. She could still die, and it didn't matter if there was no Alessi to kill him, but he certainly didn't want to be left alone with his thoughts that night.

"You alright?" the woman asked.

"Yeah," Kol said, making a mental note to ask her what happened the night before. He didn't remember anything after the pool of starshatter. He made his way to the door, only to find it was locked. He felt for the key around his neck. It was gone. Defeated, he made his way back to the balcony.

"What's wrong?" the younger woman asked.

"Door's locked, and I don't have the key to get out," Kol said. "I don't think I'm supposed to go out tonight."

"Because the red king's in town? He's already busied himself with some of the local *attractions*, so you don't need to worry," the younger woman said.

Kol swallowed, pushing down strange thoughts about Alessi. "I can't get out without a key." It had been tied around his neck, so where could it have gone? He had it just moments before he fell asleep. This had to be a dream, or one of the illusions Alessi mentioned.

"Climb down, then." The older sister pointed to some bushes below his window, perfectly trimmed in a spherical shape. "If you fall, you'll just land on the Elderbris."

Kol looked to the younger woman's pleading eyes and threw one leg over the railing. The women cheered, and Kol hoped they weren't just laughing at how awkward he must have looked. He clung to a line of decorative red wood wound up the building's edge like a seam. He looked down, though he knew he shouldn't. There was a primitive fear somewhere deep within his mind that triggered his heart to rush, and his palms to sweat. His fingers slipped. He fell backwards into the Elderbris bush, righted himself, and dusted off his filthy pants. The women chuckled.

"Have you never climbed from a balcony before?" the younger woman asked, playfully bumping into Kol.

Kol's face reddened. "No."

"Climbed a tree?"

"A few times, only recently." He had only ever climbed trees to set up camp with Alessi, and never very well. "They don't have trees where I'm from."

She made a face, and her sister chimed in. "He's kidding, Narine."

Narine. Her name was Narine. He wasn't kidding, but he also wasn't about to tell them he lived in a hole for the first twenty years of his life.

"I didn't ask you your names last time," Kol said.

"She's Narine, I'm Patina," the older sister said.

Kol looked around them, but the blue-eyed man was nowhere in sight. "Where's your friend?"

"He's waiting for us up ahead," the two sisters said in unison. This left an uneasy feeling in Kol's chest.

Follow them.

With Alessi's decision, he'd almost forgotten about his original mission—to find out what happened to his mother and brother. And if it meant taking a risk, or defying Alessi's orders, that was just something he had to do. He stepped into the forest with the two dragons.

"What happened yesterday?" Kol asked. "We were in the starshatter, and then..."

"You fell asleep," Narine said. The full moon's light showed dark half-circles beneath her eyes, as if she hadn't slept the night before. She probably hadn't. "Passed out right there. Our friend carried you back to your room. Starshatter doesn't do that to dragons, you see. We didn't know..." The younger woman's face reddened, and her sister shot her a punishing look.

"That I'm human," Kol said. They knew. And yet, they hadn't tried to eat him, or sell him, or skin him.

"Well..." Narine looked to her sister.

"We won't tell anyone," Patina said. She led them into the forest, on a similar path to the one they had taken the night before.

"Thanks," Kol said. Maybe he could trust these women. "Are we going back to the moon pool?" he asked.

"No," Patina said, her golden curls bouncing as she shook her head. "It's mostly dried up, anyway."

"Oh." Kol looked to the sisters again, but his thoughts drifted to Alessi.

"What's wrong?" Narine asked.

Did he tell her? He had no reason not to. Maybe it would make him feel better just to get things off his chest. "My friend," he said. "I wanted to say something to her but didn't. And now I may never see her again."

Patina's nose twisted. "That *woman* you're traveling with?"

"Yeah." He had been planning to say more but stopped himself. He turned his head back in the direction he thought they'd come from. They should be close enough to the village to see its yellow glowing lights, but there were only trees and mist. When Kol turned around, they were standing in a clearing.

The blue-eyed man stood waiting for them, a fire burning in front of him.

Welcome to the Valley of Dragons.

What's happening? he asked.

You'll see.

The women both looked at him expectantly. Kol took a half-step backward, every hair on his arms standing on end. Black dust fell from their forms, the same dust that fell from Alessi's wound the day it healed. He began to realize that whatever had been waiting for him in the Valley of Dragons probably wasn't everything he'd hoped for. There was no sign of his mother, and the man before him was a stranger. There was much he didn't know about this upper world. Could this all have been a trap? His muscles tensed as he prepared to make a break for the direction of the village, but the man gestured beside the fire. Kol blinked, and four seats appeared. The three dragons sat, leaving one seat for him.

"Sit," the man said. Neither he nor the women made any move as if to attack him, but still Kol remained tense.

Join them. It's alright.

The man gestured again to the chairs. "We aren't here to hurt you. Join us as a friend." This time, though with caution, Kol sat.

He felt sweat bead on his forehead. "What's going on?" He sat beside the fire. He hadn't realized how unseasonably cold the forest was on this summer night, but the fire brought feeling back to his numbing fingers.

The three dragons looked at each other, then Narine spoke first. "We were sent here."

"By who?"

"By your mother."

The tension should have been gone—he wasn't crazy, he hadn't come all this way for no reason—and yet, something felt wrong. "So, she's alive?"

Patina shook her head. "No."

Kol's blood ran cold in his veins. He'd feared this was the case. "Then she's been dead this whole time."

"Yes," Narine said softly.

"I came all this way." Kol's heart pounded in his ears. He was foolish. Whatever hope glimmered within him, of finding his mother and brother out in the wastes, vanished. Of course she was dead. She took his brother into the wastes to die, and no ordinary human survived the wastes except...

Kol.

The feeling of wrongness built within him. He thought he might be sick. He gripped his leg so tightly that it sent lightning bolts of pain up his thigh. If this wasn't real, why couldn't he wake up?

Narine put a hand on his shoulder. Her skin was ice cold. "Stop that, you'll hurt yourself."

"Is this a trick?" Kol asked. "Some sort of magic? How could my mother send you if she's dead?"

The man leaned forward, resting a finger on his chin. "What do you know about yourself and your past?"

Kol's mind raced. "I'm Kol Mendona. I'm twenty years old. I have twenty-seven siblings, most older than me. My brother Astor raised me after my mother..." What had happened that day? He didn't remember much other than the visions that haunted him, her faceless form against the sand.

"And you believe you are the son of Diego Mendona and a woman named Diwata de la Cruz?"

"Yes." Kol gripped the edge of his splintery wooden seat. "So, you know who I am. Who are you?"

"We were sent by—"

"My mother, whatever, who are you and what do you want with me?" A splinter dug into the soft flesh between Kol's nail and fingertip, but he didn't so much as flinch. He held the blue-eyed man's steady gaze.

The man sighed. "I'm Lupin. No father, no surname, just Lupin. There are places in this world where the boundaries between worlds are thin. Like this forest." Lupin pointed up, to where the moon shined brightly in the sky. There was the hint of a black sliver around its edge. "I know this is hard," the man said, "but the moon is already starting to wane, so our time is limited. Before we go any further, we should tell you that the red king is not in Wellston. Those guards were an illusion, the work of Patina here. We had to use our magic to keep you one more night."

"Your companion is safe," Patina said, "but she's probably seen through the illusion by now. She was always a clever one."

"You know Alessi?" Kol said, looking to the three dragons

in succession. Narine gave him a pained expression, but the older two maintained their stoic looks. One by one, the dragons stood.

"Your father is the human known as Diego Mendona, but your mother had another name. Diwata de la Cruz was the name she chose when seeking shelter from the red king. Her other name was Oasis."

Oasis. Kol remembered the song the men sang in Brusa, then later in the nameless city. *There once was a woman named Oasis, for where she walked, the desert bloomed.* The missing queen Oasis. He was dumbfounded, his mind spinning. Everything he thought was true was a lie. He should be furious. He should be terrified. But instead, the truth sank in his stomach like a rock.

"We know this is a lot to take in," Narine said. Her cold hand met the side of his face. "The dead and the living aren't separated for eternity, but your mother's situation is unique. She couldn't cross over with us, but she has looked forward to meeting you again."

The man turned away and began walking before he disappeared. It was as if he had walked through an invisible wall and vanished from existence. Kol blinked hard, but nothing new appeared, no object or clue as to what might have happened. Patina gave him a sad smile before she, too, walked through the invisible wall and disappeared.

Narine squeezed his hand and the tragedy of it all struck him. She must have been beautiful in life to be so beautiful in death, with her hair a golden waterfall down her back. It wasn't as brilliant as it was the previous night by the pool of starshatter and had a dullness creeping around its edges. She held his gaze with a kind intensity, and only that kept him from feeling afraid. Then she let go, making her way forward to the invisible wall, but when she was almost there, she stopped. He approached her.

"You're going to be alright." He couldn't feel her breath against his skin as she leaned forward, her icy lips meeting his. She pulled away, leaving him dumbfounded. She gave him the same sad smile her sister had before continuing forward, her arm disappearing into the invisible wall. "Hurry, Oasis is waiting for you."

"I can't see the boundary," Kol said.

"Nothing is seen with the eyes. Look with your heart." She pointed to the center of her chest, stepped forward, and then disappeared entirely.

Wetness crept around the corners of Kol's eyes, but the sorrow hit before the tears. It was a sticky, nostalgic feeling, the feeling of lost potential. He was standing alone in the darkness now, the fire's light dying behind him. What made him feel more alone than anything, however, were all the questions he didn't have answers to.

I came all this way for you, but I have a lot of questions. I need you, ma.

He shut his eyes, letting the lonely feeling take him, then opened them. Before him was a blue portal like a rounded window, and behind it were the three dragons. It reminded him of Azazel's portals, though its light was weaker.

Narine smiled. "I knew you could do it."

He tried to step through, but to him it was as solid as stone. "I can't go through."

"Not yet," the man told him. "The living cannot enter."

There was no denying it now. The three dragons were dead. Phantoms. Ghosts. A new woman stepped out from between them, her long black hair flowing behind her. Her face was familiar yet alien, like something he had seen in a dream, or in another life, and he knew this was the face he could never remember—that shadow on the woman of his memories. The other three stepped back, Narine's smile the last thing he saw of them as they faded into darkness.

"Hello, Kol," Oasis said. It was the same voice he heard in his head the entire journey, and yet, it was so strange to be standing in front of her. "It's been a while."

"Ma." His eyes watered. He had imagined meeting her during all those years. His stepmothers took no interest in him. His father was cruel. Whenever he felt alone, he would cling to fragments that remained of his young mind's memories and imagine this moment. But something was still missing. "And Caliban. He's with you?"

His mother shook her head "No. He is in your world."

Not all was lost. "I'd imagined meeting you, but I didn't think it would be like this," Kol said. The portal's light pulsed gently, more gray than blue.

"I'm sorry it took me so long to find you," Oasis said. "If fate were kinder, I'd hold you in my arms. But fate is rarely kind."

"I'm glad to see you again, but you know I need answers," Kol said.

His mother nodded, understanding in her eyes. They had the same tan skin, the same cheekbones, the same dark hair. He knew now why his father hated to look at him, because when he looked at Kol, he must have seen the woman who dared to leave him.

"First, what is this? Is this a dream or an illusion?" He looked around them.

"Neither and both," she said. "Your body sleeps, but your spirit stands before me here in the Valley of Dragons."

"Alright." She was more forthcoming than he expected. "How do I hear your voice?" Kol asked.

"My pendant connects us." She pointed to the pendant around his neck.

"Why could I suddenly hear you right before I left with Alessi?"

"I'm not sure." His mother looked down and let out a breath. She looked so young, like she was barely older than him. But if what the dragons said about her was true, she could be centuries old, like Alessi. "But that witch is the reason I had those three bring you here tonight."

"You told me to let her die, but I couldn't." The fire died behind him, and a cold breeze blew straight to his bones. He smelled smoke, thick in his lungs. "She saved my life."

"Did she really?" his mother asked.

"She's bought me food and lodging, protected me."

"From what?"

"Monsters."

"Monsters?" She stared intently at him.

"Dragons," Kol said. "And she gave me her blood so I could survive out here."

His mother sighed. "You didn't need her blood."

"Why?"

"She has told you many lies. Look into my eyes, son." His mother stepped forward, and in the full moon's light he could tell that her eyes were not brown like his father's but instead black, glowing with a fierce, dark light. "You never needed her blood. All it did was weaken the protective spell I put on you."

"But—"

"The only monster," his mother said, "is that witch."

Kol steadied himself. A coldness radiated off her, accompanied by a feeling of intense anger. He felt at the pendant around his neck, and it was hot like fire.

"She didn't mean to kill the general's wife. It was a mistake," Kol said. "She's already suffered enough."

"She murdered an innocent woman. She didn't pay, her

friends did. That's not justice, and the general's wife is also not the only person she's killed."

His mother was dead, and Alessi was a dragon slayer. Kol's heart sank. "You don't mean to say she killed you?"

"Not me. I was dead by the time we met, but she's killed countless others." His mother's voice was soft. "She is the enemy of dragons."

Kol's stomach twisted. "Who has she killed?"

His mother held his gaze, her black eyes reflecting the stars above. "You should know. They brought you here."

It was hard enough to wrap his mind around her killing one innocent person by mistake, but what exactly was her body count? "Alessi said she was tasked with apprehending criminals. What could Narine have done to deserve death?"

"Narine and Patina paid for their father's sins. Ironic, isn't it? That witch is no better than the red king himself."

"You told me to go with Alessi," Kol said. "Why would you send me with her if what you say is true?"

"It was risky, but I had to get you out of that compound and my options weren't exactly... unlimited. I had originally hoped she'd be dead by now," she said. She turned to one side, her black dress trailing like smoke in the wind behind her. "But I've had a change of heart about the witch. She could still be useful."

"Useful?"

"She thinks she's in control, but it's an illusion. Always a pawn, never the player. There's something big about to happen. Bigger than me, bigger than you." Clouds rolled across the moon as his mother continued, darkness in her eyes. "And it has to do with that witch and a wandering god. I want you to help her kill the red king. Avenge me."

Kol looked down at his hands. His weak, useless hands. Even if he wasn't human, he wasn't a fighter like Alessi, and though he had learned a great deal aboveground, he felt like he was just scratching the surface of a greater truth underlying everything. "I'm not sure I can."

"Look at me, son." She transformed her hands, black scales coating them. Kol almost fell backwards as she pressed her scaled fingers against the portal. "Don't be afraid. This is what we are. The spell I cast on you to repress your dragon inheritance and disguise you as a human is weakening. You must have begun to sense your power."

He remembered Alessi's wound, pus-filled one second and gone the next. The color of magic falling like sand from her and the Belgarri. Over the past weeks, he had begun to suspect he was not the person he thought he was, but he had pushed that thought away. Now he had no choice but to look the truth in the face.

"Yes," he said. Hesitantly, he approached the portal, and pressed his hands opposite hers. They were almost touching.

"Good."

"What are we?" He held her gaze.

She smiled. "We," she said, "are the last of the dark dragons."

His heart raced. Dragon. He was a dragon. Or, at least, a half-dragon.

"I'm sorry I left you," she continued. "I would have told you when you were young. I could have trained you."

"And why didn't you? Why did you take Caliban and leave me behind?" He'd dreamed of asking her this question since he was a child.

"I couldn't risk your life, but I had to save Caliban's," she said. "He wasn't Diego's son. Your father was going to kill him, and Caliban had a place out in Alon."

"And what about us? We don't?"

"Not anymore. They feared us for what we are, and their

fear destroyed us." His mother's taloned hands formed into fists. "The witches burned our skies, poisoned our lands. The queen started this war to eliminate dragons. She wanted to steal their power, but the power of the dark dragons was too dangerous even for her. I thought I was safe with the red king, but even he tried to exploit that power. Dark dragons restore life and have dominion over death, and there are few things those who don't understand us find more fearful or revolting. We have been both worshipped as healers and hunted as necromancers."

"So those three were..." Kol's mind drifted back to the dragons who brought him there. Patina. Narine. Lupin.

"Resurrected. Spirits returned to their bodies, able to cross freely between the worlds of the living and the dead, at least when this portal is open. As your magic matures, you will also be able to do this. Done with good intentions, this magic lets you reach into other worlds, even bring back lost lovers. But rulers rarely have good intentions. The red king wanted an army of the dead, and when I refused, he took my life instead and swore to find my son so he could take my place. Only, Caliban took after his father. He's a red dragon. You take after me."

"What do you want me to do?" Kol said.

"I want you to live freely, but for this to happen, the red king must die. If not, he will find you and use you. You will not like the person you become. Fate and my voice will bring Caliban to you. Together, you must help the witch fulfill her destiny at all costs. The red king must die."

Help Alessi at all costs. He could do that. He even wanted to, but something seemed too easy, too perfect. More clouds rolled across the moon, which now hung low on the horizon. He must have been out for hours. A purple twilight stretched across the eastern skies. With the moonlight shadow, his mother's form faded to little more than an outline, a memory of what was there.

"I'm running out of time, but there is more about the witch. Do not trust her. Once the red king is dead, she is your greatest enemy." As more clouds drifted across the moon's porcelain form, his mother's form flickered, as did the portal around her. "You must kill her once the job is done."

"I can't kill her," Kol said. "I won't do it."

"She is the enemy of dragons. If she cannot change, then she must be killed," his mother said. "Goodbye, Kol. I am always with you."

An uncomfortable reality sank in his chest, emptying his lungs. He was a dragon, and Alessi was a dragon slayer. What did this mean for their journey? Would she ever be able to accept him like he was, or would she kill him if—when—she found out? His mother's form was barely visible.

But there was one last question on his mind, the answer to which could change everything. "Does Alessi know about me?"

Before she could answer, he woke up in a pile of sweaty sheets.

19

Kol sat up gasping, clutching at his chest. His fingers wrapped around not one fraying string, but two, which he pulled off his neck and held before him. Attached to one was the strange key and attached to the other was his mother's pendant. The smell of burning pine from the campfire smoke clung to him like mud.

It was real.

Of course it was real.

Does she know? he asked.

There was no reply.

Then out loud, he asked, "Does she know?"

Still no reply.

Panic rose in his throat, threatening to choke him. This could be dangerous. On one hand, he had seen Alessi mercilessly butcher the dragon in the lift, but on the other hand, she felt remorse for killing the dragon whose magic she stole. What if she only regretted that because she was caught? What if she hated all dragons, simply because they were dragons? Would she hate him, too? Despite this, she was the only person he could talk to. He couldn't tell her everything, but he had to tell her at least some of what happened.

He made his way to his own door, throwing it open and turning to the left. He knocked three times on Alessi's, the morning's first light filtering through the translucent paneling. She would be there—there was no red king that night. It was Narine's illusion.

"What?" came her muffled voice.

Be careful.

"It happened again," Kol said.

He heard footsteps across the floor before Alessi threw open the door, leaning against its rounded frame with an unamused expression on her face.

"Sexy dragon ladies scare you again?" she mocked.

She's the enemy of dragons.

He couldn't tell her everything. "I think they were ghosts."

"Don't be ridiculous. You were dreaming."

"I smell like smoke," he said, stepping closer. "Smell me."

Alessi made a face. "I'm not going to smell you."

"I know there was no red king last night. It was part of an illusion to keep us here."

"You don't need a vision to know that. I knew something was wrong when I went to find the red king, but there was only a goat."

"But the smoke—"

"What about it? Can't throw a dead snail without hitting a cozy fireplace around here." Alessi turned around. "Get your stuff, it's time to go."

There was so much more he wanted to tell her, but now was not the time. He hurried back to his room to grab his things, and Alessi was already halfway down the street by the time he caught up with her. An uneasy feeling sank in his stomach as they walked. The empty street stretched ahead until they reached a domed archway of tan, elaborately carved stone, the sun fitting perfectly inside it. His unease grew and he looked back over his shoulder. There wasn't a person—or dragon—in sight. And the air, which had the sweet scent of honey before, now smelled stale and moist.

"Where is everyone?" Kol whispered, as speaking loudly felt strangely inappropriate.

"Who?"

"The guards, the shopkeepers, where did they go?"

Alessi looked around, as if she hadn't noticed they were gone. "I don't care, and I don't want to stick around to find out." There was plowed farmland to their immediate right, but no farmer to tend to it.

"Something could have happened to the people here," Kol said.

"Not my problem," Alessi said. "This place is abandoned. The people were probably never real, anyway. They were powerful, complex illusions. A golden dragon capable of something on this scale only comes once in a generation, so I'm surprised I haven't heard of them before."

Kol thought of Narine. Alessi *had* heard of her before—Alessi killed her. If Alessi had known Narine had such talent, would she still have killed her? Was this the old Alessi, or the new Alessi? Would she kill him, too?

"What's that look on your face?" Alessi asked, perplexed.

"I'm thinking."

"About what?" Her look was prying. "Don't lie to me. I can tell when you're lying."

A half-truth would have to do. "Whether or not I can trust you," he said softly.

She batted her eyelashes, but he knew there was not an ounce of innocence in her lithe body. "Have I ever wronged you?"

He almost snorted. "You were going to—"

"But I didn't. After all that, do you still think I'd hurt you?" Alessi asked. She leaned close to him again, their faces inches apart, their eyes meeting.

The enemy of dragons. Your enemy.

They were so close. He craved this. Despite his mother's warning in his head, despite meeting the dragons she'd killed, some part of him still wanted to kiss her. "No. You wouldn't hurt me." He wasn't sure it was a lie, but it felt like one as it left his lips.

"Then until you find your mother or realize you've gone mad, I'll keep the dragons away. Promise." She winked and increased her pace, passing him.

He watched her up ahead, oblivious to what he was experiencing. Maybe she wouldn't hurt Kol the human, but Kol the dragon was another matter. Shame, fear, and a growing fondness for her fought over his heart like starving dogs, ripping it to pieces and leaving him sick to the stomach. He couldn't hide this from her forever, but what would she do when she found out?

That is, if she didn't already know.

20

Alessi took a breath. Though they were still in the Valley of Dragons, they had stopped to rest in an abnormally tall patch of trees nestled at the base of a mountain, which stretched above them like a jagged fang. Kol had been quiet the past several days. Too quiet, in Alessi's opinion. She tried not to pry too much—everyone was entitled to their secrets—but the moping was starting to irritate her.

She took a breath, the morning air cool in her lungs. She could taste the rain on her tongue. A storm was coming. This could be bad, considering the new weather mage, Rainsinger's, temper. Damned Kai.

A twig cracked below, and Alessi peered over the edge of her hammock to see Kol, face solemn as always. It was the early morning, and he'd been out of his hammock, which was unusual for him. Did he really think he could sneak around when he was as loud as an elephant snake?

He looked at her, his face artificially expressionless.

Fine, Mr. Mystery. Two could play that game. "I didn't take you for a sleepwalker." Alessi hung halfway out of her hammock and returned her eyes to the blue morning twilight above. The pink fingers of dawn reached across the horizon, and in the distance, great shadows of mountains blocked out the stars.

"I'm not." Kol climbed the tree, clumsy as always.

"Taking a shit, then? I thought I told you to do that before bed."

"No, it's"—he shot her an irritated glance—"I couldn't sleep."

"Well, I could, and you shouldn't wander off while I'm sleeping. You'd be a tasty morsel for some dragon out there."

He shifted his weight and started climbing the tree up to his own hammock. His brow was furrowed. Alessi bit her lip, watching him fill his hands with splinters. Climb, slip. Climb, slip. She wanted to say something, but it was like she would be intruding. How could he feel so close, yet so far away? How could she ask him what was going on when she didn't know how?

Something twisted in her gut, some feeling she couldn't name, so she grunted and turned away from him. It was frustrating to be like this, like this feeling was her curse for finally not completely hating someone. It pained her to see him suffer. If she had done something wrong, she didn't know what.

She had been alone for years now, wandering aimlessly and on the run. It had been so long she was like she had forgotten how to connect with another. And now that she finally found a companion that wouldn't—or couldn't—betray her she was still alone because she was unable to break through to him. If only she could find the words, then maybe...

"You look like shit," she said.

He gave her a scowl, mud smeared across his face. "Thanks," he spat.

Fuck. Of all the things to say, why did she say that? She

pretended to be disinterested, picking her nose as he climbed the splinter-filled tree and crawled back in his hammock. A moist storm wind blew from his direction, rocking both their hammocks, and carried with it his oily smell. Then she sniffed again. Nothing.

Other feelings bubbled up, thoughts she'd had over the past few days, but she pushed them down. The facts were pointing towards a conclusion she didn't like. She knew this magic, she had seen it once before, but for it to appear in a human? Impossible.

Kol turned to her. "Can I ask you something?"

She raised an eyebrow. "Shoot."

"Who am I?"

She snarled at him. "The fuck kind of question is that?"

"What do you know about me?"

"You're Kol, the hole-boy. Your father is a dick, your much more attractive older brother is named Astor—"

He laughed. Maybe this was working.

She winked at him. Was she seriously flirting with him? She hated herself sometimes. "And you might be mad, but the best people usually are." She shot him a sideways smile, keeping a mischievous glimmer in her eye.

A smile hinted around the edge of his lips. It was working. "What else?"

Alessi brought a hand to her chin, still joking. "You have some wild dreams—"

He laughed again, and she almost saw relief on his face. "That's enough."

She sighed. They finally connected for the first time in days, but she still felt so alone. He was hiding something from her. "What were you doing out there?" She tried to keep the jovial tone in her voice, but she knew she'd failed.

"Thinking."

"About what?" she asked.

"About a girl named Narine."

There it was again, something twisting in her gut. "Who?"

"You should know. You killed her."

Oh shit. Her heart dropped. And things were going so well before he pulled this bullshit. She'd even started to think he looked rather handsome with his longer hair, not that she'd admit it. "How would you know the name of someone I killed?"

"Those dreams back in Wellston were real," Kol said. "The dragons I met, they told me—"

Alessi tasted bile. "Were they accompanied by the voice in your head? There was never a Narine." She wanted to say more but stopped herself. Over the past centuries, she had killed countless dragons—anyone with a bounty was fair game. Even if there was a Narine, she probably wouldn't remember.

"She had yellow hair and golden eyesell me why you murdered—"

"They don't call me Alessi the dragon slayer for no reason. I've been a bounty hunter for the past three centuries or so." This was too painful to talk about, so why wouldn't he just stop? "Bounty hunting isn't murder because bounties are sanctioned by the kingdoms. It's impersonal. Just business."

"How can you be so casual about that? So *technical* about murder?" Kol asked.

She wished he would stop. It was like he was growing further and further away by the second. How could she make him understand? "I don't *remember* a Narine," Alessi said in a lilting tone. "But why should I? If I killed her, then she was just a dragon, and it was just a job." As she said these words, she knew she had failed. She wanted to bring him closer but had only pushed him away again.

Moving on instinct, she climbed onto the branch, nearing him on all fours. Her claws dug into the bark like a cat's, and she leaped from her tree to his. He flinched as she neared him. Though unintentionally, she had blocked his only way down. Distant thunder rumbled, and a few raindrops hit her face.

"Why are you afraid of me?" she asked, crouching on the branch. She reached out, touching his cheek with a claw. He was so warm, she wished he wouldn't move away like that.

Kol took a sharp breath "Why do you keep me around?"

This caught her by surprise. It was a difficult question to answer because she was not even sure why. Could she tell him it was because she had the slightest inkling he would be useful to her? Or could she tell him something closer to the real reason and expose her cursed, wretched, goddamned sentimentality?

"Why?" Kol asked again.

Alessi searched for words. "I don't know."

"Why?" Kol demanded.

Alessi took a breath, about to say the most honest thing she'd said in nearly a century. It was difficult but lies would only push him away more. "I don't really belong anywhere, and people don't tend to stick around me. They say I'm trouble. So, I've been alone for a long time, and maybe I deserve it. But you... you stayed."

Kol took a deep breath, then let it out. Alessi's heart raced. The truth was dangerous—if Kol rejected this version of her, he rejected the real her. She felt raw, naked, and exposed, waiting for him to dig his claws into her back at any second.

"I'm trying to understand. Maybe I do," Kol said.

"You do?"

"I didn't belong in the compound. I was born there, and yet somehow managed to feel like an outsider my entire life," Kol said.

"What?" Alessi stifled a laugh—it was definitely not the right moment to laugh, but how could one feel like an outsider in such a tiny space?

"Our situations aren't the same, but I've had at least a taste of what it's like to feel alone," Kol said. "I wanted to feel needed, and so I helped with my siblings. But even then, I looked too much like my mother, and no one liked being reminded of her."

"You were different than the others," Alessi said. "There's nothing wrong with that."

"They expected me to be like her. Different too often means feared. Alone." Kol said. "So... I get it. At least a little bit."

It had been so long since someone pitied her, she almost forgot what it felt like. And in that moment of weakness, old emotions washed over her in waves. Memories of cruelty. Hatred. Guilt. Shame. She had once hoped for a better life, and she cursed those who made her into what she had become.

She swallowed these feelings, sending them back to simmer in the pit of her stomach. "It stings, doesn't it?" she asked. "Being hated by the ones who are supposed to love you?"

Kol nodded.

"The pain never really goes away." The wind rustled the surrounding trees, and she gripped the branch tightly with her hands. "But when I'm alone with you, it doesn't hurt quite so bad."

21

It stormed that day and the pair trudged through mud. Kol was deep in thought.

It doesn't hurt quite so bad.

His heart twinged. Sometimes, she was like a monster, something powerful and alien to him. Other times, however, she felt so human.

So *fucking* human.

He was right to be cautious, and he was still cautious, but he also hated himself for putting her on the spot like that. Of course, Alessi wasn't perfect. After all, she was human—technically—and she was like him in many ways. She was twisted up inside, just like him. Lonely, just like him. It was easy to forget sometimes that beneath those horns, they were the same.

She was hurting even more than she let on. He knew two things: he was wrong to judge her so harshly, and he believed in Alessi's potential to be good. This wasn't the same Alessi who killed Narine and the others—she had changed. He would find the right time to tell her his secret, and when he did, only then would he judge. A wicked wind swept his rough-cut hair into a frenzy. It had been months since he left the compound, and his hair was getting long around his neck. The rain ahead parted and reformed, and lightning struck the twisting trunk of an ancient oak.

"Get down!" Alessi's clawed hand met Kol's chest, pushing him into the bushes. They tumbled down an embankment, through dead branches and brambles, until they rolled to a stop in a grassy knoll.

As Kol's head stopped spinning, he felt a weight on top of him. The scent of lilacs and campfire smoke from the night before overwhelmed him, but also something else.

He pushed against her, but she remained on top of him. She was heavy. "Something smells," Kol said.

"Shh," she whispered. He could feel her breath against his ear. Her silver hair fell across his face, accompanied by her overwhelming scent and faint, silvery dust that fell like glowing light. The storm was worsening. More lightning crashed overhead, and tree branches crackled somewhere beyond. There she was, looking out for him again.

Alessi lifted her head, looking him in the eye. "Stupid Rainsinger. Goddamn you, Kai. Next time we play strip poker, you're going home naked."

"Should we," Kol began, stopping to brush away her silver hairs that fell into his mouth, "wait for the storm to pass?" He wanted her to move, but at the same time, it had been so long since they were this close. It brought all the confusing feelings to mind he felt earlier. He liked this.

He liked her.

Alessi stood, and though she tried to dust herself off, she only succeeded in further slathering her body with mud. He stifled a laugh.

"What?" Her hood fell back, and raindrops made their way

down her soaked hair, falling to the ground. There were raindrops in her eyelashes, on her eyebrows, and her clothes hung pathetically close to her body. She raised an eyebrow—he was staring.

"Nothing." Kol forced himself to look away.

"Fuck. I'm soaked." She raised her scaled arm into the air, and the rain above her froze. Then with another motion, she drew the water out of her clothes, splattering it on Kol's feet.

"Was that really necessary?" he asked, turning around. An orange light emanated from up ahead, accompanied by a thick fog.

"I've stopped around here before. There's an old statehouse up ahead. It's beat to pieces but some of the roof is still up." Alessi pointed toward the glowing light. "Let's go."

The two walked until they saw it. It was a house, once stately but now decaying, with wooden siding broken and sticking out at odd angles. Vines grew up stone columns in the front. The pair made their way over a cobblestone pathway, overgrown and forgotten, then through the empty doorway leading into a foyer. A grand staircase stretched to their right, vines growing on its railing. The floor creaked as they stepped into the room.

Alessi threw her arms wide, twirling in circles. She let herself fall backwards on the wooden floor, and Kol sat next to her. The orange glow was gone now, save for some orange dust blowing through the space. Magic had touched this place. He looked around. The decrepit house, once probably full of love and life, reminded him of a skeleton.

"There are no signs of recent habitation, no footprints up to the door, no one's trimmed the hedges in centuries... it's perfect," she said.

"It's sad." Kol leaned back as she stretched out her arms, nearly hitting him.

"It's not sad, it's an opportunity."

More orange dust drifted through the space before blinking out of existence, just like the dust he saw on Alessi and the other Belgarri. Something felt off. "I'm not sure this place is empty," Kol said.

"Other than ghosts and memories, it is."

He shot her a look when she mentioned ghosts.

"The figurative kind. Looks like we have full reign of the place."

Somewhere in the house, a door creaked open.

"Shit." Kol scrambled up, and Alessi made for the door.

"It's alright, little ones." A voice emerged from the darkness. It was scratchy, like that of an old man. "It's just me." A short, bearded man rounded the balcony at the top of the stairs, leaning against its crumbling railing. There was something off about his expression, but Kol couldn't pinpoint what it was from that distance.

"Who the hell are you?" Alessi asked.

"This is my house," the man croaked.

"This isn't your house. It's been abandoned for centuries," Alessi said.

"But I've lived here for a millennium." For a moment, the man's form rippled with light. Alessi didn't seem to notice.

"We'll be on our way, sorry to disturb you—" Kol began.

"What are you doing living in a place like this?" Alessi demanded. "No front door, vines everywhere—anyone would think it was abandoned!"

The man sighed. "I'm old, and houses are difficult to keep up with. There's a beauty in living alongside nature, though. The birds make their nests up there"—he pointed to the roof above what Kol noticed was a large pile of feces—"and deer pass through. We're all part of nature, in the end."

"Then why weren't you here the last two times I stopped by?" Alessi demanded.

"Ah! You must have been here for the party! I used to throw the most extravagant balls before the war. Even the witch queen would come, wearing that beautiful emerald dress." The man rambled on for a while, slowly turning in a circle.

Alessi stood next to him now, and she put her lips to his ear. "He's lost his mind. My mother would never go to a party." A flash of light filled the space as lightning struck again, and the following thunder loud was enough to shake the floor.

"Do you think he's dangerous?" Kol asked.

"Maybe, but he also seems pretty weak. Let me look at the storm, we might be able to find shelter elsewhere." Alessi made her way to the door while the old man continued his rambling, but lightning struck close enough to send sparks cascading inside. She froze as thunder ripped through the room. A thin line of smoke rose from the stone porch.

The old man stopped and faced her, leaning on his cane. "It's far too dangerous outside. If you choose to stay, I can't guarantee you'll be warm, but you will be dry."

Kol and Alessi looked at each other. Her eyes were wide, and it seemed even she could be shaken by a near-miss with lightning. And there were dark bags under her eyes—they both hadn't gotten much sleep the night before, though for different reasons. They needed rest.

"I would so love to have guests again," the man said. "Ever since my eyes were—well, never mind. But I was the greatest host before the war. Even the queen..."

"I think we should stay," Kol whispered, thinking of the lightning nearly striking her out front of the house. How easily that could have killed her.

"He's creepy."

"He's a lot less dangerous than lightning."

"Fine." Alessi tore her eyes away from Kol's and turned to face the strange man. "We'll stay."

The stranger smiled, stroking his thin beard. "Wonderful. Now, come here so I can see my guests." He held out his hands expectantly but made no effort to approach them.

Kol and Alessi looked at each other, then slowly neared the stranger, taking cautious steps up the worn staircase. Kol realized what was strange about the man's expression, and especially about how the man wanted to *see* them. Not only were his eyes closed, but they appeared to be shrunken, filling caverns suggestive of the skull beneath.

He brought a hand to Kol's face, but Kol tried to slink away.

"Let our host feel your face," Alessi said in a mock-polite tone. "Since you want to stay here so badly."

Kol's eyes widened, but what choice did he have? He didn't want Alessi to see him be afraid of a blind old man. When the man's icy hand made contact with his face, Kol shivered. He traced a finger along Kol's brow, his nose, his lips, and then the stranger smiled. He leaned in, and whispered, "Ah. It must be hard, being so much like her."

"What?" Kol and Alessi exclaimed in unison. Kol studied her face for signs of suspicion, but there was none. She only rolled her eyes.

Should I go?

He half-expected his mother's voice to reply, but she had been strangely silent since their meeting in the Valley of Dragons. He wasn't sure why—maybe the link that connected them had grown weaker, or maybe her mission was complete. The lack of closure gnawed at the edge of his mind.

"Now let me see you," he turned to Alessi. She made a face, and Kol shot her a look of *I did it, now you have to.* Reluctantly, she complied, and the man did the same to her. She was careful not to let him touch her horns, moving her head so as to prevent him from feeling them.

He paused, his finger in the center of her forehead. "The search for vengeance has aged you. You used to be so beautiful."

"She's still—" Kol stopped himself. "You shouldn't say things like that."

Alessi smiled, but it was more of a grimace, her fangs prominent above her lip. "I can age however I want."

The man chuckled, removing his hands. "It's always good to know what you want. Now, follow me. I have a spare room, but don't mind the cuckoo. Don't mind the cuckoo at all." He turned away from the two and began leading them down a hallway, wooden floors matching the wooden walls. Faded pictures hung on both walls, many of people with faces scratched out.

He waved his hand over the last door on the left. Kol heard a click as it unlocked and swung open, revealing a room more ornate and less dusty than the rest of the house. Kol walked inside. There was an enormous bed with a red canopy hanging overhead and around it like a tent, and six windows spanned two wide walls. The space was taller than Kol expected, the ceiling's height stretching far above where he thought the roof of the house would be. Alessi stood in the middle of the room with her arms crossed, careful not to touch anything.

The room was in impossibly good shape, considering the condition of the rest of the house. There was no dust, magical or otherwise, and even the furniture looked brand new.

"Is this real?" Kol asked.

"Yes, but it's been enhanced by an old friend of mine. Go on, try out the bed." The old man gestured to it.

It looked incredible. Kol sat on the bed, softer than the bed he slept in below Astor every night and softer than the stone inn floors and his hammock. It was already too late to realize his biggest mistake—this would be Alessi's bed. He shouldn't have gotten his hopes up. He would have to sleep on the floor again.

"There are a few rules here," the old man said, smile plastered to his face. "You can open the door to your room, but don't open any others. Those were my children's rooms, and I like to keep them preserved as they were. This was my old room, but I prefer to sleep in the attic now." The man chuckled again. "This is now the only room for guests."

"Only one guest room?" Alessi asked. "In this huge house?"

Kol thought for a moment. She had a point. He'd said he hosted parties.

"Like I said, it's been a long time since I've had a guest. And I'm sure you won't mind sharing, given that you're—"

"Fine. Whatever." Alessi furrowed her brow, twisting her foot against the ground.

"Make yourselves comfortable. Have you had dinner?" the old man asked. "This was a human house before the Darkness, and so I've learned to cook human dishes to keep with the theme. I hope you like mutton!"

Hungry and not entirely sure what mutton was—or the blind man planned to cook—Kol nodded. "Sure, we love... mutton."

She stuck out her tongue and frowned.

"Mutton it is! I'll meet you down by the piano." The man turned around, reaching for the door behind him. Orange dust fell from his skin like fine, sparkling lights.

"Piano?" Alessi asked.

"You'll know it when you see it. See you at midnight. That's when humans eat dinner, yes? Or was that supper?" The man closed the door, and as he made his way down the creaking hallway, he shrieked, "We have guests!"

"Old man's batshit," Alessi muttered. "I don't like this place."

"Neither do I." It was a lie, or at least a partial lie—the bed was heavenly, and Alessi had not yet kicked him off. It was nice to be out of the wind and rain. One more night swinging in his hammock, and he swore he'd vomit over the side. Kol threw himself back, letting the smooth, red comforter envelop him. A fireplace in the corner crackled.

"It was empty the last time I was here," Alessi said. "I was sure of it. That guy wasn't here."

"He's weird, but he doesn't seem... dangerous. What kind of Belgarri is he?" Kol swung his legs off the plush bed, letting his feet kick in the open air like a child. He remembered the orange dust falling from the man's skin.

"He's probably a dragon, but unless he shows his true form, we can only guess without seeing his eyes."

Kol felt it again, an uncomfortable twisting in his gut. "Could we ask?"

"If you want to get kicked out. It should be safe as long as he doesn't know I'm a witch, which shouldn't be hard since he's... you know. Blind. I'll just say I'm a Suuge snake woman or something. And if he's trouble, then..." She made a slashing gesture over her throat.

Kol swallowed. "Maybe he's not bad... he wants to cook us mutton, whatever that is."

"It's gross, that's what. Mutton is lamb, probably from the wild rams around here. Dragons have a sick fascination with them, eat them raw, swallow them whole. It's the worst thing I've ever seen." She stuck out her tongue.

"But he said it was a human dish."

"A dragon's take on a human dish. Don't expect much in terms of taste. I'm not sure if he's a golden dragon, or if it was his friend as he said, but this whole place has been bewitched by their magic." Alessi made her way to the window and threw open the extravagant purple curtains. Outside the window, it was sunny, despite the storm they sheltered from. And the forest seemed different somehow—greener, healthier, the rotting trunks they climbed over now trees taller than the house itself.

"That looks like one of Azazel's portals." Kol made his way to the window. "Looking through it feels like looking into another world."

Alessi sniffed the window, then ran a finger along it. "It's just an image, recorded from a better time." Alessi felt at the bottom of the window and pushed it open. Wind whistled into the room, and rain spattered across the sill. "The entire room is probably an image of the past. An illusion."

A log fell in the fireplace, sending a flurry of sparks flying into the air. The man's earlier words rang in his head. *It must be hard being so much like her.* The man had recognized him as a dragon, he was sure of it. But beyond that, Kol couldn't tell if the man was mad, like Alessi said, or if he'd known Kol's mother.

Where are you? Kol asked. *What's happening?*

At first, there was no reply, but then he heard: *She is the enemy of dragons. Do not trust the witch.*

She's changed, Kol replied, pushing down the thoughts that plagued him over the past days, the sick feeling of holding a secret and the fear of what might happen if it were exposed. *What do I do now?*

Then, for the first time in weeks, he found himself transported into his vision. He saw the outline of his mother and brother in the wastes, though this time he could see her face. His brother, Caliban, stood beside her facing away. His red hair blew in the wind.

Look for him, and fate will bring you together, his mother's voice said.

What about Alessi?

People like us are used, not loved. Do not make the same mistake I made.

But—

"What's that sour look on your face? You look like you've seen a ghost." Alessi shot him an irritated glance.

If only she knew.

22

Alessi was right. The mutton was terrible, undercooked, and far too salty. At times, it even twitched. Kol poked at the peculiar smelling lumps and made polite conversation between their host's mumbling, while Alessi lifted the whole bowl to her mouth and drank the soupy, meat-like substance as if it were second nature. And despite the old man's lack of eyes, he always turned in the direction of the two when they spoke. Kol told himself this was just a matter of politeness, or perhaps the man just wanted to hear them better, but he couldn't shake the feeling that he was looking at them. Seeing them, seeing *through* them.

The old man's eyeless gaze rested on Kol. "There once was a woman named Oasis," he sang.

Kol straightened, heart rate increasing.

"I don't know why I thought mutton was so bad, that was delicious," Alessi interrupted with a burp. "Let's get out of here. The old dude's creeping me out."

"Anything's delicious when you're starving." Kol stood. "Excuse us."

"Of course, of course, anything for the one who reaches through the darkness," the old man babbled to himself.

"It was good enough for me," Alessi said once they were back in their room. She shut the door behind them, and the sound echoed through the cavernous space. "Why didn't you eat more?"

"I don't know how you ate any." Kol's stomach growled.

"Look what I found in the kitchen," she said. She reached into her cloak and drew an entire bottle of wine and a brick of cheese.

"How the hells did you hide those?" Kol asked.

"Let's just say I've had a lot of practice." She tossed the cheese through the air, and Kol caught it clumsily with both hands. "Eat that."

He sniffed it and made a face, holding it away from him. It smelled strongly of mold. "It smells worse than you do."

Alessi almost looked embarrassed. "Pretend it's fancy cheese that's supposed to be moldy. Maybe once you eat it, I won't smell so bad to you."

"Fine." He took a breath and then a bite of the cheese. It tasted almost as bad as it smelled, and his eyes watered.

"Better than the mutton, beefcake?" Alessi asked in a lilting toe.

"No," he said, but at least he knew what this was. "And that's the second time you've called me beefcake. Don't." He took another bite, and then another. He had been starving for days—actually starving—or, at least, he should have been. He looked down at his body. He was decently well-built when he left the compound, but the amount of muscle he'd built on their journey should have been impossible while eating so little.

Alessi sat on the floor, holding the wine bottle between her feet as she dug a claw into the cork. With a good amount of effort, it came off with a distinctive *pop* and rolled across the floor. She raised the entire bottle to her mouth and drank. That was very like her, and somehow, fitting of the mood that night. She crossed her legs in a casual way, leaning back against the bed. Her silver hair caught around her ears as she drank. She lowered the bottle and raised an eyebrow.

"What?" Alessi asked.

Fuck. He was staring again. He turned away. "That's one way to drink wine."

"What, worried I'm going to down the whole bottle?" She slammed it down with such force he was surprised it didn't break or spill.

"In fact, yes."

"Then come drink some before I have the chance."

Was she really inviting him to join her? Kol hesitated before sitting across from her on the floor, cross-legged. She held the bottle out to him expectantly, her face flushed.

His face, however, must have been even redder. "Uh, shouldn't you get a glass or something?"

"I'm a lady, but I'm not that kind of lady. Hurry up."

He took the bottle out of her hand and pressed it to his lips. He took a swig. It was sweet and bitter at the same time, and though he hated it at first, he took another sip. It was better than the beer when he met the mouse-man. When he was done, he handed the bottle back to Alessi and wiped his mouth. The wine stained his hand in a line like blood, and he still tasted it around the corners of his mouth. He watched hungrily as Alessi drank, his eyes following her every swallow, her every breath, before she handed the bottle back to him.

He could smell her—that intoxicating scent. How had he never noticed it before? It was feminine and heavy, lacing the air like a silver smoke. He could see her magic, too, glimmering on her skin like dust. It fell the ground, twinkling out of sight as she laughed. They went back and forth, drinking like friends, but something still wasn't right after all he said earlier. He was unfair to her. Everything she had done, everything she had shown him, were not the actions of a monster, even if she thought herself one.

No matter what his mother said.

"I don't think... I thought it, but I don't think..." Kol fought for words, which left his mouth like strange syllables, as if he formed his lips around stones.

"Spit it out." Alessi burped.

"You said you were a bad person. I don't think you're bad, even if..."

"You keep saying that, but I don't believe it." Alessi rolled her eyes and took another drink. "Don't be ridiculous."

"Something bad happened to you, but it doesn't mean... it doesn't mean you're bad." Kol wiped his mouth. "You did what you thought was right, even if..."

"That doesn't mean I'm good."

"Then maybe everyone's a bad person."

"Yeah. Except you. You're good."

Kol finished drinking, handing the bottle back to Alessi again. "Why me?" His heart beat in his ears.

"You haven't had the chance to do anything bad yet, living in that hole." Alessi took a swig and handed the bottle back to him. The room spun, but in a good way.

He couldn't be a good person. Not when he was hiding his identity from her, not when he was hiding the fact he was one of the beasts she hated the most. It was too much sometimes.

Responding to his silence, Alessi asked, "Then what did you do?"

He searched for words. "I disrespected my father." The old man was cruel at times, but life underground was harsh. Sometimes, he wondered if his father may have come to love him if he had been a better son. Been less like his mother.

"Good. Your father is a dick." Alessi laughed. "What else did you do?"

"I took my brother for granted." Astor's memory surfaced in his mind—Astor teaching him to read, playing board games with him and Mia, Astor baking him a cake for his birthday so soon before he left. Astor taking him to the threshold to meet Alessi and warning him not to venture too far. Kol had tried to be to Mia what Astor was to him, but he knew he never could. "He deserved more thanks than he got. I told myself that leaving helped him, that I made some space for him to live a little longer. But sometimes I fear I ran away, and I worry he'll be banished anyway before I return." Kol had never even vocalized this fear to himself before, but it was like a shadow over him.

"Now we're getting somewhere." Alessi grinned. She was getting far too much enjoyment from his emotional torment, and yet, there was also a hint of sincerity in her eyes. "It's..." The last hint of levity left her face, and she cleared her throat. Her face twisted as if she were searching for the right words. "Thanks for sharing."

"Family's tough," Kol said.

Alessi laughed. "Tell me about it. My mother's eaten so much dragon flesh she practically is one."

"Yeah..." Kol's voice trailed off. There was so much he couldn't tell her, that it hurt him. It was like a dark fire burning at the edges of his soul. "For a long time, I hated myself for letting my mother take my brother into the wastes."

"The hot brother?"

"No, my full brother."

Alessi shifted where she sat. "Oh, right."

"Everyone knew that the wastes would kill you. She wasn't a good mother, and even in the end I thought she'd chosen my brother over me." Kol took a sharp breath. Even now, knowing the truth, it was hard because there was still so much he didn't understand. "I felt like I wasn't even good enough to die with her."

"Don't say stuff like that," Alessi said, swirling the bottle in her hand. The dark liquid moved behind opaque red glass, and she watched it with an empty expression. Kol laid back on the hard floor, pressing his back into it. He was anything but innocent after everything he'd been through, everything he was keeping from her. Except... he looked at Alessi, his face flushing further. The feeling he had for so long, ever since the night he cut her hair, now swept him over like a wave.

Alessi took another swig before laying down beside him. Her hand brushed his arm, scales cool and smooth against his skin, which tingled as electricity passed between them. He rolled onto his side, facing her on the warm wood floor. They were so close and her smell was so intoxicating. He swallowed. Carefully, he reached forward, taking her hair between two fingers. It felt cold despite the warmth of the room, but fine and soft, like he remembered.

"What?" Alessi asked.

She is the enemy of dragons.

He withdrew his hand. What right did he have to be so close to her? Maybe he would just say he was tired and go to bed.

"You're not telling me something." Alessi wrinkled her nose. "I don't like it."

For a second, he almost told her. A few simple words, and all this stress could be gone. Fear stopped him. Everyone had secrets, and this would have to be his.

"Let me ask you something." Was he really doing this? He wanted to melt into the floor. This could go very badly, and without the alcohol's artificial bravery, he would have given up then.

"Shoot."

"Why do you think I stay with you?"

"Desperation and circumstance." Alessi paused, narrowing her eyes at the ceiling. He was closer to her now, and she smelled like lilacs, rain, smoke, and blood. Like magic and adventures in the light. And he wanted it more than anything. "Or maybe it's boredom... could be curiosity. Why does anyone do anything?"

"None of those things. Remember the red dragon that followed us?"

"Yeah." She took another drink of the wine, then passed it back to him.

"When I met him, he felt familiar. I think I know why." He lifted the bottle to his lips and drank. "He's like you."

Alessi laughed. "Like me? Don't be ridiculous, he's a dragon!"

"Yes, but he didn't have a bad heart. He was just in a bad situation, a victim of his past choices."

"Pfft."

He took another drink. His cheeks flushed from the alcohol. "Someone hurt you. They took all your light and left you in darkness, left you a shadow of who you were. Maybe you've made mistakes, but you can change. People do terrible things when they're"—he hiccuped— "incomplete."

"That's not how you seduce a lady."

"Like..." Kol searched for the words. "You're in a process of changing, but even in this state, you're beautiful." Shit, did he really just say that? "It's a broken sort of beauty."

Alessi rolled onto her side, looking at him. Her smile held the hint of a joke. "You thought the dragon was beautiful, then?"

"Not like you." His heartbeat pounded in his ears. Logic told him not to say what he was saying, but something else pushed him forward. She brought a hand to the back of his neck, drawing him close. Heat rushed to his face, and though he felt his heartbeat in his ears, he didn't pull away. Her lips stopped inches away from his, and he felt her hot breath against his face, her eyes boring into his.

"What are you doing?" he asked.

"Tell me what you want."

"You." He swallowed. "Everything that's a part of you. The scars, the beauty, all of it." Alessi's eyes widened as he continued. "I want to understand you. I want to know all about you, the good and the bad, the past and the future. I want to watch you grow and change, and I want to see what you become."

Her expression changed into that of a wild animal, her eyes mere slits and her fangs revealed. She pushed him backwards then rolled on top of him, her claws digging into his wrists as she held them to the floor. She straddled him, and he looked at her wide-eyed with a mixture of hunger and terror.

"These claws aren't mine. These scales aren't mine. What if Viktor was right, and I'm a murderer and a savage?" She brought a claw across her cheek, letting blood well up. It dripped onto Kol's mouth, and he tasted metal and salt and that chemical sweetness he remembered from their first night in the wastes. And he loved it. She looked down at him again, more blood dripping across Kol's face. "What's keeping me from destroying you?"

The enemy of dragons. He heard his mother's voice. *Our enemy.*

"I know you," he said. This was a leap of faith, and a potentially deadly one, but he had to go forward. This feeling inside him... if he kept it bottled up any longer, he was worried it might swallow him whole.

"You don't know anything." The snarl left her face, and her eyes widened with vulnerability created by both the longing for and fear of connection. She started to pull away from him, but he sat up and wrapped his arms around her and they fell back together, her cold against his warmth.

"Didn't you just hear me? What are you—" she began, but he kissed her. He wasn't sure what exactly drove him to make such a risky move, but it was like his body was moving on its own. He pulled back, watching her reaction. For a moment she froze, and panic rose in the center of his chest. What a mistake. How could he ever think they could be more—

She kissed back with teeth and tongue, pressing into him, her claws on his shoulder, then on his neck, then tearing through his shirt and running up his back. It hurt, but at the same time it was delectably freeing. He was so tired before but at that moment, he didn't want to sleep. He came alive beneath her, and she tasted like blood and sweat as he kissed her cheek, then down to her ear, then her neck. She ripped off what was left of his shirt, then hers. He felt her fingers tracing along the inside of his muddy trousers.

His heart pounded. What was he doing? He didn't know what to do—he was only vaguely aware of what men and women did when no one was watching. Sensing this, Alessi stopped for a moment, pulling her head back. Her hair fell around him like a halo and as their eyes met, he realized how badly he wanted her, and for how long.

"What do you want?" she asked him, clawed fingers paused at his pant line in silent anticipation. Her chest heaved and her wild eyes met his.

"Everything," he breathed, and she kissed him again. Before he knew it, she peeled off his ruined trousers and threw them across the room, where they skidded to a halt by the raging fireplace.

She then removed her pants, still damp from rainwater. She stood naked other than the metal corselet he could always see below her low-cut shirt. He stumbled to his feet, reaching out a hand, but when his fingers traced the metal, she stepped back.

"What is it?" he asked. She held a clawed hand over the center of her chest, fingers curled over her heart.

"It stays on," she said.

"Why?"

"I'm damaged."

He reached again, and this time she didn't flinch. "It doesn't matter to me."

"It should." With a slight hesitation, she unlatched it on the side, and the armored corselet swung off. Patches of scales covered her breasts, growing over scars and claw marks. He traced one with his finger, feeling the mottled flesh.

"What happened?" Kol asked.

She tensed, and he thought she might step away. "When I took my first magic, the transformation was hard on me. I wanted it to go away, maybe a little too much, but the scales always came back." She turned from him. "I'm hideous."

"You're.... You're beautiful. The most beautiful woman I've ever seen." And she was. He wished he could find better words to do her justice, to make her understand, but all he could do was rest a hand on her shoulder.

She gave a tense laugh. "You've never seen a woman you weren't related to."

"I wouldn't have you any other way." He met her eyes with intensity, and before he knew it, they were on the bed. Was this really happening? Everything moved so fast, it was almost hard to believe, new sensations sweeping his body. She was on top, straddling him, and he bucked as she lowered herself onto him, moving her hips in a circular motion. It felt natural. She kissed him as she rose up and down, and his heartbeat blended with the rhythm of her movements.

Her hair was in his mouth, his ears, his eyes, as if she were a part of him. He felt her breasts and ran his hands down her curves. Pressure built, but he breathed steadily and forced it down. She enjoyed this far too much for him to end things so early. She clawed at his back, his sides, his neck. She bit him. He bled. He didn't care. He wanted her. He had her. He wanted to thrust himself in deeper and deeper, until he was a part of her—until she was complete. Her sweat dripped onto his face as she worked, speeding up before pausing to arch her back and bare her fangs at the ceiling. He felt her pulsate, and she continued.

Something triggered in him, some dormant instinct, and he put a hand on her shoulder. He flipped on top of her, her legs over his shoulders as he thrust. Pressure built again, and his breathing quickened. He forced his thrusts to slow.

"I think I'm going to... " He could barely manage more than a breathless whisper. Alessi wrapped her legs around his back, forcing him deeper, and he thought he might explode then and there. Now, being at his most vulnerable so close to her, feeling her tough yet tender touch, he knew he could trust her. Right?

"Inside," she said. "It doesn't matter, anyway." There was sorrow in her voice, and implications behind those words, but he would have to ask about that later.

He thrust faster, and she moaned and threw back her head again, baring her fangs. Her fingers curled and her legs pressed against him, drawing him closer, deeper. The next time she came, he went with her.

23

Kol woke in a tangle of blood and hair, the eternal sunshine of the strange room shining through the windows. The blood on the floor—and he was certain there must've been blood—was gone, and even their clothes were folded at the end of the bed. He could've almost convinced himself the night before was a dream if not for Alessi's naked limbs tangled up in his. She stirred and he wrapped his arms around her, pressing her against his chest. She breathed steadily, defenseless in her sleep.

Her eyes shot open, and she pulled away from him in a panic before looking around, as if she'd forgotten where she was, what had happened. "Sorry," she muttered, "I'm not used to waking up next to someone."

"It's okay, I'm here." Kol reached out to her, brushing a finger along her bare arm.

"I'm fine. It's fine." She stood, leaving him naked and alone in the bed as she walked over to her folded clothes. "Did you do this?"

He shook his head. "I hoped you did."

She sniffed the clothes, then made a face. "Someone was in here while we were... sleeping."

Kol's face reddened, and he pulled the covers over his nude form instinctively.

"Come on. We need to get going." She pointed to the door. "The storm must be over by now. That idiot Kai can't cry forever."

A massive thunderclap shook the room and rattled the windows. It was enough to send Kol out of the far-too-large bed and onto the floor, slipping on his now-cleaned trousers, then his torn shirt and leather jacket.

"What do we do?" he asked.

"We could try to go through the storm, or we could wait here until it stops." She made her way to the window, prying it open. Rain and wind splattered her face before she shut it.

Kol eyed the bed, remembering her touch the night before. He felt at his back, tracing where her claws had scratched him —there was not even the hint of a wound. He longed for that touch, and he wanted her again, more than he cared to admit. "What's the rush?"

Alessi didn't notice his interest. She picked up his folded shirt from the floor and sniffed it. Orange dust fell from the clothes and then blinked out of existence—they had definitely been touched by magic.

The clothes concerned him, too, but his animal mind now had other priorities, ones he had never felt before. "The old man must have washed our clothes for us." Kol shrugged. "A little weird but harmless enough. What if we—"

Alessi sniffed her shirt again. "I don't recognize this magic. I don't think it's dragon magic."

"That could be a good thing."

"Not necessarily."

"Well, if he's not a dragon, what could he be?" Kol thought of the mouse-man from so long ago.

"I don't know. But there are things worse than dragons out there."

Kol bit his lip, watching Alexi's curves as she stretched side to side. Fuck, he wanted to touch her. "Would those things do our laundry?"

"I wouldn't be surprised. Laundry can be an evil thing."

"Or he's nice but a little strange. He's blind, remember? He might have thought we were... out or something. And our clothes were muddy."

"He should have heard us. At least he didn't see us naked, I guess. Creepy old man." Alessi scowled before making her way to the door. Kol followed. He wanted to reach out, to touch her, to be a part of her, but he stopped himself. She acted as if nothing changed, perhaps because nothing had.

Alessi stopped in the middle of the hallway, and Kol was so lost in his thoughts, he ran into her. She didn't budge.

"Sorry," he muttered, gathering himself and trying to hide the butterflies he felt.

"Look," she whispered. The hallway before them, decaying and dusty the night before, was now clean and polished. It looked as new as the floor in their bedroom, that freshly cleaned image of the past. The pictures on the wall were still faceless but now had color, and the hall's wallpaper trim wasn't a tattered gray but a patterned blue and white. Kol yawned. There was no reason he should have been so tired.

"Good morning." The old man stood at the end of the hallway.

Kol jumped in surprise. "Good morning," he and Alessi said in unison.

"I'm glad you two are enjoying your stay," the old man said

in a suggestive voice. Kol was certain that if he had eyes, he would've winked.

Alessi crossed her arms. "That's none of your business."

"No, no, I'm glad my old bed is getting some use." The old man leaned against the railing as he set foot on the top step, Alessi and Kol closing in from behind.

"Why did you come into our room?" Alessi asked.

"Curiosity." The old man paused. "Come downstairs, I made food for you."

"Pervert," Alessi muttered, but they went down the long steps to the first level.

"More mutton?" Kol asked, his stomach churning at the thought. More pressing, however, was the word *curiosity*. Curiosity about what? What could he have hoped to find? His face reddened. *The dragon and the dragon slayer.* He felt invaded, violated, as if this old man knew all his secrets and used them to toy with him. And yet, the man seemed so senile, Kol felt crazy for suspecting him of anything at the same time.

The old man chuckled. "Mutton? No, not for breakfast! I wasn't prepared for guests when you came, so last night I did some cleaning. I found bacon and eggs from the house's earlier days, fresh as new." Then the man brought over two plates with eggs and two strips of meat. "Human food." The man smiled at them. "A delicacy."

Kol and Alessi looked at each other, then to the food. Kol raised an eyebrow. "These come from pigs and chickens, right? Those have been extinct for almost ten thousand years." And yet, even with this knowledge, his stomach hungered like never before.

"Yes." The old man nodded. "They're from the house, sometimes it reverts to an earlier state from before the Darkness. The magic brings the food back. You should see it—this house, when fully fed, is truly a marvel!"

Kol tried not to linger on the crazy old man's words. Eventually hunger took over and when they ate, Kol was surprised by the pleasant flavor. The old man's cooking skills had improved.

"I forgot to ask. What's your name?" Alessi asked him, leaning forward.

The man paused. "George."

Alessi and Kol looked at each other, and Kol raised an eyebrow.

"Alright, *George.*" Alessi stood and made her way to the front door, which not only existed now but was polished mahogany and glass. She opened it a crack, and the wind ripped it open the rest of the way.

The man hurried over and closed the door with strength Kol would not have expected from someone his age.

"Be careful!" the man yelled, the honey in his voice gone. Something moved furiously beneath his shrunken eyelids.

Alessi toed the now-wet floor, her equally wet hair plastered to her face. The rain had hit her like a wall. "How did the house repair itself?"

"Like I said, it didn't repair itself, it reverted to its original state. I rarely go through the trouble, but now that I have guests again, I thought I'd be hospitable." The man licked his lips.

Kol stood, the chair screeching as it slid behind him.

Alessi looked to Kol. "I think I need to lie down, got one hell of a hangover. Excuse me," she said in an artificially sweet voice.

The old man nodded. Kol followed Alessi upstairs, leaving his half-eaten bacon and eggs on the table.

"Something's not right," he whispered.

"I have a suspicion," Alessi said. As they neared their room at the end of the hall, she put her fist on the door opposite. "Remember how he said we can't look into the other rooms?"

"Yeah. Something about his kids."

"Right. Well, I think I know the real reason." Alessi wiped her scaled hand across her forehead, drawing the rainwater out of her hair. It formed into an ice key at the end of her pointer finger, and she jammed it into the lock.

"Why don't you make keys more often?" he asked. He stood behind her as she crouched, and he could smell her hair, same as it smelled the night before.

"It only works on basic locks. Also, it hurts," she said, twisting her finger. When the lock clicked, her fingernail broke, and she stuck her bleeding fingertip in her mouth. The door swung open to a black room, and Alessi's scent was overwhelmed by another, more pungent one. It was sweet but also bitter, as if some animal crawled into the room and lain in a pile of feces, urine, and honey before rotting.

Alessi huffed, and together they walked into the dark space. The light pouring in from the doorway stopped far too early to see anything, but as Kol's eyes adjusted, he could make out the silhouette of a bed, a dresser, a chair, and a pile of books. Alessi must have been able to see better than him because she walked to the side of the bed. A wheezing sound came from it, and the horrid smell grew stronger as Kol made his way to Alessi.

"Go..." the voice was little more than a whisper.

Kol jumped back. "That's a person?"

"It was," Alessi said. She turned away, making her way to the door. "Grab your things. We're leaving."

"Shouldn't we help them?"

"It's too late. Come on, before that's us."

Kol looked from Alessi to the outline of a human shape as his eyes adjusted. There was a lump in the covers, and something, perhaps an arm, reached out to him, bending in too many places.

"What happened to you?" he whispered.

The thing wheezed. Kol supposed it may have been a word, but he wasn't sure.

"What did you say?" Kol asked. "What is it?" He leaned in closer, and the thing he thought was an arm touched his neck, leaving a line of goo. He flinched but forced himself to lean even closer. He could smell the man's rotting breath. Maybe Kol could heal him, if he had enough time.

"You're"—the thing wheezed again—"next."

Kol stepped back.

"There's nothing we can do for him. Let's get the fuck out of here, Kai's storm is safer than this hell house." Alessi gestured to him from the hallway, and he followed. "I don't know what's going on here, but I don't like it. I think this was a trap. That old creep might just be another bounty hunter, or worse, some other opportunist."

They left the room, closing the door carefully behind them before hurrying to their own room to pack. Kol shoved the last of his things in his pack and threw it over his shoulder.

"How are we going to exit gracefully?" Kol asked.

"Who said anything about grace?" Alessi spat on the pristine floor. "We're getting out of here if we have to crawl right over the freak."

A voice made its way up the stairs. "Are you feeling any better? You should eat something, it'll help."

"You'll eat us, more like," Alessi said under her breath before saying loudly, "I'm fine, I'll be down in a minute."

"You're not planning on leaving so soon, are you?" the old man asked.

"I'm already feeling better. Let me freshen up. I'll be right down," Alessi said. She gestured to the open window, and Kol climbed out. The ledge was slick, and it was a long way to the bushes below. He looked at the bed one last time, and the room changed before his eyes, reverting to the one he remembered from the night before. Covers were thrown all over, blood on the floor.

"Hurry!" Alessi pried up his fingers, and he fell into the bushes below. Branches jabbed his ribs and scraped his spine as she jumped out, landing with all the grace and silence of a cat, and ran from the house.

"Wait up." Kol winced, forcing himself to his feet before limping after her, slipping through the mud.

"Did you break something?" she asked. For a moment, he thought she might offer him a hand.

"I don't think so," he said between heavy breaths. It only took the rain seconds to soak right down to his bones. Kol slipped in the mud again, his right ankle collapsing underneath him.

"Shit." Alessi took his hand, pulling him to his feet and dragging him forward. "This isn't good."

"It's fine. Just... give me a minute." His ankle was definitely broken, but his bones shifted and he grunted as one popped back.

This is only the beginning of what you can do.

"Do we need to stop?" Alessi asked. She was practically carrying him now, his arm over her shoulders.

"It's fine," Kol lied. His ankle was fully healed now, and it supported his weight when he tested it. "I think I just landed wrong, but it's fine now." The pain was gone, leaving him alone and facing the reality of his power. He had seen his ability, whatever it was called, save Alessi's life, and heal himself several times now, but there had always been some way he could deny it—maybe it was the druids, maybe the injury wasn't as bad as he thought. This time, however, there was no denying what had just happened. No denying what he now knew he was. With his mother dead, Kol was the last living dark dragon, alone in this world with abilities he was only just beginning to understand. He wanted to talk to someone. Tell them the truth. But if he told Alessi, something told him he'd wind up even more alone.

Or dead.

He was so lost in thought, he didn't notice he no longer walked on mud, but on dry earth. The rain had stopped. Kol looked back, and the rain fell in a perfect line. On one side, the sky was gray and the wind vicious. On the other, the sun shone gold and yellow. Small summer flowers poked through dense grasses, and insects flew about.

"What the hell?" Kol asked, looking back and forth.

Alessi reached down, taking a blade of grass between her fingers. A warm wind blew through her beautiful hair, and it sparkled in the sunlight. "I don't say this often, but we're lucky to be alive right now. I don't know what that man was, or what he wanted, but I want none of it."

24

A cool sun rose that morning, its rays filtering gray through the pillars of clouds. Three days passed, and Alessi still wasn't sure what to say to Kol. She wanted to talk about that night but couldn't bring herself to. He was starting to sense her coldness—she could feel it, and she hated herself for that disappointed look in his eye. But she couldn't bring herself to more than brush up against him.

She had been with guys before, but usually it was simple. They parted ways afterwards, and it was like it had never happened. Even Azazel fucked with a sense of detachment, their nights together like a contract to be fulfilled. But Kol? There was something more in his eyes. She would hurt him, but maybe he deserved it. She warned him she was a monster, after all.

Kol shivered, looking at the dark shape forming on the horizon. "Looks like it's going to storm again."

"No shit." There was an edge to her voice. She didn't want to sound so harsh, but hells, why couldn't she talk to him like a normal person?

"Maybe it'll snow again." Kol's eyes searched her for any sign of something deeper, some stronger desire to communicate. Whatever. She would talk about it when she felt ready.

Alessi sniffed the air. "No." She wanted to say more but left it at that. Words bounced around her head like rock snakes fighting and tangling.

They reached the top of a ridge, and twisting sands rose from the distant dunes ahead. They were nearing another patch of wastes, the eastern wastes this time. If they were lucky, they could avoid them by cutting south, but Alessi was rarely lucky. Kol's cloak whipped in the cool wind, and he shivered again. Alessi narrowed her eyes. It was getting colder. Maybe he was right, maybe it would snow. A dark shadow moved over them. Instinctively, Alessi leaped toward Kol, pulling him toward a pile of crumbling rocks.

"Get down!" she said. They crouched, pressed together in the sheltered space. She could smell him—that oily smell, the same one she smelled when they met. And that night... she shook her head. Mmm, the way he smelled. She couldn't let herself get used to it.

The dark shape passed overhead again, the wings of its shadow stretching out beside them. The shadow was black, like a darkness that absorbs all light, and she realized something had changed in Kol's face. He was different than he was when they left, but she could have sworn his eyes were lighter then. Now they were black, like endless pools, the same color as the black shadow that passed over them. She pushed the thought away, even if just temporarily.

Another shadow passed overhead, this one closer. She heard wings flapping and stood to get a better look. She bumped into him, and he gave her *that look* again. Blood rushed to her face. She was Alessi the dragon slayer. This was no time to be sentimental. Her eyes searched the sky above for a shape, some hint of the dragon hunting them, but all she found was a crow.

"You nearly scared the shit out of me, you dumb bird!" she yelled.

"Caw! Bitch be warned! Caw!" A voice came from the crow's direction.

"Ughhhhhh!" Alessi brought a hand to her forehead. A small, feathered creature descended from the clouds above, landing on her shoulder. "How the hells did you find me?"

"I can always find a bitch! Caw!" The bird-creature then turned its glowing green eyes on Kol. The light reflected and scattered off its feathers in a thousand colors.

"What is that thing?" Kol brought a curious finger to its beak, withdrawing it as the creature snapped.

"It's an Ikolki; it mimics human voices. They're used as messengers."

"Oh, like a parrot," he said.

"What's a parrot?"

"Oh. Well, they—"

"Never mind." Alessi brushed the bird off her shoulder with a hand. "If Viktor's Ikolki can find me, that means *he* can, too."

The creature settled on Alessi's forearm, which she held out in front of her. There was a time before the war when this bird was not an enemy. She spent almost her entire young life with Viktor and this dumb bird, and now... she clenched her jaw. She thought there was a future there, but she could never have a future with a dragon. Especially not one who had proven himself just as much a beast as the rest.

She leaned closer to the bird, then whispered, "Tell Viktor..." her voice trailed off. Tell Viktor to walk away from his cruel master and find another path? Tell Viktor she was sorry they became such bitter enemies, victims to powers larger and stronger than they could understand? He'd always told her she would never find someone better, and for a long time, she believed him.

She continued. "Tell Viktor I found someone better than him, but that I wish..." she looked around nervously. Kol didn't hear. "No, scratch that. Tell Viktor to go fuck himself." And with those refined words, she threw the bird back into the air. It took off, heading south away from the growing storm.

"What did you say?" Kol asked.

"I told Viktor to go fuck himself. They'll catch up soon, but thankfully we can go hide in Oniby. It's a witch merchant settlement, so we should be safe there."

Kol put a hand on her shoulder, and her heartbeat quickened. "Are you alright?"

"Yeah." She almost shook him off, but instead forced herself to let him linger there. It was nice. He was warm, and the heat radiating off his hand was a comfort. Maybe she had once loved Viktor, and every love since was like chasing that original high. But Kol was different, and it scared her. The night she shared with him was more real than anything she ever had with Viktor. It was like their one night together was the beginning of a new life, in a terrifying and unexplored world of opportunity.

She met Kol's dark eyes, and she smiled. And it was a genuine smile, because for the first time in a long time, she was happy. Still, it was hard to forget the magic growing stronger within him every day. Even with everything she'd seen and all her years behind her, in training, on her team, then as a fugitive, she wasn't sure exactly what was going on. Or, maybe she denied herself the tingling suspicion that slowly wormed its way to the forefront of her mind.

She would have to face the truth eventually.

25

Oniby was larger than Kol expected. The desert split in two before them, and at the base of the ravine sat a dilapidated town of gray faded wood built around the fork of a river, which once may have been mighty but was now little more than a greenish trickle. It took them all day, but the pair were at the canyon's base by sunset, dark clouds swirling high above.

Kol was exhausted. As he set foot on the packed-earth path leading into town, there was no glowing arch above him. Instead, they were greeted only by the remnants of a dead, brittle tree, one branch broken and hanging.

"One hell of a town," he muttered.

Alessi looked around, scrunching her nose. "It's a little emptier than I remember." She spread out her arms and twirled.

"It's creepy." A sign squeaked somewhere ahead, and Kol felt eyes on him. "We shouldn't stay here."

"What are you, afraid?" Alessi shot him her sideways smile, and he rolled his eyes.

"No, it's just... where is everyone?" The hair stood up on his arms.

"This is a city for witch merchants who were granted safe passage by the red king. Apparently, he loves money more than he hates witches. But business dries up sometimes, and people leave." Alessi rushed to the door of an inn. For a moment, Kol could almost ignore the claw marks and holes marring its dry, wooden side. "But hey, free lodging. No pickpocketing necessary." Alessi threw open the door and immediately coughed. She covered her mouth with one sleeve, and Kol peered in hesitantly.

The room smelled of ash and vinegar. Colorful dust gathered along its edges, but it didn't sparkle like what fell from Alessi and the Belgarri. He pinched his nose shut with one hand. The place smelled almost as bad as that man-creature in the house they'd escaped from. "Did something die in here?"

Alessi hopped over what may have once been a bar, its middle collapsed and splintered. She looked around, then back at him, and shrugged. "Who cares, it's free."

Kol lifted his lip in disgust as Alessi threw herself onto a sagging couch stained with crimson.

"Don't do that," Kol said.

"Why? Someone gonna stop me?" She flopped onto it again, and the couch protested, clouds of dust pluming all around her.

"No one's been here in a while, and there's probably a reason."

Alessi furrowed her brow. "You may have something there. The wastes are littered with ghost towns, most buried."

Kol thought for a moment. "And there wasn't an arch going into Oniby like there was in the other villages."

"This isn't a Belgarri village. Witch villages are different. If we're lucky, we should be able to find a Behor here to get the rest of the way."

"I don't like it here." Kol shook his head. He was sitting close to her, but not close enough to touch. "Let's get your be-whatever and leave."

"Behor. Witch mare. Fastest Belgarri in Alon." She bounced again, and Kol turned away from her. The weight of his pack cut into his shoulders, carving two itchy red lines into his skin. If not for his healing abilities, he imagined he'd have awful blisters by this point.

Alessi stopped bouncing, and rolled onto her side, one arm lolling off the filthy couch's edge. "Might as well get some sleep, there's something here I still want to see. Check out the upstairs."

"Fine. I'll go." As Kol rounded the steps, which were barely wide enough for him and his pack, the smell only grew stronger. There was a thick layer of the strange dust on this level, and he left deep footprints as he made his way to the various rooms. Each was empty, until he reached the room at the end of the hallway where the smell was strongest.

The door creaked open, and inside was a bed with the center burned out. Bits of charred paper flew in the breeze as Kol slammed the door shut again.

"Come see this!" he yelled down the hall. Within moments, the irritated witch was beside him.

"Good gods, I thought there was a dragon or something. Don't call me like that."

"No. Look." Kol opened the door, this time not allowing himself to look at the horror. Alessi stepped inside, placing one clawed hand on the door handle. It almost touched his own.

"Oh shit," she said.

"It's magic, isn't it?"

"Yeah." Alessi lowered herself to the ground, tracing one finger in the ash. She licked it. "Hunting Fire."

"So, the dragons came here, probably killed all these people?"

"Yes, and they always come back to check for survivors." Alessi's eyes darted to the open window, which she slammed shut with a fluid motion. The burned pieces of paper stopped dancing in the breeze, and Alessi returned to the door. "We can't stay," she said.

Kol let the door close behind them as they made their way back down the narrow stairs, the smell of ash and vinegar growing more faint. "I told you something wasn't right." He had sensed it before they even entered the city, though he couldn't explain why.

Alessi spun around, taking the steps backwards. She crossed her arms and furrowed her brow. "How did you know?"

How did you know? "How did you not?"

Alessi let out a snort before leaping to where she left her pack beside the sagging couch. She threw it on her shoulder. "Sure, whatever. Up the canyon we go."

"I thought your witch senses or whatever would tell you this place was bad news." To him it seemed obvious, but he was beginning to suspect magic dust wasn't the only thing he could see, or sense, that she couldn't. This distinction was still subtle but had grown increasingly obvious since he healed her wound back in the druid forest. He wanted to tell her, to talk about it again, but it was too dangerous. If he could sense her intentions, predict her reactions, only then would he be safe drawing attention to his abilities.

Alessi laughed, though quieter than usual. "Witch senses, right. Look, even if I had sensed something, there's nothing inherently wrong about an empty village. Usually it's a good thing, stuff to plunder and no one watching your every move. But this is another story."

There was movement overhead, and a winged shadow passed outside.

"Another crow?" Kol asked.

"Nope."

"So... how does one escape a dragon?" Kol whispered.

"You don't."

"What?"

"Shh, I'm thinking."

Kol heard wingbeats overhead. "Hey, there's—"

"Shh! I'm trying to remember something. There are caves near here, those should be—" The wingbeats grew louder, and Alessi's eyes widened. "Got it. Come on!"

The two began running alongside the river that cut through the center of town. The sand shifted under Kol's boots, slowing him down. Alessi slipped and let herself fall to all fours, clawing at the sandy earth like an animal.

It was no use.

Something crunched behind them, and Kol turned around, falling against his pack. A serpentine creature with a golden back and orange belly perched on the dead tree that marked Oniby's entrance. The trunk bent and swayed beneath it, and the loosely hanging branch fell with a thud to the ground below.

"Are you saying you knew? Why didn't you say something?" Alessi asked.

She had interrupted him earlier. "I did, but you—"

"But what?" she asked. He could hear the frustration in her voice.

"Nothing." Now was not the time to fight amongst themselves—something was wrong. The air was too heavy, and the flowing water too slow. The dragon didn't make any attempt to follow them, and instead watched with peculiar intent from where it sat. And, strangely enough, no matter how fast Kol ran, each time he turned around the dragon seemed to be the same distance.

Alessi looked around. Gentle notes drifted through the air, and for a moment Kol thought he would fall asleep. Then, she fell in the sand and pounded the ground with one hand. "Fuck."

"What?" Kol asked. They had run so far, he should have been exhausted, but instead his body only felt heavy. He let himself fall to the ground beside her.

"Their blue dragon isn't just a mimic, he's also a lyramancer, a music mage."

"*Oh shit,*" Kol said under his breath. He knew she was right. Somehow, this magic felt the same as that dragon they met before. It was stronger than a smell, almost as if he could *taste* the man's essence.

Alessi lazed in the sand.

"Let's get out of here! What are you doing?" Kol asked. He scrambled to his feet, but Alessi didn't move.

She laid on her back, picking up a handful of sand and sprinkling it across her torso. "Yeah. We can run all we want, but we won't go anywhere."

Kol had to step over her to get ahead. "Don't just lay there! Come on!"

"You're dreaming, Kol. We both are."

His heart almost stopped, or was that an illusion, too? "But the dragon—"

"An illusion, a dream. This is the result of that lyramancer blue dragon and illusionist golden dragon working together. We passed out along the bank, right here."

Kol let himself fall to the ground. This didn't feel like the illusions he faced in the Valley of Dragons. It felt more real, more dangerous. He collapsed into the sand beside her, the sand settling around his knees. "What do we do?"

"Calm down. If they wanted us dead, we'd already be dead. We just have to wait for them to wake us," she said.

They sat along that riverbank for what felt like hours. As time passed, it grew more difficult to talk, or to move, and eventually all they could do was lie down next to each other in the sand. Panic built up within him. If he was dying, this was his last chance to tell her the truth. At least if he died this way, she wouldn't have a chance to kill him.

"Ales..." He couldn't speak. It was like his mouth was full of mud. He regretted not being able to tell her, even if it ended in his death. And if his future was the one his mother escaped, a life of being used and hated, maybe it was better to be killed by her hand.

He used the last of his energy to roll himself onto his back. The sky was big and blue above him, and the trees swayed gently in the wind. It wasn't the worst way to go, falling asleep with the birds chirping and the water rolling beside him. Even if it was an illusion, at least he could be here with Alessi. Using the last of his strength, he rested his hand on hers. She was cold. Her eyes were shut, and she did not stir. The urge to sleep was too hard to resist. He took one last look at the great blue sky above, then shut his eyes.

26

When he opened his eyes, Kol was tied up in a dark space. Ropes cut into his wrists, shoulders, and chest. Sweat—and maybe blood, he couldn't tell—half-blinded him. He struggled against his binds, thrashing back and forth before twisting his neck to one side to see Alessi. Her cheek swelled, a cut running across it.

Koh looked up to see a man with glowing golden eyes and a vicious half-smile standing in front of her. It was Viktor.

"The little weirdo's awake," Viktor said.

Kol spat blood onto the ground. "Let us go!"

"Or you'll do what? Spit on me?" Viktor rolled his eyes. "You should have never left your hole." He walked over to Kol, tilting Kol's chin one way and then the other, inspecting him. "You could fetch some coin, if I were to sell you to a *freakshow*."

"Fuck you," Alessi snarled. "Leave him alone."

"Oh, found a new pet, I see? Will you betray this one as well?" Viktor laughed.

Alessi hissed through her teeth. "He's just a human. I'm the one you want. Fight me again, fair and square. You want to prove yourself, right?"

"I'm not falling for that again." Viktor straightened, reaching his full, lean height. He may have been the tallest Belgarri Kol had ever seen in his time on the surface. At that moment, Kol realized Viktor was the serpentine dragon he had seen in the illusion. Their essence was the same. Golden dust glimmered on his skin, falling to the ground as he walked over to Alessi and punched her in the face.

Alessi grimaced, blood red-black against her white teeth. "Double fuck you." Her shoulders cracked as she flexed against the binds. "I loved you, you asshole!"

"Don't try to prey on sentimentality I don't have. This time, ego won't get the best of me." Viktor faced away from her. "You witches are disgusting. You could have been better than that, but you had to—" He clenched his jaw, stopping himself. "Lysander you idiot, get in here!"

The blue-haired man entered the cave with a lyre in his hand. "Did you like my magic, sir?"

"Yes, yes, it was good enough until you stopped, and they woke up." Viktor shook his head. "But no matter. We are here to apprehend Alessandra, wanted by his highness the red king for crimes against dragons. Would you like to hear your list of accusations?"

"No," Alessi hissed.

"First, Alessandra, now commonly referred to as Alessi the Dragon Slayer—a ridiculous name by the way—was sent to execute General Myan for treason. Instead, she killed his wife, Myata, in cold blood and proceeded to tear her limb from limb before devouring her left arm."

Alessi's lip trembled. "You were there, you dumb shit. You know what happened."

"It was a mistake," Kol said in her defense.

"You don't know this woman, so don't defend her. Even if this was a mistake, what about all the others? What of a woman who regrets not her actions, but getting caught?" Viktor placed a hand on her head. His fingers were long and beautiful, powerful but also delicate. Then he squeezed.

Alessi threw herself against her binds and released something neither scream nor roar. Kol thought of the sounds his father's lambs made before they were slaughtered. It was an empty, helpless sound. Viktor squeezed harder.

Kol fought against his binds again, but it was no use. He could feel his skin healing where the ropes cut into them, but he could not escape.

"Your other crimes are as follows. You took underground bounties claiming the lives of the green dragon and healer Renka of the western woods, scholar and teacher Edwin of the mountain Kur..." With each name Viktor said, Alessi thrashed more. There were so many. Kol's eyes unfocused, and a numbness crept over him. The Alessi he knew was not the same cold-hearted killer, right? Only when Viktor spoke the last name did Kol's awareness fully return. "... and the golden dragon Narine of the southern seas."

Narine. Kol recalled the feeling of her lips on his cheek. It was real, all of it.

"What say you, witch?" the golden-eyed man asked.

"There were bounties on their heads! They were criminals! Murderers!" Alessi hissed. This was wrong—Narine wasn't a criminal. She couldn't have been.

"And what are you?" Viktor asked. He put a boot on her chest, putting a temporary stop to her thrashing. "Those were not real bounties, just purses offered by peoples' enemies. You're a hitman, a standard criminal, not a bounty hunter."

"What are you doing? You know you're no better than I am."

"In the eyes of the law?" Viktor pressed harder. "I don't think so."

"You don't understand what it's been like for me," Alessi growled. "You know I was set up that first time. I'm an outcast everywhere I go because of what happened, and now bounty hunting is the only work I can do. Call it murder all you want, but I did what I had to survive."

Viktor sneered, putting his fingers under her chin, forcing her to look at him. "You've stooped to new lows. I've heard the rumors... maybe after this, we can—" She bit his fingers, then thrashed her head back and forth like a wolf tearing apart prey. Viktor screamed, struggling to get away, but his hand was held in Alessi's jaws.

There was a sickening crunch, then Alessi swallowed. "You taste better than I remember."

"You bitch!" Viktor raised his bloodied hand as if to strike, then froze. He was missing half of both his middle and index fingers.

"Yeah, thought so." Alessi grinned. "I'd bet you want to kill me now, but you need me alive, don't you?"

Viktor fumed in silence.

"Come on, fucking do it." Alessi raised her chin, exposing her neck, but Viktor wouldn't strike. "You're a fucking coward. Kill me or tell that asshole king of yours to come after me himself." Blood and spit flew from Alessi's mouth and onto Viktor's face as she spoke. "Killing our friends was the wrong move. You should want vengeance, too."

"This is vengeance. Lysander," Viktor said through his teeth with calculated precision. His jaw was still clenched from the pain. "How do we find her?"

"Guilty," Lysander replied.

"And the human?" Viktor asked.

"Leave him out of this!" Alessi hissed.

Lysander thought for a moment. "I'm not sure, maybe we should leave him—"

"No!" Viktor's eyes looked like they could pop out of his head from the fury. "He's an accomplice. He wasn't part of the deal, so let's kill him and take her back to meet her fate."

Kol's hands balled into fists. A thought crept into his mind. He didn't want to die, and given the recent developments with his magic, he wasn't entirely sure he *could.* So, regardless of his injuries, he was more concerned about Alessi, her cheek swollen and blood dripping down her face.

"Take her out of here." Viktor gestured to Lysander with his bleeding hand, and Lysander nodded.

"Alessi." He looked to Alessi, but she hung limp, tied to a stake. "Use your magic."

"The rope's enchanted. As long as it's around her hands, she's useless." Viktor's neck craned until his eyes settled on Kol's, burning into them.

Instinct kicked in, and Kol's lips drew back into a snarl. "Back off." His voice was lower, like a stranger's.

"You're an odd human, aren't you?" Viktor grew closer, like a predator. No, he *was* a predator. "Though I guess that whore would have killed a regular human some time ago."

Kol searched for words. "You shouldn't say that about the princess—"

"Of witches?" Viktor laughed. "She's a bastard and a psychopath. Your naïve ass is just along for the ride."

"How could you speak that way about her? Weren't you friends?" Kol spit as he spoke, his unusually low tone wearing off near the end of his sentence. Viktor wiped saliva off his face with an impatient finger.

"You may think you know her better than me, but you don't." Viktor looked down his nose at Kol. "You're just some foolish human. Lysander."

Lysander waved his wrist, and an ice blade materialized in his hand. He brought it close to Kol's neck and moved as if to slash.

"Wait." Another man stepped into the cave. Kol's eyes locked with his, and memories danced at the edge of Kol's mind. This was the red dragon who let him go in the druid's forest.

"Red," Kol said, "don't let them do this. There's been a huge misunderstanding."

"Shhh! Go outside before he—" Lysander began.

"Yes, Red. I thought you said you wanted to *sit this one out*, in your own words. Or are you determined to ruin everything we've worked for?" There was venom in Viktor's words. "You're fucking useless. I don't know what the king sees in you."

Red's eyes rested on Viktor's bloodied finger stumps, which the dragon quickly hid behind his back. "The human wasn't part of this."

"Yes," Viktor said through gritted teeth. "That's why we're killing him."

"That wasn't part of the job," Red said, eyes locking with Kol's. There was something familiar about this man. He had sensed it earlier but now he knew for sure. They'd met before. But when? The only other person on the outside Kol might know is Caliban, and Caliban was...

Could it be?

Irritated, Viktor spun around to face Red. "You don't call the shots here, rookie."

"Let the human go." Red's presence was larger than his body, as if he took up the whole room. His eyes narrowed, and Viktor stepped back. It was at that point Kol realized that, for all his posturing, Viktor was afraid of Red. It made sense— Viktor's illusion magic was likely no match for Red's fire.

"I'd have killed you and dumped your body in the ravine if General Suta wasn't so fond of you." Viktor's lips now drew back in a snarl, serpentine fangs replacing his human canine teeth. "You're a damned mongrel bastard. I've seen every kind of mutant and creepy crawly out here, but you are by far the most annoying."

He recognizes you, even if he doesn't realize why. It was his mother's voice—it felt like so long since he heard it.

Kol's heartbeat quickened. Things just got a lot more complicated.

So, he was right. Everything clicked.

"I hope I bought you enough time." Red raised his chin in Alessi's direction, and Kol turned to see a wide grin on the witch's face. She flexed her scaled hand, raising her claws in front of her.

"What?" Viktor asked, eyes widening.

"Never turn your back on a target." Alessi made a clicking noise with her tongue before slashing herself free of her bonds. With a fluid motion, she pinned Lysander to the ground, claws at his throat. He reached for his lyre, the one he must have used to put them to sleep earlier, but she smashed it with a fist. "You idiots didn't tie me tight enough. Remember that next time."

Alessi punched Viktor in the face, sending him flying to the ground. He didn't move, but his chest rose slowly up and down —he was still alive. Alessi stood, flexing her claws, then Kol felt her warm fingers wrap around his wrist. His eyes locked with Red's one last time. He had always imagined meeting Caliban, but never would he have imagined it would be like this. He had to say something, but what could he say that could tell the entire story? A story Caliban—Red—might not even believe?

"Caliban!" Kol cried out, but Alessi was already dragging him away. He fought her.

"What are you doing?" She hissed.

Confusion spread over Red's face.

"Who are you? How do you know my name?" he asked, but within seconds Kol and Alessi were out the cave and down the side of the ravine. He stumbled over a root, barely able to keep his feet under him, his chest heaving and sweat and blood plastering his hair to his face. With a flick of her wrist, Alessi drew a spinning ball of water out of the trickle of a river and into her hand.

"That whole mess weakened me and I'm almost out of magic," Alessi said. "I'll have to eat more soon. So, make this last," she said, sending water into his ears, a dull pain radiating from them.

He winced. "Why are you blocking our ears? I thought you smashed the lyre?" His voice was muffled.

"That just bought us time. He'll put it back together."

Their pursuers were nearly at the end of the canyon, where the river emptied into a marshy, green plain.

"*Come on*," Alessi mouthed as Kol tripped over branches and brambles, sinking into the mud. She navigated the space like a cat, jumping from branch to branch.

Kol pulled himself up, then felt at his ears. Ice. Right. It felt disorienting to watch the world around him with no sound. Something shifted in the darkness, inches from Alessi. Alessi leaped from her branch. Then, in a flash of shadow, a moment of darkness, she was gone. His chest heaved, and he twisted his head back to see Viktor, Lysander, and the red-haired man reaching the first broken branches. As the ice in his ears melted, he heard the squishing of soil beneath his feet.

"Where'd she go?" Kol could barely recognize Viktor's voice, muffled as if underwater. "She's here, I can smell her filth."

"I'm not sure," Lysander said.

"And Red?"

"Taken care of."

Could Kol have come so far to find his brother, only for his brother to be murdered moments after? He pushed the thought away, but in a moment of carelessness a branch broke under his feet and both Viktor and Lysander turned their heads to look at him. He hid behind a tree and let himself sink into the muck until he could no longer see them, sheltered by the tree's great roots. He slipped, sliding forward until he rested in swampy water up to his knees.

"I hear you," Viktor said. "I know where you are. Come on out. Let's make this easy."

Gentle music started drifting his way, and his body grew heavy. If he were to fall asleep now, he would drown in the murky waters. There was a great crashing sound beyond, coming from where the dragons stood. He pressed his back against the trunk, nestling his body between its crawling roots. Something drew closer, and the trees above him swayed.

"I smell you, strange one." This was the same voice as the golden-eyed man, but also not. It reminded him of Azazel's voice, but lower, deeper, as if a thousand golden-eyed men all spoke at once. Kol took a sharp breath as a pink shape flicked overhead. A forked tongue. A golden, slit-pupiled eye followed it.

"You didn't seriously think you could outrun a dragon," Viktor, in his dragon form, said. His voice rumbled through Kol's body like thunder. Kol's terror was almost overshadowed by his sheer awe and might of the dragon's form. He held still, feeling the dragon's hot, wet breath against his face. The music grew stronger, as did his desire to sleep. The ice in his ears had mostly melted.

Viktor's tongue tasted the air. "Ah, it makes sense now."

Kol glared at him.

"You're one of us, aren't you?" Viktor narrowed one eye,

bringing it close to Kol, inspecting him. "You look like a human, but there's something else, too. I've been trying to figure it out, but now I think I see it..." Golden dust fell from his skin like a glimmering shadow, landing in the murky water below. "You see my magic, don't you?"

"Yes," Kol said after a moment.

"So you're one of us. We can let you go," Viktor said, "if you tell us where she is."

Kol remembered her vanishing overhead, as if swallowed up by shadows. Vanishing in midair, mid-jump, as if she never existed. "I don't know." A root's sharp, knobby knee dug into his side.

"You shouldn't protect her." The dragon lowered its head, its forked tongue whipping inches from Kol's face. "She doesn't deserve your protection. I learned that the hard way." He drew back, studying Kol's expression. "Or what if I offer that loser Red in exchange for her? Since you had such an... *interest* in him."

"Fuck you," Kol said.

"Bold thing to say to someone who could rip you limb from limb."

"You just try," Kol said. "I wouldn't tell you where Alessi is even if I knew."

Viktor snorted, his hot breath whipping Kol's hair into his face where it lay plastered to his skin with sweat and filth. The dragon reared back on its hind legs, craning its neck downward to look at Kol, and brought one clawed, scaly finger to Kol's chest.

"Do you know what makes dragon claws so special?" the dragon asked.

"I'm familiar."

"Good." The claw pressed against Kol's flesh, and he let out a grunt. He put both hands on the dragon's finger in a futile attempt to push him away, but he knew it was no use.

"Tell me."

"I. Don't. Know."

The dragon's claw pierced his skin, and he let out a shriek this time.

"Oh, you little lost lamb. She already betrayed you. If you tell us where she is, we'll put you right back in a *hole* where you belong." The serpentine dragon said it in a way to suggest that this hole may not be the same one he was from.

There was a noise above. Viktor roared, falling back. His tail thrashed as it rolled to both sides, and Kol soon realized why. It was severed at the base, as if by some giant, sharp blade.

"That's enough. Let's go." With her right hand, Alessi tugged at Kol's arm, pulling him out of the muck and onto tangled roots.

"I thought you left me," Kol said as they took off down the path.

"Why would I do that?"

"You were gone. Where were you?" There was a crashing in the swamp behind them.

"Above you, waiting for the right moment."

Something dark opened up ahead, a black mound amidst the sprawling roots and dangling branches. The crashing behind them was closer now.

"We're free, we just need to make it past the Esprata." Alessi looked over Kol's shoulder, meeting his eyes for a moment. "If we're lucky, it'll help us."

"The what?" Kol asked, but Alessi's foot was already on the mound, stepping once on it before jumping over it. He did the same, but the mound shook beneath him.

Alessi stopped running several meters beyond, and Kol followed suit. He doubled over, his chest heaving from the chase. Alessi dug the claws of her scaled hand into the mound's side, sending tendrils of ice shooting across its surface. The shape lifted from the water, and the dragon and his two companions beyond slowed their pace. Water dripped as the mound—the *Esprata*, Kol realized—uncurled its hardened shell to reveal a beaked face and far too many legs, twisted and reaching in every direction like a twitching carpet. It dove at them, but they nimbly dodged, and the beast quickly distracted itself with their pursuers. The pair ran forward.

"We lost them," Alessi said, looking back.

"What the hell is that thing?" Kol asked between gasping breaths.

"An Esprata. You can always find them where rivers end."

"I don't like leaving Red behind," Kol said

"He'll be fine. Dragons are notoriously hard to kill," Alessi said.

She would know. This thought left Kol with a feeling of unease, and yet, she had just saved his life again. Guilt settled in his heart. He told himself again she wasn't that same person. Her situation wasn't her fault, she was forced into it out of desperation. She had shown regret, and kindness, and tenderness, to him—granted, when she didn't know his true identity. Kol paused for a moment, feeling at his bleeding chest. He winced as his fingers slid past layers of skin and muscle, peeled back by the dragon's claw. It hurt, but already the edges of the wound were starting to knit together.

Alessi reached into her pocket and withdrew the same sort of purple fruit he saw her eating many days before. She tossed it to him. "Eat it. It'll help with the pain."

"Thanks."

"Don't thank me, I got you into this mess. You'd be safe in your hole if not for me."

Kol took a bite of the fruit, which exploded like a citrus

bomb in his mouth. He wasn't about to tell her he'd rather be out here, in the blistering sun and sanded winds, than in the hole he was born into. His foot sunk, and he looked down to see the moist floor of the swamp give way to muddy sand which dried up ahead. They walked out of a basin and into dunes like where they were before.

A shriek came from behind them, between the roars of the Esprata. "You can't run from fate forever, Alessandra!"

She took a stone in her hand and hurled it in the voice's direction. "Bastards!" She looked at him, and smiled, but something sank in his gut.

"Did you hear anything back there?" Kol asked. His body ached all over—he was still tired from the music.

"Not much. Why?" Alessi asked.

"Uh." What could he tell her? If she'd heard Viktor's words about Kol being a dragon, this could be a problem. "Just... curious. Did you see Viktor attack me?"

"Sort of. I was busy throwing Lysander's lyre off a cliff."

"Alright. Thanks." He wasn't sure what else to say. At least he wouldn't have to explain why his chest wound had already closed, or why he had no scrapes or scratches from running through the forest. Hopefully the filth and grime on his body would cover for him, at least for now, and he could blame the tear in his shirt on a branch. He had to tell her. He would tell her. Eventually.

"What's wrong?" She raised an eyebrow. "And why did you call that red dragon by another name?"

He was silent. If Alessi knew that his brother was a dragon, it wouldn't be hard to put the pieces together. And yet if he didn't, he wasn't sure how long he could stand this pressure building in his chest, threatening to eat him from the inside out. She rested her head on his shoulder, wrapping her arm around his chest.

She wasn't ready. Maybe she would never be ready.

"I was worried back there," she said. Her wrists bled where she was bound, and her left horn had a nick on it. This was the closest he had come to dying. He wrapped his arm around her, and they embraced each other. Her smell overwhelmed him, and her magic glimmered on her skin like silver dust.

He couldn't keep lying. He exhaled, holding her apart from him with his hands on her shoulders. "There's something I have to tell you."

Branches snapped behind him, and he turned to see a commotion in the woods. Not only had Viktor survived, but so had the Esprata. This time, the creature had deployed, membranous white wings lining its body, large and plentiful as its vicious legs. It flew through the trees with grace, diving at Viktor and Lysander, who had adopted the form of a squat blue dragon.

"They're leading it to us," Alessi said. "Let's go!" They ran away from the forest, which turned to a grassland, which turned to stone. The greenery disappeared in front of them, replaced by a cliff and a crater in the ground that stretched as far as Kol could see. Pillars rose from the crater, and clouds drifted between them, obscuring many of the further ones.

They were close enough to the edge for him to see the bottom—only, he couldn't. There was only an eternity of mist. "We can't go down there," Kol said.

"We have to." Alessi made as if to climb down the cliff. No way he was doing that, but maybe if they took one of the vines that webbed the space, connecting the various stone islands...

"We can swing across!" He gestured to the vine. One of the pillars wasn't too far, and there was a sliver of a chance they could make it. Given those odds, however, he wasn't entirely sure he didn't prefer to face the dragons.

Alessi looked at him incredulously. "We'd be a splat on the side of a distant cliff. We'll have to fly."

"Fly?"

She let go of Kol's hand and dug her heels into the rocky earth, pebbles tumbling into the abyss as she changed direction. The dragons were so close, and so was the Esprata.

"Have a taste of your own medicine, witch," Viktor roared. His face bled. He tore at the Esprata's wings with his claws, sending the now even more furious millipede creature flying toward them.

"Perfect timing. This will be the last of my old magic." Alessi leaped into the air. She landed on the Esprata's back, slicing off a pair of small white wings with a thin blade of ice. It threw back its head and shrieked. She opened her mouth, unhinging her jaw.

In that moment, she was an animal, a beast. His blood ran cold, but Kol forced himself to keep watching. This was a side of Alessi he had only seen once, the devouring side, where her hunger led. Bones cracked as she tore into two wings—flesh, membrane, and bone as if it were nothing. It was unnatural looking, maybe the most unnatural thing he had ever seen. And yet, she was still dignified, even beautiful, with black blood dripping down her chin. The creature's tail whipped him in the gut, sending him sliding nearly over the edge of the cliff. He caught himself on the edge, chest heaving and tasting bile.

Survive, he heard his mother's voice. *Kill the dragons and the beast if the witch fails.*

All of them? How?

Destroying life is easier than fixing it.

What?

You've done it before. You should know.

His mind flipped to the dragon in the flats. He looked over the cliff and into the blackness looming beneath. There was nowhere to run, and if he were to jump—he imagined his broken body lying below in the darkness, found only by ravens. He stood, feeling his organs shift as his ribs knitted back together, and made his way to the edge of the cliff. Maybe he would find this sensation less disturbing someday, but it was unlikely.

Alessi broke off two sticks from the tree and jumped over the still screaming Esparata, jamming them into its eyes. She changed directions, leaping toward Kol. In an instant, he knew what she was going to do. Her shoulder met the center of his chest, and the pair tumbled into the abyss below.

27

Kol and Alessi fell through the mists.

"What were you thinking?" Kol yelled over the rushing air. "We're going to die!"

"We won't!" Alessi said, wind whipping her hair in a stream above her head as they spun.

"We will!" Kol wrapped his arms around her. They spun faster. His eyes watered from the brutal winds.

"Just give me a second." Alessi shut her eyes.

Fog enveloped them, moist air clinging to Kol's skin. He could have imagined they were floating, just the two of them, if he weren't so terrified.

"What are you doing?" he yelled.

"I'm sorry." The wind dried tears on Alessi's face. "I thought this would work. I need you to do me a favor."

"Anything." Kol looked down at the white nothing below. They could hit the ground in an instant, or in a lifetime. He had no way of knowing.

"Pain speeds the transmutation. Bite me!"

"What?" Kol's voice broke. "No!"

"Then I'll do it." Alessi dug her teeth into the soft flesh of her upper arm, ripping it side to side like a wolf tearing apart a corpse. Blood soaked from her fresh wound and onto his shirt.

There was a moment of clarity, then another cloud. Alessi screamed and arched her back. Two shapes, white and covered in mucus, tore through the back of her cloak. She stretched out the membranous appendages and let the wind dry them.

"How did you do that?" Kol held on tight as their descent slowed.

She smiled, her teeth stained with black blood. "I stole the Esprata's wings. I'm a witch, after all."

With powerful beats of her new, blood-smeared wings, their fall slowed. While they looked far too small on the Esprata, they were just the right size to keep the two of them in the air. Kol twisted his head to see jagged rocks and a river below them. As she pounded her wings, and they moved upward, he held onto her for dear life. The clouds twisted around them, swirling in little eddies as she flew.

"Thank gods. I didn't actually think that was going to work," she said.

His heartbeat quickened. "*What?*"

"Well, I had a suspicion."

"You threw us off a cliff because you had a suspicion?"

"Transmutations are fast, but they're faster when I'm in pain." The new appendages shined crimson-white in the sun's light as she flew over the mists, toward one of the rocky pillars stretching from the white nothingness below.

Kol reached a hand up, tracing the white flesh. Scales covered these wings, as inhuman as her arm, though smoother in texture.

"I hope you like 'em, because I'm stuck with 'em," Alessi said. "Unless I cut them off."

"Why would you do that?" Kol asked. "You can fly! That's incredible! You're incredible!"

Alessi's face reddened—or at least he thought so. She was so covered in blood it was hard to tell. "Stealing power works in a pinch but steal too much and you turn into a beast. Some of the older witches look like dragons, others like mountains or trees. Steal too much, and you forget yourself, the legends say. I'd say my mother already has."

This power was incredible, but she was right—it had a cost. His imagination drifted. What did the queen look like? How many sets of wings did she have by now? He imagined another version of Alessi, more dragon than human. If that happened to her someday, would she still be the person he knew?

She set him down, then landed a few feet further on the one of the flat-topped spires dotting the landscape. Besides a few shrubs, it was as wind-whipped and barren as the wastes.

Kol fell to the ground, letting his body go limp. With the tension gone, it was like there was nothing holding him together. The fog obscured the cliff they fell from. The world around him was one of gray and brown-green, white-water vapor floating on updrafts around them. Alessi sat beside him. Kol let himself lay back, looking at her wings. It was still hard for him to move, as if he was the one who had flown them across the chasm. At their base, where they'd ripped through her cloak, they met her skin in a heap of mottled tissue.

"Those wings look like they hurt," he said.

Alessi laughed. "Not as much as getting our skulls crushed at the bottom of the cliff."

28

Something twinkled through the mist that shrouded the stone spire-island. Kol squinted, but it was just out of sight. Alessi stayed behind as he stood. Dry brush crunched beneath his feet as he made his way toward the light. The sound of running water grew louder as he neared a silver pool in the center of the pillar-island, large and round enough to capture the rising moon's reflection. He stuck his hands in it, the cold water running over his skin. For a moment, he could almost imagine he was back at the starshatter pool with Narine and the others, but this water was muddied and impure.

He drank, then ran his wet hands over his face and sat back. So much had happened. The warm wind rustled his hair and cleared some of the mist to reveal the edge of the island and the blackness beyond. Alessi was incredible—she had probably saved his life twice in only the past day, but questions still nagged him. What would happen once they reached the red king's palace? To her? To him?

Something caught Kol's eye, a glint underneath the water, likely what summoned him to that spot. He leaned forward, wincing as he placed his hands on sharp stones, cutting into the soft flesh of his palms. The bright white object glinted again, reflecting the silver moonlight. With his hand, he pushed a layer of the sharp stones off its smooth surface.

It was a skull.

Kol scrambled out of the water, eying it like it was about to bite him. It didn't move—of course it didn't—so he cautiously approached it again.

Kol withdrew, but curiosity got the best of him. He let himself back into the water, crawling towards it. The skull was humanoid, and a bleach white—it had been there for some time.

He tried to pick it up, but it was stuck, so he cleared pebbles and silt off it. Only its eyes and forehead were visible at first, the rest buried in the sands and pebbles of the shallow pool, and he felt the slippery bone as he slipped his fingers through its eye sockets, trying to pick it up again. He twisted the skull, shaking it until it came loose. It was then he saw the reason it held so much weight, the reason it fought against him.

Two horns came free from the rocks and debris. They were longer than Alessi's and almost twice the length of the skull itself, curling backwards and around themselves. Its two long fangs were the only teeth left in its grinning, lipless mouth.

"You found a witch grave," Alessi said, startling him. She crouched in the dry sands beside him, red streaking her new white wings. "This all used to be witch territory."

"Really?"

"Yeah. It used to be a witch's greatest desire to be buried in the floating islands when she dies."

Kol released the skull, and it sank below the waters.

With a flick of her wrist, the stones freed themselves from the bottom of the pool, carried to the opposite end by her strong and sudden current. More skulls emerged, with horns of all shapes and sizes, some straight and others twisted into intricate shapes.

There were so many. Too many. How many skulls was he standing on, and what was in that water he drank? Kol stepped backward until his feet met soil.

"Jumping was risky, but I thought that maybe, if we'd died, it wouldn't be so bad if we rested among the great witches of the past. Our only other option was to get torn apart by the Esprata. Life's full of shit choices." Alessi forced a stiff laugh, then twisted her arms to feel under her new wings. The bleeding where the wings exited her body had stopped, and now thick scabs marked where the wings had torn through her flesh. "Sometimes I wonder about the choice the first witch made."

"First witch?" Kol could tell being a witch wasn't always something she was proud of, so it was nice to see her open up. Maybe it was being so close to death, having so narrowly escaped it, that urged her on.

"She was a human, a regular one, just like you," Alessi said. Kol's stomach churned, but he tried not to show it. "And she had to choose between killing her lover and being powerless. She killed him, but always regretted her choice. They say it ate her up inside, and I'm sure it did."

"Sounds like your mother and Fenvir," Kol said.

"You're right. There are differences to the stories, but I wouldn't be surprised if she was the first witch. She's gone by a hundred different names, and no one knows how old she is." Alessi stretched out her wings. They were still damp from their early growth, glistening in the dim light.

Kol reached out a hesitant hand.

"Go on," she said. "You touched them earlier."

Kol felt the cool leather against his fingers, running the membranes between his thumb and index fingers. They shined so brightly in the moon, above the pool of silver water. "They're amazing, the things you can do. So much more than me. And now you can fly."

Then it struck him. Why he hadn't thought of it before, he wasn't sure, but he was a dragon. Maybe he *could* fly.

Can I? he asked.

There was no response. He felt at his mother's pendant around his neck, something he hadn't done in some time. It was like her voice, their connection, was growing weaker. Above, the moon was only a sliver.

Alessi raised an eyebrow. "There's something odd about you." She was smiling, so she couldn't suspect the truth, right? "You've changed. What's on your mind?"

He had changed. He knew it. And if he let her talk about it too much, he feared the adrenaline in his veins may make him say something careless. He couldn't tell her why—he couldn't tell her the whole truth—but he had to tell her something. "I was thinking about my mother. I did find her in the Valley of Dragons."

"Why didn't you tell me?" Alessi almost sounded hurt, her face adorning a callous mask.

"She was dead."

Alessi pried no further, and the two sat in silence beside one another on the lonely rock. She knew something, or at least suspected, but as long as he didn't ask, the two of them could pretend nothing was wrong. They could pretend they were the same people they were when their journey started.

Eventually, Alessi wordlessly left his side and made her way to the edge of the pillar. And when she took to the sky with her new wings, her hair the same silver as the moonlight filling the sky, the unsettled feeling in Kol's stomach made it almost impossible to appreciate the beauty of her magic.

29

The soft silt around the moon pool was more comfortable than Kol expected, forming an indentation around his body as he slept. He woke to the sound of distant songbirds, and a feeling of emptiness. Even Alessi's boot in his back would have given him more comfort than that.

"Are you ready?" Alessi asked. "It's time to go."

Kol groaned, rubbing sand and sleep from his eyes. The sun rose some hours ago.

"Gods, we're high up." Kol peered over the edge, feeling his heart lurch in his chest. "How are we getting out of here?"

Alessi walked up to him, wrapping her arms around him, face-to-face. Did this mean everything was fine?

"Same way we got here," she said. He could feel her breath against his lips—they were so close. She leaned into him, and their lips touched before she unfurled her wings and took to the sky. An unsettled feeling was still in the back of Kol's mind, yet Alessi was acting like everything was normal.

"Fuck, you're heavy," Alessi said.

"Is that why you like being on top?"

She laughed, and he could feel her voice reverberating through him. They were so close together. The sun shone in his eyes as they continued east, passing over countless rocky spires and clouds of mist which curled around Alessi's wingtips. A cliff rose ahead. Nearly its entire face was a waterfall, and Kol realized where the mists came from, curling up from the fall's base and rising into the sky in a milky fog. Alessi spread her still wings wide, riding the draft up before banking right and heading toward a clump of trees. He twisted his head, squinting at them. Where he may have expected varying shades of green, there were instead blacks and purples.

"That was the red king's forest," Alessi said, "but it's just ash and charcoal now."

Kol watched the black and purple trees grow closer, and they landed at the top of the basin by the bank of the shallow sea. The forest's darkness was oppressive, even in daylight. The shadows had a strange color about them, too, like oil on water. Every color, but muted and dark.

The sun beat on them from overhead. It was hot here. Wet, too. The sea's waters lapped against black sands, oily like the shadows of trees, strange little shelled creatures crawling in the shallows. Shadows darted about the forest.

"What are those?" Kol asked.

"More feral Belgarri. Stay close."

Shiny, black eyes peered between purple leaves and around black trunks. The creatures stayed out of the sunlight, relegating themselves to shadow, but Kol could see they were the same iridescent colors as Alessi's now-missing cloak, which she must have discarded after her transformation.

With a flick of her wrist, Alessi summoned a sizable chunk

of ice, throwing it ahead of her. The ferals scattered. "It's good I got these wings when I did. I was nearly out of magic."

Kol adjusted his pack, running his finger along where Alessi had sloppily repaired it with string.

"We can't fly over. We're too close, the guards will see us if we do." Alessi stepped into the shadows, and Kol followed. "We'll have to walk."

Ferals darted as they walked through, most small, dirt-covered animals with a certain madness in their eyes. They looked nothing like the first feral he met—they felt weaker, and their colors were all wrong. Kol jumped as they passed a larger one, who appeared like the shadow of a cat. Minutes passed like hours as they pushed through the black forest.

Occasionally, six-eyed and many-legged things would come out to watch them as they walked, and Alessi would summon another chunk of ice and send them scattering. Even when no creature was apparent, Kol couldn't shake the feeling of being watched in that oily, dark place. When they reached the end of the forest, the sun's setting rays caught on a river that forked ahead of them. Between the forks was a delta, and on that delta were the withered remains of a wooden dwelling. It had taken them all day to cross the forest, and it would be dark soon.

Alessi stepped into the shallow water. "We'll stay there for the night. I'm going to the red king's castle tomorrow, so get some sleep."

"*I'm?*" Kol asked.

"Yeah. You shouldn't come with." Something flashed in her eyes. Sorrow? Fear? She turned away from him. Was that... guilt? "You've already found your mother, so your journey has ended."

Go with the witch. You know what you must do, but there's something she must do first. Help her, for now. Kol heard his mother's voice for the first time in a while. He didn't need his mother's voice to compel him, however. Now, Alessi wanted to march off to her death alone. Was there any chance he could still talk some sense into her?

"You can't seriously still be determined to throw your life away. If you don't want me to go with you, you should turn back," he said.

Alessi snarled. "I can't turn back now!"

"You can, and you know it."

"I won't."

"There's no way I'm letting you go through this alone."

"Don't be foolish," Alessi said. "I'm giving you a chance to live. Don't—don't do this."

"I have to," Kol said.

"You'll die. We'll both die."

"Maybe." Kol set a foot on the cabin's creaking steps, the entire building of dried wood squeaking in protest.

"Fine." Alessi laid down in the corner, facing the building's gray wall. Her wings curled around her, shoulders slumped. "A man has little choice in anything but the manner of his death. Who am I to deny you that?" There was a bitterness in her voice, the voice of someone making a difficult decision. She was right, earlier—life was full of shit decisions.

When sleep didn't come, he opened his eyes again. Alessi, far away from him, shivered in the cold breeze drifting through the building's many holes. Kol stood and walked over to her, laying with his back against hers. He draped his sleeping bag over them both, and she stopped shivering. There was a lot on his mind, too. What would happen tomorrow? What would he say to his brother, if he was waiting for him, as their mother said? Would Alessi die, and if she did, how could he continue living on the surface when she was everything he knew? It was too much, so he laid there with his eyes open. Beneath his web of emotions was fear—fear for Alessi. Fear for her future—for their future, if there could be one. Maybe he was foolish to believe in anything, but he knew one thing.

"I love you, Alessi," he whispered.

She stirred, but there was no response.

30

Kol woke to a cold breeze on his face. It was still dark, and now Alessi's form wasn't there to shield him from the cracks in the wall.

"Alessi?" He stood. What if this was it? What if she had left him there to go on without him? He cursed himself for being so stupid, tears welling up at the edges of his eyes. "Where are you?" He burst through the rotted door and into the open night air.

"I heard you." She leaned against the building, and her eyes turned toward the red king's palace, towering in the distance. There were fewer trees here, and mostly shrubs dotted the hilly landscape. The grass was yellow and dry. Words sat on the tip of Kol's tongue, unable to escape his mouth. Time became suddenly too real to him, like he was drowning in the sand of an hourglass.

"Couldn't sleep?" she asked.

He had slept, if it could be called that. He had been plagued by nightmares he could no longer remember. "I woke up," he said. "It's cold."

"Nights are colder in eastern Alon. We're at a higher elevation than where you're from." Alessi's voice was flat and sterile, scientific even, but there was no way she wasn't experiencing turmoil at least as bad as his. He stood next to her, then leaned against the building beside her. Her hand brushed his, and he turned to look at her. She wore a brave face, but there was sadness underneath. And she was so beautiful. Indescribably beautiful, in a way only deadly things were.

He had to tell her how he felt, before... well, while he still could. Just in case. And he wouldn't do it like a fucking coward this time—he would say it while she was awake, to her face. It was fate they were both awake this night, even if it meant they would get no sleep before the morning. He didn't care if he was a dragon, and she was a dragon slayer. He would rip the words straight from his soul if he had to.

"Alessi." He cleared his throat, and she looked at him. Her silver eyes glowed like miniature moons, outshining the crescent moon above. His face reddened. "There's something I have to tell—"

"It's okay," she said. "I said I heard you."

His heart pounded in his ears. So, she was awake earlier. It made sense, who could sleep the night before their probable death? And if she heard him, why didn't she say anything? Was this a rejection? Maybe she felt nothing for him. Maybe she wanted nothing to do with someone as weak as him, or maybe she was hung up on Azazel—

Her hand met his, pulling him from his thoughts. "Come," she said. "There's something I want to show you." She took his hand in hers, leading him over hills and ruins. A cave opened up in the side of one hill, and the pair stopped walking. The air was moist, and Kol's feet sank into the soft soil. Moss lined a path into a dark space.

Alessi let go of his hand and ran ahead. Somewhere behind

them, the sun started to rise. She led him into the rising dawn's shadows, purple shapes stretching like dark fingers against the far walls. The cave's floor had the texture of soft paper in parts, but water pooled in others as they ventured deeper. Cracks in the roof let in moonlight and increasing amounts of sunlight. Other caves, some so narrow Kol could not imagine squeezing through them, veered off at various angles.

"We're almost here," Alessi said. "Not so bad for our last night in Alon, right?"

Kol's blood ran cold, but he said nothing. If she had already made up her mind, there wasn't much he could do. The sandy earth gave way to a sea of soft white, and for a moment Kol almost thought it was snow. Dust danced through a ray of light filtering from high above as it came to rest on the trunk of a giant tree, gnarled and twisting and covered in silver-white blossoms the exact color of Alessi's hair. Alessi ran to it, twirling and falling into the soft piles. She leaped onto the side of the tree, gripping it with her claws and hoisting herself onto its great boughs.

"What is this place?" Kol looked around in awe. The tree was massive.

"This cherry tree was planted by a witch, a long time ago. It doesn't look it, but it's dying. A real shame considering everything it's been through," Alessi said. "The cave protected it when the red king burned the rest of the forest and the hinterlands. I used to come here, sometimes. A long time ago."

"Alright." For a moment, Kol almost forgot about the horrors of the coming day, about his secrets and the mysteries of his magic. He was a boy, and she was a girl, and they were going to climb a tree.

"Come on." Alessi grinned at him from the branch above and offered him a hand up.

The pressing heat told him it was summer, but when he

saw Alessi amongst the blossoming boughs, though the flowers were nearing their end, it felt like spring. Her claws dug into his skin as she lifted him to the branch as if he weighed no more than air. The diffused light shone white on her hair, speckled shadows falling across her face as she sat opposite him, straddling the branch with her legs.

"How did you find this place?"

"By accident," Alessi said.

Petals landed in her hair, and she cast her silver eyes down. She plucked a flower from a branch below them, twirling it between her claws. "Legend says cherry blossoms used to be pink, a long time ago. Magic made them lose all their color." She dropped the silver blossom, but Kol caught it before it could drift away.

Alessi swayed, one hand on a branch above for support. Kol remembered when they were in the forest, sleeping high above the ground in their hammocks, when she threw herself off. Azazel caught her then. Would he catch her this time if she fell?

Hesitating, he tucked the blossom behind her ear. "They look like you."

Alessi shook her head, and the flower fell out, drifting all the way to the ground. "They're unnatural, just like witches. Humans aren't supposed to have magic; we have to steal it, or be given it—either way, it has a price."

"It's still beautiful, though. Magic." Kol stroked another blossom in his palm. Its delicate petals felt soft against his skin. Silver dust glimmered on its surface, and he realized something. It glowed, just slightly, the same color as Alessi's eyes.

"If you like that sort of thing." Alessi sniffed, then wiped her nose on her bloodied sleeve. "We missed the main bloom, anyway. This tree's almost done for the season." She stepped forward, her wing catching on a branch. She lost her balance and began to fall.

Kol wrapped one arm around one of the tree's great branches, and the other around her waist, and they stood there. They were so close. His heart raced. She heard him earlier, so what did it mean that she brought him here? What was she going to say, or do, that could only be said or done here?

"If this was the last thing you ever saw, would you be happy?" she asked.

That was not what he expected. "No."

"Why?"

"Because." Kol pulled her back toward him. "You keep acting like you're going to die. Like we're going to die. I'm not stupid, I know that's a possibility if this guy is as strong as you think. But you have to go there, and you have to *fight*. Fight to win."

"But—"

"I know you won't turn back, but don't let this be the end. I'm not happy until you are."

Alessi made a face. "Then you'll never be happy."

Kol smiled. "I take that as a challenge."

She pressed her lips against his. He craved her touch more than he realized, and he shut his eyes, reaching his fingers around the back of her neck. She pressed him against the tree and kept going. Warmth blossomed in his chest, consuming his body as she leaned into him. His wrist stung as her claws wrapped around it, and he felt blood drip down his skin and onto the bark below. Deadly. Beautiful. And such a deep crimson, it was practically black.

He startled. His blood was no longer the blood of a human.

He withdrew his wrist before Alessi could notice, trying not to think about it. All around, above and below them, the dying tree turned a silver-white as fresh blossoms emerged from between its leaves, larger and more brilliant than the ones before. Kol couldn't deny the beauty, but also knew it exposed him more than he would like. This was his magic, his power over life. His truth was raw and on the tip of his tongue, his desire to tell her everything becoming almost a compulsion, even though he still didn't know how his magic worked, or how much he was capable of.

"Alessi, hear me out—"

When he looked back to Alessi, her expression was one of sorrow and horror. "What are you?"

His heart dropped. He brought a hand to his face, finding his own black blood smeared across his cheek. This wasn't how he wanted her to find out. If only he'd told her earlier.

"I can explain." He stepped forward, and she stepped back.

Fear flashed in her eyes. Betrayal. A look of suspicions confirmed. Her wing caught on another branch, and she struggled with her balance. She started to panic, trying to get away. The cherry tree was tall, and the pair had climbed almost to the top during their conversation—if they were to fall from here, it could have fatal consequences. She stretched out her wings as she fell, but they folded underneath her as her body spun.

Kol threw himself forward, extending his hand with black blood still dripping, but not in time to catch her. He couldn't even catch himself. His weight carried him over the edge, and soon the pair fell together, Kol mere feet above her but helpless to do anything but wave his arms through the air. Time slowed down, and each heartbeat was an eternity. Them falling, black blood droplets spattering the air around him. When she landed with a sickening crunch, he followed only moments after. However, while she had managed to somewhat right herself, Kol fell headfirst. The pain was overwhelming, and for several seconds all he could do was lay there. His nose bled. He must have broken it. He couldn't move.

"Kol?" Alessi asked. There was concern in her voice, but beneath it was a mixture of horror and fear.

He couldn't move, but he could see her limp towards him from where she fell. "I'm sorry," he said—or wanted to say. All he could do was groan. The pain was being replaced by a numbness, starting at his toes, and moving up his body.

Alessi placed a hand on his shoulder, then removed it like he was on fire. "Oh shit."

Bones shifted in his neck and feeling returned to his feet. He sat up and coughed out blood as his nose snapped into place.

The look on her face was horror. "You lied to me."

"There's more to it than that," Kol began, "I didn't know until recently—"

"Spit it out."

"I'm a..." He couldn't say it. Not with her looking at him like that.

Alessi's claws were out. She hissed at him, then took a step towards him before her ankle gave out and she collapsed to the ground. "I didn't want it to be true," she said.

He kneeled beside her. "Me neither."

"I tried to ignore it. I tried to pretend I didn't notice how quickly your wounds healed, or how your eyes grew darker over the past weeks," Alessi said, "But..."

"You can't ignore it," Kol said. "I hoped..." That she would overcome her hatred of dragons for him? He realized how stupid that was, and yet, there was still a glimmer of hope in him. She was not lost. He had seen her do amazing things—selfless things—on their journey. She had saved his life even after he was of no use to her, more times than he could count.

She stretched her leg out in front of her. Her ankle was definitely broken and had already started turning purple.

"Here, let me help. I think I can heal you," he said, but

when he reached for her ankle, she hissed at him. So easily could those fangs pierce his flesh.

"What are you going to do? You'll die if you face the red king in this condition," Kol said. "I can help. Look, I don't totally understand this myself, but this is the least I can do for you after all that you've done for me."

"Fuck off." Alessi stood and put weight on her broken ankle, inhaling sharply through her teeth.

"I don't care if you hate me, just let me help."

"You kept this from me," she said.

"I had to," Kol argued.

Alessi narrowed her eyes. The cave's roof made a hollow sound as the wind blew through it. "I'm going, just like this."

"You'll die," Kol said.

"What if I want to?" Alessi roared. "Who are you to stop me?" She bore her fangs, but water beaded around the edges of her eyes.

Kol moved towards her. "I can't let you." His voice wasn't wild like hers—it was cool and strong—composed.

"Why?" Alessi said. She didn't move back. "Why do you care what happens to me?"

He moved closer. "Because I love you."

"You shouldn't," she said. Something flashed in her eyes. She felt something, too, even though he knew she would deny it even to herself.

He moved closer. "Maybe, but I still do." He wrapped his arms around her. She flinched but didn't pull away.

"You know what I've done," Alessi said. "I don't regret it."

"You do," he said. "You aren't a monster. You knew I was a dragon for a long time, didn't you? Yet you didn't kill me."

She only buried her face in his chest, leaving bloodied streaks on his shirt. She gripped a fistful of his cloak in each hand.

"You knew," Kol repeated.

"Yes," she said after a moment.

"I know this must be... hard for you." Hard was probably an understatement.

She gripped him tighter, her eyes focused on the distance. There was more going on in her mind, an internal debate only she was privy to. Even though suffering must have changed her over the centuries, the monster within her likely lived on like a voice in her head.

"You fixed it," Alessi said. When he looked at her ankle, previously swollen and turning purple, it was already as if it had never been broken in the first place. She rotated her foot.

"I guess so," Kol said. He hadn't even tried, but his magic was strong enough now to act on its own.

Alessi paused. "I shouldn't expect you to tell me everything. You have your secrets, and I have mine." She took a breath, her fingers gripping his cloak tighter. She buried her face in his chest. "Can we... stay like this for a moment?" Around them, there was nothing but blossoms, as if there were nothing in the world but the two of them.

Kol twisted his boots for traction. "If you need to." He stroked her hair, which smelled as it did that night in the house, like lilacs and smoke and rain.

"There's one more thing. This is high queen Oasis' magic, isn't it?" she asked.

Kol paused. "Yeah." He wanted to say more, but this said enough.

Alessi gripped him tighter, claws cutting into his instantly-healing flesh. "I'm sorry," she said under her breath. "I'm so, so sorry."

It wasn't like her to apologize, but they walked out of the cave hand-in-hand and accompanied by silence. The few birds that lived in the hinterlands had left, and all Kol could hear was the wind and a distant river. Ahead, the red king's palace—a fortress—rose like a spine on the horizon, dark against the lightening sky. Even the castle was red like blood, and Kol wondered if the king's scales were the same. An uneasy feeling returned, like bricks tied to his ankles.

The king. The father of his brother.

"It'll all be over soon," Alessi said. In the morning light, her hair was more gray than silver. She let go of his hand.

They walked until they were close enough to see the guards. Two dragons watched from guard towers. "A witch!" one yelled, leaping from the wall in his human form. His claws cut into the stone as he skidded down. The other did the same.

"Who are you?" the second dragon asked, long blue hair cascading down his back. He was obviously the same kind as Lysander, but unlike Lysander, this man lacked no grace or beauty. If not for his voice, Kol might have thought he was a woman.

"I'm here to see the king." Alessi stared at the two men, her eyes hard.

The two dragons looked at each other, amused expressions in their faces. "And just who are you, to demand an audience with the king?" the first said before turning to Kol. "And who's he?"

"I'm Princess Alessandra of the witch kingdom." Alessi feigned a curtsey, which didn't fit her at all. "He's been expecting me."

The guards looked at each other and snickered. Alessi took a step back.

"He's been expecting you, all right." A forked tongue slipped out of the first dragon's mouth, rust-colored hair curling past his ears. "Expecting you dead, that is. Tell me why we shouldn't kill you right now."

Alessi's squeezed Kol's hand. "Because I have something you want."

"You're a murderer, but not too bad to look at." The blue-haired dragon raised an eyebrow. "This better be good, or you'll wind up on the king's stake one way or another."

Rage welled within Kol, but Alessi's gaze was cool, calm, that of a serpent about to strike. She walked over to Kol, inter-twining her fingers with his. This touch brought him comfort, but she looked at him as if he were a stranger—but only for a moment. With a swift motion, she wrapped her clawed fingers around his wrist, and a crushing pain ran up his arm.

Sweat beaded on Kol's brow. "What are you doing?"

"I'm sorry," Alessi said, "but you know what I am."

"Get on with it!" the rust-haired dragon yelled.

She squared her shoulders, standing tall before the guards. "I have Kol Mendona, son of High Queen Oasis, and I'm here to collect his bounty."

31

"Selling out your fucktoy to save yourself?" the other dragon said. "Kind of low, even for you."

"Shut up," Alessi hissed. "You don't know what it took to get here."

Kol was too stunned to speak. Emotions swam through his mind—confusion, fear, shame, hatred, and love, soon betrayed by numbness. Alessi couldn't mean it, right? This had to be part of some plan, or had everything she said to him been a lie? A cold, hard substance encased his hands and ankles, and he felt himself being dragged to the floor. Instinct took over. He roared. It was a rich, deep sound which echoed off the walls of the fortress. He didn't feel like himself. He felt alien, different, like a spectator watching someone else's tragedy from the sidelines.

"Shut up." Alessi kicked him in the side, expelling the air from his lungs. She ripped off his pendant, holding it up before crushing it in her hands. His only connection with his mother was destroyed. In seconds, everything he had was taken from him.

He looked at her with wild eyes and remembered his mother's words back in the Valley of Dragons. Breaking her would be easier than healing her. He could pull the life right out of her body, and yet, he couldn't bring himself to do it. Some sense returned to him, and he looked at his binds. They were metal and far too tight—he felt his fingers break and heal, break and heal again. The bones in his ankles were crushed, and he felt them trying to return to their former state.

It was torture. Enough to drive most men mad. He gritted his teeth. "What have you done?" he asked Alessi.

She ignored him. "What are you waiting for?" Alessi said to the dragons. "I got more than my hands dirty bringing him here. I demand an audience with the king."

The dragons sniffed the air, then laughed. "More than your hands is an understatement," the blue-haired one said. "Dragon slayer to dragon layer. You really are something. The king will have a field day with this."

Alessi's hands balled into fists. "Tease all you want, but business is business." Her expression was cool, but her face was red.

The blue dragon lapped the air with a forked tongue, his pupils turning to slits. "The humiliation suits you. It's delicious."

"Stop fucking with me. I demand an audience with the king," she repeated.

"I get it, I get it." The rust-haired dragon crossed his arms. "But you can't just walk in here and demand an audience with the king. He's busy, and there's no reason to think that this"—the man toed Kol's limp form—"is a son of Oasis. Everyone knows your word is good for nothing, and if you're an assassin, you're a shit one."

"Fine. Let me prove he has her magic, then," Alessi said. She kneeled next to Kol, who struggled against his binds.

"Don't do this," Kol said through gritted teeth. "Please."

"Shut up," Alessi said. Her claws dug into Kol's shoulder, holding him still. There was no love in her eyes, not even recognition. He was a lamb, and she was his slaughterer. He was a dragon, and she was his slayer. She dug her claws into the sensitive flesh of his throat.

"Alessi, please..." he whimpered, but it was no use. She slashed through his throat, his veins, his arteries. Cartilage ripped and flesh tore.

First, he tasted blood. It poured out of his nose, his mouth, and dripped down his body and into a growing pool of black around him. It was warm and sticky against his skin. He tried to yell, to scream, but only blood bubbled from his throat. He couldn't breathe. His energy left him with the blood, and soon he could barely move. It grew harder to think, and all that was him faded until nothing was left but a simmering hatred for the woman he once loved. His vision faded to black.

The next thing he was aware of, he coughed. He spat black clots of blood onto the ground in front of him, his lungs clearing themselves of the carnage they'd endured. It took him several more coughs before he could finally take some semblance of a breath, his brain still aching and his thoughts slow. He was alive, but his energy was gone. His will to fight was also gone. There was nothing left in this world for him. He laid there numbly.

"I thought he was dead for sure," the blue-haired dragon whispered.

"This is Oasis' magic. Do you not understand?" Alessi stomped.

"Fine," the other dragon said. "You may enter, but not freely. You're a dangerous woman, Alessandra."

"If you've really heard so much about me, you must realize

I'm nobody's prisoner," Alessi said, wings outstretched, and claws brandished.

"Except your mother's," The red dragon teased. "Pathetic, isn't it?"

Alessi clenched her jaw. Her pupils were dilated and sweat plastered her hair against her skin. She stood there, cruel and beautiful. He hated himself nearly as much as he hated her. She hadn't changed, and he should have realized that.

"You're a murderer," the blue dragon said. "We're not about to let a criminal enter the king's castle unbound. There's a bounty on your head, too."

"And I've brought him to pay it," she said. "This moron for my freedom. You have to honor it."

If she had a plan, it wasn't working. Even Kol knew that. This sacrifice—her surrendering him to the dragons like this—would be for nothing. They'd both wind up in whatever prisons they had here, or worse.

"That's not how this works," the red dragon said. The dragons looked at each other, smirked, then tackled Alessi to the ground. She fell, thrashing, wings beating in vain, one dragon on her neck and the other pinning her legs. One licked her cheek with a forked tongue, causing her to hiss. "I'm going to have some fun with you later. That's something you're familiar with, aren't you?"

She whipped her head back to bite the man's hand, but instead he pressed her skull into the ground. Her eyes met Kol's with furious intensity, blood dripping down her face. She hissed and writhed, but the dragons were unphased, the rust-haired dragon binding her arms and wings in the same iron as Kol's hands and ankles.

With the flick of his wrist, the rust-haired dragon attached a chain to the two prisoners. The binds on Kol's ankles turned into a chain, which slithered up his body and attached itself to his wrist bindings. The gates uncurled like fingers as the dragons dragged the two across the stone ground, worn smooth by years of use. Kol faced backwards as the dragons dragged them, letting his body go limp.

Alessi twisted furiously, spouting expletives he'd never heard. She hissed. "Do you treat your mother this way?" She spat blood on the ground. "I'd treat her better than that, and when I'm out of here, that's exactly what I'll do."

The rust-haired dragon laughed. "My mother is dead."

"Do I look like I give a shit?" Alessi hissed, but the dragon rolled his eyes before binding her mouth closed with a bar of metal. She only thrashed with more fury, muffled curses flying from her mouth.

The dragons talked, but Kol couldn't follow the conversation. It was like listening to voices underwater. How could Alessi do this to him? What was going to happen to him? This wasn't at all like he imagined. His neck ached in phantom pain, purely psychological at this point, that moment bleeding into the earth seared into his memory forever.

She told him not to come. Why hadn't he listened? Every warning sign, every red flag, was there. His eyes searched Alessi's for some sense of remorse, some semblance of humanity, but only saw a monster hissing, thrashing, and growling. Some part of him still wanted this to be part of her plan, but he knew he just didn't want to face the truth. She was not the person he thought she was.

A tall, square doorway led to a narrow hall, which grew narrower before it grew wider again, its edges lined in torches and framed with spiderwebs, several of which caught on Kol's legs as they moved. They seemed to be in a labyrinth, hallways splitting to the left and right, curious faces turned towards them as they progressed. Some stones on the walls were newer, but others were older and stained with soot. At least one fire ravaged this castle—probably the same one that burned the forest outside. After what felt like an hour, the hallway widened and they passed through another doorway, this one taller and more elaborate than the first.

"I'm surprised." A low voice came from within the room. "Who captured this wily bitch?"

Kol felt his heartbeat in his ears, heat in his palms.

"We did," the red-haired dragon said.

"Don't lie to me." The low voice was reduced to a growl.

"Sorry, sir. That's not the full truth. She came to the castle—"

"—and practically threw herself into our claws." The two dragons' voices tripped over each other, and Kol couldn't tell who was speaking.

"She thought she could bargain with us by bringing this guy, but—"

"Let her speak," the low voice demanded. The dragons dragged Kol and Alessi to the center of the room, then spun the pair around. Ahead of him was a tall, pale man with long, red hair every shade of fire. It was more brilliant than that of any other dragon they saw on their journey, its color metallic and shifting with the light. He had a smirk on his face, the smile of someone who knew something no one else in the room did. His every beautiful movement emanated power and terror. At his feet were at least a dozen scantily clad women with hair and eyes every color of the rainbow, brilliant reds, blues, and teals like the ocean. They scattered as the man stood, making his way over to Alessi. He inspected her, and she spat on his shoe.

"As pleasant as ever." The man made his way over to Kol, leaning over to look at his eyes. "Who is this?"

"He has Oasis's magic," one of the dragons said.

The king's eyes widened, and he straightened. "You're sure?"

"Yes," one of the dragons said. "The witch, uh, proved it."

The king stooped low again, eyes darting over the blood on Kol's throat. "Barbaric..." the king's words trailed off. "I'd expect nothing less from her, of course. Are you alright?"

Kol wasn't sure how to answer. It was like his tongue was made of lead.

"The boy's a mess; he's so stunned he can't even talk. How could you two idiots let her do this?" He turned to the guards, and with a wave of his hand, said, "You're dismissed."

"I'm sorry—" one began. Kol couldn't even bring himself to look at them.

Alessi gasped as the rust-haired dragon released the binding over her mouth. The iron fell apart like sand before returning to the dragon's palm.

"You owe me a hearing for bringing him in," she said. "It's against dragon law to keep me like a prisoner when I brought you a bounty."

"There's only one thing we have in common," the king said. "Neither of us gives a shit about dragon law." The king looked over her body. "You're a waste of beauty, you know that? You threw your life away like an idiot."

She was set up, Kol wanted to say. Only, he didn't say it. Whatever happened to her, she deserved it.

"Haven't you been looking for him for twenty years?" Alessi hissed. "I've done you a favor. All I want is forgiveness."

"Forgiveness? For slitting my son's throat?"

Son? Kol didn't understand at first, but then it dawned on him. The king didn't know about Red. He thought *Kol* was Oasis' first child, and the red king's son, but Kol's father was a human from a compound in the western wastes.

"You're just going to eat him anyway," Alessi said. "What's the point?"

"Eat him?" The king was taken aback.

"Yes! Because of the prophecy he would kill you—"

"A rumor! This boy is the prince." The king gestured, and the binds left Kol's wrists. "He looks just like his mother." He still lay there on the ground. It was hard to move, to say anything, like he was drowning in emotion. The king stood over Alessi, looking at her over his nose.

"Are you going to kill me?" she asked. "Fucking do it. I'm not afraid of you."

"No," he said. "We're not animals. And you may be useful to me yet."

"What?" Alessi was stunned.

"Yes. This is one reason we dragons are above you witches, regardless of whatever lies you tell about us," he said. "Mercy. I'll hold a trial for you in a few days, and until then, you'll make yourself comfortable in prison."

Prison? Mercy? This man wasn't at all like Kol expected. He expected a vindictive monster, a snarling creature. He looked from the king, to Alessi, then back to the king. The only monster he saw was Alessi. And still, if the king was this merciful being, why had he killed her friends in her place? Had that even happened? Alessi seemed so sincere when she told him the story, but now he had doubts.

"Get her out of here," the king said. A muscular, golden-haired woman took Alessi's chains in hand. Alessi didn't seem so strong now, as the woman easily overpowered her every attempt to fight or escape.

"Red," the king called out. "Take my son somewhere safe while the servants prepare his room."

32

R ed?

For a moment, Kol thought he was hallucinating but it really was Red—the same orange eyes, the same strong but narrow build. Red looked so much like the king, and yet the king seemed unaware he was his son. Still, Kol wasn't about to tell him. Not until he had a better grasp on the situation. Too much had changed, and too quickly.

Red smiled, and for a moment, Kol felt a semblance of ease. A familiar face might mean safety. "Hey Kol," Red said. "Let's get you out of here."

Kol, still stunned, could only manage one word. "Caliban..."

Red helped him to his feet, eyes darting over the blood soaking his now-ruined cloak and shirt. The same ones Alessi bought him back in Vico. When Kol felt like he would stumble to the ground again, Red brought Kol's arm over his shoulders, supporting him.

"It's alright," Red said. "You don't have to talk."

"Caliban..." Kol repeated, clenching his jaw to fight back

tears. Red had spared his life before, even when they were enemies. Viktor was easy to demonize, but Caliban? No. Kol met the man's eyes. While Caliban's hair was the same color as the king's, his face was different. He and Kol had the same nose, the same tan skin, the same soft expression he remembered seeing in a mirror. This was the face of neither a killer nor a monster.

"You know mine, but what's your true name?" Red asked.

"Kol Mendona."

"Kol's an unusual name. I thought it was also a nickname or something." Red was obviously trying to make light conversation, but Kol wasn't feeling it.

"No." Kol managed to shake his head. "It's... my mother named me after a dark mineral."

Red stopped. His eyes met Kol's, and they burned like embers, the orange within them shifting like living fire. As Kol looked into the man's burning eyes, set in a face so much like his own, it was like he found a piece of himself, a piece of his past. He remembered that outline of his mother and brother in the fiery sands. That wasn't an end, but a beginning.

"Are you alright?" Red asked. "I... heard what happened."

Of course he wasn't alright. Just because his physical wounds had healed didn't mean his mental wounds had. "No."

"The look on your face says everything." Red continued forward, taking Kol with him. "I was worried I wouldn't make it back in time to talk to you."

"What do you mean?" Kol's voice was soft. The pair made their way down a staircase, then another. The air was damp, and Kol struggled not to think of his time with Alessi in the cherry tree. That was a lifetime ago, now.

"You were sighted traveling in this direction, so we headed back. I told the king I wanted to talk to the man traveling with Alessi but didn't say anything more," Red said. They entered a small room with bars on the doors. "I prepared the room myself. I know it's not much, but"—he tapped on the metal bars that made up the door—"it's safe."

"It's a prison cell," Kol said.

"Yeah." Red led Kol to a cot suspended from the wall. The room was clean and not so uncomfortable, despite the dampness. They must have been under the citadel. "No one in, no one out. It's a logical choice until more permanent lodgings are arranged. Don't be surprised if people come for you, since they think you're... you know." Red looked at him curiously, sitting on the floor. He swung his legs forward, slouching in a sitting position against the wall, and rested his chin on his fist.

Kol laid on the cot. "You're wondering if it's true."

"I'm wondering about a lot of things."

"So am I. You start."

"No one knows my true name. So, I must ask, how did you?" Red asked. "It's like I recognize you from somewhere, but I can't place it."

"I remember you," Kol said, "even if you don't remember me. I thought you were dead until recently. I thought she'd taken you to die out in the wastes."

Red's eyes widened, that spark of recognition growing into a timid flame. "Who?"

"Our mother."

"*Our* mother? But your mother is Oasis." Red's expression hardened. "That's impossible."

"Why don't you remember?" Kol asked. He wanted him to remember so he could tell Red, the only person he might be able to trust in this brutal world, everything. He wanted to blurt it out, to tell his brother he had searched for him for months, to tell him about his journey, about meeting Oasis in the Valley of Dragons. But Kol was too broken now to trust the king, and truth could put his brother in a dangerous situation.

"I don't know," Red said.

"Do you want to know the truth? I could stop right now," Kol said.

"You're joking. This can't be real." Red shook his head.

"No, I'm serious," Kol said. "I'm your younger brother."

"Lies. Bullshit and lies." Red crossed his arms. "But at the same time, I could have sworn I met you somewhere before."

Kol could tell by Red's blank expression that he wasn't faking. "You don't remember me. So, what do you remember?"

"Nothing but a faint impression, and the slight oily scent of magic." Red sniffed the air. "My mother—Oasis, if what you say is true—abandoned me in the western wastes with no memory. Or at least that's what I was told. I was raised by a family of Weasel belgarri before my magic matured, and they had to hand me over to the dragons."

"Oasis didn't abandon you—she died. And what do you mean, they had to?"

"It's law. An untrained dragon is dangerous, and all orphaned dragons must be handed over to the eastern kingdom by the time they're ten and trained as soldiers. My family hid me, but unfortunately, I had a knack for gambling even at that young age and landed myself in some debt. Also illegal, I should mention. I got caught and shipped off to the military, and had to serve for ten years, lest the government seize my family's home to pay my debts."

"That's awful."

Red shrugged. "Life can be. Military training was rough. Some take to it, but unfortunately, I'm not really cut out for the job. I don't know what they're going to do with me, but if I'm lucky, maybe I'll get shipped off to Carpacia or something."

"I'm sorry." Kol thought of his time with his family. They weren't always kind to him, and his father was cruel, but he couldn't imagine being torn away from the only family he ever knew and raised as a soldier.

"It's not as bad as it sounds, though I'm not the best soldier." Red sighed. "I should have been a bartender, but I probably would have sucked at that, too."

Kol might have laughed if the events of the day weren't still heavy on his heart. His brother didn't remember him. Is that why he gave a fake name, too? He didn't remember his own name? Kol sat up in the cot and slouched against the wall. It had been so long since he saw his brother—the brother he thought dead—and here he was, with no memory of their time together.

"You must have had a hard time out here, huh?" Red asked. "But I'm not sure where you came from was much easier. I saw the compound you left behind. Small, crowded."

"Yeah."

Red was right, but there was more to it. Kol's father would have happily sacrificed him to the sands, unknowing that Kol was, in fact, immune. But Astor loved him, and so did Mia and his other siblings, even if their father was cruel and their way of life hard.

Was this his life now? One cruelty after another?

"And then you trekked over the entirety of Alon by foot, with that monstrous witch. How did you do it?" Red asked. "Why didn't she kill you some time ago?"

"I'm half human. Oasis cast a protection spell repressing my dragon aspects, so I don't think she knew, at least for most of it. I was stuck with her when she had to escape you three and stayed with her after that."

"You didn't go back?" Red asked.

"No. She said if we went back, you'd follow us and kill my family." Kol's mind raced. Was that a lie, too? Was she manipulating him?

Red shook his head. "That's ridiculous. Maybe Viktor would have tried, but I wouldn't have let him. She was our target, not the others."

Everything had been a lie. Of course. Anger welled within him. Kol remembered her crushing grip, her throwing him down and leaving him at the mercy of the dragons.

"Maybe you should have killed her," Kol said.

"Look," Red said. "I know you've had one hell of a day, but you look like you haven't slept in weeks. I asked to personally guard your door so you can rest a while. The king let me because, well, it should be a pretty easy job with you locked in a cage. Just don't try to escape on me."

Escape? Kol didn't have it in him. He was tired. So tired. All the healing magic in the world couldn't rid him of that sensation. Foreboding twisted in his stomach. Without the sun or moon visible, it was impossible to tell the time, but sleep gnawed at the edges of his mind, and he fought back a yawn.

"Get some sleep while you can." Red stepped outside his cell, then to the right, standing like a statue.

Kol shut his eyes but couldn't escape his thoughts. Alessi was not who he thought she was. The king was also not who he expected. And his brother? A dragon. A new emotion bubbled and frothed in his chest—a pure, seething rage. Alessi hurt him. Unimaginably so. He could still taste the blood in his mouth, feel it running down his neck and onto his shirt. He thought of everything that happened to her, everything she told him about, true or not—and for the first time since leaving his hole, he thought she deserved it. And maybe he needed answers, maybe he just needed to spit on her, but he had to see her one last time.

"I need to see her," he said, half-hoping no one heard him.

33

Kol woke to the sound of metal on metal.

"Get back here, assholes!" Alessi yelled, clanking chains against her iron gate. The sound echoed through the hall.

Something twisted inside him. He wanted to talk to her—he asked to talk to her—but so soon? And it sounded like she was thrown into the cell next to him.

"You look tired." Out of sight, a man chuckled. "Bed a little hard for you, *princess?*"

Alessi roared, iron bars clattering as she slammed against them.

"Come on." It was Red's voice. "Leave her alone. She's practically dead already."

Kol sat up, resting his eyes on Red, who stood just outside his cell. He wore a new uniform, a stately red and white one with two rows of buttons going up the front.

"You're awake." Red leaned against the wall, his eyes turned toward the sight.

Kol's heart raced in his chest, a cocktail of emotions

flowing through his veins like fire. He rubbed the last remaining sleep from his eyes. This was the woman who betrayed him, who slit his throat like he was an animal. The memory bubbled up in his throat along with the taste of blood.

"Hey, Kol." Alessi's voice was too sweet, the voice of a manipulator. "Who's your new friend?"

Kol gritted his teeth.

"Red." Red waved a hand. "You should recognize me."

"I do." Alessi picked at her nails. "I was just trying to be conversational."

Kol wanted to snap at her. To tell her exactly what was on his mind. But he gathered himself and managed in a low voice, "Little late for that, don't you think?"

"There you are." With an open hand, Alessi gestured to her body from her head to her feet. Her wings had been severed at the joint, leaving bloody stumps on her back.

"You look like hell," Kol said.

"Yeah. Seems there was a bit of a mix-up."

"Mix-up?" Kol said. "I doubt that."

"The plan was—"

"No. I don't give a shit about your plan," Kol spat.

A week ago, the sad and bewildered look on Alessi's face would have broken him. Now, it just made him angrier.

"You know it's not like that," Alessi said.

"I know?" Kol's voice broke. "I know nothing. I thought I knew you. I trusted you. And then you threw me to the ground and slit my throat."

"I knew it wouldn't kill you," Alessi said. "I had to do it."

"That's not what this is about." Kol's voice was a growl. "You're not the person I thought you were. The person I wanted you to be."

"Well, that's your problem, isn't it?" Alessi snapped.

Red let out a long whistle. "You two slept together, didn't you?"

"I'll tell you what, *Red.*" A fake smile was plastered to Alessi's face. "How about you shut the fuck up and let us talk?"

Red whistled again, only leaning in. "What's that, princess?"

"*Go. Away.*" Alessi hissed at the man, who summoned a flame to his hand.

"I don't think so." The flame twisted in his hand, and its reflection danced in Alessi's eyes. "You were a little scary before, I'll admit, but not right now. Not in a cage without your magic."

Alessi peeled back her lips, showing her fangs in full, eyes narrowed. She looked more like a mad dog than a person. *This* was the real Alessi. Violent. Broken.

Inhuman.

"Why is she here?" Kol asked.

"She was transferred up here. King's request." Red shrugged. "He decided that, since she's still technically a princess, she should get the nicer cells. But I suspect you're the reason."

"I want her gone," Kol said through gritted teeth. In the cell beside his, he watched Alessi fold into herself. Once, he may have felt pity, but no more. "Get her out of here."

"Unfortunately, I can't do that." Red sighed. "And there's something else you should know."

Kol's heart raced. "What?"

"The king has invited both of you to dinner tomorrow night. Unfortunately"—Red eyed Alessi—"it's not optional."

34

Kol spent the rest of the day curled in his bed, facing the wall. He said what he wanted to say, but now she wouldn't shut up. The moment she betrayed him replayed in his head, over and over, over and over, and the taste of blood wouldn't leave his mouth. It was hell. And he was angry.

He didn't know what would happen at the dinner. Maybe this would be Alessi's trial. Maybe she would be executed. Though he didn't acknowledge her, she tried to explain herself, to convince him everything was part of some larger plan, but her words slipped through his mind like water through his fingers. If there was a plan, she would have—should have—told him. He told himself he didn't care what happened to her anymore.

He felt some relief when Red and three guards came to get them. Kol walked freely beside them, and Alessi fought against her chains, her claws bound and a wire mesh over her mouth like a muzzle. After making their way through the dusty, labyrinthine hallways, they arrived in the banquet hall.

"Sit, sit!" The king gestured.

A blue-haired servant, now dressed in a silk uniform as brilliantly blue as his hair, pulled out a chair. Red ushered Kol to it, motioning to it with an open hand. A group of women took Alessi away, then Kol sat in silence for several minutes until they entered with a dress wearing Alessi and proceeded to wrangle her into a chair. Her chains tightened around her wrist every time she struggled. When the women were done with her, she spat at them.

Alessi sat across from Kol. Their eyes met briefly. A mark above Alessi's eye, caused by the skirmish at the gates, was covered up with a colored paste. Her dress was green and covered in sequins—he couldn't imagine what strength it must have taken to get her into it. It clung tightly to her body, a sea of green shining in the light, accentuating every curve. Something twinged in his chest. A beast like her didn't deserve to be so beautiful.

"Welcome to my table," the red king said.

"What's going on?" Kol asked, but the king only whispered to one of his attendants, who nodded silently. Servants rushed about, putting platters here and there. The table was long enough to seat a hundred people, but there were only the four of them in the echoing room, and a few select women from what appeared to be the king's harem. The king sat in a throne at the end, and women sat around him on the floor. He ate, and everyone watched hungrily.

"What are you waiting for?" the red king boomed. "Eat!"

Kol and Red eyed each other but didn't reach for the food. Something was wrong; Kol felt it in his bones. Why would the king feed someone he's probably planning to kill? Or did he really need them for something? Alessi was less bothered. She reached forward, taking a bird thigh, larger than a chicken's, into her clawed hand. A plump female servant stepped forward, and slapped Alessi's wrist. Alessi hissed, but the servant brought a finger to her lips and gestured to Alessi's other hand—her human hand—and Alessi stopped hissing. Kol could hear her stomach grumble even from that distance.

"Use your civilized hand, witch," the king said.

"Fuck you." Alessi pushed her plate off the table, and it fell to the floor and shattered. "I don't want your poisoned food anyway." The servants rushed to get her another plate, their faces cold and devoid of emotion.

A woman poured a thick, red liquid into the king's wine glass, and he took a sip. "It's not poisoned. But if you don't eat, I'll cut off that stolen arm of yours. It's an atrocity."

"Fine." Alessi paused, then reached for the thigh and took a bite. Hunger overtook her and she tore into it, ravenous. "And whose blood is that, you sicko?" she asked with a mouthful of chewed meat.

"It's blood wine. It only tastes real." The king smiled, crimson on his teeth, his hair every shifting color of fire. "You might be wondering why I invited you to my table tonight."

"No shit," Alessi mumbled. "If you're going to kill me, kill me, but don't torture me with formalities."

"This is a royal dinner, the first dinner I've ever had with my son," the king said, looking at Kol. "And you, the princess of witches, are our guest."

"Do you always chain up your guests? A little kinky for the dinner table, don't you think?" Alessi smirked at him.

"Just the dangerous ones," the king said. "I'm not an idiot."

She huffed, hunching over her meal before tearing back into the corpse of whatever bird was on the table, iridescent feathers strewn about. Kol, however, only poked at his food, weaving his fork through strange fruits. Beside him, Red stood, eying the conversation with suspicion. Red looked like he wanted to say something, but stopped himself, and this was good. It was better if the king didn't know the truth quite yet.

"Kol." The king smiled. His teeth were too white. Too sharp. "When I heard my first wife, high queen Oasis, died out in the wastes, it broke my heart... but a piece of her lives on in you. You're special, and you have rare gifts. I can give you the training you need to make a difference in this world."

"Training?" Kol asked. For a moment, curiosity overtook his tension and anger.

"Of course. Every dragon should be trained. I can get you the best tutors and even send you to the royal academy if you'd like. Abilities like yours shouldn't go to waste."

School. Kol never imagined himself going to school, and yet the thought was appealing. He had never thought he could be privy to the sort of education that belonged only to fantasy, and to the past before the Darkness.

"School's for prissies and—" Alessi began.

"Enough from you." The red king gripped the wine glass so hard Kol was surprised it didn't break. His eyes were cinders glaring at Alessi, smoldering in his skull, and yet he did not act out against her.

"What do you think I can do?" Kol asked.

"Everything Oasis could. You could turn the wastes into paradise, make sure no one in Alon ever goes hungry again."

This was good. The king was giving him information, and though Kol told himself his curiosity would only hurt him here, he couldn't stop himself. "Why did she leave?" he asked after a moment.

The king took a breath. "You must understand, Oasis was not a bad person. Her magic, however, had a cost to it. She said the voices of the dead spoke to her, that they told her things, drew her out into the wastes..." The king shook his head. "Children don't often come to dragons. She was pregnant with you at the time, and her disappearance left me broken for many years. I thought I would be childless forever. And despite all these women, and all our attempts, no dragon child of mine has survived until birth."

He looked at Red, who watched wide-eyed. "You really had no other children?" Kol asked.

The king nodded gravely. "No. You will be of use to this kingdom in ways only she could before. You can save us."

Blood rushed to Kol's face. This was a lot to take in, and the lies he had not yet corrected stung his heart like needles.

"Mister red king, sir—" he began, trying to diffuse the situation.

"You can call me father." The king turned to him. "Or Bakar, if you're more comfortable with that."

Kol took a sharp breath, and Alessi sat back in her chair. Kol continued, "Bakar, what do you mean? What was my mother to you, really?" He looked over the king's harem. With so many women, how could one be so special?

The king set his glass down, tracing its rim with his finger. "She was my savior. Or I thought she was. But now, all that's left of her is you." He spoke slowly, adding, "Her magic was the key to immortality, the end of death, the bridge between worlds." His eyes widened and unfocused, and he took another sip of blood wine.

"And now you think I can be... your savior?" Kol asked.

The king's demeanor changed. "That's what I want to find out. If you're really like her, if you can really do what she could do, you will be incredible, maybe the most powerful dragon in a thousand years." The red king stood, making his way around the table. He circled it like a cat about to pounce, slow despite the table's length. "Oasis could have been great, but she was afraid of her own power."

Alessi watched with narrowed eyes.

"Do you see those flowers in the center of the table?" the red king asked.

"Yes, sir." Kol's back straightened as the red king passed behind him, sending a chill down his spine.

"Good. I want you to look at them," Bakar said.

Kol was already looking at the wilted flowers. "What am I —" he began.

"*Look,*" Bakar ordered, his voice a growl. "Form a connection."

Across the table, Alessi flexed her claws as much as she could in those binds.

Kol focused his eyes on the flowers. They may once have been beautiful, but now they hung limply from their stalks. Their shriveled petals were pale in the yellow light, some lying in a pile at the bottom of the vase. Kol wasn't sure what, exactly, Bakar expected him to see.

As Bakar passed behind him and out of sight, Kol felt every hair on his body stand on end. Claws dug into his skull—brutal, sharp, violent claws—and he let out a cry. Warm blood dripped down the back of his neck. Alessi shouted curses, but Kol was in too much pain to hear more than a mumbling, as if she were underwater.

"I'm looking," Kol said through gritted teeth.

"*Look harder.*" Kol could feel the dragon's breath against his ear. The red king continued. "With the army Oasis could have built us, we would have already dominated the continent. We would be unstoppable. Not even the witch queen could stand up to us."

Kol gritted his teeth. Everything his mother had warned him about was right. And not everything Alessi had told him was a lie.

What do I do? he asked in his mind. There was no response. He then remembered his pendant, his only connection to his mother, was gone—and with it, her voice. He could feel her absence like a void within himself. Alessi had robbed him of her guidance. He was truly alone, with nowhere to turn to and no one to trust.

"Hey!" Alessi stood on the other side of the table, and it took three dragon servants to hold her back.

Kol thought his head might explode as the king continued digging his claws into his skull. "I don't know what you want me to do!" A forked tongue flicked his ear.

"See the possibilities," Bakar instructed. "Not just of what's there, but what could be. Your mother was always... good at that."

Kol thought of other occasions he had used his magic. He healed Alessi's dragon venom wound, her broken ankle, healed his various wounds and broken neck, but there was no conscious intention. It just happened. But he didn't heal all wounds—he hadn't healed Alessi's wounds in the cell earlier. There was a commonality between the times his magic worked. An intense emotion, an unconscious connection.

So, what was he supposed to do with a bunch of dead flowers?

"I told you to *do it!*" The red king shoved Kol's head forward, and with the growing pressure Kol saw black dancing at the edge of his vision. "Reach through the darkness."

Panic rose in Kol's chest. "I can't!"

"I have to see for myself that you have her power." The king pressed harder. "If you can't do this, you'll force me to do something I don't like. You wouldn't want to do that, would you?" So easily could the king's claws crush his skull or sever his spine.

Alessi wasn't entirely wrong. This was not a kind man—this was a powerful tyrant hungry for power. Kol's power. And Kol didn't feel like almost dying again if he could avoid it.

Kol imagined himself back in the cherry tree. The wonder of what once was, the wonder of what could be. He slowed his breathing and heartbeat until they were little more than that of a dead man, and before his eyes, color seeped back into the wilted petals. They were every shade Kol had seen, and every shade he had not. They were more brilliant than he could have imagined.

"Promising," the king said. The pressure on Kol's skull reduced to nothing, and he fell back into his chair. "You will bring us to greatness like your mother never could. Guards!" The king waved a hand to the servants. "Take them back. This could be interesting."

Kol couldn't listen. There was no rest for him, no peace. All he could think of were the flowers, and his mother, and what the king might use him for as a bustling group of servants rushed the three away. He felt at the spot on his chest where his pendant used to lay. He had so many questions, and no answers.

<h1 style="text-align:center">35</h1>

The cell door clanked shut, and Kol crawled back into his bed while Alessi hurled expletives at the guards. He hated her, but what he hated most was now he had two enemies—Alessi and the king.

"He's harsh, but the king means well," Red said.

"Means well?" Alessi spat. "I don't think someone who clearly wants to raise an army of the dead means well."

Kol weighed his options. The king wanted to use him, but maybe it wouldn't be so bad. Even if under false pretenses, the king offered him power, training, and a home. He could lean into this and maybe survive. Or maybe be killed once the king found out Red was his real son, or if Kol wasn't useful enough.

"I see that look in your eye, and I can't blame you if you want to join the king. Training, school, a family... it sounds nice." Alessi took a breath. "But there's something you should know about Oasis's magic before choosing that path."

More lies. "And why would I listen to you?"

"Because Red should know this story," Alessi said. "He can confirm that it's true."

Red raised an eyebrow.

"About thirty years ago, there was a plague in an enclave known as Ostendon. It was an ancient city of white and red, built into the side of a desert cliff. Oasis would often visit cities to cure plagues, but this one was different. By the time she got there, it was already too late." Alessi slumped against the wall, knees drawn in to her chest and her chin propped on top.. "She had never used her magic to bring back the dead before. I don't know what changed that day, but the story goes she brought a little girl back to life and came back to the king's castle with the child in her arms."

"This part is true," Red said. "I wasn't there, but I've heard it."

"People started disappearing. A guard here, a maid there, one of the king's attendants. It was a few weeks before the bodies were found, laid in rows just outside the fortress, their skulls smashed and their bowels missing. Soldiers laid traps around the bodies, and one day they caught the little girl, but they realized something else had been living in her body. Something older, something stronger, that used the little girl's memories to manipulate people into doing what she wanted. It was then that the king realized an army of these would be unstoppable." Alessi finished, and the room was silent.

"Is this true?" Kol asked Red.

"I've heard the older soldiers talk about it," Red said, "even though it's forbidden. The king did his best to keep it a secret. How did you hear it?"

"I didn't meet Oasis, or the girl, but I was there." Alessi said. There was a glint in her eye. "I watched the plague take the city, and I was there when Oasis arrived. I saw the little girl, who was no little girl. That thing was not of this world, nor any other world I've ever heard of."

"So, he wants me not only to raise an army of the dead, but

an army of... possessed undead?" Kol asked. "I don't even know if I could do that."

"You might not be able to," Red said. "This is just a rumor, but they say there were experiments afterwards, and she brought back other people. Sometimes they were themselves, sometimes other people. It seems getting the right soul in the right body is the hard part. She couldn't bring back another monster before she disappeared."

"And joined my father's compound, where she gave birth to you," Kol said. He scratched at his chest. "I can't let this happen... I don't know what to do. Nowhere is safe, and everyone wants to use me."

"Welcome to the real world," Alessi said. "But thankfully, I know a way to get you home."

"I don't trust you," Kol said. "I don't even like you."

"Look, I'm sorry about earlier. You never would have agreed to it, and you had to play the part—"

Kol rolled his eyes. "Fucking hells, just stop about that."

"I know planning in advance isn't really my thing, but I swear I thought it through. I needed a way in to kill Bakar, then a way out. Security here is phenomenal and I was struggling with the first part until I realized what you were. Can't blame me for being an opportunist," she said.

"Sure, I can," Kol replied.

"You were just my ticket in here. I'm still working on the second part, but the third..." Alessi's voice trailed off. "I have a way out."

"Bullshit," Kol said.

She leaned in, then whispered, "It's Azazel."

"Who?" Red asked.

"Do you want out of here, too?" Alessi asked Red. "Away from soldier training, guard duty, all that, even for a little while?"

Red looked down. "Depends."

"Do you want to see all of Alon destroyed by monsters from another realm?" she asked.

"No," Red said.

"Then join us. Help us tomorrow, and we can get you out of this, too."

"Since when is there an 'us'?" Kol snapped, meeting Alessi's steely gaze.

"Since your only other option became to raise an army of the dead to take over the world," Alessi said. "I'm your best bet."

As much as Kol hated it, she was right. He remembered Azazel's promise a month ago, and for a moment, thought Alessi might actually have a plan.

"I'll go with," Red said. "I'm curious enough. But if you turn on me, I'll burn you alive."

"Not going to go crying to daddy, I assume?" Alessi teased.

"Without telling the king?" Kol asked.

"He's an asshole. I saw the way he treated Kol tonight," Red said. "Fuck 'em. And I don't even have Oasis's magic. I'd only be a disappointment."

"I doubt it," Kol said.

"I'm not like her, and I'm not as talented as him, or anyone, really... best case, he'd see me as a mediocre replica that pales in comparison to the original." Red ran his fingers through his hair, his eyes far away. "And a man like that isn't capable of loving something more than it's useful."

"Red!" A voice came from around the corner. "Get some sleep. Shift's changing."

"Fine," Red answered.

"Help us tomorrow," Alessi said, "and we'll get you out of here. Just play along."

Red nodded, then left, walking down the long hallway.

There was an electricity between Kol and Red, and when Red left his view, it was as if the rope attaching them snapped back in Kol's face.

"Finally!" Azazel squeezed out from under Kol's bed. "I thought I'd have to stay under there for all eternity."

Kol jumped into the air with such force he almost hit the ceiling.

"Azazel!" Alessi said.

Irritation flickered in Kol's eyes. Why did Azazel have to portal under his bed?

"Where've you been?" Alessi asked.

"Busy. You should know by now you're not my only concern. I was dealing with my sister," Azazel said, dusting himself off. He took the form of the tawny-haired man. "Unfortunately, it was dealing of a more literal kind. I lost two games of cards, and she wouldn't even listen to me. She wants another trip into the human realm, but after last time—"

"I thought you'd never show up." Alessi's tone was biting.

"And yet, I'm here. Just on time," Azazel said. "I looked everywhere for you. Why aren't you in the dungeons like you told me?"

"Dungeons?" Kol asked. "You wanted to get thrown into the dungeons?"

"Close enough. Part of the plan, remember?" Alessi said. "Get captured, not killed, work my way in?" When he didn't respond, she rolled her eyes. "Ugh. You didn't listen to a word I said."

Kol gritted his teeth. Once, he may have found this endearing, but now anger overwhelmed him. He was being torn apart. Part of him hated her—truly hated her—and part of him wanted to believe her. Wanted to believe that this was all part of her plan from the beginning, wanted to drink her sweet little lies like honey. But who slit someone's throat as part of a plan?

She was his torment. Yet, despite it all, he still wanted her, and this denial hurt more than anything.

"So, you want me to portal out the dragon boy, too?" Azazel asked. "That wasn't part of the plan."

"They're both dragons, catch up. Take them, and only them. I can take care of myself," Alessi said.

Kol would be separated from Alessi, but he knew he should be ok with that. That's what he should want after everything she did, right? She looked down the dark hall. "Won't the guard be coming soon?"

"The next guard is experiencing an unexpected delay." Azazel shrugged. "Most unfortunate. His pants are nowhere to be found."

"Why can't you just portal us out of here now?" Kol asked.

"That's not part of the plan," Azazel said.

"Then just portal me," he said. "Get me out of this wretched place. I just want to go home."

"No," Alessi said. "Not yet. I need you."

Those words didn't mean what he once hoped they would. "I see I'm still just a tool to you."

"It wasn't like that." She drew her lips back into a snarl. "You should know it was never like that."

She had said she would do whatever it takes. He was a mere casualty to her ambition. But as he looked closely, there was something else in those silver eyes. Sadness and depravity. He didn't care if she never wanted to do this, using him was a choice she made. He wanted to leave, but at the same time, he traced the place on his neck where his pendant used to rest and remembered his mother's words. *The enemy of dragons.* Conflicting emotions ripped through him.

Azazel looked from Alessi to Kol. "You mortals make me depressed, so I'm going to return that poor boy's pants. I'll be watching." He disappeared.

"You hurt me," Kol said. "Used me, threw me away. I don't want to help you."

"And I'm sorry," she said. "But you were fine. I knew you wouldn't die."

"Sorry is not enough for what you did," Kol said. His eyes met hers, and he remembered her back in their first weeks together, her rough-cut hair against the night sky, their days spent haggling with innkeepers. The look in her eyes was a hard acceptance, one calloused by years of betrayal and pain and never expecting anything better from people.

And he cracked. No matter how much he wanted to hate her, some part of him couldn't. No matter how much he wanted to wish she had never taken him from his hole and into this strange world, and that they had never met, he couldn't. He had to get away from her, from everything, and just figure things out.

"I want out of here," he said. "Then I never want to see you again."

"Then help me." She gave him a sad smile. "One last time."

36

The next day, the king summoned them to the dining hall again. This time, Alessi was clothed in a new white dress with a black rose embroidered up the side. Even her hair was brushed and parted to one side. Kol watched her as she turned, the dress tight and perfectly shaped to her body as if she were a serpent with white scales.

He knew what she looked like underneath, and he couldn't stop himself from imagining it. And of course, she must have known this. She caught his leering eyes and smiled. He frowned at her then looked away. She wasn't going to soften him like this.

"I was hoping to test another of your abilities," the king said. He circled the table, clicking his claws against the wood as he walked. "But first, some insurance. One of my guards overheard part of a discussion last night while searching for his mysteriously missing pants."

Kol's heart nearly stopped beating and sweat beaded on his brow. Maybe he had overlooked the fact that Red could have betrayed him, too.

The king continued. "I'd hate it if something were to *happen* tonight." He put his hands on the back of Kol's chair. "An assassination attempt, for example."

Alessi squirmed in her seat, and Kol leaned forward, feeling the table press a line into his chest. He twisted his head, neck cracking as he looked back at the king. A flame appeared on the tip of the king's finger, and he brought it to his own chest. Kol winced, hearing the king's flesh sizzle.

Then he brought the finger closer to Kol. Kol gritted his teeth as the king pressed his burning finger to the base of Kol's throat, just above where his pendant used to rest. His flesh stung as it melted away and knitted back together. Maybe, just maybe, Kol could escape whatever the king had in plan. Maybe the king underestimated him. Maybe—

"You have your mother's gifts," the king said. "Some say your kind are immortal, but I know how to kill you."

"Because you killed her," Kol said. "Didn't you?"

The king smirked.

"What did you do to him?" Alessi hissed. She started out of her chair, but two chains snaked their way around her arms, binding her to it.

"If I die, he dies," the king said. "This is why I put you two together, Alessi. To see if your bond is enough to muzzle you."

Kol's heart dropped, a sick feeling spreading from his chest.

Alessi growled. In her eyes he saw the dissonance within her, her old self fighting with her new self. If she decided to go forward, Kol could actually die. He didn't want to die, but at the same time, he had nothing—no friends, no certain future. What reason did he have to live? To be used as a weapon?

His mother was dead, and he was finally reunited with Caliban. Maybe that was his journey. Maybe it was okay if this was the end. But then... how would he help Alessi accomplish her destiny, like his mother wanted him to?

The king shrugged. "Only if you were going to kill me. Now, where were we?" He smiled at Kol, and a shiver ran down his spine. "Ah, right. Let me tell you a story. A century ago, your mother walked through my gates and demanded that she marry me. She had no name, no origin, no family she could remember."

"I said no at first, but it soon became apparent she could perform miracles. First, a stable boy fell off the roof and broke his neck. He walked home that day because of her. The people heard and started coming to her with all ailments and she became rather famous. She had no name back then, but people took to calling her the dark queen. Scholars said she was a dark dragon, but it's impossible to know since history says the last of those died with the Neon Empire. All I knew for certain was that she was my wife, and as time passed, I grew to love her.

"One year, there was a plague out in the wastes. She traveled to heal the sick, and as she walked, life bloomed around her—sand turned to grass and cactus flowers, trees sprouted from roots far below our feet. It was the most amazing thing I've ever seen. From that moment forward, all knew her as Oasis, healer, and savior of the dragon lands."

"And you killed her," Kol said, eyes narrowed. "You murdered the savior of the dragon lands."

"Do you want to know the truth about your mother?" the red king asked. "The truth no one talks about?"

The king's eyes met Kol's with intensity, but Kol didn't answer.

"There was more to her than you know... all while I knew her, she had nightmares. Sometimes, she'd wake with what she took from the realm of dreams. Usually, it was insignificant items, like a seashell or a handful of soil, but one morning she woke with something... else. A small pendant. I found her whispering to it in her sleep, and sometimes a voice would whisper back. And no matter how many times I tried to destroy the pendant, it always came back.

"That was the first spirit. Then there came others. She said they were the key to all ancient knowledge, that they remembered a time before the Darkness, before Belgarri and Humans. It taught her about the colors and vastness of the space beyond the stars. I lost her long before she left these gates."

"Why are you telling me this?" Kol asked.

"Because you will face the same danger," the king said. "There's a war coming, and our kind needs you if we are to survive."

"I don't know how much help you need fighting witches," Kol said.

"No. Bigger," the king said. "My prophets tell me the beast of Alon will return, and with him, the Darkness."

"Nobody even knows if that's real," Alessi said. "And Kol would never help you. He's better than that."

"Kol Mendona will do whatever I want him to do." The king grabbed Kol's shoulder with one hand, claws digging into his flesh. "I have one more test for you."

"He's not your trick pony," Alessi said. "Kill us or let us go but stop playing games."

"Don't tell him to kill us," Kol hissed.

"This is no game," the king said. He summoned fire to his palm, walking closer to Alessi. She struggled against her chains as the fire's light licked her face, the king's hand drawing closer to her. Her eyes widened, and she hissed as he held the flame in her face, singeing her hair, before he extinguished it. He transformed one finger, a razor-sharp talon emerging from its tip.

"Don't do this!" Red yelled. "She's the princess. What would this mean with the witches?"

"Do not speak to your king that way." The red king sent a

wall of flame in Red's direction, sending him skidding back several feet as he struggled to contain it.

Kol's eyes widened. This was a dragon. This was a monster about to spill a woman's blood the same way she spilled his. Even after everything she did, even after she hurt him, he couldn't let this happen. But before he could react, the man ran his claw through Alessi's heart.

"Alessi!" Kol screamed. He struggled against his chains, snapping them in half, and ran over to her. It wasn't fair, even after everything. Tears fell from Kol's eyes and onto Alessi's still form. The sheen vanished from her hair, leaving it a dull stone-gray. She opened her mouth as if to say something, but only blood bubbled from her lips.

"What is it?" Kol leaned in closer.

Her lips moved, and she whispered something barely audible. "I'm"—she wheezed— "sor—" She coughed, a cascade of blood running down her chin.

"I shouldn't have doubted you about him, I shouldn't have..." He remembered the night they met, how she stood up to his father. Their adventures in the wastes, cutting her hair, buying his jacket. And now she lay in his arms, heavier than in life. He held her hand.

"Justice has been served, but will you still save her anyway?" the king mocked. "Show me what you can do."

Is this how it ends? Kol thought. I didn't get to say goodbye. She never got to. He remembered their night in the demon's house, and of how he wanted to heal her, to make her complete, to give back what the queen took from her. He didn't know how to bring her back. She would never have that, now. There was no future for them.

And though she had done the same to him not too long ago, betraying and abandoning him, he couldn't do the same to her. He wasn't like her. He would be better and save her life even if he knew he would never be able to trust her in the same way. He wasn't the same person anymore. He turned to the king— her murderer—with fury in his eyes.

Stroking Alessi's hair, Kol thought of the dead flowers on the king's table. He imagined her blooming like they had, and yet the story about his mother's necromancy stayed on his mind. He knew the creature that came back may not be the woman he traveled here with, the woman he spent a night with in the house of a monster. However, it was a chance he had to take. He had to talk to her again, even if she didn't deserve it.

Alessi's eyes opened.

"Alessi!" Kol exclaimed, but she didn't respond.

For a moment, her colors were dull, and her expression bewildered.

"You're just like your mother." The red king gave a crooked smile.

"Alessi?" Kol asked. Her eyes narrowed, and she snarled like an animal, tearing herself from his arms. In an instant, she was on top of the red king, claws at his throat.

"You killed me, you bastard!" Spit flew on Bakar's face as she roared. Relief flooded Kol. That was her, alright. "And now I'll kill you, like I should have all those years ago."

The king smiled. "If you kill me, you kill that friend of yours, and that's no way to repay a favor."

Alessi paused, her claws cutting into the man's flesh. The light was back in her eyes, and her hair was almost its lustrous silver again.

"It's okay, Alessi," Kol said.

Alessi hissed again, wrapping her fangs around the man's throat. The king scrambled backwards, unable to move as she pressed his shoulders into the floor. The sound of cracking bones echoed through the cavernous space. He wasn't dead, but Kol hesitated to think how many bones she must have broken.

She stopped as quickly as she started. She stood and spat on the man's face. "Asshole," she said, grabbing Kol's hand. Then to Kol, she said, "I'm sorry. For everything."

"I know," Kol said. His heart twisted. Things could never be like they were before. "But it's still not enough." In the end, she chose him over revenge, but his heart ached. She had crossed too many lines. He couldn't stay with her. He had to heal, to get stronger, and then meet her on her own level.

There were tears in Alessi's eyes. Genuine tears. She looked up. "Azazel, it's time."

Kol heard the whirring of a portal opening behind him.

"Take Kol and Red," Alessi ordered an unseen Azazel. "I'm better off alone."

"But Alessi—" Azazel's voice came from behind him.

Alessi hissed, pushing Kol into Azazel's muscular arms. Red ran toward them. "Take them and go."

"But—" Azazel pleaded. More guards arrived, weapons in hand. One transformed into a blue dragon, and a bewitching melody filled the air.

Kol could see Alessi breaking. He broke, too. Everything they had on this journey was lost in a split second, and Alessi was again the feral beast she was when they met. He would find her again, some day, when he was strong enough.

"Go!" she roared at them, fangs bared.

Red leaped through the portal, but Kol couldn't take his eyes off Alessi, her eyes lit with the fire of an internal torment. She slashed at the dragons, but there were too many. She was exhausted. He could see it on her face, and in her silver magic losing its sheen.

"It's time to go, Kol." Azazel's feathered arms pulled him back. "When she's made up her mind..."

"...there's no changing it," Kol finished.

The portal closed, and that was the last he saw of Alessi.

Acknowledgments

There are many who deserve thanks for this book, and I know I'll miss at least a few and feel terrible about it. To those – you know who you are, and I love you.

I'd first like to thank my family: my parents, grandparents, cousins, and partner, with whom I have lived at various points while working on this book. My various pets who sat beside me while I drafted and edited also deserve a mention here.

Next, my teachers, especially Dr. Nancy K. Greer, the first to encourage my interest in creative writing. Also, a special thanks to my beta readers and online writing community members who kept me writing through law school. In a mix of real names and usernames and in no particular order, these people include: Skyler Clark, J. Amaryllis, rowdyrevy, Sasopsy, Lotsa Matcha, Merron, Verena, Ann, Natasha Eagle, Ian Kinder, goose, Willy, Bubbles, Sushi, Ryan Patrick, Jellyfish Jo, Kay, Empress Crazydog, HICABIL F FETL, and many others.

And of course, I couldn't have done this without Brittany Weisrock and my fellow LCP writers.

About the Author

Kit enjoyed writing as a child and rediscovered her passion during the COVID-19 lockdown. She has a degree in finance from Southern Methodist University and recently graduated from Georgetown University Law Center, where she was the administrative editor of an academic publication. When she's not writing, you can find her running barefoot, taming stray cats, or listening to paranormal podcasts.